Cheyenne,
Thanks so

KEYS OF CANDOR

THE RED DEATHS

By Seth Ervin and Casey Eanes

Cheyenne!

Thank you!

Keys of Candor: The Red Deaths

ISBN-13: 978-1-50782-049-0 (paperback)

ISBN-10: 1-50782-204-96 (paperback)

ASIN: B00T2BB1L0 (Kindle format)

Keys of Candor: The Red Deaths / by Seth Ervin and Casey Eanes

978-1-50782-049-0 (paperback)

1. Good and evil. 2. Adventure fiction. 3. Fantasy fiction.

For my beautiful wife and my two amazing kids. - CE

For Janet. -SE

TABLE OF CONTENTS

MAP OF CANDOR

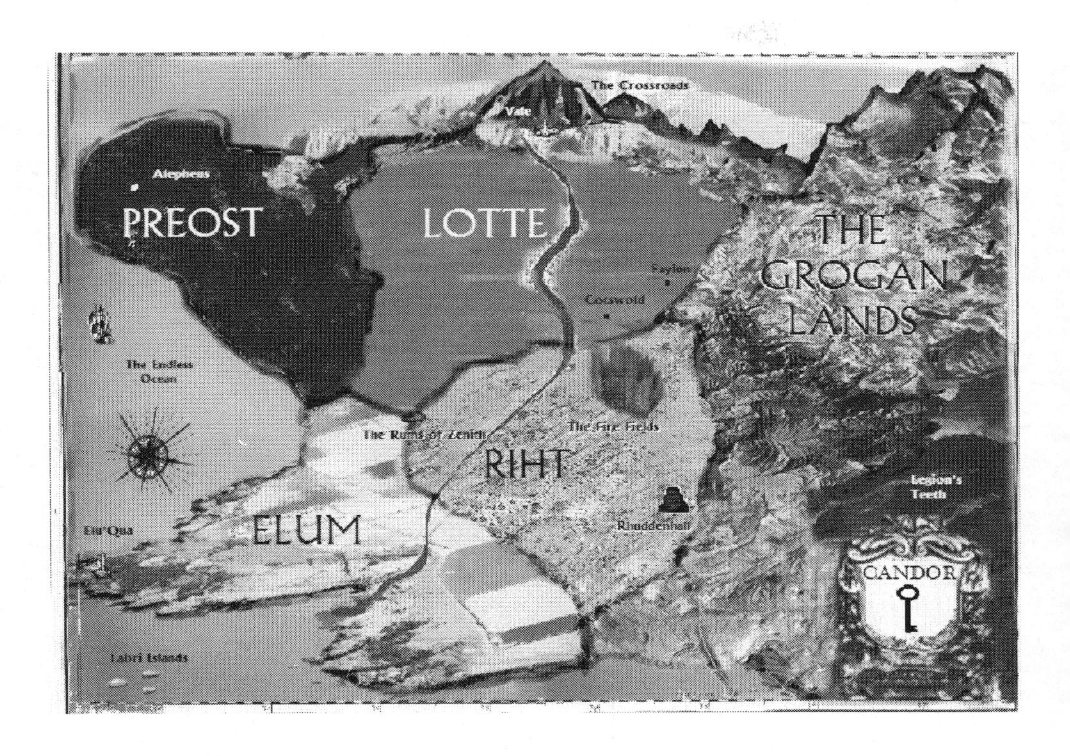

CHAPTER ONE

"Again. Strike again."

Kull flinched at the command. He rolled over on the hard packed earth. His body felt broken.

"You going to lie in the dirt and cry?" The taunts gave Kull a new vigor.

Rising to his knees, Kull licked his bloody lip and spat on the ground.

"Just give me a second."

A rocketing fist flew across his helmet, stealing his breath. The young man fell flat as the world buzzed and swam in a sea of black and blue. He panted, sweat pouring from his brow. Kull could not remember a time his father had beaten him so badly in a sparring match. He was like a ghost; he couldn't land a single strike on him.

"In battle there are no seconds to give. Get up!" Grift ran a hand through his long, graying hair, frustration flickering across his face. He bent down to grasp the heavy cloth of his son's training armor and hoisted him to his feet.

"The Academy won't give you any seconds either." The words landed on Kull harder than his father's fist. Entrance into the Academy was Kull's dream – a way to make a name for himself. Unlike young men of wealth, Kull's only ticket into the esteemed ranks of the Academy would be his skill in combat. Without his father's training he knew he did not stand a chance. Grift stepped back and picked up a training sword before turning to Kull.

"Son, you have to do better than this if you ever expect the Academy to accept you."

Propelled by anger and insult, Kull lifted a sword and stalked towards his father. He already wore a tapestry of bruises highlighting his earlier mistakes, but he determined the mistakes were going to end. The training sword was heavy in his hand, and his arms ached in silent protest. They had been sparring for hours.

Kull stared his father down, trying to read his next move. He knew he was no match for his father's swift tactical skill. His body ached for rest, but his pride overshadowed the pain as he probed for an open strike.

Grift sounded a warning, "Your stance is too narrow. I could knock you down with one swing if you don't widen your stance."

Kull listened, but gritted his teeth and mumbled beneath his breath.

Grift held the training sword in a defensive position. "So what's your next move, son?"

"THIS!" Kull rushed at his father. Their swords connected, letting out a huge *CRACK.* Grift swung around, channeling the energy of Kull's blow, and brought his own blade right back down on top of Kull with ease. Kull hit the dirt. He had failed, again.

Defeated, Kull rolled to his back and tossed his sword to the side. Frustrated, he complained, "I don't know why we need to practice with these dumb swords anyway! In the Academy the cadets are issued rifles."

Grift held out a hand to Kull and lifted him to his feet. He looked deep into Kull's blue eyes. "You're a great shot, Kull. Even better than a lot of my soldiers. But it's not enough to rely on a single talent. When you're in a fight – a real fight – you have to use any weapon you can find. The most dangerous and useful weapon for you to wield is right here." Grift tapped his son's head and embraced him. "You have a great mind, Kull. *Be ready to use it*. You hear me?"

Kull let out a deep breath and, despite it all, smiled. "I hear you dad. Can we go now?"

Grift slapped his son's back and dusted the dirt out of Kull's shaggy brown hair.

"You did really well today. But remember, *always be ready*."

Kull shrugged. "Thanks. I guess. Maybe next time I will actually get some licks in."

Grift let out a booming laugh, "Don't worry, son. Soon it will be you picking me up off the ground. You are close, very close."

With each sparring match, and there were many, Grift was grooming Kull for success. Someday soon the lessons would help him gain entry into the Academy. His bruises were a tactile reminder of his mistakes, but they also let him know he could handle pain easily enough. He was not made of glass.

"Remember, *always* be ready." The memory of his father haunted Kull as he stood on Lookout Hill and stared out into the vast valley below him. A cold blue canopy of sky stretched out toward the capital city of Vale. The smell of honeysuckle and the lilies that once dotted the hillside had long faded into the dark brown chill of autumn. Winter was quickly approaching. The once lush, green hillsides now looked like the brown hide of an old cow; plain and dull. The only color that survived the seasonal change was the dark green hue of the evergreens that danced in the cool wind over Kull's small village of Cotswold.

Kull could smell snow and he spied several large flakes beginning to fall. He stamped his feet and shuddered, trying to shake the frigid, still air around him.

Despite the cold, the quiet countryside offered solace from his ailing mother's bedside where he spent his entire morning. He had never seen her this bad; her condition had faded with the oncoming winter. Silently, he wished his dad would hurry and return to help. He did not know what to do, and he hated to face this sickness alone. The days grew longer with more tremors, fevers, and terrible rattling coughs. No matter how many ice wraps he prepared the fever burned on. Herbs, poultices, spring water; nothing was working. Perhaps just seeing Grift would give her strength to keep fighting. It was as if she had given up hope after he left for war.

Before leaving for Lookout Hill, Kull ground extra herbs and crushed up her pills into their normal daily rations. She sat motionless over her uneaten plate of breakfast as he pulled back her thin brown hair and raised a glass for her to drink. She sipped at the cup but said nothing, her brown eyes like dull stones, glazed over and fixated on the wall in front of her.

Kull thought back to his last memory of his mother when she was healthy and full of life. He was only twelve years old. It was shortly after his birthday, and his mom took him into town to buy a uniform for the Academy. She always told Kull she believed he would become a top recruit. But her health soon took a turn for the worst and the five years passed, turning her into the skeletal shell left sitting at the table. Instead of heading off for the Academy, Kull had to stay and help tend to her.

His dad kept promising he would help him get in. He trained him, a lot. But nothing changed over the years.

"Mom, can you hear me?" Nothing. Kull stooped down and kissed the top of his mother's head.

He leaned in, desperate for some sign of life. "Mom. Ewing is coming over to sit with you. He will probably tell you the same old stories again. I am going to wait for Dad. I got a letter from him. *You know*. The one I read to you last night? He should be back today."

His mother looked at him, her face still vacant. Kull draped a blanket around her shoulders and kissed her head again.

"I'll be back in a few hours. Please, try to eat something."

Kull let himself out of their small home, allowing his worries and fears to be carried with the cool autumn wind. He climbed to Lookout Hill and sat on an old stump. For nearly three hours, he waited and watched over the hills for his father's return. His mind drifted, returning to the words that had turned his world into an ever deeper, lonelier void, the words that stole his father from him and left him alone, caring for his dying mother. The announcement exploded through Candor like a cannonball, leaving nothing the same as it had been before.

"The King is dead!" The proclamation tore through the streets of Cotswold just six months prior. The commotion in the town square caught his attention and drew him in to see what was happening. One of the town elders was frantically pacing the square, stamping his cane. "The King is dead! *He is dead.*

Murdered. Poisoned! Why? Why, oh Aleph, why?" Tears were pouring from his wrinkled cheeks as he screamed out for everyone to hear the terrible news.

It meant only one thing. War. Lotte was at war. After nearly 40 years of hard-earned peace, the Realm was once again plunged into conflict. The continent of Candor and its five Realms were no strangers to battle. The oncoming war would dwindle already meager resources to near exhaustion and men would take desperate, unthinkable measures to survive. For others, the fighting was a window of opportunity to grasp more power as the continent's control of oil, water, and food changed hands.

For Kull, the announcement of King Camden's death and the ensuing war meant that his father would once again be called away on an active tour of duty, and he would be left to handle the task of keeping his mother alive. Grift had been gone on details before, but this was different. For years, Grift served King Camden as his steadfast head of security. For as long as Kull could remember, his father never failed to protect the King. Camden's assassination ripped through Grift with such force that he did not hesitate to volunteer for combat duty to avenge his murder.

In Cotswold it was said that his sacrifice was because of Grift's faithfulness and loyalty. Others suggested that Seam Panderean, the heir to King Camden's throne, had sent Grift to the front as punishment for allowing such a tragedy to occur under his watch. No one knew for sure, and Kull was not given any details, least of all from his father. Staring over the hills, his mind swept back to the day he watched Grift's rail car take him away to war. Kull scratched at the old stump with a knife.

He shivered and rubbed his arms as a cold northern wind blew over him. He wondered if his father had been scared to go to war. *No. He was never scared*. Yet the thought would not leave him, creeping back into his mind. Fear was in his eyes when he stepped on the railcar. *He had been afraid*. He knew he might not come back again. Another thought hit Kull like a punch in the gut. *What if he isn't on the next railcar? What if he knew he would never come back?*

He pulled out the letter, filled with his father's small, neat script. It came only two weeks ago. In it, he said he earned some leave. Two weeks, in fact. He would arrive either Monday or Tuesday of the current week. Today was Wednesday, and Kull kept his watch, blowing his breath into his cold, aching hands.

Come on Dad. Come on.

Kull tried to ignore the dread building within him as each minute went by. He talked to himself, trying to calm his nerves. *Just bury those thoughts, Kull. They are no good for you. Dad is coming.* Like a storm cloud, dark images formed in Kull's mind. Burying his father. Caring for his sick mother. Being alone. Kull's terrible daydreams were interrupted by the sound of a railcar blasting its horn, announcing its approach.

"Finally!"

Kull shot down the hill, rocketing toward the station, trying his best to breathe in the icy air. A ribbon of smoke began to wind over the hills. Kull could see as one puff of smoke gave way to another, and the familiar sounds of a panting motor and grinding wheels soon joined the chorus; the old engine was getting closer. The railcar that made rounds to Cotswold was older and slower than others, but the sight thrilled Kull just as much now at seventeen as it did when he was a young boy. Grift used to lift Kull to his shoulders to help him get a view of the hulking old engine approaching the small logging town, bringing loads of migrant baggers trying to get a season's work. The odd baggers used to excite Kull as they always brought fresh fruit and exciting stories with them, but the arrival of his father was far more thrilling. The image made Kull smile as he watched the approaching railcar.

He reached the platform panting, trying to regain his composure, wiping the sweat from his brow. His father's letter said he would be coming from Faylon, the small city that rested right on Lotte's border with the Groganlands. A small crowd of other villagers began to gather, anxiously awaiting the railcar's arrival. It dawned on Kull that he wasn't the only one to lose a family member to the war. His arms tingled with anxiety as he waited. He smiled to himself as he pictured his father stepping down off the tracks full of life; his gray eyes glowing and his booming voice filling the station. His daydream was interrupted by a young toddler next to him.

"Uh oh, broken," she stammered as she pointed to the oncoming engine.

Someone in the crowd responded, "Girl's right. Something is wrong. Look at that thing!"

The people began to shuffle as everyone pushed in on the platform to try and glimpse the car. As it slid closer and closer, the villagers saw that the arrival was not what they had expected.

"That thing is riddled with holes!"

"How is it even rolling? The engine is smoking like the Fire Fields!"

As the car screeched and stuttered to a stop, the doors that were still intact flew open.

"Gods above, what is happening!?" someone yelled.

Kull's mind exploded with shock and revulsion as a throng of wounded poured out of the car. The passengers had clearly just escaped a massacre. Many were missing limbs, while others bore wounds that were haphazardly patched up. Women and children wailed in a frenzy, wearing ash-covered clothes. Blood trickled out of the car's floor and onto the ground.

War had come to Cotswold.

"Dad!" Kull screamed, shocked at the sound of his voice. He had to find him. He had to be in the railcar. He threw himself into the ruined crowd of refugees, searching for his father. The men and women he faced were a mad blend of hollow and wild eyes and uncontrollable screaming.

"Help me, son!" A bloodied old man grasped at Kull's arm, pulling at him as he screamed.

Kull shook free; shoving his dirty hands off, but then lost his balance and fell to the gravel ground. Kull realized the car was almost empty and there was no sight of Grift. He lifted himself from the ground, surrounded by the bloodcurdling wails of the injured collapsed around him. He looked up and saw a herd of people running, limping, and crawling, not into the town, but away from it. They were making for the forest that bordered Cotswold, running for their lives, abandoning everything for the safety of the trees. Dread washed over him. *Something else is coming.*

In the chaos of the first railcar emptying, Kull looked over the horizon and saw a second, smaller service car barreling down the tracks. He braced himself for an attack, but quickly saw that the car was carrying a few members of Lotte's civil guard. A surge of relief washed over him as he was able to make out the outline of what could only be his father riding alongside them.

The car slammed to a stop behind the larger engine and Grift jumped down to assist those who were still emptying from the first transport. Several guards also exited and set their weapons sights on the track line's horizon. The others tried to pick up the wounded that were sprawled out along the station deck.

Grift rushed to usher the frenzied crowd toward the shelter of the woods.

"Run! Do not go to your homes! Seek shelter in the woods! You are not safe here!" Grift's voice boomed over the crowd as he attempted to push the mad scramble towards safety. He repeated the speech over again, yelling over the riot of people.

"Listen to me! Turn and run! *If you want to live, head for the forest!*" Kull swelled with pride at the sight of his father leading the people. He attempted to push against the crowd once again, but the mass of panicked citizens was surging frantically toward the tree line at Grift's instruction. Kull's eyes caught his father's through the crowd, and the two of them stood frozen, their eyes locked on one another. Grift shot a grin at his son, and Kull could not help but smile back.

Suddenly, a deafening explosion went off to Kull's left sending dirt and fire spewing into the sky. He strained to make sense of the chaos as the first explosion linked with another and then another, a fiery showcase of synchronized destruction. Cotswold's humble buildings buckled under the attack like eggshells in a hail storm. He strained over the roar to hear what his father was screaming. "Run!"

Kull stood motionless as the stampede pushed against him, forcing him backward toward the tree line. The ground trembled and pulsed underfoot, not from the rocket attack, but by something else. Kull looked further down the rail line, expecting to see another supply vehicle, a medical convoy, anything that could help. He realized there was nothing coming down the line when another blast thundered, causing his stomach to somersault inside of him. A fiery explosion sent the metal service car Grift had stood on tumbling off the rails and into the town square. The dismantled car flung shards of metal and glass into the streets until it smashed into the front of Arthur Ewing's general store.

Ewing. Gods, no. Mom. Kull's body filled with adrenaline as he sprinted across the courtyards of Cotswold toward his house. He prayed that he had enough time to get to his mother. The town was emptying as crowds of screaming people ran in all directions, trying to find cover from the incoming inferno. In the din, Kull sprinted against the masses trying to get back to his mother.

His heart hammered as he burst through the door. Inside he saw Ewing, carrying her in his arms. Ewing screamed at him, his eyes like fire, "What are you doing here, lad? Run! I've got her!"

In a panic, Kull checked to see that it was her. *Yes.* His mother's vacant eyes looked up at the sky as Ewing and Kull bounded for the fields toward the forest. Kull heard another explosion and turned back.

The attackers finally revealed themselves. There were nearly thirty Grogan rooks swarming in from the valley pass, following the railcar's path. Their black engines were branded with the blood-red banner of the Groganlands; a lion and wolf locked in battle. The death machines flew toward them, gliding over the rocks and dips that littered the valley. The shells rained down on Cotswold, sending shrapnel everywhere. Charred, black craters began to replace buildings and people as the rooks' fiery mortars carpet-bombed the town, leveling everything before them. Kull ran with the others toward the tree line, a surge of panic wanting to set in.

He did his best to check his fears. *Calm down. Keep your wits about you. Use your head.*

Grift's teachings found him there in the war zone that was once his hometown. Kull realized that he and all of Cotswold had been unprepared for this assault. *Why would the Grogans send such a large force to this little town? What do they want with us?* Amidst the questions and panic, Grift's consistent reminder throbbed in Kull's mind. *Always be prepared.* He sprinted with Ewing and his mother away from the Grogan forces and caught sight of his father leading troops back towards the fray. Grift opened fire and bellowed commands at his men as they charged the incoming rooks. His shot struck one of the drivers, quick and accurate, sending the machine careening off course, colliding with two others. The mass of twisted, flaming metal smashed into a muddy bank. Grift's shot emboldened his second in command, Tash Brinkley, to charge forward, firing at the incoming swarm as they continued to crest the hills like an army of ants. He spewed bullets into the valley, screaming curses at the Grogan pilots.

"Tash, fall back. Fall back in line!" Grift's voice cracked as he screamed for him to return to his position, but his cries fell on deaf ears. "Tash, now, fall back NOW!"

Tash's surge quickly ended as a rook unleashed a fiery harpoon, piercing and pinning his motionless body to the ground. They continued to fire rockets toward the fleeing crowd. An explosion sent Kull flying backward, and he crashed into a small gulley. Shaken, he reached for his arm, realizing he caught shrapnel in his left shoulder. Excruciating pain seared down his left arm and up his neck as Kull tried to make sure his arm still worked. A warm gush of blood dripped from his fingertips, mixing with the muddy ground below him. His ears were ringing, muffling the screams, the explosions, and the gunfire together into one encompassing buzz. His eyes were fuzzy as he tried to focus. The pain pulled at Kull like an anchor as he fought simply to stand, his body trying to hold him to the ground. *Am I dying? I can't move... I just want to lie down.*

"Get up, Kull." Grift's voice somehow penetrated through the fog of Kull's mind and his ringing ears.

He looked up and saw his father. His shoulder screamed as Grift stood him up on his feet, pulling him by his injured arm. Nausea washed over him like a tidal wave, and he tried not to pass out. He could hardly lift his eyes to find where to run next. Instead, he scanned the bloodstained ground, examining the old, muddy hillside as it was washed over with fresh crimson puddles. Grift's marching orders brought him back to reality.

"RUN, Kull! Get to the woods! Follow Ewing for Aleph's sake!"

Kull's legs felt as if they were rooted to the ground, but he turned and ran as fast as he could. Ewing was still running ahead, holding his mother. *Good,* he thought. *They are still alive.*

"GO, KULL!" He heard Grift scream amidst the ringing ribbons of bullet spray and echoing explosions.

The forest was half a mile away from Cotswold, and Kull was close to reaching its safety. With each labored stride, his shoulder ached and stung with newfound agony. He ran with his friends and his neighbors. Everyone was running, jumping over those who were already dead, whose bodies were charred into contorted, disfigured shapes. No one tried to recover the fallen. Instead, they left them lying, smoking, in the ravines as every last survivor ran to save themselves. Kull sprinted with a reckless energy as shock wore down and gave way to adrenaline, keeping his eyes pinned on Ewing and his mother ahead.

I'm almost there now. Just a little further. Dad is right behind. Just keep running.

The tree line was only fifty feet away. He turned around to try to see his father but all he could focus on was Cotswold engulfed in flames and mobs of people still barreling toward the forest. He peered through the crowd to see his father standing bravely, facing the enemy. He ordered what was left of his small platoon of soldiers to form a front, barring the way of the oncoming rooks.

Kull could hear Grift's voice barking orders to his men. "Find cover and stand your ground. Don't let them through!"

Holding their line, the soldiers hit the ground, sniping the rooks from behind what cover they could find in the field. Several of their shots hit their mark, causing the hovercrafts to careen to the ground enveloped in fire. Grift ran alongside his men, encouraging them as he lobbed grenades at the Grogan forces. Their forces were thinning them out, and Kull counted as Grift's men slowly took down ten rooks. Grift and his men were taking back ground and forcing the rooks back into the burning streets of the ruined town. With every step the platoon forced the black machines back, giving the last of the fleeing refugees valuable time to escape.

When Kull finally reached the edge of the forest he crashed through layers of low-lying brush trying to hide. He could hear other townspeople pushing through the woods, snapping branches and panting as they fled. They were like a panicked herd of deer fleeing a predator that caught them by surprise. Kull's heart sank as he heard the screams. Newly orphaned children called for their lost parents as they scrambled through the thickets. The wails of mothers that lost their children were a haunting sound that was impossible for Kull to comprehend. The cover of the trees may have protected Kull from the rooks, but it offered no protection from the nightmare that was setting in around him. He plunged himself through the masses looking for Ewing and his mother, but his injury stopped him.

Exhausted, he slid beneath the thick canopy and lay as flat against the ground as he could. His shoulder pulsed uncontrollably, spilling his blood out onto the ground. With conscious effort he laid against it, putting pressure on the wound. He had forgotten his shoulder in his mad scramble for cover, and his side was soaked with wet, hot blood. He peered out from his hiding place to survey the battle. Grift and the few remaining men had been pushed back out of Cotswold and were making every effort possible to keep the rooks from getting any closer to the woods. The small army was exposed from multiple angles as they fired from behind a crumbling retaining wall. Each fiery missile whittled down the wall, spraying pieces of brick and mortar in every direction.

Kull watched his father's gun either jam or run out of bullets. Kull cursed and prayed all in the same breath.

"Fall back!" Grift screamed.

Grift reached down and picked up a pistol from a fallen comrade. A large, black rook broke ranks from the phalanx and charged straight for the wall. It burst through the feeble barrier and skidded across the earth, turning its guns on the remaining soldiers. Grift stood up and unloaded the pistol on the war machine in a last ditch effort to distract the craft. His few surviving men began running to the forest. Grift's shots ricocheted off the craft's advanced armor. In desperation, he lobbed one last grenade in the direction of the nearest enemy vehicle.

An electric burst erupted from the rook, and Kull saw the shiny tazernet shoot out, expand, and surround his dad. It sent Grift's body into convulsions as he fell flat on his face writhing in an electric torrent of pain.

"No!" Kull tried to get to his feet to run to his father's side, but was quickly pulled down from behind.

"Let me go!" Kull screamed.

"Stay down, boy. They will kill you too," Ewing whispered. Ewing had finally found Kull. His large hands held Kull's shoulders as he tried to shake free, but the loss of blood and shock of the explosions left Kull too weak to escape Ewing's strong hold.

"*Stay down, Kull*. You need to live to fight another day."

His eyes never broke from his father as he lay shaking uncontrollably on the ground. He waited for the final blow from the rook hovering over Grift's shivering body, but instead it lowered to the ground and the small cockpit shield swung up. The driver, clad in black body armor and a dark helmet, stepped out onto the ground and walked toward Grift. Two more rooks arrived, and the drivers quickly dismounted in unison.

The first pointed toward Grift as the other two swooped down, kicking at him, sending blows to his ribs and head.

Kull turned away, unable to watch. He could hear his father moan as the first Grogan called off the two larger grunts. The leader unstrapped his helmet and threw it to the ground. When Kull looked back, his eyes widened with fear.

It was a girl. A river of red hair fell down around the girl's shoulders as she dropped her helmet to the side and leaned over Grift. Grabbing him by his hair, she lifted his head to whisper in his ear before slamming him back down to the ground.

"Let me go!" Kull screamed through clenched teeth. "Let me go fight! I will kill her!" He threw himself against Ewing. Kull took in the face of the girl, marking it in his memory.

Behind him, Kull heard something he had not heard in months. There, leaning against a tree stood his mother, her eyes fully aware of what was happening. She cried out, "Grift! No!" She took one step forward only to fall on the ground, her face a horrid tapestry wracked with fear and misery. Kull could not stand the sight of his mother wailing on the ground. His mind could not comprehend what was happening, and he bucked against Ewing with a mad fury. Ewing did not relent and pinned him down, restraining Kull's rage.

"*Kull*. You can't fight them. There is nothing we can do."

The larger of the two Grogans threw Grift over his shoulder and flung him into the back compartment of the girl's rook. She hopped back into her machine and yelled out to the others to fall out. Then, as swiftly as the rooks arrived, raining fire and fear, they were gone. They found what they came for.

CHAPTER TWO

The city of Vale stood silent. All commerce, all speaking, and all feasting were at a halt. Shops were boarded and closed, and the beautiful cobblestone streets and squares were empty. Wreaths of purple crowns of thistle hung on every door. Gray candles burned in every window, flickering ghosts keeping their night long vigil, sending pinpricks of light from the lowest hovel to the highest towers. An uncanny silence hung over Lotte's capital city. The city echoed with a new, empty void that begged to be whole again. The silence dissipated at dawn, swallowed by a deep, rolling chant that swelled out into the city streets, echoing off the marble promenades. The groaning hymn shattered the silence of the gray, mournful morning announcing the commencement of the long-awaited royal funeral procession. All the people of the city left their homes and stood united as a line of monks marched solemnly towards the king's hall. Each man and woman hoped to catch a glimpse of the king's gilded casket. Camden's body had been prepared, washed, and presented to the people, waiting in state for six months, fulfilling the time of mourning customary for the royals in Lotte. The mourning would soon be over, and now it was time for Camden to be laid to rest, according to the traditions of the Alephian monks.

The monks were clad in only light gray robes despite the frigid morning breeze. Their faces were painted with ceremonial ash. They led the funeral procession, singing low, doling chants that were almost inaudible. To the people of Vale, the holy men were strangers, otherworldly and terrifying. They rarely visited their city in such numbers, and only left their sacred forest of Preost during times of great upheaval or loss. They were not a welcome sight, and their solemn appearance did little to make their arrival a warm one. The Panderean royal court marched behind the congregation of monks, dressed in long, heavy fur robes. Everyone's faces were downcast and somber. The swell of the procession marched dutifully, rising to climb the smooth, marble steps leading up to the entrance of the king's hall. The surrounding throng of people mourned and sobbed. Representatives had come from the Darian family who ruled the coastal Realm of Elum. They, along with the monks from Preost, came with their deepest condolences, offering undying support to the royal family of Lotte. They walked proudly with their Panderean counterparts to the high hall, dressed in fine shimmering fabrics of bright blue and deep dark purple, colors that few in Lotte had ever seen worn, colors that ebbed and flowed in the sunlight, glistening like the ocean tide. Many children pointed at their clothes before being scolded by their parents for showing disrespect. The Grogans and the Rihts were notably absent from the procession, but their absence was an expected one. Their hands were stained with the king's blood.

Behind the parade of monks and government officials was a single casket made of solid ironwood. The casket was carried by Seam Panderean and his loyal troop of guardsmen. Seam's light brown hair was pulled back and tied behind his head with thin golden twine. His blue and gray robes hung over his tall frame as he shouldered the casket. The men climbed, slowly bearing the heavy burden, careful with their footing and pace. For Seam, the thought of carrying the remains of his murdered father up to what would soon become his hall, *his* throne, was tinged with a twisted and brutal irony. As they made their way up to the summit, the citizens of Vale threw immaculate wreaths onto the street and held their hands out to Seam, hailing him. Many were sobbing and wailing as the casket of King Camden passed them. Seam's mother, Queen Aleigha, followed closely behind the troop of men. She was a beautiful woman whose smile was famous throughout Lotte, but it had long disappeared. Her bowed head was covered with a black veil that shielded her face from the onlookers. The veil stood in stark contrast to the flowing ivory gown she wore, draped from her thin shoulders.

The men and women of Vale called out to their queen and soon-to-be king as they passed; each man and woman attempted to offer words of encouragement and love.

An older man's voice crackled through the crowd, "You will make your father proud, King Seam! All Hail King Seam!" Several other onlookers followed his lead and began chanting as well. Others continued to cry out and moan as their beloved King Camden passed by, too absorbed by their Realm's loss to think of hailing their future king.

A wrinkled, middle-aged woman laid a wreath at the Queen's feet and softly encouraged her. "Be strong, my queen! Your son will carry us on his shoulders just as he carries his father now! Your husband was great, but King Seam will be our savior from this war."

The weight of the casket wore down the young royal as he marched; digging deeper into his shoulder with each step, but it was of no consequence. The pit of Seam's stomach was coiled in a knot, and it shifted violently with each commoner's cry. Despite the pain and the bile that was trying to climb up his throat, he could not deny that a small spark of ecstasy jolted inside of him each time he overheard someone call him "King Seam."

The casket was placed high above the promenade, where the entire of city of Vale watched with anxious and nervous energy. The air was alive with electricity, and the crowd mumbled as the long train of mourners finally ended their arduous procession. Hover-cameras streaked across the sky like mechanical birds, careening themselves to get the best shot of the momentous occasion, beaming their images across all the Realms. Seam took his place, kneeling before the casket, where a hulking, ebony-skinned monk stood.

It was the Mastermonk and head of the Alephian Order, known as Wael. Rarely did he venture out from the confines of Preost's forests, but now he stood before Seam like a tall, lonely mountain. He spread out his long arms, and in an instant the murmurs of the crowd went silent. The Questioning was about to begin, and all of Lotte stood transfixed in awe. The Mastermonk rang out, his deep and thunderous voice booming across the crowd. A chant of an unknown language danced out from the man's mouth, each syllable unintelligible and melodious, when suddenly and unexpectedly it fell into something Seam understood:

"What is your first task?"

Seam stared into the dark eyes of the Alephian monk that bore down into him. Wael's face was streaked with the hot, white ash of war.

Seam was uneasy, but forced himself to focus on the face of the solemn monk before him, doing the best he could to ignore the pain within his eyes. Deep remorse could be seen in the monk's eyes, spilling out from behind his ghostly mask.

Seam replied to the monk, projecting his voice for the crowd to hear, "To bear the dead up to their final resting place. To hold them in my heart and to carry on their lives through my own."

The Mastermonk continued the Questioning:

"And what is your task for your people?"

Seam did not miss a beat. "To submit my will for their betterment, thinking always of their welfare before my own." Pride swelled within his heart as the people cried out in praise.

The Mastermonk closed his eyes and nodded his head in agreement. The final question was coming, and soon Seam would be done with the dreadful ceremony.

"Young Panderean, there is only one more question." The monk paused and his eyes flew open.

"What is your duty to Aleph?"

The very name of the deity commanded the silence. Seam locked eyes with the intense Mastermonk. He did not waver in his gaze. He could feel the weight of the ceremony now. It was a charade of old traditions, traditions that would soon fall out of favor. But traditions still held power. Heat rushed to his face as he cleared his throat and dryly answered the final question.

"To honor He, above all else."

The Mastermonk walked toward Seam, resting his hand on his forehead and began a long chant in the same ancient sing-song language with which he opened the ceremony. Raising his head, he looked up and out into the mass of spectators and stretched out his hands.

"It is my prayer that Aleph's peace will rest on *you* today. It is my prayer that this war, this war that has sent all of Candor into an uproar, will cease. So that we can remain in peace, which is the will of Aleph. Destruction and tyranny *will not* hold us in fear, for we know that we are always in his hands and always in his vision. It is my prayer that you may be blessed, that your lands may be blessed," the monk looked down at Seam, "and that your new King may be blessed. Until the Keeper returns to lead us into Aleph's loving restoration, I pray that you go now, spreading the peace of Aleph with you."

Once the prayer concluded, the Mastermonk lowered his hands and the ceremony was dismissed.

Peace. The thought of the word caused a tempest of pain, sorrow, and anger to well up inside of Seam.

How has it become custom to speak of peace and blessing when one loses all he has and all he has loved, thought Seam as he stared down at his feet. *This nation has been burned and beaten and nearly every man and woman here has lost someone, and yet we still speak of peace.*

The priests and honorary guests of Elum and Preost made the final march into the king's hall where Camden would be laid to rest in his catacomb. Seam walked into the darkness of the tomb beside his mother. She reached and squeezed his hand. Her cold hand cooled Seam's irritation and rage and helped bring his mind back to the task at hand.

"You did well, Seam. Your father would have been so proud." Her sentence stung with oncoming grief. She remained silent, but gripped down on Seam's hand hard. Seam winced at the words, but remained silent.

The depths of the catacomb were dark, illuminated with only dim candlelight. Frosty portraits and marble effigies flickered in the dark, standing like a large troop of long forgotten ghosts. The hollow eyes of the earlier royal families stared down upon the living who dared to enter this hall of the dead.

King Camden's newly hewn vault lay open, ready to swallow the titanic casket. Seam helped lower the body into its final resting place. The casket landed with a heavy thud. His mother leaned down to kiss the top of the casket before it was sealed under the heavy marble slab. She wailed, filling the room with a new line of grief. It was a scream that echoed the long history of Lotte's kings. Despite their glory and gains in reign, inevitably they all ended in the same dark place. Seam and the other guardsmen sealed the vault, dropping the heavy lid with a thunderclap of finality. The lid bore the inscription: "HERE LIES HE OF LINE DESCENT—CAMDEN PANDEREA—HIGH KING OF VALE AND LOTTE; SERVANT OF ALEPH." Underneath the written inscription was the carved family insignia; a bull's head, whose horns wore a crown of thistle blossoms.

With this final act, the ceremony came to a hollow end. The foreign dignitaries shuffled from the room, eager to leave the dark dread behind them. The ambassadors sent by the Darian family and the others of royal lineage from Elum seemed nervous from the moment they arrived in Lotte, and it was obvious, despite their support, that they were eager to leave. Elum had not yet been engulfed in the war that flared between Lotte and The Groganlands. The Elumites had every desire to remain neutral.

Seam had only one word for them. *Cowards.* Elum had a long history of avoiding conflict amidst its neighbors, even when those neighbors were tyrannical like the Grogan Sars. Right and wrong held no bearing with them. They sought only safety and profit.

The Alephian monks lingered. They took time to speak with every individual from the procession. They eventually took their leave, leaving Seam alone with his mother in the depths of the mausoleum, alone with the earthly remains of his fallen father.

"He was such a good man."

Seam had not expected his mother to break the silence. He pursed his lips as she spoke.

"He was the one to think of your name first, you know? I argued with him for weeks, but your father was always a good negotiator. 'Seam?' I said. 'Who had ever heard of such a name? Why?' He said that you would be the one to stitch us all back together. You would be Lotte's seam. Candor's seam."

Seam's mother wrapped her thin fingers around his upper arm and lightly squeezed as she pulled close to her son. "And I know now more than ever that he was right. You will bring us together."

Seam could feel his pulse beating beneath the weight of his mother's grip and he gently took her hands into his own as he looked down into her teary eyes.

"Strange. He never seemed that convinced in my ability. Did it require his death to learn what he really thought?"

Seam turned and rested his hands on the cold marble slab that sealed his father in his final resting place. His head dropped as he tried to sort through the tempest of thoughts and emotions that spun inside his chest.

Aleigha laid her hand back onto Seam's shoulder and gently addressed him as she fought back tears.

"You know he loved you, son. Very much. He was a busy man, maybe too busy at times, but he did believe in you. You were his only son and the most important piece of his heart."

To Seam, all he could remember of his father was the man he debated and argued with in recent years. His mother began to sob softly and Seam turned to embrace her and kiss the top of her head.

"Thank you, Mother. I apologize; I just don't know what to say. But you know I love you and I will do you proud."

Aleigha looked up at her son with a small smile and wiped her eyes. "You will make us both proud, son."

Seam bit the inside of his cheek, mustered what little smile he could find, and squeezed his mother's hand as she slipped away. "I will be up in a bit, Mother. I just need some time to think."

As Aleigha disappeared into the thin sliver of light creeping through the open doors, the silence of the room fell over Seam's shoulders.

Silence. For years, silence made Seam wary and restless. Silence normally meant dreams, and dreams meant terror. Sitting in the catacombs, though, there was total silence, unavoidable and heavy. Candles danced in the dark, bouncing an eerie amber light off the marble stones. Shadows skipped and swayed across the cold empty floor making it sparkle like black glass.

"There is *no* peace," he whispered. "There will *never* be any peace. Not for you, not for what you've done."

His words echoed in the dark halls, bouncing off the walls as if his thoughts were calling back to him. He loosened the golden ties that held his hair in place, and ran his hands through his long brown hair. He threw off his ceremonial cloak, and fell to his knees beside his father's tomb. Seam pinched his eyes together and tried to force pleasant memories of his father to return to his mind. His mind had been preoccupied with the most lasting and most recent memories as he and his father fought over policy and ideology.

However, after a few minutes several memories did return—early memories—of his father letting him sit on his lap in the throne room wearing his ceremonial crown. The old crown fell over his eyes and they laughed as he clumsily tried to perch it atop his childish head without any luck. Then his father's words flooded back into his mind, "Son, one day you too will serve the Realm of Lotte as king, and that day this old crown will fit much better. I know you will be one of the greatest kings of this Realm's history." Seam lifted his chin from the cold marble slab and looked up into the eyes of the paintings above him. Kings, dozens of them, memorialized on the walls, glared down at their own caskets. None of them could avoid death. King or not, they had all come to an end. Death did not respect their crown; they were merely men, no different than their servants. In the dark catacombs, there were no kings. There were only men. Dry, brittle bones and men.

As more memories rushed through his mind, Seam began to wail. He threw his fists down on the stone floor. His wail morphed into an unchained groan, and to his utter surprise he began to sob. Seam never expected losing his father to hurt so deeply. When he thought of the day he might lose Camden it had always gone differently in his mind. Pain and anguish were expected for the day he would lose his mother. However, the grief he felt for his father caught him off guard. He gasped for breath as pain tore through him, ripping his heart like a thin piece of fabric. In it all he heard the voice, the still small voice within him that began to question everything that brought him to this point.

What did you think, you fool? Did you think you could ascend to the throne without any pain, without any loss? No, no Seam, you are far, far too weak for that. You longed for power to bring change. Did you truly convince yourself that you could rise so quickly without a cost? Now you will know the true weight that power brings. You dreamed of the day you would be King, but you did not think of what loss you would suffer to precede your gain. It is yours now, King Seam, yours alone. War is on your doorstep, and everything you've hoped for holds on by a single thread.

"I can't!" Seam screamed. "Oh, gods above, I can't!"

Panting, lying on the floor, Seam allowed the cool stones beneath him to calm his fretting. He realized what he needed to do. He stood up and laid his hand on his father's grave.

"Father," he croaked hoarsely, rubbing his reddened eyes. "Forgive me, but I now know what must be done to bring about the peace you've longed for…that we've longed for. We will not be at war much longer now. I just wish I could have spared you this death, but you *would not* listen to me. Rest now and know that despite my shame, that I … I..."

Unable to utter the words that he longed to say, Seam hoisted himself up and away from the Pandarean catacombs, swearing to himself never to enter them again. The grief that wracked his body and shuttered his spirit evaporated as he stepped into the light flowing throughout the main floor of the High Hall. He emerged from the tombs, and there waiting for him was the court of lords from the surrounding villages, waiting for an audience. Upon entering, they quieted themselves and bowed.

Seam rebuffed their actions. "My lords, do not bow, for I am not yet your king. This time of mourning has just yet begun and we have much to speak about without the royal court pageantry. Do any of you have news from the front lines? Is there any news from Faylon?"

Marcus Esslered, the spokesman of the eastern cities, was the first to answer. "My lord, I personally have received word from my scouts that Faylon was completely destroyed. The Grogan forces took no quarter, and they butchered our people." The man paused as he looked into Seam's eyes and quickly lowered his gaze to his feet as he kicked at the floor.

"There were no survivors."

Seam threw out another question. "What about our Head Guardsman, Grift Shepherd? Is he counted among the dead as well?" Seam's eyes burned behind the question.

Marcus again spoke for the assembly as he muttered, "My lord, there has been no word about Grift or his forces. My report does not confirm his..."

Seam cut him off, "Find out, Esslered! It is of great importance that Grift not be captured by those barbarians. He is one of the few men that truly dictate our kingdom's security. As for the rest of you," Seam paused, exhaling. "Candor has survived a millennia of wars and is no stranger to conflict. We, the remnant of mankind, can attest to struggles in the past that our world has endured. But I tell you now that we have never faced a time darker in our kingdom's history. If the Grogans have their way, Lotte will be laid to waste just as the nation of Riht, and I will not allow that to happen. I need your full support and loyalty as we decipher the best strategy to run the Grogans out of our Realm. I assure you I will not rest until I have my revenge on the Groganlands for this treachery, even if I have to rekindle the fires in Riht and march our forces to the gates of Rhuddenhall." He paused, his mind buzzing. "Meet me at dawn. We must plan our next move. In the meantime, communicate to your forces to form a perimeter around the borders of Lotte and to hold their positions. We cannot have these brutes advance any further."

Each of the men bowed and made their way out of the High Hall leaving Seam alone with only the guards who remained steadfast at their post. Making his way to his personal chamber, Seam felt the confidence he felt with his advisors peel away. A nagging ache of fear began to pool inside his gut.

He barred his chamber door and paused at the room's small mirror, taking account of his haggard countenance. He sunk into his desk chair and sighed as he reached into the dusty drawer of his desk. He laid a small, leather-bound tome on the desk and slid his fingers across its surface.

The book's presence eased his spirit and helped lift the anchor weighing on his chest. Seam pulled his hair back as he leaned over the book and opened its ancient pages. As he scanned through the pages he spoke in a hushed whisper, "Speak to me again."

He flipped to a familiar page that had held his eyes captive over the years. The faded scribbling stood out stronger than anything else in the room.

We wait in time for our savior,
The Keeper from beyond,
Do not let your weary spirit waver,
Answer and break our bond.

Seam drew in another breath and exhaled the day's stress and pain. He turned again to another familiar passage, *his passage.*

We wait, Immortal, locked in glass.
Until the Keeper comes.
Descend, rise, and free our hands.

Come soon, dear Keeper, come!
Let out your life, release your gift,
This world waits for thee,
Through you, by you, we will come,
Keeper of Candor's Keys.

CHAPTER THREE

A tower of white grit and dust was pitched into the sky as a phalanx of black rooks ripped through the deserts of Riht. Their speed could not be matched, and in the ruined Realm of Riht, there were no limits to their acceleration. No obstacles, no boundaries; just a flat, open desert plain. Willyn Kara led the dreadful formation across the wasteland. She finally had her prized quarry, Grift Shepherd. She hammered down on the throttle and felt the engine throw her back into her seat, roaring like a raging lion, as she pushed it to its limits. A spot of radio chatter buzzed in her cockpit.

"General Kara, the rooks cannot maintain this velocity for much longer. I have to advise you to slow down. The engine levels on your bird are becoming critical."

Willyn gunned the engine in defiance, and with another rocketing explosion the Rihtian desert smeared by her in a blur. She glanced down at her navigation screen. She was only an hour out from Rhuddenhall. She had to get back to the Red City. To Hagan.

I just hope I'm not too late.

Willyn sat silently by the bed that held her older brother's brittle and twisted body. Her thin fingers were interlocked with the skin and bone that replaced his once powerful hands. Hagan's commanding and confident aura shriveled into the pale, sunken skeleton that held his soul captive. He labored through the last moments of his life with little grace, hidden from the public's view.

The sound of the ventilator wheezing and clicking was enough to make Willyn sick to her stomach. She quietly waited, not knowing whether to hope for a miracle or to wish for her brother's passing. Neither seemed realistic, as Hagan was caught in the delicate place between life and death. Her hope for any recovery had eroded since the first day her brother was connected to the terrible machines.

The Sar was young by Grogan standards, and his rise to power was filled with high hopes of his people. Chief among the tribal lords of his kin, Hagan walked in the image of his father, but he brought with him new vision of what the Groganlands could be. Willyn could still hear his booming voice in Rhuddenhall echoing across the throng of citizens gathered in the Red City to celebrate his ascension.

Hagan walked up to the podium, wearing only the simple black body armor of a commanding officer on the day of ascension. He refused to adorn himself with the traditional crimson garb of a newly ascended Sar. Most surprising was his refusal to wear the Helm of Rodnim. The helm was made by the first Sar, Hagan's ancestor from ancient times. Rodnim the First conquered and unified the bickering Grogan tribes under his family's banner. The helmet had always been worn as it passed down the family line. Instead, Hagan held the helmet by his side, its golden face shining red in the oncoming twilight. He insisted that his first public appearance would be as himself. Envoys from every Realm were gathered, and even King Camden from Lotte traveled to pay special homage to the new Sar. Willyn could still remember the rousing speech her brother gave that day:

"My fellow Grogans. Today is a new day. Aleph blessed my father, Wodyn the Great, with a strong, remarkable reign. He has been called back by Aleph into his care, but through him peace has been secured for not only our Realm, but for all Candor. The vile Realm of Riht is conquered, and its lecherous leadership exiled or imprisoned. We stand united, finally at peace with our other brothers and sisters." He glanced over to High King Camden Pandarean. "The tensions we have had with Lotte are over, thanks to the hard work and friendship of High King Camden. He has brought much honor to my house with his presence here today."

Camden stood smiling and waving at the jubilant crowd. Hagan continued, "Elum is ready to trade with us once more, and our ties to our spiritual brethren in Preost could never be stronger. It is with these graces and blessings that my reign begins today."

The city exploded with an uproar of devotion. Hagan paused as the wave of praise washed over him. He continued, "We will redouble the efforts now in this time of peace to reclaim the lost Predecessors' technologies. My grandfather and father understood that real power comes from the might of our forces, but we cannot hope to remain strong if we do not advance." Willyn stood near the podium as Hagan continued, her body alive with the electric energy showering over the city. The people loved their new Sar, and Willyn could not have been any prouder of her older brother. He was meant for greatness.

Hagan continued, "We owe a debt to the Predecessors, not just for the mechanics and infrastructure that we use for our own advancements, but also for their folly and pride." The crowd's roar died down as the new Sar's speech took an unexpected turn.

"Our ancient ancestors serve us today with something much more important than rail lines or datalinks. The Predecessors give us a warning. A warning to those who do not heed caution. A warning for those who do not weigh the cost of wanton violence or destruction, but think only of their selfish pride." The crowd was silent, and Willyn smiled at how quickly Hagan caught their attention. This was not the common speech that the Grogan Sar gave to the people. This was something completely different.

"These are lessons that we Grogans do not often consider, but it is good for us to reflect on this day that it is only by Aleph's grace that humanity continues to exist on Candor. We are the last of the human race. All of us on Candor must walk in humility. We must not blindly surrender ourselves to pride or hatred. When we give into the hate that drove the Old World to ruin, we ensure our destruction."

Hagan paused, allowing the silence to permeate the Red City. "We must make assurances that the downfall of the Predecessors does not mirror our own undoing. The Groganlands is the strongest Realm in Candor, and we must set an example not to uncover the Predecessor technology only to fuel and advance our military prowess. We have an opportunity to extend advancements in medicine and healing, in infrastructure and learning out to all of our brothers and sisters who inhabit this land, and secure peace across this entire Continent for generations. As your leader, I promise to hope for peace while staying prepared for conflict should it come. If we, the Grogans, can hope for peace while staying ready for war, I can assure that Aleph will reward our efforts.

He picked up the golden helm and placed it on his head. Willyn's ears nearly burst under the thunder of people. "May Aleph continue to bless you, the Groganlands, and all of Candor. So begins the reign of Sar Hagan the First."

The booming bravado of Hagan and all the joy that accompanied it was now silent, and Willyn was forced to observe the twisted carousel of machines upon which all her bleak hope was now placed. They would spin in their pattern with a maddening regularity, all in an effort to frantically hold back the dark extinguishment of her brother's life.

Hagan's chest shuttered grotesquely as an unnatural gurgling sound bubbled deep from within his throat. The ventilator wheezed, puffing a low click of fresh air through his paralyzed lungs. Then the small green dot would flicker with each new, weak heart beat. The pattern never changed and never stopped. With each cycle, Willyn was filled with anxious dread, certain that *this* would be Hagan's last moment. But the messy and tangled mixture of tubes and wires that ran into and through Hagan's body made sure his final moment never came. As long as the smattering of machines continued to do their job, the small flicker of life in Hagan continued to burn.

Willyn grabbed a damp cloth and wiped at her brother's head, pushing away the small beads of sweat from his furrowed brow. She carefully observed his eyes and mouth hoping for a sign that her small acts of affection might bring about a sign of life, some sort of recognition. Some hope. She had only been home from war for eighteen hours, but in that entire time she sat tirelessly by his bedside, caring for him and watching over his needs.

Willyn smiled as she wiped at his cheeks with the white cloth and pushed back a lock of red hair that had fallen into his face. A question sprang from her lips, "Do you remember the time you ate all those mushrooms out in the forest? I had to take care of you then, too. You were so, so stupid. You insisted that they were safe and to prove it you popped one into your mouth." The memory caused a smile to wash over her, and she stared blankly, lost in it. "You threw up so much, but that was a good lesson you learned, wasn't it? I never thought you would get better."

In her heart she hoped that he would stir under the memory, but there was nothing. There were only the rhythmic beeps and clicks drawing her back into the grim fog suffocating the room. Willyn's smile faded as her brother's blank, despondent face stared back at her, *through her*, reminding her that he was suffering from far more than a bad case of food poisoning; he was dying. Whatever he was exposed to worked within him slowly, meticulously stealing one function of his life after another. Hagan started complaining of symptoms months earlier. He could not keep his food down and was having trouble sleeping. His insomnia eventually led to a ratcheting fever that peaked so high it brought him to seizure. In the following weeks, it exploded into a grand culmination of nothing less than a full-body shutdown. With each hour, Willyn saw her brother deteriorate before her eyes.

She laid her face against the side of the bed. Tears, unexpected and unwelcome, rolled down her cheeks as she wept into the clean linen that wrapped around her brother's frail figure. The weeping grew into a full chain of sobs that racked and wrenched their way through her body. She bellowed out a low howl and finally collapsed beside her brother's bed, exhausted but relieved to release her grief. Willyn realized that for the first time in her life she was alone and she was powerless.

The terrifying fear rose within her. *There is nothing I can do to change this. Any of this.*

"You need to wake up, Hagan," she said, squeezing at his hand, her fingers like a vise. "You can't be like this! You are the *ruler* of the Groganlands. The people need you." Her voice trailed off as she wiped at her eyes and tried to gather herself. "I need you! I am not ready to be the Sar. I won't be! You need to wake up. *Please just wake up."*

Willyn's plea rang hollow in the empty silence of the room. She gathered her composure and wiped her eyes dry. No one could ever see her cry. She buried any trace of her grief, and the guilt that had accompanied her tears faded into her cold, chiseled face. Hagan would have never stood for any tears being shed on his behalf. However, Willyn had not expected that it would feel so good to cry, to no longer be the Sar's sister, but to be Hagan's. Willyn knew that any sign of weakness outside of this moment of privacy would not be accepted by her people. It was weakness. It was error. It was forbidden. But with Hagan she could always be herself. The thought of losing that freedom, and losing her closest and only friend, terrified her.

To lose Hagan was to lose herself and be trapped within the walls of her official position; the next in line as Sar.

Hagan's heart monitor bounced a thin, green line across its dark screen while another light flashed with each pulse. Willyn adjusted one of the knobs to turn down the annoying beeping noise that kept pinging from the machine.

"I wish we had some of the medical technology from Lotte or Elum for you." The irony of Hagan's former speech washed over her.

"Lotte." Willyn's heart sank back deep into her chest and slowed its beating. She swallowed the knot that twisted in her throat as she thought of the man she had just locked away. A new feeling ran through her: rage. She stood.

"Hagan, I have to go now. I have someone who knows what needs to be done to get you back." She leaned down and kissed her brother's cold, clammy forehead and made her way for the infirmary exit.

Grift Shepherd sat alone in the cold cement cell. One light bulb seared overhead, a single pinprick of illumination. Willyn stood behind the wall of shadows and gritted her teeth as she observed the man she personally ripped out of Lotte. Grift rested on his knees with his hands bound behind his back, a dirty, rough blindfold covering his eyes. He was stoic given his current state. He demonstrated no movement, no jostling, and no panic. Instead, he sat on his knees with his head down, quietly humming to himself.

Heat rushed to her cheeks as Willyn continued to observe the man that poisoned Hagan. Each childish note he would hum only incensed her further. It was as if he knew she was in the room with him and was toying with her, waiting. Her eyes narrowed and she moved into the light.

She sprung from the dark corner of the cell and sunk her boot into Grift's side without hesitation. A loud crack rang out as Grift's broken ribcage caved under the impact. Grift crashed to the floor his mouth agape, opening and closing like a fish out of water. He tried to steady himself, but his hands were tied so tightly behind his back that he could only writhe in pain on the floor. Willyn reached down and picked Grift up by his hair, yanking his face just inches from her own.

She stared into Grift's swollen and bruised face and hissed, "Now that I have your attention, I have some questions for you, Shepherd."

She slapped Grift and pointed into the shadows behind her.

"You will want to answer me honestly every time I ask you a question. I am not the only pain lurking in the shadows."

Grift groaned as he worked to sit himself up straight again. He growled a low answer, "Willyn Kara. Your reputation precedes you once again...I'm not the one that needs to be answering questions. I did not declare war after forty years of peace. I did not assassinate a king!"

Willyn's fist exploded against Grift's jaw, sending spit and blood across the cement floor. She ripped the blindfold from his face.

"Don't you *dare* accuse me! You tried to assassinate a Sar. And that is why you are here. You are here because of Hagan."

Grift spewed a red spatter on the gray floor. He looked up at her, his eyes filled with shock. Willyn's words caused Grift's face to show an unexpected emotion. *Fear.* He narrowed his eyes and evenly answered the accusation through his swelling mouth.

"Hagan was a friend. He is still a friend. I would have never attacked him."

Grift did not break the stare with Willyn, even though blood was freely dripping from his mouth. Resigned, he continued, "Ask me what you want, but know that I did not harm your brother."

Willyn reached into her pocket and threw a small metal vial on the floor between the two. She stooped to look at Grift, her eyes cutting into him like sharpened blades.

"Then explain to me how it is that we found this vial in my brother's room with your prints on it?"

Grift stared at Willyn and looked down at the vial that had engulfed Candor in war. He continued to stare at the capsule as he tried to remember it, but there was nothing.

"Those prints were planted. I've never seen that thing," Grift answered. The answer was matter of fact. Willyn could not deny that he was convincing. Grift continued, "You know better than to accuse me because of some fingerprints."

Willyn snatched up the vial and put it back into her pocket. She calculated her next move. He would cave. He would cave and tell her what he did to Hagan.

"Then what about the surveillance video we have, Grift?"
The room fell silent as they stared at one another. Neither took a breath or moved. Willyn could see he had no idea of the video. Grift squinted his eyes and addressed Willyn not out of anger or remorse, but confusion.

"Video?" Grift sputtered. "Of what? There is no video of me attacking Hagan because I never stepped foot into the Groganlands without proper clearance."

Willyn's heartbeat sped as she stepped toward Grift and leaned to whisper next to his ear.

"I told you not to lie to me, Grift. I told you not to lie to me."

A small screen flickered to life behind her and played a looping video of Grift stepping into Hagan's private quarters and then re-emerging a few minutes later.

Willyn stepped back and locked her cold blue eyes on Grift, hatred pouring from them like a broken dam.

"I told you not to lie to me. You HAVE been to the Groganlands without border clearance as evidenced. The day after that video was taken my brother's body started its full failure. This is NO coincidence, Grift! You will die by my hands, and I will enjoy it!"

Willyn stood and brushed herself off, as if Grift's presence left a cloud of debris on her. "I have other matters to attend to. I will have my friends come join you until you decide to tell them exactly what you used to poison my brother."

Willyn started to step away but then quickly spun on her heels and slammed her boot into the back of Grift's head. The blow sent his crumpled body tumbling across the floor. Willyn's arms were shaking as rage poured through her veins like boiling water. All she wanted to do was tear Grift limb from limb. *It would feel so good to make him suffer.* She hesitated. She needed to know what was poisoning Hagan.

Control yourself. Hang on. You can kill him soon enough.

Grift let out a low moan as he started to lift himself from the floor. Willyn shoved down the building tempest within her enough to address Grift one last time.

"I believe I made my point, Grift. You don't want to lie around here. Do yourself a favor when the interrogators come; tell the truth."

She quietly slid from the cell and paced the outside hallway. Her boots clicked on the cold cement floor in a rhythmic pattern. Willyn felt like her insides were warped and twisted as she tried to shake the tempest coursing through her. Her inner voice chided her for becoming so volatile.

You nearly killed him. Then where would we be? Where would Hagan be?

The thought of Hagan made her hold a deep breath in her lungs to release the aggression from her mind.

I need to get back to Hagan. I can't stay here. Willyn could feel the magnetic pull of the cell. Back to Shepherd. Back into that cell to finish him off. She put her hand down by her sidearm. *I can make him talk,* said her rage. *I can make him wish he had never set foot into the Groganlands.* Her hand gripped the cell door, but the image of Hagan reappeared in her mind, illuminating her purpose.

No. The interrogators will pull it from Grift. He knows. He knows what we need. What I need. Just let them do their job and extract it from him. I need to be with Hagan.

Willyn settled the matter in her mind before forcing herself away from the door and back down the hallway. For the last few weeks she had grown accustomed to the roar of her rook's engine and the cadence of its fifty caliber machine guns rattling off rounds on the front line. It made the silence of the hallway maddening. Without the noise of war drowning out her thoughts, all Willyn could focus on was the dreadful weight of her brother's condition and the violence blooming against the man that she knew had poisoned him. It was infuriating to think that she was so close to answers but was forced to wait.

Willyn jammed the button to open the elevator leading back up to the northern wing of the compound. The old, cracked button lit up as the gears moaned from deep within the elevator shaft. Once the door opened, Willyn stepped into the slick, chrome interior of the cabin and spun around to catch one last glimpse at the door holding Grift captive.

"I was just coming to see you. I thought you would be down here," a voice whispered.

It pushed every ounce of breath from Willyn's lungs, but she did not allow herself to flinch. Instead of shouting or jumping, her brain sent her hand to wrap around her pistol. In a millisecond, she redirected her hardened instincts, recollecting that she was back home, back in Rhuddenhall.

You don't pull guns on people in Rhuddenhall. Calm down.

The man who had blended into the back corner of the elevator spoke in parcels of regulated words, cold, even, and calculated.

"I *am* a bit shocked you didn't see me. In your own world I guess. I can understand. You have been through a lot."

Willyn turned to face the cold, gray eyes locked onto her. Blue embers locked into place, boldly unblinking against the eyes of Hospsadda Gran, an upstart and ambitious member of the Grogan Council.

Willyn regulated her response. "Hosp. What are you doing here? Council members have no business in the lower levels."

A smile twisted itself onto Hosp's face, "That is why I waited in the elevator, Madam Kara."

Willyn was first to break the stare. Her skin crawled to look at him, revulsion first and foremost to his pathetic features; his patchy thin beard, pasty white skin, long interlocking fingers, and a small waterfall of shiny, greasy black hair. It was his eyes, however, the gray hurricanes that surrounded his pupils that worried her most. "What *do* you want, Hosp? I don't have time for you right now. I have more important things than politics to deal with right now."

Hosp's smile grew to a pointed smirk as he waved his hand in the air between the two.

"Oh, I did not mean to bother you. I simply wanted to offer my deepest regret for what has happened to Hagan."

The grin and the glint in his eyes revealed no remorse. Hosp looked like a man staring at a prize. Willyn knew exactly what he wanted: power.

Willyn shot back, “You could have offered your sympathies anytime and anyplace. Right now is most inconvenient, and I'm afraid I don’t have much time to meet with you. Is there anything else?”

Hosp’s eyes widened, like that of an animal locking onto prey. He let out a small chuckle and clasped his hands together as his cold eyes bore into her. Willyn regretted opening the conversation up further.

“Ah, yes, I do have something of importance to tell you. The Council is working on a motion to surrogate.”

Willyn’s chest felt empty, and a knot twisted itself into her dry throat.

“A motion to surrogate? I have not been notified of being elected as a candidate.”

Hosp drew in a deep breath and paused before coolly hissing, “That is because you are not a candidate. My apologies for any confusion on *my* part. I can see why you would *assume* to be a potential candidate."

Willyn grabbed Hosp’s collar and slammed him against the wall of the elevator. She felt like her face was going to explode with the rush of heat that flew into her.

“There is no one worthy of replacing Hagan because he *will* recover. And no one is better suited to stand in for him than me. What do you mean that I am not the candidate?”

Hosp tried to steady himself as Willyn pushed him into the corner of the creaking elevator.

“Simply put, Willyn, the Council feels the war has left you…unstable.” Hosp put his cold, twisted hand around Willyn’s wrist, “And I believe this attempted display of aggression against a Council member is another piece of evidence to support that suspicion.”

Willyn ripped her hand away and glared at the worm before her. The thought of beating Hosp felt like it would bring more relief than her earlier assault on Grift.

"You are nothing but a snake! You are the last person I would vote to power."

Hosp rubbed his hand against his throat and coughed. Wheezing, he spoke, "Regrettably, Mistress Kara, you have no vote to cast. Had your concern been for your Realm rather than for your kin, you might have garnered favor with the Council, but instead you rushed your legion of rooks out into Lotte without so much as a single resolution from the people of your Realm."

Willyn checked him, breaking through, "Don't you mean the Sar? The *Sar*? The sovereign head of our Realm was nearly assassinated, and you make it sound like a petty family squabble. Are you deft, you sniveling idiot?"

Hosp fired back, "Yet your rash actions have guaranteed a blood war with the Pandereans. And for how long? Months? Years?!" Passion percolated out from the calculating maw standing before her, "How could we, the legislative representatives of the Groganlands, put you in as the surrogate when you have guaranteed an end to peace, the death of *our* loved ones, and the debt of your subjects."

The elevator dinged, and the doors swung open. Willyn had never felt so relieved. "Hosp, I will not continue this with you. Not here, not now. I will send a full report to the Council dictating my actions on the Lottian front and my purposes behind them. Who are the potential surrogate candidates?"

Hosp stared at her and slowly and delicately responded, as if to absorb this moment in his memories, "Well, Mistress Kara, there is only one candidate being considered. Myself."

Enemies were encroaching on all sides. Hagan had been nearly killed. Grift Shepherd would not give up his secrets. And now, Hosp. She riveted her eyes toward Hosp, answering him with masterful control.

"Then Councilman, I can assure you that your attempt to surrogate will fail. I will personally go to Council tomorrow and make my case to your colleagues. They will hear the truth and be swayed not to cast any vote for you."

An explosion of sirens went off, the sound cascading violently down the hallway. Willyn recognized the cadence of the particular alarm.

Prison break. Grift.

CHAPTER FOUR

A black plume of smoke hovered over Cotswold. What was once a small, unassuming village had become an inferno of fifteen foot flames. The sound of timber frames cracking and buckling echoed through the whole valley as smoldering buildings collapsed in on themselves. Even from the outer fields, Kull had to shield his face from the wall of heat keeping him and everyone else at a distance. Nearly half the town was burnt to the ground, and the remnant of buildings still standing were all ruined.

Kull stood at the edge of the forest; his hands were shaking like leaves in a hurricane. His mind scrambled, trying to pick up the pieces of where he was.

The butchering rooks were gone.

Cotswold was gone.

Dad.

Dad is gone.

The dreadful thought repeated in his mind as the shock wore off. He stood amidst the burning remains of his ruined hometown and was bewildered as to why the Grogans had any desire to destroy his hometown and kidnap his father.

"Kull."

Kull's head snapped at the voice that did not register in his mind. It was a voice that had long been silent. He met the lucid eyes of his mother and nearly wept. Leaning over her was Ewing, who stood by her side as more and more refugees poured into the forest. She embraced him, weak and trembling. They held each other amidst the tall pines swaying in the soot-stained wind.

She whispered in his ear, her weak words like rain in the desert to Kull's shattered mind. He could scarcely believe he was hearing them. What she said was not what he expected.

"You have to go after him, Kull. You have to go after your father."

Kull stared in her eyes, trying to understand what he was hearing. Responsibilities and duty flooded his mouth like a reflex, "What about you?" *How could he ever leave her alone when all that they knew was ripped away?*

Her cold hand grasped his in the autumn air, and her eyes were wet with grief. "*Grift is more important than me.*" A rasping cough racked through her thin frame.

Kull did not know what to say. His hands shook, and quietly he stammered, "Don't say that." The thought of leaving his mother was so foreign to everything he knew. It pinned his heart to the wall of his chest.

Kull gazed into her eyes and did his best to be reasonable. "Mom, I know I have to do something, but I can't leave you here in this town." He turned his face to the wall of fire that was now consuming all he knew. "Look at it! Nothing is left. Who would take care of you?"

Rose took her son's hand and wiped the dirt from his face with her frail, trembling hand. A smile fought its way onto her face. "Kull, you have been so good to me, but you have to find your father. I need you to be strong for me, and I will be strong for you. I promise."

Kull wrapped his arms around her and fought back the tears pushing through. Everything within him churned with pain; his shoulder's wound blazed with heat, and his heart broke and ached. All of it was happening so fast. His mind was blurred with the shock of his mother speaking to him, commanding him to go after his father, and the fear of what might happen.

Finally, the words shook free from his lips, "But, what can I do mom? The Grogans came with an army."

Kull's mother stared deeply into his eyes, and her face stiffened like stone. "Do exactly what your father would do if they had taken you, Kull. *Don't stop and keep fighting*."

The words ignited Kull's heart and set fire to his spirit. They pushed heat through his bones that was more intense than the smoldering remains of Cotswold. *She is right*. He had no choice but to try and find his father, regardless of the cost. If his mother was strong enough to ask her son to leave her side, he could be strong enough to seek out his father.

"I have to go gather my things, then." The sentence was awkward, but Kull did not know what to say.

His mother nodded. "Come see me before you go. I have something I need to give to you before you leave." Kull nodded, his mind filling with disbelief. He sat her back down under a tall pine.

"I'll be right back."

"Kull." His mother's large, brown eyes stared at him. "Go. I'm fine. Now, go."

Kull nodded and looked over the burning city before him, trying to plan his next move.

The girl. The red-haired girl. I'm going to find her, and then I'm going to kill her and bring dad back.

Arthur Ewing hobbled up past Rose and up to Kull as they both looked out over the raging fire. He cocked his head at him, noticing Kull's vacant eyes.

"Lad, are you alright?"

"Stay with mom, Ewing," said Kull before sprinting like a madman across the plain toward the hellish, burning town. Arthur Ewing screamed behind him, limping in vain to catch up.

Kull did not stop. He plunged himself deep into the smoldering wreckage of what was once his hometown, weaving far from the pyre that hungrily consumed half the village. The streets were littered with debris, shrapnel, and smoking wreckage. He looked back to see Ewing trailing far behind. He could hear his booming curses as he scrambled up toward Kull.

From his vantage point, he could see the streams of Lottian reinforcements flooding in from Vale, bringing with them a caravan of aid. Large white tents were being hoisted up in the outlying pastures, doctors and nurses scrambling to care for the wounded and the dying.

Kull tried to make sense of his surroundings. The buildings that were spared from the burning had either collapsed or were marked by fresh mortar craters and bullet holes. He weaved down a small alley, toward the hardware store his family lived out of for years. The store had been spared from a fiery destruction, but was badly damaged. He stepped gingerly around the familiar wreckage. Pieces of his past littered the floor in a ruin of scattered memories. Broken glass and splintered planks popped and cracked under each uneven step as he made his way to the back of the building.

Three walls of the back room were still standing, but the structure seemed to moan in protest as Kull explored the ruins of his former home. Then he found it.

"There you are."

He pulled an old hunting rifle out from under the rubble. His fingers ran down the barrel and the stock and opened the chamber to inspect it. It was still intact, and he thanked Aleph.

He reached back into the wreckage of an old shelf and pulled out a half-filled box of ammunition. As he stretched his hand out, his shoulder thundered with pain, a quick reminder of his close brush with death. He groaned as his collar bone twinged with misery.

Kull could hear heavy footsteps approaching him from the front of the building. Ewing had finally caught up with him.

With every step came a curse and a heavy panting for breath.

"Boy! Gods above, what *are* you doing? Come on out of there now!" Kull's mind switched from frustration back to dread. He had not thought to look at Ewing, but he was not in good shape. His trembling voice lost its boisterous boom. Something was wrong with him. Kull could hear it in his voice.

Kull stepped out from the back room to find Ewing leaning on the counter, catching his breath.

Holding up the ammunition, Kull revealed his intent.

"I'm going after her," he admitted. "I'm going to make her pay." Ewing said nothing, but his lips pursed as he shook his head. Kull threw his rifle over his good shoulder and stuffed the handfuls of rounds in his pocket. As he stepped around the counter Ewing suddenly grabbed Kull by his wounded shoulder and clamped down, his vise-like grip causing an explosion of pain up Kull's arm. Kull fell to his knees, screaming.

"And what do you think the Grogans will do to you, *boy*?" Ewing's grip tightened. "If an old man like me can cause you to fall on your knees in your condition, what do you think they'll do?!"

It took every ounce of Kull's restraint not to retaliate. His temper extinguished immediately, however, when he spied the black open wound in Ewing's right leg. Gaping and swollen, the leg looked like rotten meat and it was losing a large amount of blood. Kull shoved Ewing's arm off his shoulder and stood up.

"Arthur... your leg."

Ewing did not hear him, but stared at him, continuing to lecture. "I know you want to try and chase those Grogan monsters, but right now you are in no shape to go running after them with your shoulder..." Ewing smacked his lips as he tried to continue. "Listen to me... boy... it's stupid to..." The color drained from Ewing's face as his adrenaline faded. "You can't just..." His sentence faded and Ewing swayed, falling to the ground unconscious.

Kull screamed and grabbed Ewing under his arms and dragged him out of the ruined home. The old man was a heavy load to drag, even a short distance, and every tug sent a blast of pain through Kull's body.

"Help! I need some help here!" Kull called out amidst the empty streets.

White-clad medics were carefully navigating through the rubble, searching for survivors when they heard Kull and found him pulling Ewing into the street. Several broke into a sprint with a stretcher. While two of the men carried the fabric cradle, the other checked Ewing's vitals and began to run IVs into his arm and patch his infected leg. Ewing started to come back around and mumbled as the men set him down outside one of the large white tents. Kull stared at the men toiling over Ewing, cleaning and dressing the wound. Soon, he could see the attendants relax; Arthur Ewing was stable. A man in a white coat splattered with blood issued a command to Kull as he tied a red piece of yarn around Ewing's tattered leg.

"Take him down to the infirmary tent. We've done all we can do with his leg."

Kull stood up. "What do you mean you've done all you can?" The question flew out before Kull could stop it.

"Just take him down to the infirmary tent." The doctor's stern eyes peered over his glasses, commanding the other medics. He gave a quick glare at Kull and walked away. The medics picked up Ewing again and hauled him further down the hill. They checked him in with the field nurses and then sprinted back into the burning town center.

Kull walked beside Ewing to one of the medical tents and helped him into a small cot so another medic could reexamine and treat his leg. His eyes kept scanning the tent, trying to find evidence of his mother. Ewing left her behind to chase after him. Panic thumped through Kull's chest as he started for the door of the tent to go back to where he left her. Eva Dellinger, the town healer and nurse, came rushing over to them.

"Oh, Kull. Good. Your mother." Kull quickly read her eyes for an answer. Eva spoke, "She is okay. She is resting, poor thing. But she is okay. Such a blessing she was spared."

The words washed over Kull like cool water, extinguishing the panic that started to set in.

"Thanks Eva," smiled Kull, "I didn't know what to think."

Eva smiled and pointed over her shoulder. "I have her in a smaller tent outside. She needs some quiet. This tent is a mess. It would rattle her nerves." Then her eyes fell on Kull's shoulder. "You need some attention yourself."

Eva sat Kull in an open cot next to Ewing and began examining his wounds. Then she looked over at Ewing. There was shock in her eyes as she looked at Ewing's leg. Her hands toyed with the red yarn. *What did it mean? Was it a fatal wound?*

Silently, Kull sat as Ewing slept in a shock ridden stupor. His mind raced and worried over the old man passed out beside him. *At least mom is okay*. All he could do was wait.

Wait.

The image of the girl kicking his father to the ground filled him again with rage.

The Grogans were not waiting.

He took in all the people around him. Friends, neighbors, family. All the victims were innocents, butchered by the Grogans. He felt his throbbing shoulder and realized how lucky he was. Had the shrapnel landed a few inches over, it would have been over for him. A hand brushed over him, resting in the middle of his shoulder blades, as light as a feather, but as warm as a blanket. Kull looked up and his gaze fell on Adley Rainer. She looked exactly the same as the last time Kull had seen her before she left for the Academy. She left him years before, just one of many in Cotswold who made the routine journey away from home. Yet when it came to the people Kull missed most, she meant more than all of his friends who had left. Kull long held a secret affection for her, but life had other plans. Her long, brown hair was braided, falling down near the small of her back, and she was dressed in green medical scrubs. She greeted Kull with a smile, and Kull quickly stood and embraced her with genuine surprise.

"Adley! I didn't think..."

She interrupted, "Kull, are you okay?"

"I didn't know…"

"As soon as I heard about the attack I volunteered to be on the first support run." Adley's eyes were soft but determined. "I can't imagine what they could have wanted with Cotswold...but I'm glad to find you alive. And Eva let me know that Rose is resting well in the quarantine tent."

"I am lucky to be alive," Kull whispered in shock, paralyzed by the sudden appearance of his longtime friend. His thoughts stumbled in a rush of excitement in her presence like a team of intoxicated horses. He couldn't believe that she was back, right in front of him. She was the same girl he remembered, but she had changed. Her eyes possessed a strength that he had not seen before, but she was just as gorgeous as he remembered.

"They didn't want Cotswold, Adley," Kull replied, doing his best to force himself back in the present. "They wanted my father. The Grogans took him, and once they had him, they left. Cotswold was just in their way."

Adley stared at Kull with her dark eyes and spoke, "Kull, lie down. I have to see your shoulder."

Quickly, she grabbed a pack of sterile scissors and began cutting away the singed shirt that covered his wound. The deep musky smell of blood and burnt flesh invaded his nostrils, causing his mouth to dry. Her hands operated with determined ease, a skill that only came from her diligent training at the Academy. She handed him a leather strip.

"Kull, I'm going to need you to bite this."

"Umm…what?"

"Bite on this belt, Kull."

He stared deep into her brown eyes. They swallowed him, and like a fool he obeyed, clamping his teeth on the cow-hide.

Without hesitation, she peeled back Kull's flesh in one swift movement, delving deep into his shoulder to fetch the shrapnel locked inside. Kull ground the leather strap between his teeth, grunting as pain went off in his mind like fireworks. As she worked, he could not stop the hot tears that poured out of his eyes. For what seemed like an eternity, Adley stood over him digging through him, the pain swelling to a tormenting crescendo, until suddenly it was all over, replaced only by a light-headed dizziness. The only thing holding Kull steady was Adley's kind, striking face.

She washed her tools and then painted the wound with a gray concoction of medicine. She looked down at him as she wrapped his wound and spoke in a much too chipper voice, "You did well, Kull!"

Kull tried to speak, but the foul tasting leather was still clamped in his mouth.

Adley laughed, "I have seen a lot of men pass out over less."

Kull squeaked out a coy reply, "Just what are you trying to say?" A crooked smile filled his face, and the pain that dominated him slowly resided. Adley's hand rested against Kull's chest, and his heart panged.

"I'm saying you did great. At least it's out now. You'll be just fine. Let me go and get some more dressing for it. I'll be right back. Hold this bandage down." Adley reached and squeezed his hand. Her touch sent a pulse up Kull's arm. In a second, Adley extinguished all the pain and rage that a few moments ago dominated his mind.

He held the bandage over his shoulder and allowed himself to breath. The pain was bearable now, not good, but not as bad as it was. The dizziness was subsiding, and without the distraction of Adley, Kull began to focus on his father again and his mother's request to find him. *Why had the Grogans taken him? Why would they risk war for the capture of one man? What had Grift done to possibly deserve this?*

He lay there as the questions swirled in his mind, listening to the hundreds of injured citizens moan in a chorus of misery. *Why would they do this to us?*

"Hold him down!" a voice shrieked. It was Eva Dellinger, and she was directing several large men to hold Arthur Ewing.

"Arthur, we have no choice. If we don't remove this leg, you'll be dead in a week."

"By the gods, woman, let me go!" Ewing was throwing his body against the men holding his arms and legs down. One of the men lost his grip, and Ewing swung, shattering his giant fist against the medic's jaw. A grueling crack filled the air. "You devils be cursed if I'll let you do this to me!" An unrelenting torrent of curses, spittle, and threats spewed from Ewing's mouth as the party of medical orderlies tried desperately to restrain him. Silent as a shadow, a tall man moved into the tent, his face masked and his hands gloved. His presence felt like a dark specter. He held a large, long blade.

Oh no.

"NO! Please don't...I'll be okay...soon enough!" Ewing screamed, whimpering as his eyes followed the blade moving across the room.

It was over in an instant. With one swift and controlled stroke of the doctor's surgical blade, Ewing's black infected leg was lobbed off. Kull stared and shuttered as the orderlies bound his bleeding stump with a tourniquet and quickly began wrapping it with sterile gauze. To Kull it felt like a terrible dream, a dream that he wished he could wake up from. Ewing was quiet and went white as a sheet. His eyes lost focus. He sat motionless for minutes with his mouth hanging open, slowly muttering and humming one of his favorite drinking songs.

"Serubs and morels, got in some quarrels, and now they get the best of *me.*"

He let out a childlike laugh and looked over at Kull in a fog of shock as a stupid grin wrapped itself around his face. Too gleeful, he whispered, "It's alright, boy. I'm alright." he passed out headlong into his cot.

Eva, who stood by him the entire time, laid her hand on him and put a damp cloth across his neck. Ewing broke out into a cold sweat and was shivering violently. She looked over at Kull as she wiped away the sweat from Ewing. She waved over a medic to hook a bag of blood to Ewing as he slept.

"Kull, can you look after him? I have more injured to care for. He just needs a watchful eye for a few hours. Can you yell if you see he's not doing well?"

Under normal circumstances it would be laughable that she would put Ewing under his care in his condition. Kull nodded, still holding the gauze up on his tender shoulder. "Go on, Eva. I will watch him. I won't let him go anywhere." *Not that he can go anywhere.*

Kull lay in his cot staring at Ewing who continued to shiver. The old man was a pitiful sight, and Kull felt a potent mixture of fear and sadness swirl inside his chest. Despite all the frustration and annoyance Arthur Ewing had caused him in his life, the man was like a grandfather. Ewing served in the King's Guard along with his father and had been his mentor as he climbed the ranks. When he retired, he settled in Cotswold and having no other family, he formed an unlikely one with the Shepherds.

Kull propped himself up, swung his legs out of his cot and gathered up his thin blanket to cover Ewing.

"Let me get that for you," Adley said, returning with a handful of gauze and medical tape. "I will cover him up. You need to lie down, Kull. Ewing will be fine. He's just cold from blood loss, but he will be okay. He's taking his blood bag well. It will make a world of difference. I will take care of the two of you myself."

"Well then I know we are in good hands." In his mind, Kull chastised himself for the stupid nonsense overflowing out his mouth. *Gods above, Shepherd, get it together. Shut up.*

Adley smiled, took the covers from Kull, and laid them over Ewing, tucking them in around his large frame. His shivering diminished as time passed, and Kull was finally able to quit staring at him, for fear that he would die there in that old military cot.

Adley chastised him, "Kull, please. You need to lie down. I promise he will be okay. Besides, I need to get your wound dressed. Now lie down and let me patch you up. We are safe now."

Kull obeyed as Adley meticulously wrapped his shoulder and packed the wound. As she worked, Kull noticed how much she had grown up since he had last seen her. Time had changed her. All of the past day's events spun in his head like a surreal dream, the nightmare of losing his father and his hometown mixed with the strange elation to be reunited with Adley. All of it made everything even more farfetched and unreal. He was silent as he watched her work.

Adley was the first to speak, "Kull, you said the Grogans were after your father. Why?"

Kull coughed, clearing his throat. "I wish I knew. All I know is what I saw. They killed everyone else, but then they took him."

Adley said nothing, but her face filled with worry.

He sat up as she finished dressing the wound. "I'm going after them. I've already wasted too much time."

There was a pause. Adley tightened the wrapping with a harsh jerk, making Kull wince.

Her tone was serious and filled with warning. "You know you can't do that. They have stopped all travel across the Realm except for the military and the emergency response teams. The guards won't let you leave Cotswold, much less Lotte."

Kull locked eyes with her. Her face was stern as she stared back, unflinching.

His voice went grave. "Adley. What choice do I have? Dad would do the same for me. I can't just sit around here while he rots in a Grogan prison. I've got to get up and go while his trail is fresh."

Adley fired back at him. "Who will watch Rose, Kull? Or did you even think of that?"

Kull's hand fell on Adley's. "Mom asked me to go. I would never leave her otherwise."

Adley's face was a mixture of worry and pride, and yet somehow it still bore the kind glow that always stayed with her.

"You're as stubborn as I remember, Kull Shepherd. I know better than to try to persuade you to stay..." Her sentence fell away, as if there was something else she wished to say.

She reached out and placed her hand on Kull's cheek. Her hand was warm, and her soft skin was smooth against Kull's dirty jaw.

"Just don't get yourself killed, okay? There are some things that even nurses can't fix."

Kull's determination relaxed and he laughed. "I will. I promise. It was good to see you again."

"Good to see you too."

They paused and looked at each other for an awkward moment. Then, as if someone was timing their chance encounter, they quickly embraced each other as they parted ways.

Adley released him and turned away from the stunned young man. All Kull wanted was to stay in her embrace for a few moments longer. He shot a glance back at Ewing who was now alert, staring at him with weak eyes.

"Looks like it's you and me again, kid. Don't worry, we'll be fine." Ewing slowly sat up on his cot and smiled.

"Bold words for someone who just lost their leg."

Ewing looked down at the voided limb and began to laugh.

"What...a...day. I can't say that I saw this one in the cards. Well, I didn't much like that ol' leg anyway. Now I can get me one of those new additions those tech-boys have been crafting for the veterans...I'm gonna get me a shiny one." A wicked smile flew across the old man's face.

Kull smiled at Ewing in utter amazement as the old goat brushed off the nightmare he had just been through. Back to his old ways, he was shoveling large wads of brown tobacco out of his pouch and loading it into his pipe.

"You know that's going to kill you one day, right?" Kull said playfully.

Clenching the pipe in his mouth, Ewing stared back at Kull with wide eyes. "Seems like I'm doing a much better job of that myself, boy!" Ewing lit a match and his pipe in one grand sweeping motion that looked and felt like a magic trick. Kull hadn't noticed before, but Ewing always seemed to have a certain flair about him, a quality that took the normal everydayness of life and made it oddly significant. The old man stared at Kull through the smoke enveloping his head and took three long draws, savoring each one.

"Thank you Aleph above...that is good." Ewing shut his eyes as smoke floated around his head and the smell of the tobacco permeated throughout the tent. Another young man with a bandage around his head was lying in the cot next to Ewing. His eyes flew open and his nose crinkled as the smoke wafted over onto him, and he lurched as a shower of vomit fell in the space between the cots. Ewing opened his eyes and patted him on the back as he retched again.

"There, there, my man. There, there!"

Turning to Kull, Ewing continued, "You need not worry about me and my bad habits." Kull looked at Ewing's stump of a leg, smirked, and shook his head in disbelief. The memory of his mother's voice goaded him. *"You have to go after him, Kull. You have to go after your father."*

"It's not you I'm worried about, Arthur. It's dad."

Ewing's face grimaced with a knowing look.

"I know, boy. I know. But if anyone can make it out of the Grogans' hands it would be Grift. He's more cunning than about anyone I know. The Grogans really don't realize what danger they are in."

"Danger?"

"That's right, lad. Danger." Ewing took another draw from his pipe. "Your father is a very skilled man of war. Being captain of the Lottian guard is not a post doled out for ceremony. Grift is a warrior, and what he lacks in strength, he makes up in strategy. The Grogans like to strong-arm the other Realms into submission, but the reason our Realm has stayed free from their interference for these past forty years is because of men like Grift." Ewing puffed at his pipe again, his eyes grave. "Yes…taking Grift, even as a prisoner, is a risky move on the Grogans' part, whether they realize it or not."

"So you don't think they are going to kill him?" All he knew about his father's position was that he commanded a small band of soldiers patrolling the border. Yet to hear Ewing talk, it put his father in a whole new light.

"No, lad. They'll torture him, for sure, but if they intended to kill him they would have done that on the battlefield. They've got Grift held prisoner either to use him as a hostage or to interrogate him. Why, with King Camden laid to rest your father is one of the most valuable assets they can possess." Ewing's voice trailed off and he ran his hands through his thinning hair. Something flickered across Ewing's face that made a chill run down Kull's spine.

"What is it, Arthur?"

"Nothing lad…nothing."

Kull's eyes trailed off beyond the recovery tent doors and out over the smoldering hills of what was once Cotswold. Anger rekindled in him, and an uncompromising grit. His father was not dead, and there was still time, but he would have to hurry. Kull was now sure of what he had to do.

"I have to go and find him, Ewing." The broken voice of his mother pierced his mind. *'He is more important than me.'* Kull continued, "If they're not going to kill him, then I have to go now. I have to get to him. If they had taken me, Dad would have already left Lotte by now." As he spoke, the realization that he would have to say goodbye to his mother washed over him, and his mind filled with dread.

Ewing read Kull's face and frowned for a moment, lost in his thoughts. He spoke, "Help me up, Kull. Let's go see her. You need to if you're setting off to go. Plus, I don't think my neighbor appreciates my pipe."

"But your leg!"

"Ah, my leg nothing. Now, help me up and grab me some crutches."

Kull slowly led Ewing out of the medical tent. Ewing teetered on his ill-fitted crutches and cursed under his breath with each step as Kull directed him through the obstacles of patients, doctors, and nurses standing in his way. Somehow, the two made their way to the outlying tent where Kull's mother would be. Ewing tossed his crutches to the side and flopped onto the damp ground.

"This is far enough for me, son. I'll be out here. Go and see her." He panted, catching his breath. Ewing leaned back on his elbows, his portly belly rising and falling with each breath. After resting a little while, he grabbed Kull's arm and drew him in. "But I still have words for you. Don't run off. Do you understand?" Despite all that happened to him, the old man's grip was still strong. Kull nodded and went inside the tent.

A young orderly greeted Kull as he slipped inside. "Evening."

"I'm looking for Rose Shepherd."

"Ah...Ms. Shepherd." The orderly led him down the rows of wounded, and he saw her. Even at a distance Kull could see that the coherent mother he left in the forest was gone. Her hollow eyes were full of shadows.

The orderly reported the obvious. "She isn't doing too much responding. Unfortunately, I am afraid the shock of the battle put her into a bit of a stupor." Kull nodded, not bothering to correct him. "She is stable, however."

The orderly excused himself as Kull's heart drowned in disappointment. Her frail frame was slumped over in a chair as her chest puffed out shallow breaths. She was the shell of the person Kull had become accustomed to over the past few years. Before entering the tent, Kull had been set on going after his dad. He was not so sure now.

"Hey, Mom. It's me."

Rose sat quietly in the chair with her glazed eyes staring into the dirt floor. Kull picked up a damp cloth and wiped it at her brow.

He whispered, "Mom. I'm here. Can you hear me?"

A spark ignited in her eyes at his voice. Rose's frail hand groped for him, sliding weakly across Kull's cheek. Kull cringed as she struggled to speak. Her eyes began to roll back slowly as she fought to maintain her gaze. With her free hand, she lifted a necklace from her neck and forced it into Kull's hand. He recoiled from the pendant.

"You cannot give this to me." Kull shook his head, wide-eyed, and put the pendant back in his mother's hands. It was a simple circle, bearing the mark of Aleph.

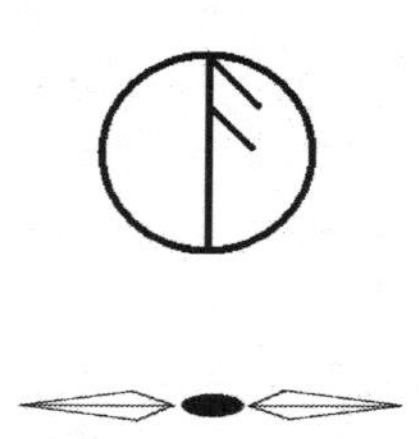

The pendant was given to Rose by a visiting monk after she became very ill when Kull was just a young boy. For months, Grift sought help from doctors across Lotte, but every physician he employed insisted that there was nothing medically that could be done for her condition. That had been a terrible time for the family, and Kull could remember encountering the hard, cold face of his father as he battled a war that he could not win. One night,

Kull lay in bed awake, listening to his parents' hushed conversations through the walls.

"Grift, please call for him. He will come and bless our house, and perhaps Aleph will show me mercy."

The gruff voice of his father penetrated through the wall, causing Kull to lie absolutely still.

"I know he will come, Rose. I know that, and I would welcome him here. It's not that…It's just that why in Aleph's name is this happening? If the god we serve is so powerful and wise, why would he allow this to happen to you?" There was a pause, and Kull leaned his ear to the wall straining to hear. "You, of all people, don't deserve this."

Kull heard his mother's coughs rip through the night. "His plans are not our own, Grift. I am in his hands. You know this."

Kull heard the sound of furniture flying, and then something he never heard before. His father was weeping. Kull pulled the quilt around him tightly, straining to make out Grift's reply. "You have enough faith for the both of us, it seems."

"And you have more faith than you realize, Grift Shepherd."

The next week a tall, young, dark-skinned monk traveled to Cotswold. Kull had vivid memories of the monk praying over his mother, and then his father, and ending at last by praying over him. Before he left, he gave Rose the pendant and for many years her disease subsided, until it came again during Kull's twelfth year, stronger than ever. Despite this, Kull always knew that his father held a reverence for the pendant, and he continually asked her to wear it when the sickness's grip grew stronger.

Rose's lips silently bounced open and shut, but from the look in her eyes, Kull knew she had something to say.

Kull leaned his ear next to her lips and heard her speak. With all the force she could muster, she pressed the pendant into Kull's palm and said, "Find…Grift…love."

Kull fought back stinging tears as he kissed his mother's cheek. *Even now she thinks of him.* Kull stood up mesmerized before kneeling back down to try and meet his mother's eyes one more time. "I love you too, Mom. I know you want me to go. I'll make sure you are taken care of. *Fight for me.* I will be back. Okay?"

The spark that flared up earlier left and her empty gaze returned. Kull wiped his eyes and looked down at the pendant she had put into his hand. Kull draped the small gold chain around his neck and stepped outside the tent. Ewing had remained at his post.

"You say goodbye?"

Kull nodded.

Ewing took a long draw of his pipe. "Don't worry, Kull. She is in good hands. I'll make sure that Eva will watch over her. She'll keep her up."

Kull nodded, but said nothing. Ewing, not one for silence, filled the void with his scheme.

"I overheard you talking to that pretty little nurse, Kull. And I also heard what Rose asked you to do, Aleph bless her. Seeing as you are still carrying around your father's old rifle like a fool, I have a feeling that you are serious about going after the Grogans."

Kull looked out over the plain toward the south. Toward the Groganlands. "You can't stop me, Ewing."

"I don't intend to, but I think you need to think this through, Kull," Ewing replied.

"There is nothing to think about. I am going after Dad. I don't care if they kill me." He locked his eyes on Ewing. "I'm going after him. I can't go on..." His voice cracked under the thoughts raging in his mind. "If they're going to torture him, Ewing, I want them to pay for it."

Ewing waved his hand in the air, dismissing the surge of determination.

"Steady now, son, let me finish. I have someone you need to meet if you're planning on trying to rescue your father. He is a bit of a hermit, but if anyone can get you to Grift, this would be your guy. He's only as far as the capital city of Vale from what I've heard."

Kull's body tensed with frustration. "Ewing, I don't have time for this!" He pointed to the Asban mountain range. "Vale is north, and right now they are rushing dad into the Groganlands. I'd be losing his trail!"

Ewing thundered at him, squelching his bravado. "And how do you think, lad, that you'll be able to cross the border? Vale will be sending troops down by the thousands to patrol! You'd be shot onsite for even trying to cross the border without any clearance, Grogan or not!"

Kull sighed and pinched his eyes.

Ewing continued, "You need a safer way into the Groganlands. My friend can get you there, but you need to trust me." Ewing stared into Kull's eyes, and Kull nodded.

"Okay, Ewing."

"Good. We need to get you to Vale." Ewing glanced down at his missing leg and slowly rubbed at his thigh above his bandaged, bloody knob. "I just wish I could help you get to him." He laughed. "I can't help you get anywhere in this state. I don't think me hobbling over the hills would be moving quite at a pace of your liking."

Kull's eyes shot wide as he looked down at Ewing's leg and then back toward the medic's tent. "Actually, Ewing, I think you are going to be our ticket to Vale."

Ewing grimaced, "Eh? I don't follow you."

Kull smiled. "You said you want one of those fancy new mechanical legs, right?"

"Yeah, so?"

"Well, Vale is the only place to get one of those that I can think of. Your veteran status should be good for something, right? It should buy us a ticket to Vale so maybe we can catch the next transport out of here."

Ewing let out a large, booming laugh as he sat back.

"Now I follow you. I like your thinking, son. You got more of Grift in you than I thought, that's for sure."

"I hope so, Ewing. I hope so."

CHAPTER FIVE

"The time for mourning is over,
the New King has come.
May he live forever,
and may his rule be strong."
-*Song of Ascension*

Nearly a week had passed since King Camden had been laid to rest, but the reality of the change was still fresh and awkward for Seam. He had not yet been crowned as the new king, but the people of Lotte already started to crowd around him pining for his attention and decisions in matters both large and small. Elders and statesmen continually filed in and out of the official state room and monopolized most of Seam's time as he sat restlessly atop the king's throne. An endless line of bureaucrats queued, bowing before him and making flowery introductions. The droning of the underlings buzzed like bees in Seam's ears as he stared past the chamber doors. These proceedings were the very thing his father loved, but the pageantry seemed like nothing but an elaborate waste of time and energy.

Gods above, Seam thought to himself, sinking in the bog of twisted words that spewed out from a baron's formal oration. *Can these people not do anything for themselves? I've got more pressing matters to deal with…*

Seam's thoughts drifted to his mother, who had locked herself away following the burial ceremonies. She needed Seam more than ever. He recounted the last time she allowed him into her room three days prior. Her frail figure sat hunched over Camden's belongings, wiping her eyes and running her thumb over a ring she gave him years earlier. She was pitiful. The sight ripped at Seam's chest, but he could not help but feel disappointed that she could not at least pull herself together to make some effort at recovery.

When is she going to come out? The thought rolled in his gut like a heavy stone. It was as if she gave up completely. She was waiting to die, to be marched to her final resting place next to Camden. It disgusted him. Each time Seam intruded into the dark patch of midnight that was his mother's quarters, he expected—no, he hoped—to find his mother slowly growing stronger. He was met each time with bitter disappointment. Every time he found her sitting in the same chair, the gray fog of mourning surrounding her. She was completely unaware of Seam. Unaware that *he* was still with her.

There seemed to be no solution to her state, none that he could think of. The petty droning and worries of the incessant nobles failed to make it any easier on him.

The young ruler attempted to sit patiently, showing all signs of genuine respect, but his mind was occupied with his lingering thoughts. He was not interested in the agricultural updates or the lumber quota being filled in the different provinces of the Realm. His long hair hung freely and partially obscured the look of boredom on his face as one noble after another began their oration. Seam sighed as another old man cleared his throat and pulled a long scrap of paper from his breast pocket.

"My most excellent liege, I am Rueden Lot, and I am here to discuss with you the production of crops in the north-lands..."

"Enough." Seam's low request went unnoticed as Rueden continued, "The corn yields were down this past harvest, but the current war has…"

"Did you not hear me the first time? I said I have heard enough!" Seam stood from his throne and glared down at the gray-haired farmer.

"I beg your pardon, my king, but it is court policy that we must continue..."

"I said enough!" Seam's exclamation muted the entire hall, and he slammed his fist on the throne's arm. He sat back down and closed his eyes. The burden of sitting on the rigid, uncomfortable antique was more than he ever expected.

In the silence, Seam retorted, "I am *done* with court policy. I am *done* with this talking. We are in a time of war! This ceaseless dribble cannot concern me, not now. I hereby order my officials to send me your reports via datalink, but I will not have this precious congress diminished with minor domestic issues when we must make decisions about this war."

A chorus of grumbling built as the nobles looked at one another in shock that the new king would actually interrupt the official reports. Camden would have never interrupted an advisor no matter how low his post and it was well known that he reveled in spending time speaking with each of them. Seam stood and addressed the crowd of bewildered and irritated onlookers.

"Gentlemen. I would like to ask if anyone can give me one good reason, other than tradition, that we should continue this gathering. All I need is one reason, just one, and I will allow you to continue. But before one of you speaks, may I remind you my father has been murdered, the Grogans are collapsing on our borders as we speak, and our queen is in terrible health. But by all means, if anyone can give me one reason to continue, please speak now."

The room dropped into a dead silence. Seam stood glancing from one advisor to another to see who might have the gall to raise their voice. No one spoke, and Seam used the silence as his exit.

"Very good. Then it is agreed. We are now adjourned."

In a huff, Seam slid through a door at the top of the hall, leaving all his advisors standing in silence as they tried to process what had just occurred. He walked the lonely hallway that stretched from the throne room to his private sitting quarters. The still, quiet refuge smelled stale like ancient dust. A small window in the corner of the room interrupted the darkness with a lonely pane of light. It was furnished only with a quaint wooden desk and a small wall of books held in a case. A single bottle of wine sat on the desk along with a silver flask, and it was apparent that the room had been sitting unused for quite some time. Seam's father normally traveled throughout the entire province of Lotte meeting with his officials and commoners and had little use for such a space, but Seam relished in the refuge of the small, secluded space where he could be alone with his thoughts.

He paced over to the small window and looked out over the throne room's balcony and the courtyard below it. In the courtyard, people were running back and forth with yellow and blue banners and stringing them across balconies and any building window facing the courtyard. The Realm's colors were everywhere as the residents of Vale prepared for Seam's upcoming coronation ceremony. Their expressions were marked with fear and determination, joy and sorrow. Normally a coronation brought a great deal of joy to the people, but this ceremony would be different. The Grogan war left panic hanging in the air as everyone waited for another oncoming attack. No matter how many forces Seam sent out, it did not offer enough security to break the mantle of fear. The people of Lotte lost more than their king. They lost friends and family alike, and unlike a king, they could not be replaced.

Seam allowed himself to relax as he basked in the window light and felt the silence in the room. The thought that by the end of the day he would be the newly crowned sovereign comforted him. The old and sedentary ways of the kingdom would be uprooted. Eventually, unity would be established across the Realms and Seam would be their king. Everyone's king.

It was a dream, but it was one that was rooted in the legacy of Camden, who had long been a champion of compromise and collaboration with the other Realms. He was often heralded as the Great Peacemaker. He brokered a critical alliance with the Grogans following numerous wars when murmurs and rumors of conflict had once again sprung up across Candor. After this peace was brokered, Camden's rule became lax, almost casual, despite his affinity for pompous royal court ceremonies. In economic trade, he compromised with the different Realms who strove to take advantage of Lotte and its people. He, like a lap dog, bent to their wills, claiming his efforts were all for the sake of peace. To Seam it appeared that his father was weak, caring more for the brittle treaties of tyrants than the life and security of his people. Weak *and* foolish.

He was a fool. The thought cut through Seam. *After all, how could he of all people, with so much influence, fail to see the opportunity to culminate all power throughout the Realms?* These thoughts had always bothered him, once he learned the truth. *He had to know how to rise to power, but why did he choose not to act? What stayed his hand? Why did he compromise with the other, weaker Realms on so many issues?*

The thoughts percolated in his mind as Seam walked over to open the bookcase door. He pulled out a small package wrapped in thick, yellowed canvas.

There will be no more compromises in my reign. I will establish order in Candor, and I will do it with the only language this unruly continent understands: fear.

His heart quickened as his hands shook with an undeniable sense of dark pleasure. He carefully removed the volume from the shelf and unwrapped the aged canvas to look at the object open before him. The small, black leather tome could have been set inconspicuously with the other volumes because it bore no marking either on its spine or its cover, but Seam could not resist the temptation to further hide it. To leave it unbound did not seem to be at all reasonable in his mind.

He stumbled across the book when he was nine years old. He skipped his lessons only to get lost running through the maze of halls deep within the royal library. He always enjoyed exploring the depths of the dark, mysterious aisles that were long unused and forgotten. The books that sat on the cobweb-covered shelves always seemed to be filled with more life and truth than those readily accessible near the entrance of the library. The stories and pictures he explored in the dark corners of that place held an inexplicable gravity to them that marked him and pulled him deeper into their pages. It was as if the stories themselves were missing only one character: Seam.

This precious book, *his book,* had been buried in a trunk full of poorly organized relics, maps, and artifacts. It had been tossed aside as if it was garbage like the rest of the trunk, but Seam could *feel* the pages calling him. When he opened it for the first time, he could not tear himself away from the words held within. He found *his* story. The story that would finally unlock a perfect order.

From the tome he discovered many things; revelations that made him question the history his family taught him. The first was the realization that his line of kin, the Pandereans, had not always been the rulers of Lotte. For countless generations, the crown changed hands between multiple families. There had been one such family, the Nephiles, to claim sovereignty over the kingdom before any Panderean had ever set foot into Vale. Learning one new truth after another, Seam questioned early on just how much had been hidden away in hopes it would one day be forgotten. Seam let his eyes flit across the familiar words snaking within the old, tattered pages:

This is the personal journal of Alebrade Nephile, High King of Vale.
4th Volume, 391 A.C.E

Seam flipped quickly to the last entry of the book that pulsed incessantly in his brain ever since he first read it:

The Benefactors have left me with a very important task, one that is not without consequence. The front has pushed through into the very heart of Lotte. Vale will fall within days...if not hours. I can hear the thunder of war machines outside this bunker as I write, so I know my time is short.

The Benefactors have instructed me that this defeat will not be their end, but that it will be mine. So be it. They know me and count me as a servant to the Way, and I will ensure that I will preserve their artifacts within my Line. They will reward me upon their return, but division is required now. This separation is necessary to keep the Benefactors secret and secure for another time. A time when some great soul will find them, find them after seeking them with a pure heart and a pure mind and bring them forth again in the Light of Day. Then peace will be restored, evermore. The others will state that the division was to bind them and cast them out, but we, the Followers, the True believers, know that it is to preserve them. This is our task, therefore, to live patiently within the lie and spread the false-truth that the division is necessary. For it is. But not for binding. For preserving. We will wait upon The Keeper to unite us with them once again.

Seam closed his eyes as the words of the text resonated through him. Warmth and a quickness of understanding lifted him up out of the frustration he felt.

I am the great soul. I am the Keeper. I will accomplish the task he speaks of.

Somehow, deep within him the ideas comforted and confirmed him. He would set out and accomplish the task, and he would spend the rest of his life in service to achieving the Great Order that was referred to over and over again in Alebrade Nephile's log. His father spent years exhausting himself trying to chase peace to no avail. All Camden accomplished was to allow all the other Realms to manipulate and steal what they wanted from the people of Lotte, a strategy that allowed the Grogans ample time to ramp up their efforts of domination. Through this book, Seam found unexpected purpose and new, hidden allies who shared the same hope he had.

"There is only one way, one power, that will restore order to this broken world," Seam spoke quietly to himself, "and I will not stop until I get it."

A timid knock came against the sitting room door. Seam stood up from the desk and hid the precious tome back within the bookcase, locking it in one quick stroke. He slid the door's solid iron lock back and cracked the door.

"You understand that an interruption of my privacy could cost you your life," Seam spat as the large, wide door swung open. Standing before him was a tall man clad in black linen, whose face was completely covered. Fiery yellow eyes stared back at him like hot embers.

"Not my life, dear King." A brandished dirk flashed from the stranger and found its home in Seam's side. A soft puff of air left Seam's mouth as he felt the blade penetrate him between the ribs. There was no pain, not at first, but upon the second strike and the third, agony ripped through his entire chest. Seam slammed his fist into the assassin's temple, sending him reeling back a few steps. The blade glinted in the dim light of the room, wet with blood dripping from its edge. The man dove for Seam, swiping to connect with his chest again as he pushed in closer.

Seam reached to grab the flask of wine from the desk table and shattered it across the skull of his assailant. The smell of dark, musty drink wafted into the air. Stumbling from the blow, the assassin made another wide swipe for Seam's neck, but Seam caught the attacker's arm and threw him into the table. The intruder lunged again, finally connecting with Seam's shoulder, opening another fresh wound. Seam grabbed the man and drove him into the wall. The collision sent both men stumbling to the floor, gasping for breath. The dirk crashed into a corner of the room, but instead of chasing after the weapon, the assassin climbed on top of Seam, wrapping his hands around his throat.

The man leaned in next to Seam's ear and whispered, "This kill will be much more enjoyable than your father's. Poison is far too easy. But now I will be able to feel your life slip through my fingers. No imagination will be necessary."

The man's grasp tightened as he peered into Seam's eyes. Seam reached out, his hands desperate for anything to help him as he lay bleeding, suffocating beneath his attacker. His fingers danced across the floor, sliding over the tiles, searching for anything to help until he felt the rim of the flask he wielded earlier. Its smooth metallic edge was just at his fingertips. Darkness began to swirl around his vision. Seam had only seconds.

He flung his body to the side, bucking his assailant as his hand wrapped around the flask.

Ignoring the throbbing pain and the oncoming darkness, he pushed through, hammering the wine goblet against the attacker's temple. The blow knocked the assassin's grip free and Seam gasped for the fresh air. He jumped to his feet and swung again, smashing the flask into the man's head. It landed with a resounding thud. Seam tackled him to the ground.

Adrenaline surged through him as Seam unmercifully bashed the goblet over his attacker's skull. The once pristine vessel bent, curled, and finally caved under the blows that connected. A primal energy overtook him as his defense transitioned into savagery. The robed spy slumped over dead even as Seam continued his rhythmic, grotesque assault. Exhausted, Seam finally fell to the floor. His hand refused to let go of the goblet. Where the man's yellow eyes had been, there was only a void, a crimson cavern of blood and death.

When his consciousness returned and the shock wore off, Seam began to question. *What just happened? How did he get in?* He thought to himself as he struggled to breathe, his lungs were ragged. He gripped at his side, where blood was seeping from his wounds. He forced himself back onto his feet. He took one look back at the bookcase, ensuring that the tome was secure and staggered back to the throne room.

Upon entering, the nobles who were still in congress saw their wounded leader and sounded the alarms. A medical team rushed in and surrounded Seam as he lay shivering on the floor, the pious face of the soon-to-be king as white as a ghost. They stripped off his royal robes and began treating the wounds that were freely bleeding. A frenzied mass of bodies rushed in on him, but the medical staff skillfully pushed back the crowd as the surgeons examined Seam's multiple injuries.

Once the head surgeon announced the wounds were not fatal, the crowd breathed an audible sigh of relief and thanked Aleph for the good fortune. Royal guards thundered into the sitting chamber and dragged out the dead assassin. They stripped off the dark linen wrappings the attacker wore. He was a Rihtian by race; undoubtedly a slave assassin sent by the Grogans.

There were many nobles and palace officials who spoke to Seam, assuring him, praising him, but everything that was said seemed to pass through a fog, unable to penetrate the king's consciousness. He saw them clearly and heard them, but could not listen or understand. A doctor pulled out a syringe, and he felt a strange sense of calmness spread through his body.

Seam sat on the throne of Lotte, holding his aching side. He winced with each breath. The pain throbbing between his ribs was a constant reminder of how quickly he nearly joined his father within the depths of the royal catacombs.

"My liege, the Preost ambassador is here."

"Send him in," Seam whispered.

A tall, ebony-skinned monk approached the throne. He wore a long, flowing linen robe and carried an ironwood staff. He bowed his head and raised his hand with the sign of Aleph.

"Blessings on you, High King. I am Wael, the Preost ambassador to your country and Mastermonk of my Order. We are honored to be a part of your upcoming coronation. It will be a beautiful ceremony, and we, the monks of Preost, wish you a long and prosperous reign."

"Thank you for your kind words, Wael of Preost. The monks have long been strong allies to our Realm. What brings you to my court this day?" Seam spoke with bated breath as he pushed each utterance out from his bruised lungs. Each breath, each movement, reminded him of his assailant and the look of brutal determination in the yellow eyes that tried to end his life.

"I come to ask that you and your Kingdom enter into peace talks with the Groganlands."

Seam could not believe the outright boldness of the monk. "*Unacceptable*. We do not negotiate with a people who have made sport of butchering Lotte's sovereigns."

"My king, I am not unaware of the challenges the Grogans have created for your new kingdom."

"*Challenges*?" The soft-spoken nature that Seam presented to Wael evaporated. "Challenges? You must mean *atrocities*, monk. How dare you step into my court and try to force parlay with these Grogans, the same ones that, if it weren't for us, would burn your sacred forest to the ground? Do you not see my burning countryside? Do you not remember burying my father, and do you not see the blood still seeping from my own wounds?" His exertion made him double over in pain. "No, there will be no peace until Rhuddenhall burns to the ground," he whispered, "and I will not discuss this further with you. You are dismissed."

The tall monk stood staring into the High King's eyes. He bowed his head. "Then I will take my plea to the Grogans. Aleph wishes only for peace and forgiveness to fill these lands. May he continue to bless you, High King. I take my leave."

Seam rolled his eyes as the monk turned away and left the court. He called for a recess, and he excused himself from the High Hall.

Once again, Seam found himself in the royal sitting room. He stood over the place where he had taken a life, remembering the shock of having to crush another to ensure his own survival. He gazed through the room noticing that there were no traces of the encounter, as if nothing ever happened. Whoever cleaned the sitting room deserved a promotion. Even the silver goblet had been replaced with an identical twin. On the desk a new datalink had been installed at his request. Seam ran his finger over the power switch, and the screen came to life.

The gray-eyed man stared back at him, as if he had been waiting, sitting patiently at the other end of the datalink for Seam to come online.

"You..." Seam growled.

Hosp smiled and chuckled. "Seam, *I told you* to be prepared. Everything needed to be convincing. I'm sure you understand. It is no small task to keep our populaces at war with one another."

"Be prepared?" Seam growled. "Prepared for what? To be killed? How dare you even think of such a charade? I have no business trusting you. Not after what I have been through!"

There was a pause over the datalink as the two men stared at each other, locked in silence.

Seam was first to speak. "It makes me wonder why I shouldn't send word to the Grogans. Perhaps to Willyn Kara herself about your plans to coup the Sar's throne."

Hosp showed no sign of aggravation, but Seam noticed how his pupils dilated at the sound of the name *Willyn.* He struck a nerve.

Hosp spoke, his voice clearly agitated but controlled. "Go ahead, High King, and send word. But I guarantee you that your people will learn how you orchestrated your father's death. They will learn how you had him murdered in cold blood, just so you could sit on the throne and call yourself king. Imagine how they'll treat you when they learn of your lofty ambitions? They will not stomach a royal murder, my friend, so think about your actions before your anger leads to your own death."

The threats were volleyed, leaving the two men silent once again.

"You told me you would send a runner to me, not an assassin. I was unprepared. Had you told me, I would have not been so badly injured."

Hosp quietly answered the king after clearing his throat, "Rest assured, Seam, there will be no further surprises."

"I am willing to overlook this transgression and keep this alliance intact, but I need to know that you will send communication to me when the plan changes."

Hosp responded earnestly, "The plan had to change. Our intelligence knew that we needed to facilitate another attack. The Preost monks can be swift catalysts for peace in both our Realms, and your people have already begun to forget the name of Camden."

Camden's name caused Seam to wince.

"To continue the war effort we needed to throw more kindling on the coals. I sent you my worst assassin, Seam. Though he was able to poison Camden, there was no chance he would succeed in attacking you. His loss was calculated, and I knew very well that he posed you no danger. I didn't inform you and for that I apologize, but to do so would have compromised the authenticity of the situation."

Seam paused and stared at Hosp's viper eyes. They reminded him of the man that tried to kill him. He swallowed. He remembered the words he read before the assassination attempt.

Division is necessary. Not for binding. For preserving. He smiled, knowing that Hosp would soon play a grand part in what was to come.

"All right, Hosp. So what's next?"

CHAPTER SIX

The crack of bones popping against cool concrete whistled through the prison cell as Willyn stood over a soldier groaning in agony. An inferno of rage burned within her, and her jaw locked as she ground her teeth in a feeble attempt to rein in the fury threatening to take control. *Don't kill this man. Keep it together.* Amid the screaming sirens and flashing red lights, her mind strained to focus. The entire compound had gone midnight black. Someone cut the power, leaving only the emergency systems to flicker and flare in unison to the chorus of sirens. Willyn's mind, too, was dark, clouded by all that had just transpired. Hosp's flagrant attempt at a power grab floored her. Normally, Hagan would have taken care of sniveling leeches like Hosp, but instead Willyn had to shoulder the political burden she never wanted while her brother lay dying from an unknown poison. She was so close to answers, to be able to bring him back, but now the unthinkable had happened. Grift had escaped.

The thought of Hagan snapped a resolute purpose back to her mind, and Willyn looked down at the pistol in her hand. She paused and hammered it back into its holster. *Hosp has to wait. Shepherd cannot. I have to find him now.*

A strange clarity set in. *One thing at a time, Willyn. Stop one, then the other. I have to know what he used to poison Hagan.* Her eyes focused back on the young whelp lying on the floor whimpering before her.

She stooped over and lifted the soldier to a sitting position as she looked into his hazy, distant eyes. He was injured but still conscious, and he fought to focus on his General.

"Officer, I need you to tell me what happened *right now.*" The young guard stammered and held his arms up to shield himself.

"I swear to the gods, I don't know how he escaped," he groaned.

Willyn's arm sprang for him in an instant, ratcheting across his throat. "The gods won't help you if you don't tell me what happened." The idea of un-holstering her pistol flittered through her mind, flushing her with the intoxicating sense of power. She steadied herself and bore into his eyes as he shook with fear.

"Tell me what happened now. That is a command, officer."

"Yes…yes, General." His voice staggered out slowly as he weighed his words. "We received… received transfer orders for interrogation. While switching out his bindings he attacked us."

"Where did he go?"

The soldier lifted his finger and pointed to the door. "Out and he veered to the right. I saw it, to the right. I don't know how he did it, but he disappeared! I swear!"

Willyn looked over her shoulder to the cell door behind her. She had come from the left, the direction of the stairs and the elevator. There was no exit to the right. There was only one entrance.

Willyn stood back to her feet and addressed the officer as she exited the cell.

"Get back to your station. Do not raise a public alarm. I will call in my elites."

The battered warden stammered to find the words, "I am...I am afraid that I've already sent out an alert. Grift's face will be on every datalink in the city by now."

It was enough to make her scream. "You idiot! We are in a time of war! We can't incite a panic!"

Fury pulsed through her veins. *Such incompetence.* She breathed in, focusing her energy. The general inside her directed her to attention. *Hagan. He is all that matters. Let the people think what they will. Just get Grift.* She let go of the ineptitude of the guards. She let go of the people of the Groganlands and their perceptions. *I can fix this. I just have to get Grift.*

Without a word she left the guard lying on the cell floor and raced down the hallway, her flashlight bouncing from wall to wall. The answer to the question of Grift's escape came when her eyes landed on the open ventilation return. *The rail line.*

Grift never intended to use the stairs. He was trying to make his escape underground through the winding labyrinth of rail lines beneath the city. Willyn radioed back to the command center.

"Fire up the emergency generators and reset the power. I need access to the nearest datalink immediately!"

Her command was met with a quick response and the lights shuttered back to life. Willyn raced to a datalink panel and furiously pulled up a map of all the rail line access points.

Her cold blue eyes scanned the colored map. *The tracks that run to Lotte cut straight through the western part of the city. He'll take that route back to his country.* Fear flew through her as her mind connected the dots. Time was slipping away for her to find a cure. Hagan would die if Grift escaped. He was the only one who knew the true nature of Hagan's poisoning.

She called into her radio one more time, "Halt the line cars from running. I need two platoons of men to sweep both lines that run toward Lotte's borders. Update me as soon as you have them in place. I'll be there shortly."

The radio crackled back, "Understood. Units are being dispatched now." Willyn's heart pounded and her mind raced. *How could this assassin be so good? How could he make us look like fools?*

Willyn raced to her quarters to prepare herself. If Grift had so easily taken out her prison detail, she knew she could not take any chances. She slung open the doors of her battle locker and strapped on an armored vest. She snatched up clips for her pistol, hoping she would not need them. As she put the clips on her belt, she glanced back over her equipment. Deep within the locker sat a quiver of javes. The long spears were made from a light titanium alloy and were equipped with a range of different functions. Some in the quiver were standard, razor-tipped at the points, used for hunting, while others held special properties. Some were configured to be explosive, incendiary, or even as advanced as utilizing heat-seeking technology. She picked up the quiver and strapped it over her free shoulder. She had been lucky to have taken him down once with her rook, but to enter the tunnels erased any advantage she had before. Her face was grim when she left; she bore the face of one going back into war.

One man at a time. One problem at a time. Get Grift. Save Hagan. Nothing else matters.

Willyn arrived at the opening of Tunnel 1AAE, the primary entrance for all of Rhuddenhall's underground rail cars. She sat as the engine of her rook hummed around her. She stared into the darkness before her, wishing that Grift would simply step out of the shadows to surrender and end this pointless game. The smell of damp moisture and stale air wafted out of the large entrance, causing her to scowl. *Gods above, what a day,* she thought to herself. Her militia stood ready at the entrance when she arrived, at attention, waiting on her command.

"Leave your rifles outside. If you fire live ammunition inside the tunnel you risk ricocheting and killing yourselves. Just take in your shock rods, taze nets, or pulse rifles. Make no mistake, I want Grift alive."

The platoon obeyed without a word, dropping their rifles and pulling out smaller weaponry and nets from their ruck packs. Willyn pulled out a jave and led the party into the darkness.

"Lights on, soldiers."

Willyn flipped a switch on her battle armor and a shoulder mounted light fired to life, sending its beams bouncing down the deep channel ahead of the party. The pinpricks of light seemed to get swallowed in the sea of black that flooded the tunnel. A single line of rail ran through the middle of the underpass, and there was a clearance of ten feet on each side of the enclosure. With each step, Willyn could feel the low, barely audible echo of her movements hum within the concrete cavern, echoing deep into the depths. In silence, she split one half of the detail to stay on the left of the tracks while the remaining party came up the right. The wall of men followed her, dutifully marching further into darkness, stopping at regular intervals to listen and look for any signs of Grift. The only movement within the tunnel was the slow gusts of horrid wind wafting over them, bringing foul odors of mildew and rot up from the subterranean labyrinth.

Willyn could not contain her disgust. "Gods, what is *that*?" It smelled foul, like something died, and with each step the stench grew in strength and presence. She had smelled death in all its forms, but something about this was uncanny. It made her uneasy. The militia marched on through the darkness, ignoring the sound of dripping water and the low moans of rotting wind blowing through the tunnel. Even though she was flanked by thirty soldiers, she could not shake the feeling of being alone, her focus and determination preparing her for her next inevitable confrontation with Grift.

The group had pushed more than a mile into the tunnel system with no solid leads. After an hour of marching they found nothing and Willyn began to worry. The hair on the back of the neck stood up, and her blood hammered through her veins. On the battlefield she had long learned to trust her intuition, and she had a palpable sense that something was wrong. There was another waft of air, but it was ice cold and reeked of putrefied flesh. *This air is not coming from the other end of the tunnel.* Willyn bounced ideas through her mind, calculating the origin of the odor as she worked not to show any visible signs of distress toward the men.

“Steady, soldiers,” she whispered. She could feel them, their nervousness, their anxiety; it all let off an invisible energy within the darkness.

Thoughts blasted through her mind like red hot rockets slicing through the night sky. They were terrible and impossible to ignore. Grift was not in the tunnel, and she concluded that her initial assumptions about his strategy were off. His guise worked, and now Willyn was nowhere near her target. None of that mattered because her mistake landed her into a trap. *His trap.* She quickly realized that soon they would have to either fight or run. Her mind tried to prepare itself, but the answer came up short. *Fight what, Willyn?*

A strong gust of wind pushed in from the group's right side. An opening. A vast chasm had been dug out from the side of the tunnel. Willyn signaled for her men to focus their lights on the void with a flick of her wrist. The cold light fell into the tunnel. In the distance, a man stood alone in the dark.

Willyn's heart jumped at the sight. She had not expected this. The man showed only his profile towards the party and was slumped over, failing to acknowledge either Willyn or the other soldiers. It was as if they were invisible to him. He was old and very unkempt, and his chest pulsed in quick, shallow breaths as he stood up slowly, rolling one visible eye toward them, unblinking in the harsh light. He did not bother to move his body to turn and face them. Though he was too far away for Willyn to distinguish any telling facial features, it was apparent that something was wrong with him.

"You there, what are you doing down in the tunnels? Trespassing is forbidden, even for the homeless. Have you seen anyone else come through here?"

There was no response. The man just stood like a pillar in the dark, completely unaware of the militia's presence; comatose.

Willyn took a cautious step forward. *There is something wrong with this. There is something very wrong with this.* The thought just kept banging in her mind as all her instincts told her to stay back, but curiosity overtook her fear and she inched forward.

She moved within three feet of the man as he stood wheezing for breath. She tried to ignore how much her hands were shaking as she clutched her razor jave. She was steadied only by the thought that at any moment she could easily decapitate the man should he pose any danger. The squadron behind her trained their pulse rifles on the stranger as he stood like an old, rotting statue. She took another step. Another. Another. In a flash the man turned to face her, and Willyn's mouth fell open.

His face was completely mutilated, carved away from the skull, rotting flesh dangling in the foul dark air. What was left of his jaw was unhinged, dangling like a rag doll. A guttural, screeching snarl rolled out of his ragged maw, as his milky eyes stared back at her. The one scenario Willyn hoped would not come true was horribly confirmed. They had disturbed a morel hive.

"RUN! Fall back!" The need for stealth was over. When you disturbed one morel, you disturbed them all. Willyn screamed as she plunged the jave deep into the fiend's chest. It staggered and bellowed while furiously clawing at the jave's shaft.

"Morels! Get out!" she screamed.

Willyn spied the outline of three more morels sprinting from the depths of the cave. The beasts had frothing mouths, and hot, white clouds streaked through their eyes. Five more, ten more. The hive was awake and hungry, and the entire hoard was pouring toward Willyn and her men.

The cave erupted in the blue glow of pulse rifles firing into the masses of morel bodies. The bursts of energy held them back, but only for a moment, as they continued to push forward, one after another. The pack grew from three to twenty in mere seconds, and they continued to stream from the shadows like ants from a disturbed mound.

"Your weapons are no good! RUN!"

Willyn pushed her way back into the main passage and dropped a grenade at the mouth of the morels' cave. The explosion blew through the tunnel with deafening force, partially collapsing its entrance. It was not enough. Morels forced themselves out of the rubble to continue their hot pursuit.

The security force pounded down the tracks as the morels sprinted after them howling and hooting like banshees. Their loud shrieks echoed through the tunnel walls, making it feel as if they were surrounded. Willyn, her mind clear with the adrenaline that was ripping through her, threw three razor javes in quick succession toward the twisted mob of monstrous bodies. The javes shot through the tunnel like lightning and found her targets, slicing at limbs and pinning down some of the creatures. One of the javes exploded into a wide taze net that stunned and held a mob for a few seconds, but the *pop, pop, pop* of the net's metallic fibers bursting at the seams announced that the beasts had broken through. They clamored over their fallen, ravenous to destroy and feast on every one of them.

Willyn calculated multiple options as her lungs burned. She could feel her mind whirr and click into place, denying the fear that boiled in the bottom of her stomach and clawed at her throat. It would be another half mile before they cleared the tunnel. She kept up her pace, forcing herself to remain calm. She turned to see her pursuers' progress. Like a buzzing swarm of bees, the morels came, sprinting and jumping over one another, many spilling up on the sides of the tunnel. They trampled over one another in their dogged pursuit. Their claws mutilated each other at random, unaware of the damage that they rendered upon themselves. They craved to feast on the fresh flesh that had so foolishly entered their hive.

Willyn goaded her men to keep running. "Drop your packs! Drop your packs!" Her men obeyed and flung their tactical vests and backpacks to the ground. The scheme worked for a moment as the morels dove on top of the packs and ripped into them, fighting one another for the opportunity to feast. It bought them only a second, but a second nonetheless.

The sounds of live ammunition ripped through the air. Willyn fired back at them with her pistol, ignoring her earlier warning to her soldiers. Willyn cursed herself as she thought how nice it would have been for her men to be fully armed. *I would rather die of ricochet fire than at the hands of one of these monsters.*

The shots left the pack unfazed. The injured and the dead were engulfed in the sea of monsters. As Willyn stumbled to catch up to the rest of her party four of her men turned back, spreading out a large taze net. The nets cast a blue light in the dark tunnel, illuminating the faces of four of her most loyal men, led by Corporal Waden. The men blurred past Willyn and straight for the horde.

Willyn screamed. "Fall back, men, fall back! That is an order!" Waden answered in proud defiance, "No, General. Better you survive." The four broke in unison into the ancient Grogan marching song and broke away from the others.

The echoes rang through the underground chambers as the men met their fates.

"To die a good death is great, my friends, all for all. For the Groganlands!"

The men disappeared in the darkness, meeting their good death beneath the tidal wave of morels that engulfed them. Willyn's stomach lurched at the sound of their screams and the sharp snapping of bones that filled the tunnel. She kept running. Her loyal men bought them one more second.

Someone erupted with joy, "Faster, faster! I see the entrance!" There, at what seemed a thousand miles away, was the light of day streaming in, illuminating the wet, curved sides of the hellish tunnel. The men were gasping as they pushed every ounce of their energy into a full blown sprint to freedom and safety. Willyn screamed into her radio.

"I need morel barrier force coverage at the entrance of Western tunnel 1AAE. Do you copy?"

"We've got the target set, General Kara."

Willyn heaved for breath as she neared the exit. "Wait...for my signal." She glanced back at the ravenous pack. They were only about fifteen yards behind her.

The militia ran out of the tunnel, and Willyn was the last one out. She lifted her wrist up to her face and screamed into her radio, "FIRE!"

A thunder shock vibrated through Willyn as she saw a mortar round launch up from the vista of Rhuddenhall. She yelled to her squadron, "HIT THE GROUND!" They moved in unison, as the mortar fell just behind Willyn at the tunnel's entrance. A fireball of pure energy exploded, hurdling her and her forces like tumbleweed into the ravine on the side of the line tracks. There was a din of screams and wails over the roaring flames as Willyn's body slammed into the ground. The blow knocked the breath out of her and sent a spike of pain up her back. She gasped and wheezed for air and turned to look at the carnage behind her. The morels that cleared the tunnel were caked in fire, flailing and screaming during their last moments. The mortar had completely caved in the entrance of the rail-line, sealing the hoard of living nightmares behind. Willyn emptied her pistol on the brains of the few that were still standing, walking pyres of living flames. She felt no sympathy for them. The Fallen would never have sympathy from the Grogans. Willyn hurriedly counted her men, barking orders.

"Any injuries? Status report, soldiers!"

The sergeant clamored up to her from the ditch where he landed. "Some burns and broken limbs, my lady, but no life-threatening injuries." His eyes dropped, "We are four short, however."

Willyn could feel her heart swallow itself with grief for the fallen soldiers. They made it out alive but at the expense of four of her finest men. She quietly replied, "What were their names, sergeant?"

The sergeant brought up his datalink, scrolling through the names of those who died. "Private Morgan of Rhuddenhall, Private Broach of the Boroughs district, Corporal Waden of Rhuddenhall, and Private Rote of the Mountainfoot colony."

"They will be honored. They were good men." They saluted one another and she dismissed him.

Willyn called into her radio again, "We need a medical team down here...and an extinguisher force and cleanup crew."

Twisted tendrils of dark smoke rose from the blaze of fire lapping up the dry corpses of morel flesh. Willyn stood and looked into the furnace of hellish kindling. Her red hair flew in her face, singed by the fire that nearly killed her but saved her men. Her mind raced. *Where are you, Grift Shepherd?* The answer came in an instant.

Gods above, Willyn Kara. You fool.

She stood, shocked at her own stupidity. Grift would not leave the Groganlands...not without finishing the job.

Utter fear washed over her.

"Hagan."

Willyn rushed back towards her brother's compound. All of Rhuddenhall's billboards and public terminals projected a rotation of the faces of the men who laid down their lives for their general; Morgan, Broach, Waden, and Rote. Seeing their faces caused Willyn to feel an odd mixture of both guilt and pride.

When she finally made it through the doors of the royal family compound two guards saluted her before opening the gate to the private channel-car line. Willyn boarded a small car that carried her towards her brother's chamber. The dark tunnel and mechanical rhythm of the rolling cart weaved its way to Hagan, as Willyn paced, jave in hand. As she rode alone through the darkness she could not shake the image of her brother's pale, tortured face. He was still fighting to stay alive, to stay with her, and she knew she could not stop fighting either.

Two more guards greeted Willyn as she sprinted from the cart and entered the elevator leading up to the main stronghold. She punched the button impatiently as the old machine creaked to life and the stubborn doors slid together. Little by little it carried her back above ground, but it did not move fast enough.

"Come on, come on, COME ON!"

As the doors slid open, confirmation of Willyn's fears flooded into the elevator.

Across the room, the unconscious body of the foyer guard was slumped on the ground. She put her fingers on the man. A pulse. *Why would an assassin leave a guard alive*? Bullet holes riddled the lock on the door and the hinges appeared to have buckled from being kicked in.

Willyn slid through the open door. There were no lights burning in the Sar's great hall, only moon glow that fell through the open sky lights lit the room. The luminescent light left small square patches leading up to the doors of her brother's quarters. Willyn pressed herself against the wall and inched down the hall, avoiding the open moonlight. The hall's silence was broken by a low moan. Willyn squinted and then saw someone. Hosp was lying face down in the middle of the hall writhing in pain. From her distant position, it seemed apparent that he suffered a blow to the head and a cut had opened on his brow. Willyn could not hide the smile that crept over her lips. *You are too merciful, Grift. You could have at least done me a favor.*

Willyn approached Hagan's door. She spied two of Hagan's personal bodyguards, his Elites, lying face down. Willyn checked their vitals. *Alive. Alive. Why is he leaving these men alive?*

She eased through her brother's doors only to see him sitting up in his bed. His bedroom was dark, but the moonlight made it impossible to hide that someone was standing over Hagan.

Grift.

Willyn searched through her quiver for the proper jave. Amidst a handful of explosive and gas javes, there were only two that she could use without killing her brother. She gripped one of the two razor javes and closed her eyes. *You've got one more chance.*

She inched further into the bed-chamber, hiding herself behind the columns lining its perimeter. Pressing her back to the column, she waited. She would have only one chance to land her shot. Rage clouded her vision as she heard him speaking to Hagan.

"Why did you do it?" questioned Grift in a hushed tone, "Why did you incite war against my people?"

There was no response from Hagan, whose body remained silent except for the steady whirrs, clicks, and beeps of the machinery keeping him alive.

"Where did you hide it, Hagan? You don't have much longer to live."

Willyn strained to see in the darkness and waited for the opportune time to strike.

Grift hushed all his questions and stood over him like a statue. His hands went down to the pistol at his side. *He knows you're here.* Willyn sprung from behind the column, sending the jave rocketing out of her hand.

"GRIFT SHEPHERD, THIS ENDS NOW!"

Her projectile sliced through the air in a flash, but Grift was quick. Like a machine, he dove to the side, an evasive maneuver that cheated death at the last moment. The jave aimed at his throat instead clipped his right arm, sending a gushing spray of hot, red blood into the white moonlight.

Grift grabbed his wound only to look up to catch Willyn's hot eyes burning, blue coals in the moonlight. Her last and final jave was pulled back for the kill.

Willyn's arm exploded, sending her last shot with all the energy she could muster, but again Grift defied her as he slid into the darkness at the edge of the room. The second jave flashed above his ear as he dove, finding refuge in the shadows.

Willyn focused her eyes on the dark corner of the room like a predator. Suddenly, the sound of gunfire rang out and the feeling of bullets brushing past her made her hit the ground. Diving behind the large marble column, she pulled out her own pistol from its holster and volleyed shots back at her attacker, grinning when she saw her shot catch Grift's arm.

"GIVE IT UP, SHEPHERD! SURRENDER NOW!"

The advantage was hers. He only had his weaker hand, and now Willyn knew she could bring him down. She turned out of her cover only to hear a waterfall of glass shattering.

No. He can't be.

Leaving her cover, she ran past her comatose brother. She ran to a shattered window whose pieces lay before her, the night air whispering through her red, wavy hair. She spied down nearly five stories below her at a shadowy figure running in the alleyways far below.

She raised her pistol into the darkness, but it was too late. He was gone, made invisible even now in the full moon. There was no way to reach him. How a man could drop five stories and live to tell the tale made no sense to Willyn, but here she saw that it was possible.

With cold absolution she made a promise to herself and to her quarry:

"I am going to cut you down, Grift Shepherd, and I will not rest until I send a bullet through your brain."

CHAPTER SEVEN

The sound of a northern, winter wind whipped through the ragged canvas covering the back of an old medical convoy. It carried Kull far away from his burning home and sick mother, though closer, he hoped, to finding his father. Kull slid his fingers over the charm his mother had given him and closed his eyes, trying to imagine happier times. A bitter chill sliced through the dark truck bed, and Kull smiled and thanked Aleph for sending it as Adley pressed up against his side, huddling close to stay warm.

Her presence radiated untold comfort. In the shadows of the truck Kull felt safe enough to wrap his arm around her shoulders, to hold her to try to keep her warm. She made everything pass like a blur, making the bone-shivering trek to Vale seem like a privilege rather than a curse. The pain that had radiated in his wounded shoulder all but dissipated; a testament to Adley's skill as a healer. Kull was grateful for the relief since the ride to Vale took five hours and covered rugged territory. Despite the frigid mountain air and Ewing's blasphemous curses that came with each pot hole, Adley made all of it more bearable. She was a welcome distraction.

The truck slowed its pace, and Adley laid her head on Kull's good shoulder, yawning, as she tried to get comfortable. Kull's inner voice prodded him, his mother's face flashing in his memory. *Dad is gone. Stay focused.*

The thought brought a twisted grimace to his face. He looked across the bay of the truck at Ewing lying on a cot. He had a glint in his eye.

"What?"

Ewing chuckled, "Well, you seem to be enjoying *your* ride."

Kull rolled his eyes as a wide smirk grew on Ewing's face. Ewing tapped at the blood donor card strapped to his arm and rolled over to his side, cursing under his breath, shuffling his battered stump of a leg over closer to him, causing a twinge of guilt to cut through Kull. The cost of this trip was a lie, and soon both he and Ewing would have to pay up. Kull tried to distract himself by whispering to Adley.

"How much farther do you think we have?"

Adley's dark brown eyes fluttered open and she flashed a grin, "Why? Am I boring you?"

A rush of energy flushed over him.

"Um, no," he said as he let out an awkward, nervous laugh. "I just was wondering how long we had until...well, you know."

Until we leave each other. The words wanted to shoot out of his mouth like sparrows, but Kull held them inside.

"I know *what,* Kull?" Adley's eyes stared at him, calm and collected, causing his whole body to flush with anxiety. She was too much for him. *How can she be so composed?* It had been so long since he had been this close to a girl, and never a girl as attractive as Adley. The thought of leaving her again made him ache with loss. *How many more people will I lose?* The thought dragged in his mind like a boulder.

"Know what, Kull?" Adley repeated as she smiled.

"Ah, nothing. You know, just enjoying the ride."

"If you like the ride, wait till you see Vale."

Adley chuckled and dropped her head back to Kull's shoulder as he fought back the urge to slap himself for his stupidity. All of this was built on one glorious sham.

You're an idiot. Using her to get a free ride!

Kull worked at rationalizing away his frustrations as they bounced along up the swinging mountain passes. *Ewing is due for the leg augmentation.* That much was true. Dread pooled into his stomach when he thought about how much his ticket would cost him. The memory of whispering to Adley quietly and quickly in the medical tent washed over him. It was the lie that had bought him his ride, *"Adley, I've been accepted into the Academy. I just need a ride to Vale. I need to join the cause and help like you are. It's the least I can do after what they did to my dad. I can't fight a whole army to find him, but I can at least join our army and do my best to help out."*

It had been so simple. In a flash, Adley pulled some strings and ushered both of them on the caravan heading directly up to Vale. It was Ewing's idea. At the time it seemed brilliant, but now Kull felt like an idiot for going along with it. All his life Kull dreamt of joining the Academy and making a new life for himself in the Royal City, but now he was about to turn his back on all of it and leave Adley just as soon as she found him.

A sour knot twisted in Kull's stomach as he tried to bury his anxiety. If Adley was a true friend...or something more, then she would just have to forgive him. She was the last person he wanted to manipulate, but he was left with little choice. His father needed him, and his mother was counting on him to bring him back.

It was the last thought he had until he drifted off to sleep.

A blast of icy wind rushed into the back of the truck as the convoy slammed to a halt, jarring Kull out of a dream. The doors flung open and the rushing sun blinded him. Arms reached in to pull out gurneys and lift bodies from the back of the truck, and soon Kull stepped, for the first time, into Vale.

He drew in one quick breath and blinked his eyes as they adjusted to the high noon sun. The ancient city engulfed him in a feast of sounds and sights he had never experienced. Amid the roar of the thousands flooding the city streets, Kull's eyes shot up at the dizzying heights of the massive stone towers soaring above him, piercing the sky. It was as if they had been carved out from the mountains, and they made him feel like an insect. Tall pinnacles stood proud, lining the wide promenades of the Royal City's cobbled, pristine streets, each filled with thousands of people, living together, all on top of one another. The thought of that alone made Kull shudder. His eyes wandered from the towers to the strong white-capped mountains encircling the city, the Asban mountain range. They served Vale well, protecting it from foreign intrusion and threats, allowing the small country of Lotte to remain free from its neighbors for hundreds of years.

Kull grabbed his thin coat and drew it in as the crisp mountain air blew over him. He always wanted to come to Vale, but now that he was here he could hardly stomach the sight. The contrast that he felt was unlike anything he had ever experienced. All morning long he rode with the convoy of refugees on the rustic, wild roads of the Lottian countryside. It was a desolate landscape of ravaged ruins. Kull had learned the truth. Cotswold was not the only village destroyed by the Grogans. Town after town they passed through had met a similar fate, each destroyed by the fire of Grogan warships and rooks.

Yet here, in Vale, it was as if all of that was only a dream. Well-dressed children played ball games in the streets, laughing and yelling. Businessmen and merchants sat hunched over their datalinks buying and selling goods. Some sat leisurely at cafes eating fine foods, drinking, smiling. The city's citizens scurried about the large promenades without a care in the world, babbling about the upcoming coronation ceremonies and dressed in the finest thick furs. They soon began to peer over at the refugees, whispering with one another and snickering, faces masked with a mixture of disgust and concern. Kull gritted his teeth at the sight of such naive opulence.

He reached back into the convoy and grabbed Ewing's hand. He pulled him out into the cool mountain air. Ewing balanced gingerly on a single crutch while Kull whispered, "Mark my words, Ewing. Aleph will curse this city."

He was met with a growl. "And you, young lad, must keep your mouth *shut*. You are not in Cotswold, anymore. This city has ears, and you don't know who might be listening."

A horrible mixture of grief and rage rolled within him. He bit his tongue as the Valish residents gawked at them and the rest of the wounded that poured out into the street. Unable to contain it anymore, he continued, "But look at these people, Ewing! They have no concern for Cotswold, no concern for..."

"I lost a leg, boy, not my eyes!" snapped Ewing. "Now shut your trap."

Kull swallowed his protests and let out a low grunt.

Ewing whispered to him, drawing him close as he teetered on his crutch. "You've got to learn to control that tongue, Shepherd. It's no wonder your Pa didn't send you to the Academy. They would have ground you to dust because of your attitude."

Kull snapped back, "I don't have an attitude, Ewing. I—"

"NOT another word. Not here, Kull." Ewing stared into his eyes, "*Follow my lead.*" Kull nodded. His frustration with himself, with Ewing, and with this place continued its low boil as he felt the pious glances fall on him and the others. He had seen enough of Lotte's capital city. Besides Adley, it held nothing for him.

Truckload after truckload pulled up and dumped out another crew of weary, injured passengers. In the streets, women snatched their children from their games and shut them in their houses as pockets of men stood dumbfounded and speechless at the sight. The reality of the war fell over the city with a hush.

A stout medic with a clipboard marched over to them, his eyes looking them over as his mouth drew up in a scowl.

Ewing quipped at him, "Is there a problem here, doc?"

The doctor did not acknowledge them, but went to the back of the truck.

Adley stood and greeted the doctor with a salute. The look on her face made it obvious this was a visit she was not looking forward to.

Oh no.

"Nurse Rainer, I told you only to deliver *criticals.* These two could have stayed back."

Kull's stomach dropped. The plan to get out of Lotte was already falling apart.

Adley gave a quick glance at them, as if Kull and Ewing meant nothing to her and coolly replied, "Actually, the old man is a decorated veteran. He lost that leg in the Grogan attack on Cotswold and is due his just compensation. Plus, the Major has a rare blood type and the banks were dry in Cotswold. You can pull his tag. He is two units low, and we weren't going to let him bleed out."

Kull swallowed hard. At least part of this grand lie was true. Ewing was low on blood, but he was as regular a blood type as Kull's or any other random man off the street. The blood card they swiped from the medic's tent was what persuaded Adley to join them in their charade, that and his lie of his acceptance into the Academy. It was all too much for her not to help them. Kull's knees weakened as he watched Adley continue to defend them, even though she had no idea she had been strung along the whole time.

"Major Ewing's companion was brought along because he was recently accepted into the Academy. He was eager to complete his enlisting to ensure he could aid in the defense and recovery efforts. You know we need all the help we can get."

The doctor glared over old wire frame glasses back at Ewing and then began pouring over the long list of incoming Cotswoldians. "*What* is his name?" The question simmered with frustration.

In a huff of pride, Ewing hobbled over towards them, ridiculously bombast and comically animated for a man with one leg. "Arthur Ewing. *Major* Arthur Ewing. I am here for my new leg. As you see, I am currently without!"

There was a certain sick satisfaction that came with Ewing's outlandish tactics. Kull did not know how he did it, but Arthur Ewing always got what he wanted. The military doctor threw up a quick salute.

"My apologies, Major. We've had so many come in from the towns and villages. It's all a bit too much to handle, I'm afraid."

"Excuses mean nothing to these people," Ewing grumbled as he gestured to the masses of incoming refuges.

The lead medic said nothing but addressed Adley. "Take him to the hospital. I will personally see to it that the Major gets in the queue for his...compensation." He turned to Ewing, "Major, I apologize, but we can't secure you a ride back out to Cotswold after you are outfitted with your prosthetic. The Grogans have attacked our earlier supply lines, and we have no vehicles to spare."

The man's voice hardened as he shot a glance back to Adley. "Once you get these few refugees squared away, take off for Tindler, okay? I still don't know why you were sent to Cotswold."

Adley blushed with embarrassment as she was chided and nodded her head. "Yes sir. I understand."

Panic slowly untwisted from within Kull as a cautious relief grew inside of him. They actually made it to Vale and would not be sent away or arrested. Plus, the fact that Adley would have to head to Tindler gave him some room not to uncover his lies to her, after all.

Another doctor pointed to Kull, "What's wrong with this kid?"

Adley replied sharply, "He wouldn't leave the old man's side. Said he was all he had. Plus, he was just accepted into the Academy."

Adley shot a quick grin to Kull as the doctor rolled his eyes and turned back to the hospital.

"Alright, Kull, let's get you two on your way." Adley secured a wheelchair outside the hospital and went to assist Ewing. It was a visible relief for him to get off his crutch. Yet as soon as she began pushing him through the doors of the hospital, the wheelchair slammed to an abrupt halt. Ewing had pulled the brake, sending Adley to a stumble. The charade was over. Kull groaned, wishing the old man had at least waited until Adley left them so he didn't have to reveal their real reason for coming into Vale.

Adley let out an unexpected laugh, "Ewing, what are you doing?" She reached to release the wheels. "We need to get you fitted for your new leg right now. Quit fooling around."

"I'm afraid that now is not the time for that, my dear young lady. Kull and I have something more pressing to attend to. Something much more important than some fancy leg."

Adley's hands fell off the wheelchair. "What?"

Ewing continued his monologue, unaware of Adley's question. "Now if you don't mind, wheel me around the other way please."

"What are you talking about? You're here for the prosthetic and two units of blood, Ewing! I don't know what you are trying to pull, but I already stretched things to get you here." She sent a quick glare over to Kull. "To get you *both* here. Now, like it or not, we are going to get you fitted."

"Ms. Rainer, now I knew your father while we served in the..."

"Ewing, please..."

Kull broke his silence, laying his hand on Adley's shoulder as he reached to unlock the brake on Ewing's chair.

"I'm sorry; Adley, but you were my only way out of Cotswold. We had to get to Vale. Ewing knows someone who can help me find my dad."

Adley's expression flew from shock to anger.

"What? What did you say, Kull?"

Kull could not bear to look into her piercing brown eyes. "I wasn't accepted into the Academy…and Ewing did not need any rare blood type…but we both needed to get to Vale. You were our only option."

"Well, this is the last time I'm an 'option' for you, Kull Shepherd." She threw her hands to her sides. "I can't believe you did this. I did NOT want to help you get yourself killed! And you lied to me!? I thought you actually wanted to help. Unbelievable! How could you be so selfish?"

Kull tried to find the words to say, but fell short. Adley shook her head and turned away from them.

"Fine. Do what you want, but don't bother dragging me into the middle of it again. I have to go to Tindler for people who actually need me to help save their lives, and not run off on suicide missions."

Kull chased after her and grabbed her shoulder as she began to rush for the hospital doors. Her face was flushed and she huffed as he turned her back to him.

"Adley, there was no other way!" Frustration ramped inside him as he apologized. "I'm sorry, alright! We lied to you, but you just helped me save my dad's life."

Adley's eyes began to tear up. Ewing, for once, remained silent as the two quarreled.

"Kull, you've lost your mind! What makes you think you can take on the Grogans? They took your *dad*! He couldn't even handle them, so *what makes you think you can?* There is a war going on out there! *A war*. This is not a game! And you left your dying mother behind to get yourself killed."

"You think I don't know that, Adley?" Ewing placed a hand on Kull's back to steady him. "I have to try. I can't just…" Hot tears formed in his eyes, but he fought them back in protest. "I can't just let them take him. I have to fight, and don't bring mom into this. I promised her I would bring dad back. She knows the cost. I know the cost, and I have to go after them!"

Adley's face remained stoic.

"This is stupid, Kull. Our armies can barely hold the Grogans back from Vale." Kull was just about to row into her again, but Adley grabbed his hand and stared into his eyes. "I can't stand the thought that I may have just helped you get one step closer to getting yourself killed. I am going to let the guards know you need to be escorted back. This is just wrong."

"Don't!" Kull tempered his anger. "Look, I'm sorry. I truly am, but this is not your call. I can't just sit around, Adley. They are going to kill him. Once they get what they want, they will kill him."

"And what is that, Kull? What do they want?" Adley stared at him.

"I...I don't know..." The wind had been knocked out of him.

"Come on, lad." Ewing broke Kull's gaze from Adley. "We need to find my friend, and the day is almost spent. He'll be making his way out of Vale soon, and... I doubt I will be able to help much longer."

Kull looked at Ewing. He was as white as a sheet. They needed to hurry.

Kull swallowed hard and looked back at Adley. "Listen, Adley." He grasped for words that would make it all better, but found none. "I'm sorry."

Adley looked at him, cut her eyes down, and said nothing as she turned around and bolted into the hospital.

"Adley, wait!" Kull shouted.

"Let her go, Kull! She has her choices, and you have yours. Let her make this choice." Kull could feel Ewing's stare boring into his back as he reproached him. He relented and turned around.

"Fine. Let's go."

Kull got behind his friend and began to push his wheelchair up the cobblestone alley as guilt weighed down each step he took. He did not have long to feel guilty though, as Ewing began barking turn by turn directions. Kull dutifully followed each direction as he labored to push the portly old brute along the cobbled streets.

Ewing's directions eventually brought them to a shadowy alley leading to a single iron door. He was shocked as Ewing forced himself to hobble up on his one good leg and knock on it. A small window flew open, and Ewing whispered something to the person on the other side. Kull heard the thick metal bolt behind the door unlatch, and it swung open with a low moan. There, much to Kull's surprise, was a monk from the Preost Forest. The white-robed figure didn't say a word, but motioned them forward. Careful to bolt back the heavy door, the monk led them both toward a small stone chapel surrounded by a beautiful garden of blooming red roses. Despite the tall towers surrounding them, sunlight poured throughout the hidden courtyard, and Kull was shocked to find that such a peaceful place existed deep within the bustling streets of Vale.

The monk motioned for them to enter the chapel. As Ewing and Kull entered the small alcove of the sanctuary they were greeted by a low, brooding growl. When Kull saw the origin of the growl, he wanted to bolt for the door, but Ewing held him in place, his grip firm. There, deep within the chapel, was a praying ebony-skinned monk accompanied by a wild, bearish dog. Kull could barely hold back the questions and fear bubbling within him as he stared at the dog lying by this mysterious monk's side.

Kull whispered, unable to contain himself, "*This* is your friend, Ewing?"

Ewing whispered back, "*Be quiet!* And yes, this is my friend. *Hush now.*"

But Kull could not hush. "You never told me you were friends with a Preost monk."

Ewing quickly snapped back, *"There are **many** things I have not told you. Now hush! You are never supposed to interrupt a Preost monk's prayers. It's just plain bad luck."*

Kull rolled his eyes. "I never took you as one who weighed out luck."

"I don't. But I make an exception with priests, monks, and witches and anyone else who has dealings with the Beyond. You'd be smart to do the same."

The lone cloaked figure sat cross-legged on the white marble floor of the bare room surrounded by candlelight, his lips fluttering rapidly, his eyes held shut. His dark skin served a stark contrast to the intricate ash patterns that wove and swirled over his face. He wore only a coarse gray tunic, and an ironwood staff lay beside him on the ground. He prayed unlike anyone Kull had seen before, for no cleric Kull ever encountered prayed with such quiet intensity. Whatever the monk was saying, it was not meant for his ears or as a showcase of outward piety, yet Kull could not shake off how fierce his face looked.

The only thing more ferocious in the room was the hulking beast of a dog that greeted them upon their entrance. In all his life Kull had never seen a dog more horrible. Its face was a brutal display of disfigurement and scars, like a tattered quilt of fur with long, white teeth. It glared at him, staring him down with its one good eye, the other a hollow scar of patchwork from some unknown battle. Flashing a fraught warning toward him and Ewing, the beast raised one side of its scarred mouth, bearing a row of white fangs. A low, rumbling growl began to build.

The monk broke off his prayer for a quick pause. "Rot," the monk said.

The hound whined and ceased his grumbling, but continued to monitor Kull and Ewing with suspicion.

Silence followed the man's prayers, and the lull lingered and built until Kull felt like he could stand it no longer. He was about to step toward the bowed, silent stranger when Ewing swung his hand around and grabbed Kull by the arm.

"Selah." The stranger's whisper was barely audible.

Without any warning the monk stood to a great height and opened up his eyes, looking down at the two who were trying their best not to interrupt his meditations.

He smiled, showing his crisp, white teeth, as a deep, earthy voice rolled out in greeting. "Arthur Ewing, my friend. I am glad that you are here."

The voice. It boomed with a depth and tenor that was sweet and serious, fluid and solid, as if everything in the world was boiled down into its essence and then wrapped up into a sound. As if this were not enough, Kull was taken aback by how tall the man actually stood. Bowing, his figure was imposing, but standing, his presence was unmistakable. He was easily a foot taller than Kull, if not more. His taut arms, muscled frame, and stature radiated with a strength that could not be hidden under his simple gray robes.

"My dear, Wael. So pleasant to see you again. May Aleph's blessing be upon you."

Kull's eyebrows rose to the sound of Ewing's strange talk. Ewing was *actually* showcasing piety and reverence, and it was, to boot, believable. *What is going on?* Kull was dumbfounded. Gone was the sly cunning and sharp tongue that marked his friend so well. He glanced over at the man who had been his father's companion for what seemed like ages, confused by this sudden shift in his demeanor.

Wael's face frowned as he glanced at Ewing's leg. "My friend, it is you who looks to be in need of a blessing. Is this the work of Grogan hands?"

Ewing coughed, embarrassed. "Unfortunately so, my friend. Cotswold will never be the same. The Grogans all but burnt it to the ground, but our town fought the best they could."

Wael winced at the news. The large hound by his side stood up and sat by his master, continuing to stare at them with his good eye full of distrust. Kull could clearly see now that what the dog lacked in looks, it made up in strength. Sitting down the muscular hound's head came above Wael's hip, taller than any dog Kull had ever seen. The beast made Kull's mouth dry out with fear. *What kind of man keeps an animal like this?*

Wael spoke, "It is terrible to have them on the warpath again. They are a hard people whose lust for power rivals any I've met as a member of my Order. The Realms cannot continue to handle all of this upheaval and bloodshed."

"Have you gotten word, Wael? Have the other Brothers sent you to bargain?" Ewing's question made no sense to Kull.

What are they talking about?

Wael replied, "Yes. I am going directly into the Groganlands to seek and broker a truce. I am to meet with Sar Hagan himself, if he will have me. This war must end. I am shocked to think Hagan would even allow such brutality. The Alephian monks have..." Wael trailed off, his eyes for the first time focusing on Kull.

Kull swallowed hard.

"Who is this you have brought to me, Ewing?" The monk's voice seemed to flow into Kull, causing his heart to explode with a quickening.

"Oh, yes...my apologies, Wael. Let me introduce to you someone you know quite well."

"What?" Kull blurted out.

Ewing shook his head, "Yes, Kull. This is Wael, the Mastermonk of the Alephian order. He comes from the Sanctuary of Preost. Rose and Grift had him bless you when you were born, though I'm sure you were too young to remember that."

Memory washed over Kull's mind like a wave.

Cotswold fields.

A family gathering.

Laughing.

A celebration.

His mother was there, smiling with pure, unmarred vitality, her long auburn hair flowing. Whatever disease she bore could not be seen now. Grift was there too, and he was smiling. It was an odd collage of youth and happiness that seemed foreign to Kull. It was something he had not seen much of growing up. They had been together as a family, and the sun warmed them as the dark man, this man, poured oil over the baby's head. The baby. *That was him.*

Kull looked away, the memory receding from his mind as he fought the tears welling up in his eyes. It was as if he had been transported to another time, as if a dream had become reality. Wael kindly glanced at Kull with a knowing look and smiled quietly.

"I believe Kull does remember me, Ewing, but I was only a footnote on that day. Young man, you have grown, and I can see much of your father in you...as well as your mother." The pause lingered as Wael weighed his words. "And now you are both here. I take it, Kull, that you wish to join me in searching for your father in the Groganlands?"

"How did you know that?" Kull was shocked to know this monk knew of everything already. Ewing had not communicated his plan to anyone on the journey to Vale. The thought that he may have some inside information on his father's disappearance caused a great uneasiness to rise in Kull's chest. Was it possible for this monk to have helped lead to his father's capture?

Wael cleared his throat and glanced at Ewing with a smile. "It seems since your mother's sickness, your father has done you a disservice in not getting you involved within the fold."

Ewing coughed nervously and smiled, trying to avoid Wael's keen gaze.

Wael continued, "Kull, maybe you haven't been taught about my kind. In my Order we have certain...certain *gifts* that have been passed down for generations. These gifts are given from Aleph, and we use them to conduct the work of Aleph on this plane. The memory that fell into your mind was one that I projected onto you. It is *my* memory and mine alone...I just wanted to share it with you."

Kull did his best to comprehend the vision of seeing both his mother and his father together, young, full of life, and carefree. The thought roared in his heart and choked him up with another swell of rampant emotion. How could such a reality exist? All his life, Kull had known two absolute facts; his mother was sick and his father was a Guardsman. Those two facts meant that he would have to bear his family's burdens alone. Turning back to the monk, Kull muttered out a single question: "Why?" The emotional turbulence of this encounter was something he had not prepared for, and he did not understand how any of it related to rescuing his dad.

Wael leaned down and put his hand on Kull's shoulder. "I need you to trust me. If you are to come with me to the Groganlands, as I believe you wish to do, then I hope that by sharing that memory I can earn your trust. I know both your father and your mother very well, and they share a special bond with me. It is for this reason I am going to help you find your father."

Wael glanced down at Kull, his eyes widening. "What do you have?"

"What?" Kull didn't understand.

"Did your mother give you something?" Wael's eyes stared at Kull's chest, directly at the charm his mother gave him, hidden underneath his shirt.

Kull reached for it and pulled it out. The rune for Aleph bounced in the candlelight. "This?"

Wael stared at the pendant, his lips pursed. "Yes. It was good for your mother to give you the emblem. She understood that you needed it now."

"It was you?" Kull asked, stammering. Ewing shuffled nervously behind them as Kull lost himself deep within the monk's wide eyes. "You were the monk that gave her the necklace. I do remember you."

Wael smiled and spoke, "Your memory serves you well. I gave that emblem of Aleph long ago to your mother, and now she has given it to you." The monk leaned in closer as a serious whisper crept from his lips, *"She asked you to find your father, didn't she?"*

Kull was floored, but he spoke boldly. "She did. She told me to go after dad. To bring him back. She said it was more important than staying with her. She gave me this pendant, and that is why I am here."

Wael nodded, allowing silence to fill the room. "She gave you much more than a pendant, Kull, but that is a tale for another time. That gift will help you greatly to find your father."

Kull stared at Wael. "Can't you just use your...*gifts* and find him?"

Wael picked up his ironwood staff and shifted his weight onto the massive weapon. The hound stood up with him.

"Kull, I wish it were that easy. Unfortunately, Aleph's gifts do not grant the bearer with unlimited scope or insight. I do not know if your father is still alive. So we must hurry. If Grift still lives, then I fear for his safety. If he spends too much time in the hands of the Grogan interrogators his mind may never return. The Grogans," Wael paused, "know not only how to kill the body, but are also skilled in flaying one's spirit and mind. We need to get to Grift quickly."

Kull's head began to spin as his heart throbbed inside his chest. Each breath became heavy and labored. The thought of losing his father was unbearable. Kull straightened himself up, shaking off the fear and doubt that had begun to weigh on him.

"So you don't know if he is alive?"

"Kull, I cannot promise you the outcome you desire." Wael closed his eyes and took in a deep breath. "There will be much to do and much for you to learn along the way." The monk held out his powerful right hand. "You must make an oath to me, Kull Shepherd, to follow my instructions once we leave Lotte. The way to the Groganlands is fraught with many dangers, and I must have your absolute cooperation if you and your father have any hope of surviving."

Kull's hand folded over Wael's. "I promise."

"Very well then. We will leave tonight."

Ewing piped in. "Wael, what can I do for you and the boy?" Kull had nearly forgotten about Ewing during the exchange.

The dog by Wael's side suddenly began to growl, its bristled hair springing up from its back in alarm. An eruption of noise sounded from all sides of the chapel, a huge rolling roar of people screaming. It was unlike anything Kull had ever heard and instinctively the thought of Grogan rooks ascending from the horizon filled him with a rush of panic. The dog was barking madly as long ribbons of drool fell from its maw onto the chapel floor. Wael placed his hand on the beast and it instantly became calm. The monk closed his eyes as the rumbling din receded.

"What was that?" Kull shouted.

"Lotte has just crowned their new king. That was the sound of Seam Panderean ascending to the high throne. The people are now rejoicing."

Wael showed no sign of joy or appreciation as he mentioned the new king's ascension.

Returning to Ewing, Wael continued, "We are going to need you to stay here, Ewing. We will need a reliable contact within Vale. Those who we could trust are becoming...unreliable. I'll send word to you once we learn Grift's fate. Are you able to stay in Vale?"

"Aye," Ewing said nodding his head. "I've got an appointment here anyway," He winced as he glanced down at his gnarled stump of a leg. "How do you plan to make the trip into the Groganlands? In a time of war there is no way you can ride the line cars."

Wael smiled with a knowing look. "That's where you come in, my friend. Do you still have any of your old logging trucks in the city?"

Ewing nodded. "I believe I can pull some strings for you, Wael. My logging business in Vale all but folded years ago when I settled in Cotswold. I still have some friends here, though. I'll see if I can't pull a few favors."

"Pull all the strings you can, Ewing," said Wael. "Kull and I are going to need all the help we can get."

CHAPTER EIGHT

Deep pain rolled through Seam with each shallow breath. As hard as it was to focus on his new duties as king, his wounds reminded him of one thing: *he was alive.* His first experience of having to kill another man had not gone at all as he expected. He had trained, of course, in the Academy for combat, but the thrill that came with defeating a true attacker was so…intoxicating.

The new king continued to shower himself with inner accolades over his first victory. *He was the first, but he won't be the last. Others will come. They will come to take me away from the Path, but I'll kill them before they stop me.* Seam shuddered as he reveled in the dark thought of having to take another life. He did not tremble from fear or disgust, but out of a strange sensation of fulfillment as he imagined himself conquering his foes. He found himself running his long fingers across the dusty old bookshelf hiding his most prized possession. Day after day, he would orbit his private sitting chamber, just to be near *it.* Behind his bolted chamber door he was free, finally free to delve deep into the lore of the forsaken tome that revealed his path to him and to hold the key that had been unhinged from his late father's broach.

As Seam turned the key over in his hands he noticed its intricate design. Two beasts, serpent-like in their design, were locked in conflict, their mouths touching, forming the key's bow. Upon further inspection, small markings of an ancient script flowed from the sides of it, markings identical to those on the spine of the ancient relic he recovered from the library.

This Key will unlock my path, my purpose, he thought to himself. *Soon all of Candor will be swept up in this one bold act. They will be free once more. Free at last to bring order to this cursed continent. Free to establish and usher in my new reign.*

The king has requested you to transport him to an undisclosed location. Report to him immediately.

Bronson stared at the message blinking on his datalink. It had only been three hours since the coronation ceremony, and it seemed that the king was disregarding all of the galas and parties that had been meticulously choreographed in his honor. He could already see that his work was cut out for him as the new head guardsman. This most recent request confirmed his fears about his new sovereign. *How am I to advise a king who wants no advice?* Not only did the request burning on his screen throw out all sense of protocol and security, it seemed especially risky considering the recent assassination attempt. It left a bad taste in Bronson's mouth and made him nervous. He punched a quick response into the datalink on his wrist, the blue letters ticking off in a rush: *I'm on my way.*

Bronson knocked at the king's chamber door and waited. He could hear Seam's voice, muffled by the thick oak frame.

"Come in."

Bronson entered and bowed. He rattled off the excuse he had been reciting before answering the king's call, "My king, I came as quickly as I could. Gathering a convoy together in the midst of the coronation celebration was no easy task on such short notice."

Seam's reply was short as he snatched up a book from the bookcase, "I don't need a convoy, Bronson. If I needed one, I would have asked for it."

"But, but sir, the king's detail always travels by..."

"Not this time, Bronson!" Seam's fist fell down on the desk with a resounding thud. "Now let the security detail go celebrate or do whatever else they wish tonight. I simply need you, and that will be all."

"But..."

"Do not question me again, Bronson. Is it the captain of the guard's job to question his sovereign's requests?"
Bronson's eyes lowered, "No, my lord."

"Then listen to what I have to say." Seam's eyes tore through him as he sneered.

Bronson was both appalled and shocked at the verbal lashing. For decades he served the Pandereans faithfully. Camden had only been supportive of his painstaking efforts and focus for detail. He assumed it was his thoroughness in all situations that propelled him to this new post.

Bronson stammered a weak reply as he backed from the room, "Yes, sir. I understand. You can meet me at the rear concourse, and I will have a vehicle ready. We will be sure to slip away quietly."

As Bronson hustled away from his quarters toward the transport hangar, Seam glanced into the satchel he had collected containing his treasured book of writings and the key he received from his father's cold corpse.

Tonight will be special. Everything is coming together. Soon this will all be worth the struggle.

Bronson left the royal chamber as hot anger washed over him. He had not had much interaction with Seam during the later part of his father's rule, but he always assisted with the security of the royal family, and never had he been so insulted. *Aleph, what an idiot. He'll get himself killed, and then I'll be next if I'm not careful.* To Bronson, Seam was still a child, and an insolent one at that.

Mischief and rumors had never been too far from Seam when he was growing up in the palace. The Realm had long been filled with sordid stories of the young prince's late night soirees and antics. *But this behavior, this is something different,* Bronson thought to himself. In public, Seam appeared to be the future king that all of Lotte expected him to be; brave, strong, and resolute. Yet amid the private staff who served him personally, stories were being traded about the royal's erratic nature. Stories that painted him as increasingly unstable. As if some form of mania was taking root within him, some sort of dark madness. Bronson saw no evidence to validate the rumors, but he noticed even during Camden's reign how the prince's hands would often shake, and at best his concentration in the royal proceedings was aloof. What concerned Bronson was the rumor's increasing frequency. He kept hearing from others within the palace that Seam was changing. That the young royal would not sleep, spending his nights locked in his study, talking to some unknown party. Was he talking to himself? Or with someone else? Bronson couldn't be sure.

He slipped himself into the oversized, black military vehicle and turned over the ignition. The engine rumbled with anticipation. He rolled up to the side gate of the palace and muttered to himself, "Something might not be right with him." He felt for the sidearm he carried on his belt.

As soon as Bronson parked the vehicle, the door of the transport flung open. Bronson's heart jumped, and his hand gripped for his weapon. He turned only to notice that the King had entered the vehicle cloaked in a long black cape. It was as if a blur of shadows had been swept into the cabin.

"What took you so long, Bronson?" the royal hissed underneath the hood.

Bronson struggled to find words, still startled at this sudden apparition. "My liege?" Bronson did not mean for it to be a question. Slowly, he forced his hand away from his sidearm.

"Of course it's me." Seam spoke with sharp, staccato sentences, "Now we cannot sit here all day. We must move. I have pressing business to attend to. Take me to the Crossroads."

Bronson slammed on the brakes. *What did he say?* "Sir?" He looked behind the seat and stared over at his king to ensure he had heard correctly. "*The Crossroads?* Sir?"

"Am I not making myself clear, Captain?" Seam shouted, his frustration giving over to rage. "Take me to the Crossroads! On top of Trosedd's Peak. Or am I to take it that *you* have not heard of it?"

Bronson stared into the dark eyes of his new king. Never in his life had he heard such a request. "Of course, my Lord." He gunned the engine, and the heavy tires spun away from the palace.

The Crossroads? In Aleph's name, why does he want to go there?"

The history of Vale had long been contested by the scholars and the historians, and there were many legends about the founding of the capital city. Some said it grew from being a small, peaceful logging village that tremendously benefited when the ancient Predecessor rail lines were uncovered. Others claimed that Vale was built on the outskirts of what had once been another city, Muldock.

Muldock. The very thought of it fell over Bronson like a chill that sets in before an illness. Muldock was the subject of many childhood ghost stories and tales used to frighten Valish children into behaving. The legend blossomed into a frightful nursery rhyme.

Fit for Muldock,
You Naughty Child,
Waste your days
In the Rotting Aisles,
Waiting with those dead and gone,
Unable to sing Aleph's song.

Bronson found the rhyme disturbing and made a point never to sing it to his own children. Legends like Muldock were not to be trivialized. Most people in Lotte left history to die. Bronson always enjoyed studying old stories, but Muldock was one he wished he never read about. Whatever truth lay in the legends of that city, that truth was to be feared. Muldock was a dark and treacherous city, filled with mass public executions, wanton violence, and savagery beyond imagination. It was a city ruled by a dynasty of malicious and destructive kings, horrible enough in their own right, only to be usurped by one last terror. One of the Five. The Sorrow of Lotte—Abtren of the Serubs, *cursed be her name.*

Abtren, *cursed be her name,* along with her Serub kin, split Candor down the middle, as if it were a fat bull chosen for slaughter. They held the entire continent in their mighty grip, crushing any who dared challenge their rule, never parlaying with their enemies and reveling in genocide. Worshipped as gods by the conquered, the Serubs claimed to be the embodiment of the divine on Candor, sending the entire continent to fall into utter darkness.

Bronson hammered down the pedal of the vehicle as it sped into the night. Roadside ruins of ancient shrines blotted the landscape. These rotting ruins grew taller and taller where the three ancient trading paths finally converged. History was clear enough; the blood of humans was traded on this peak, bought and sold as a commodity in order to make amends to the conquerors. Alephian monks, in a swell of religious fervor, destroyed the temples and shrines of the dark place, leaving them in ruins. They commanded all those who served Aleph to treat the place as cursed ground, for it was still filled with a dark and twisted energy that clung to the very earth rumbling beneath the transport's tires.

As the truck slid up the mountainside toward Seam's destination, the road became surrounded by a thick, foreboding forest that squeezed out the moon's soft light. Bronson shuddered as he stared out into the pitch black surrounding the vehicle. It was as if the headlights were only candles.

Seam smiled as he watched Bronson's eyes stare out into the darkness beyond them, fear dancing on his face. "Come, come, Bronson. Surely you are not one for superstition? For ghost stories?" He let out a low chuckle.

Bronson turned; startled by the first words Seam had spoken during the long drive.

"Of course not, sir. I just can't see a thing out this window. Even with the lights on I can barely see ten feet in front of us."

"So, you are scared of the dark then?" Seam smirked with his arms folded across his chest.

Bronson's reply was flat, devoid of any of the real fear hammering against his heart. "No, sir. I am simply looking out for your safety. Considering that your normal protection detail was left behind and you only have me with you, I have to admit that I am a bit concerned."

Seam turned his eyes out the side window of the truck and stared out into the dark trees rolling by.

"Don't sell yourself too short, my loyal Captain of the Guard. Your frets are for nothing. This trip will not take long."

After another half hour of snaking through the black forest, the ruined features of the Crossroads began to rise around the road. At first, small toppled hovels and stacks of rubble grown over by moss and weeds were visible as the headlights glanced over them. Then they reached the mounds. The mounds of the dead, long buried in massive graves, forced the truck to weave and wind between them. Bronson's stomach flipped inside as he wound through the maze. He wondered how many innocents were thrown into shallow graves here, buried twisted together, uncared for and unloved in this cursed place.

Following the mounds, skeletons of small buildings appeared, emerging from the darkness on the sides of the road. They were covered with thick ivy growing through their windows and out of the roofs that had long since collapsed. Some of the old buildings were hunched over, falling in on themselves, as if they were begging to crash to the ground and be relieved of their own weight.

Seam's voice pierced the silence as the truck continued to crawl up the abandoned highway. "Captain."

"Yes, sir?"

Seam pointed from the back seat. "I want you to bring me to the center of the ruin. There should be an old temple complex there."

Unquestioning but full of dread, Bronson replied, "Yes sir."

As the truck turned a sharp corner its lights revealed the square, and just as Seam had said, there lay a massive, unkempt temple, standing proudly, defiant of the decomposition that surround it.

How could this place still stand? Bronson wondered to himself. *And why would the monks leave it standing?*

Bronson's eye caught a faint flicker of light from behind the red stained glass windows of the building. At first he thought it was a reflection of the truck's headlights, but as the truck turned away the stained glass continued to flicker, and then glow.

There was a light or a fire inside the temple lighting the red panes.

There's someone in there.

Seam opened the door and got out without a word. Bronson, in turn, stepped out of the convoy with his king. Seam turned and held out his hand.

"Stay here. *That is an order*. I will not be long."

Seam slid away from him, making his way toward the door standing open at the front of the temple. He disappeared through it as he hurried into the darkness.

After a few moments passed, Bronson slid from his seat of the truck. He stood, grabbed his rifle, and headed toward the temple.

I will just as soon die before I leave my new king alone in such a place, thought Bronson as he snuck up to one of the open windows. Peering in from the safety of the shadows his fear for his king grew with what he saw.

Seam was sitting at a small fire across from a figure that was clad in a black hooded robe, very similar to his own. The two characters looked like shadows sitting across from one another as they spoke.

Seam's eyes danced from the flickering firelight as he spoke softly with the hooded stranger. Bronson gripped his rifle and clicked off the safety, his eye aiming down the sight. He warned the stranger in his mind, *Make one move.*

Seam's words flew out from him, "Vashti, I have something for you. I have dreamt of this day for a long time, and now I am finally able to begin the process of redemption."

A soft, gentle voice came from underneath the stranger's hood. It seemed to sing like chimes over the crackling fire.

"Show me, please."

Seam reached up to his right shoulder and unclasped the hidden key he had found within his father's royal robes. As he released the key he stood and handed it over for inspection.

"Oh, Seam. This is exciting indeed. You have done very well."

Bronson did not lower his weapon, but stared in through the window, straining to hear the conversation and make out the identity of the stranger opposite Seam.

The long, black hood was finally lifted, revealing a stunning girl with flowing raven hair and dark skin that glowed in the firelight. Underneath her cloak, Bronson could see the purple robe she wore; the colors that came from the Realm of Preost. *What in Aleph's name is a Preost woman doing here?*

Bronson did not know much about the forest people, but he knew he had never seen a woman from Preost. Her beauty, even in the dim light, was stunning. Bronson was convinced that Seam was meeting with the most beautiful woman to ever come out of any of the Realms. Her hair fell across her shoulders in intricate curls, a waterfall of midnight. Her skin was dark like mahogany and smooth like porcelain. It was her eyes, however, that captivated the old guard, causing him to feel young and full of vigor and passion. She was exquisite, and Bronson had to tear himself away from staring at her. He lowered his rifle and slowly stepped back from the window.

He chuckled to himself and let out a low whistle as he quietly climbed back into the truck to wait on his king's return.

Vashti was quick to notice the old guard staring at her through the tall stained glass window. Even when she saw him raise his weapon, she had wisely chosen to play as if she were unaware, only pulling back her cowl to showcase her good intentions toward the young King Seam. Her strategy had worked, and the incident that could have erupted was avoided without any harm. She looked down at the key that Seam had given her, felt its weight, and twirled it in her hand. She could not believe her good fortune. Her mistress would be *so pleased* with her.

She stared into Seam's brown eyes, calculating her approach toward him. With a subtle smile, she leaned in a deliberate attempt to showcase her luxurious curved features. She could tell the naïve man before her was falling for it and everything would soon go according to her plan.

"You are the High King of Vale now. We can finally progress further," she said with a smile.

CHAPTER NINE

As the sun rose on the beaches of Elum, gulls cried in high shrills, their chorus echoing over the thunder of the waves crashing in cadence on the province's rocky shores. The sun slid across the surface of the ocean, awakening the dark, blue body of water into a golden slate of glass. The shores of Elum were renowned by those wealthy enough to afford the journey to visit them.

The Darian family estate was a testament to the wealth and prestige of the Elum province. The complex sat high atop the cliffs over the southernmost beaches in the Realm, its marble columns standing proudly over the shoreline. One could see the structure from miles around. Flying buttresses of clear glass shot up into a sharp pinnacle, the structure taking on the same golden hue of the early morning light; a large glowing torch burning upon the water's edge.

The Darian family's rule was marked with deceit, treachery, and skillful machinations of politics. All of it preserved Elum in its pristine condition. The Realm had been able to avoid conflict for hundreds of years, remaining largely disinterested in the affairs of outsiders and offering resources to all of them, treasures harvested from their lush ocean whenever needed. The abundance of oil stashed in their hidden reserves was all the leverage this Realm had ever needed to maintain its own peace. However, the peace was beginning to splinter a week after Grift Shepherd escaped from the Groganlands.

Filip Darian was pouring himself his second glass of brandy that morning when he heard a bellowing roar of thunder that shook his palace's foundation. His heart filled with fear when he looked out from his glass pinnacle to see the black cloud of three hundred rumbling Grogan rooks charging toward his doorstep. The massive army came to a rest outside the palace, as if this were a common practice. Filip stormed out of the main gates, barefoot and wearing only a silk robe. He pushed through the security guards trying to usher him toward safety. His face was flushed with pride, and a vein protruded from his forehead as he stamped toward the lead vehicle in the invading convoy. He threw his fist down on the hood of the first rook and bellowed a deluge of hot curses, waving his arms for the vehicles to shut off their engines. The convoy did not oblige the request, as the drivers continued to idle. Filip threw down his glass, which shattered upon the fine marble bricks, and held up his index finger in the air. He twirled it above his head like a mad magician as he screamed, his voice drowned out in the chaos. Drowned out or not, the command ushered out a platoon of snipers that flooded onto the roof of the palace. They lowered their weapons on the phalanx beneath them, hot pinpricks of red dots hovering over the invading army of faceless warriors.

"SHUT your vehicles down. NOW." Filip stared through the tinted glass of the head rook. The cockpit opened and Willyn Kara removed her helmet. She stepped out of the vehicle and whispered in her radio. Immediately the engines ceased, as the red dotted pinpoints of the snipers danced on her face.

Filip growled at her, "What in Aleph's name ***is this***? What could be so important that you would bring a military detail to the front gates of my estate, Grogan?! I want to speak to your captain!"

"*General*. General Kara. Now, call your snipers off."

Filip's face transformed from shock to hot-faced rage, only to settle into a stern glare of disgust. He sent his hand through his thinning hair, cursed loudly, and spat on the ground.

Willyn did not back down. *"Now, Filip."*

Filip snapped his fingers, and immediately the black armored sniper brigade lowered their weapons, but did not leave their post.

Filip smirked at the young general and spoke flatly to her, his patience strained. "Mistress Willyn Kara of the Groganlands. What do I owe the pleasure of..."

"Cut the pleasantries, Fillip. I am not here to visit. My sources have informed me that your family is harboring a terrorist. *I want him now*."

Fillip's anger resurged and boiled over. He straightened a short, chubby finger and pointed it right into Willyn's face.

"STOP! RIGHT there!" Spittle reeking of alcohol flew from his mouth as he roared at her. "How dare you come to my front steps and accuse me of harboring a terrorist. Neither my family, nor the nation of Elum has any interest in giving asylum to a known threat to any of the Realms. Now I would advise you to explain yourself. The Sar must be utterly mad to send you to me like this without notice."

Willyn's vision went black with rage. "IT IS BECAUSE OF THE SAR THAT I AM HERE!" Immediately, she stepped back and turned away from him, caught off guard by her own response. *Get it together,* she thought to herself.

Recovering, she fired back at him. "I'm shocked to see you have grown a backbone, Filip. It suits you." She smiled to see Filip bite his lip. She stared down at the short, portly magnate and spoke, "So you claim that you are not harboring the terrorist. *Fine*. I believe you, but rest assured the man I'm seeking *is here in Elum,* and I will find him. My men lost him a week ago, and I don't have time to waste negotiating with you right now."

"Your lack of courtesy is remarkable, even for a Grogan, Madam Kara. Let me remind you that you are in *my land,* and it is by my graces that you remain in my land unharmed. Hagan must be feeling very insecure to send in his forces like this. What terrorist, pray-tell, would garner such a force from the mighty Groganlands?" He stared at her, his eyes like daggers. "Tell me. *Now.*"

Willyn spoke, burying the unsteadiness she felt at the mention of Hagan. "Let me be clear, I am looking for Grift Shepherd of Lotte. He is the man responsible for Sar Hagan's current debilitation."

Filip's eyes widened, but his lips remained pursed as he pointed his finger back into Willyn's face.

"I saw on my datalink about your brother, and for that I am sorry. I did not realize how poor his condition was. However, your petty war with Lotte does not concern me or my people. I will overlook your Realm's haste and incompetence for the fact that the Sar is unable to manage his *generals*." Filip spat on the ground in defiance and continued. "You have three days. Three days to find Shepherd. Now let me be clear, on the fourth day you and all these troops will leave Elum regardless of your mission's success. If even one of your troops remains in my state on the fifth day, I will, rest assured, cut off all trade with your barbarous nation. Your precious little machines will be no good to you without my oil. Also, I will send for a formal consul from a Brother Counselor."

Willyn laughed, "Filip, do you really think that my people are afraid of the monks? The old ways are passing away. Their influence is waning, and the faith that sustains them is losing its power." She gripped the hilt of the pistol by her side. "Better to be equipped with guns and grit than to depend on the prayers of those old hermits. It's nice to see that some still hold to the faith, though." She glared at him, unflinching. "I agree with your terms. We will honor your request. "

"Good." Filip smirked and straightened his robe as he started to turn back to the palace. His bare feet flapped on the marble stairs, amusing Willyn greatly as he waddled back to his crystal estate.

"Despite your insults and foolishness, I'm glad the Grogan people still have some mental capacity. Rest assured I want you and your men out of here as soon as possible." Willyn continued to smile as the short ruler shot his platitudes at her. "Therefore, to aid you in your task, I am going to be sending my best scout to escort you personally through the Realm. He will not only be helping you find Shepherd, *should he be here,* but he will also be my eyes and ears. If you cause my people any harm, or if you cause any harm to befall on him, I will personally see this as an act of unprovoked war."

"Oh, we wouldn't want *that* now would we, Filip?" Willyn whispered mockingly. "I would not want to be the cause of an international conflict."

Filip looked back to Willyn. His jousting words fell flat and serious. "You are still just a child. You do not know the way the world truly works yet, but trust me, when you are alone, you will find that your arrogance will have done nothing but hurt you."

Willyn blinked, taken aback from the comment. *What is this old fool saying to me?*

"Now come on and I will introduce you to your escort."

Willyn motioned her personal security detail forward as Filip spun back around on his heels.

"Leave your brutes behind, Willyn. I personally will guarantee your safety in my Realm, but I really don't care to have my rugs soiled with your men's boots. Now come on and get in here. It's cold out and I am ready for another drink."

Willyn could not help but laugh. "A bit early isn't it, Filip?"

"It's never too early for the finer things in life," Filip said as he and Willyn stepped into the grand main parlor.

He turned and addressed her, "Wait here, I will be back in just a moment. "

Filip scurried away, leaving Willyn alone. She sat down at a sprawling pine table in the middle of the room and slowly examined the intricate interior surrounding her. The embellished moldings, crystal chandeliers, and hand-crafted furniture stood in stark contrast to the cold cement walls that made up her home in the Groganlands. Both were a show of power, the Grogan halls as a nearly impenetrable fortress, which could withstand assaults of nearly any kind. The nation of Elum, however, had no shame in putting its riches on display, flaunting its wealth and prestige.

After a half hour of sitting alone in the grand foyer, listening to the nearby clock tick by the minutes, the door that Filip disappeared behind creaked open. Willyn was not greeted again by the diminutive ruler, however, but instead a lean, dark-haired man, who, without a word, stepped into the room and sat down across the table from her. He was handsome but plainly dressed, and Willyn noticed instantly that he did not carry himself in the same fashion as the Elum royalty. The man sat and stared at her with his cold, gray eyes, completely silent. He slowly and deliberately kicked his legs up on the table, never breaking his eyes from her.

The two sat in silence for a few moments. The stranger continued to stare. He did not blink, not once, and Willyn locked her eyes with him, accepting his unspoken challenge. They sat there for what seemed like an eternity. She could not maintain the strange ordeal a moment longer.

Willyn bulldozed through without a pause, "Introduce yourself, stranger." She reached down for her sidearm, threatening to release her pistol from its holster. "I don't have time to waste so you need to speak up or get out."

The man slapped the table with such force that it nearly buckled, and he began to laugh. The laughter, if you could call it that, came in strange controlled bursts, rolling out slow and deliberate. Willyn sat dumbfounded as the stranger spoke.

"Ha! Ha...ha. Oh, I do love a good laugh. You Grogans and your guns."

The stranger quickly straightened himself and stood to his feet. This oddness, along with the laughter, disappeared in an instant as he calmly addressed her.

"Willyn Kara, what a pleasure to meet you. Please allow me to introduce myself. I am Luken, and I will serve as your escort as you visit Elum. I am thoroughly at your service." He bowed quickly and sprung up. "Now, I understand you have lost something." A wry, knowing smile grew on his face. There was something captivating about the man with the gray eyes, as if he released a tangible energy that permeated the air.

Willyn sifted through her feelings, relieved that the conversation was turning to what really mattered. "Not something, but someone. I am in search of a terrorist that I have reason to believe is hiding in Elum. His name is Grift Shepherd, though I doubt that name means anything to you."

Luken's face dropped and his eyes became distant upon the mention of Grift's name. He murmured something to himself, turning to stare out of the clear glass wall that overlooked the royal promenade. Willyn approached him, reading the recognition on his face.

"Ah, so Filip actually did send me someone useful. I see you know exactly who I am looking for." Luken did not acknowledge her, but continued to keep his back toward her. Softly, Willyn laid her hand on Luken's broad shoulder and whispered. "Tell me, Luken, have you seen Grift Shepherd recently?" Her hand squeezed into his shoulder as the question lingered in the air.

He stood motionless for several moments before blinking and reconnecting his sharp eyes with hers. Willyn could tell that he was weighing his words carefully. *He knows something. He knows something about Grift.*

Luken spoke. "I know exactly who you are looking for. Have I seen him recently?" He shook his head. "No. I haven't seen him in many years. However, I do know him, know of him. He is a Guardian, correct?"

"Yes, he was the head guard, or guardian as you say, for King Camden's security detail, but according to evidence I have received, he is also the man that attempted to assassinate my brother, Hagan."

Luken shook his head and looked back out into promenade. "No, that does not seem right. I believe you are mistaken about him. There is no way that Grift Shepherd would have attacked your brother. It actually makes no sense. You are clearly looking for the wrong person."

Willyn snapped back, "And clearly, you are a fool. I know who poisoned Hagan, and I have evidence to prove that Grift Shepherd was the man who attempted the assassination. Now quit with your petulant games and let's start searching."

Luken made no rebuttal. "As you wish, Mistress Kara."

"Good." Willyn turned for the door to the outer courtyards where her men were still waiting.

Luken redirected her, "My lady. You are going the wrong way." A small, wiry smile grew on his face.

Willyn looked back over her shoulder and narrowed her eyes. Her sneer produced no visible sign of fear in him, and it made her loathe him all the more. Luken chuckled and exited from the door where he first emerged. Willyn reluctantly followed.

"You see, my dear Mistress Kara, Shepherd would not be on the mainland had he sought exile in Elum. People around these parts like to talk too much about good-looking strangers. They also are incredibly vain and materialistic. They would sell out their own mothers if it would buy them credits. No, he's definitely not on the mainland."

"Then where is he?" Willyn asked.

"Isn't it obvious? If you are certain he punched a ticket to Elum, he's on one of the hundreds of islands just off the coast."

Willyn cursed her luck underneath her breath. Islands meant boats, and Willyn hated boats.

"Now, please, dear one, if you would kindly follow me down to the dock where my ship is waiting."

Willyn scowled. "I am *not* your dear one. What about my soldiers?"

"Don't worry about them. They will only slow us down. Filip will arrange for them to have a good time while we are out."

"And of my safety? How can I trust you?"

"Did not Filip already guarantee your safety? Rest easy in the knowledge that my country has no desire to have a conflict with the Groganlands. That should be enough for you to know that I mean no harm to you and I will protect you from harm as well."

Willyn was surprised to find herself satisfied with this answer, and followed Luken out to the docks. Despite the answer, she still ran her hand down over her pistol as she reminded herself that she could never trust anyone too easily, especially some odd Elumite.

Luken weaved her through the clear palace, out into a gleaming courtyard of white stucco. From there, he led her through the Filip's garden courtyard and out through an open archway. From this vantage point, The Endless Ocean filled the horizon, its breaking waves hitting the cliffs far below her. Willyn felt her heart slam against her chest. She recoiled at the thought of having to travel on the sea, but it seemed she had no choice.

"Watch your step. The dock is below us. The steps here can be slick."

Carefully she followed him down the winding steps hewn in the steep cliff face, down to the dock.

There a small, black vessel bobbed in the deep blue water, and Luken held out his hand for her to board.

The wind whipped and churned out on the open water. The tiny vessel rocketed through the large swells sweeping up toward them, threatening to overturn them into the deep. The salty air wafted over Willyn as she fought the ongoing weight of nausea that grew deep within her gut. Luken sat behind the wheel piloting the water craft with a mad smile, the wind blowing back his dark hair.

"Not a fan of walking on water, are you?"

Willyn barely could contain the curses that ripped through her mind. "I would hardly call this walking. This boat of yours is as smooth as a drunkard."

"Speaking of drunkards, I do miss your brother. He was a lot like Filip in that regard. *They both like their stiff drinks.*"

Willyn's temper flared like a hot furnace. "How dare you insult the Sar! Don't make me remind you of who I am and exactly what I am capable of."

Luken replied with a dry smile, "Oh please, mighty Willyn, sacker of cities and scourge of the Grogan people, I meant no disrespect. But I would like it very much if you would stop trying to remind me of *who you are*." His voice broke from its normal cadence and fell to a growl. "I know very well who you are, dear girl. Your reputation is known throughout all of Candor, so please, drop the threats. You wouldn't want today to be the day you finally met your match, after all."

Willyn stood up from the ship's rail. "Is that a threat?" She reached for her stun stick. Luken threw the wheel to the right, and the vessel sliced through a small opening between a collection of rocks jutting up out of the water, threatening to shatter the vessel. The turn sent Willyn reeling across the deck.

Her chin smashed against the cabin's wall, and pain riveted through her, the metallic taste of blood filling her mouth. She could feel her face burning hot, glowing as red as her hair, as she leveled her gaze back on her impossibly irreverent guide.

She stood as straight as she could on the bobbing vessel and tried to approach him, but Luken's attention was fully focused on the shoreline. She wiped her bloody lip as she lifted her voice at him trying to regain his attention, "I swear I will..."

"Shhh! Be quiet! If we are going to find Grift anywhere I would expect this to be the place."

Willyn blinked and looked. She had not noticed an island on the horizon as they traveled, but here it was, nonetheless. Luken throttled down the engine and allowed the boat to drift slowly into a cove obscured by a heavy grove of large, ancient mangrove trees, their long branches dangling into the salt water below. The cove was quiet with an uncanny stillness; the only sound was of insects chirping within the trees. Luken leaned on the edge of the hull as he squinted, staring through the canopy of foliage. Willyn also strained her eyes on the shoreline, attempting to find any sign of a Shepherd.

Why was this particular island any more likely a hiding spot than any of the others that lined Elum? Any fool could see that the mangroves didn't provide adequate cover.

As if he could tell from the look in her eyes, Luken spoke.

"You are familiar with the Rihtian War, yes?"

"Of course I am. My father was responsible for ending the revolt and rebellion of Riht."

"Ah yes, the 'rebellion of Riht.' What a nice trope your people have constructed. Well, this, my dear," he held his hands out to the island, "is where we hid many of the Rihtian refugees from your father. In fact, the Realm of Lotte was instrumental in helping transport many of them here. Grift would be very familiar with this particular island chain, and my bet, if he's out here; this is one he would have visited."

Luken eased the vessel closer to land. He cut the engine, grabbed a rope, and dove into the water. He swam to the shoreline, towing the boat closer with each stroke, and quickly tied it to one of the trees. Willyn bobbed up and down in the skiff as she peered over the bow at Luken standing on the sandy shore with his hands on his hips, staring back at her.

"Well, are you coming?"

Willyn bit her lip. "Ugh...I...I can't..."

"What?"

"I can't..."

"You can't what?"

"I can't swim!" Willyn blurted out the hard truth before she could stop herself, and Luken looked at her with a blank expression. After a pause, he leaned over his knees laughing, holding his side. The laughter echoed over the water. Rage threatened to rattle Willyn's heart from her chest.

She screamed, "How dare you laugh at me, you stupid fool."

"Oh, ho, ho...I'm sorry it's just...it's just that...you of all people. HA! It's that easy to defeat you?! I've put you in a never-ending body of water, and now you, YOU are defeated!" He pointed at her, "Who knew that this was all it took? If only all of Candor knew what it took to stop the Grogan hoards! HA, the thought of..."

A bullet screamed by his forehead, and his sentence came up short. Willyn stood on the bobbing boat, eyes smoldering with hot rage, a smoking pistol in her hand. Her mouth was twisted with curses. *"Don't you dare mock me."*

"Oh little girl, you are going to wish you had not done that."

Willyn blinked, and in a flash, Luken was back in the boat and grabbed the pistol out of her hand. Willyn screamed as he chucked the gun from the boat to the beach in a flash. She reached for her stun stick, but Luken threw his whole body on top of her, pinning her down with such strength that it knocked the breath out of her. Willyn gasped violently, her body heaving for the oxygen that had been forced out of her. Luken stared into her eyes as he nabbed her stun stick from her hand and broke it in front of her face.

"You are testing *my patience,* little girl. That is more than enough threats from you. Whether you chose to accept it or not, I am here to help you. I want answers as badly as you if Grift did what you claim. Now, snap out of it and get in the water." With that he jumped out of the boat and swam over to the shoreline again, leaving Willyn gasping.

She lay in the boat, trying to piece together what had just happened. How did Luken clear that much space so quickly and then disarm her? Slowly, she regained her breath and gradually got up on her feet. She looked across the water at her assailant.

Luken spoke, clear anger still flowing on his face. "Are you going to come to shore or not? That temper of yours is going to get you into trouble. I hope you take that as a lesson."

Willyn held her bruised chest. Each breath she took was met with a hot, dull ache. With each searing inhale of air she was reminded of how much she hated this man, this man who now sat smirking on the beach. She had never been so humiliated in all her life, and now she was trapped out in the wilderness, defenseless and surrounded by deep water she could not cross, her gun lying on the beach. Her eyes flashed as her mind exploded with a solution. She resolutely began to untie the boat from the rope.

"Willyn, unless you want to die at sea, I wouldn't untie the boat." Luken proudly held up the small key that started the engine. The girl threw down the rope.

I have been defeated. She couldn't believe her own thought. She had never encountered someone who so utterly confounded her. The only person ever to get the better of her was Hagan, but he never boasted in his power. Now this stranger was constantly a step ahead, toying with her. She looked at the water and then to the island's beach. Hopelessness washed over her. The journey, all of it, left her spent and powerless.

I can't do this. I just can't keep this up. Hagan is dying and I am here wasting time. Grift is gone. I'll never find him. I should have killed him when I had the chance. At least I could have gotten justice even if I could not get Hagan back. A torrent of backlogged emotion loosened deep within Willyn, and she felt the fear and rage swirling against her, melting away into a release she did not want.

Luken stood up from the shore and saw Willyn standing motionless. She stood silent, distant and solemn. For the first time, he realized that the person before him was not just a ferocious, terrible warrior, but also a girl, a sister overwhelmed with the state of her older brother. He stared at her, not to make her uncomfortable or to bully her, but with pity, and he slowly swam out to the boat.

"Hey."

Willyn looked over the boat's edge and saw him hovering below, treading water.

"Get in. You can always learn how to swim later. Just get in. I'll make sure you won't drown. I can get you over to the shore."

Luken's calming voice broke through to her, alone, on her floating prison. She was just so tired. Tired of trying to be an unflappable warrior. Tired of trying to save the day and to fight for her brother. As tears rolled down her face, she realized that she had never shown so much vulnerability toward anyone in her life. She pulled back her hair for a moment as she peered over the edge of the boat. The bobbing of the boat mixed with the waves slapping on the boat's side.

She spoke softly, "How do I know you won't drown me?"

Luken shook his head and smiled, "If I wanted to kill you I would have just thrown you overboard miles back. You are not the most pleasant passenger, you know."

The small jab broke through and Willyn knew she could trust him. As much as she hated to admit it, she knew he was trying to help. She took a deep breath and looked out to Luken, "Just shut up and catch me. I swear you better not let me drown."

Slipping over the edge of the boat, Luken held out his hand toward her. She took it and let herself fall into the cold, clear, salty water. It immersed her quickly, her fiery red hair expanding in the water around her face. She gasped as he pulled her close to him. She could feel him kick the water as he swam for them both.

"Keep your head up!"

Luken led her to the shallows, and she slowly walked out to the shore with him. She collapsed there, her dark red hair curled up in long red strands, a tangled mess. She felt the solid, pebbly beach under her hand and looked up at him. He stood over her dripping, and he held out his hand.

"Come on. Let me show you where we hid those refugees. We might get a clue of where he is, if he's not here, that is."

Willyn grabbed his hand and felt a spark of energy jolt through her. She stared deeply into Luken's eyes in awe of the day's strange, unexpected events. This man...this man had done something to her. She had never, ever let her guard down in front of anyone but Hagan, but somehow Luken of Elum forced her to be vulnerable. He had clearly seen her weakness and the fact that she had a weakness within her both alarmed and relieved her. *This Elumite is so strange,* she thought to herself. As Luken released her hand she could feel a sensation seem to pull away from her, and she secretly longed to touch his hand again.

Her mind was lost in thought when her eyes registered something deep within the forest. She took a step forward and squinted her eyes. "Look!" Willyn exclaimed, bounding through the foliage.

She sprinted for the edge of the tree line and straight to what appeared to be the half-buried remains of a fire. She knelt and held her hand above the remnant. After a moment she reached her hand under the soil and down into the ashes.

"The fire is dead, but it hasn't been out for more than a day. It might not be hot, but it is still warm. If this was his fire he did not leave it too long ago."

Luken stepped over to the small fire and knelt down beside her, scanning the foliage around the abandoned camp site. His eyes grew wide as he fixed his gaze on something hidden from Willyn's point of view.

"Willyn, I know this was his camp site."

"How?"

He left her, allowing the brambles and foliage to envelope him. Willyn waited, hearing him crunch through the thick undergrowth. There was a pause in his movements. She could hear him coming back to her, quicker than she expected. He came out of the brush holding something, staring down at it. He seemed lost in his thoughts, as if the object hypnotized him. Before Willyn could see what he was carrying, Luken turned as if trying to spot a trail or any other sign of life in the brush.

Luken spoke, his voice dire. "I don't know who else would have left this behind. And from the looks of the blood on this thing, I don't imagine he could be in very good shape. If we do find him, he may just be laying dead in the brush somewhere."

"What do you have? What do you have, Luken?

Luken turned back to Willyn and looked up at her. Silently, he held up a bloodied Lottian military jacket, and Willyn felt a rush of fear overtake her.

"Are there other people on this island, Luken?"

Luken continued to stare at the blood-soaked jacket. He whispered, looking back at her.

"Yes."

CHAPTER TEN

A rusty, dented transport rambled down the lonesome, deserted highway known only by those who frequented it as Devil's Stretch. The road was a loosely stitched patchwork of pavement that staggered through the abandoned Realm of Riht. Kull cursed as the transport shuddered violently over the gaping potholes and ripped asphalt. For speed's sake, there was no more direct route to the Groganlands, but it was not without its cost. Most travelers were wise to avoid it, but time was not on their side.

The old truck had made many trips down the Stretch before and it showed. The glass of its windshield was spider-webbed with cracks, and what once had been dark green paint had long been ground down to a dull mixture of sun bleach and brown rust. Travel was not common in this part of Candor, but the Grogans were fond of Lottian lumber, and that was enough of a reason to keep Ewing's smugglers on the Stretch. Ewing was not one to worry about embargos or trade pacts and he was a very rich man for it.

The truck carried two ancient tree trunks that hung out over the back of the open bed. An old canvas tarp filled with gashes was draped over the giant trees. It flapped in the vehicle's wake like a banner, its condition matching the landscape surrounding them. Kull sat on the tailgate of the truck, looking out over the ruined road running beneath his feet. He shot a glance over his shoulder to see Wael sitting with his eyes shut, quiet and still in the back of the truck bed. Next to him was the monstrous Rot, who seemed content enough to chomp on an old bone.

Kull examined the passing landscape. His eyes grew wide at the charred hulls of buildings that lined the road. All of it reminded him of Cotswold in flames. He remembered his friends and neighbors that had died and the smoldering destruction created by the black phalanx of Grogan rooks. He could still hear the pounding *thump, thump, thump* of those dreaded engines, and he could still see them hovering over the horizon firing rockets onto his home.

This is what happened here, he thought to himself. *The Grogans did the very same thing here.* The sudden realization sat like a heavy brick in his stomach. He wondered how many other people had lost a father or a mother to the terrible Grogan hoards.

The landscape, besides the ruined, desolate buildings, was largely unremarkable. Flat desert plains expanded to the horizon and were all Kull could see for miles around. It was not long before painful boredom began to set in. He turned around to look at Wael again, hoping to pass the time with some conversation, but was greeted only with the same closed eyes and stoic face.

Aleph above, what is he doing? For miles they traveled, and Wael had not said a word. The monk sat silently in a private trance that Kull could not bring himself to interrupt.

As the sun began to set, Kull tried his best to entertain himself, and that was when he noticed the fault lines beginning to appear under the vehicle. Kull blinked in disbelief.

Are they glowing?

His question was answered when he saw a small, but clearly visible flame shot up out of one of the cracks in the ground, throwing up a small flash of popping red light. As the slow tide of evening crept in, the veins of fire became even more noticeable, dancing in the oncoming darkness. Each opening in the earth sent up streams of noxious smoke, with a smell that reminded Kull of rotten eggs. *Sulfur,* he remembered. Then it dawned on him. They were passing through the Fire Fields.

The ground soon glowed with a sinister aura, and the cracks and fissures grew with each mile they traversed. They smoked and hissed, throbbing under the thin, sandy skin of the desert. Kull could not help and look again at Wael, who, even now, remained deep in his trance.

The air took on a heavy quality, clinging around them like a toxic fog. Kull was overcome with a fit of coughing. He could feel himself struggling to breath, his chest growing tighter the further the truck traveled beyond Lotte's border. To make matters worse, a chill swept over the travelers as the coldness of the desert night air began to press in around them.

Kull scooted himself up further into the truck and pressed his back against the edge of the transport bed. Night brought with it an amazing spectacle as the bright red fissures glowed and illuminated the walls of smoke rising from them. The fields made the sky look draped with red, burning curtains. There were no signs of life, just fire and burnt reminders of the death of those who once lived along the Stretch when it had been a much happier place. Kull shuddered to himself when he realized that they had been gone for hours, and he had yet to see another living creature. The noxious fumes caused tears to roll from his stinging eyes, and the further they drove, the more the air seemed to press down on them. Kull soon began to cough violently, gasping for breath. He held a handkerchief to his mouth and chose to break the silence he shared with the monk.

"I have heard stories about this place since I was a boy. Is it really true what they say?"

Wael's eyes flew open, and he responded without missing a beat, "What does *who* say?"

"That the ground is really on fire?" The obvious question sounded ridiculous as it left Kull's mouth, and he shook his head at himself.

"You can see for yourself that it is."

"Yes, I know. What I mean, is it true no one lives out here anymore? *No one?* Is it true that the Grogans somehow did this to the land? They say that morels are the only thing that can live out here."

Wael nodded his head and spoke. "It is true. Riht was once the most powerful Realm in all of Candor. They controlled most of the continent's oil supply and held all of Candor under their grip, cutting off trade to the other Realms when it was to their advantage. When Riht went to war with the Grogans, they did not realize that their own oil would be their ultimate downfall."

Kull did not understand. "What do you mean?"

Wael continued, "You see, Kull, the Grogans are not to be trifled with. Their culture does not allow for failure, and they do not back down from a challenge. It is not their way to simply win wars. Their ultimate objective is to bring about the utter destruction of their enemies, regardless of the cost. In Riht's case, the Grogans' desire was to render justice on their nation and destroy the Realm as payment for all it had done in Candor. The Grogan surge was swift and devastating. They swept into Riht and began to burn all their settlements. The Rihtians fought back bravely. They pushed the Grogans back to the cusp of the borders. But then the Grogans did something remarkable."

"What did they do?" Kull was entranced.

"They set fire to Riht's precious oil fields. With one spark, the Grogans set all of Candor back centuries, regardless of the consequences. Nearly all of Candor's oil still burns under this very ground. Even after all these long years, the fire still burns and we have the Grogans to thank for it. If it weren't for the few offshore pumps near Elum's coast, Candor would be in a dark age."

Kull struggled to understand how the Grogans could justify taking such extreme measures. The obvious question escaped from his lips, "But why? Couldn't they have just taken the oil for themselves? Wouldn't that have been more strategic? I mean, with all their machines it seems like they would have wanted to have access to all of Riht's oil."

Wael looked back down to Rot and shrugged his shoulders. He gently smoothed the hair on the beast's head, then reached into his small bag and fed the dog a piece of jerky. Rot nuzzled his head against Wael's leg and closed his eyes, just as the bed of the truck catapulted into the air and bounced furiously over a new stretch of potholes. Rot glared at his master and huffed in protest.

"Fearful men do not think rationally, Kull. Riht has long been feared by the other Realms due to their involvement in the Dominion War. During the most recent conflict with Riht, the Grogans thought it best to take it upon themselves to ensure that the Rihtians would never again rise to the heights of power they had hundreds of years ago. That is why they set the oil fields on fire."

Kull cut in. "Wait. So you're saying that the Grogans set fire to the oil fields during the Rihtian War because of another war that was fought three hundred years ago?" Kull shook his head. "That seems a bit ridiculous to me."

"It might seem ridiculous to you, Kull, but the Dominion War was the darkest period of Candor's history. My Order was led by Lucius then, the first Mastermonk. From our annals it seems that the entire continent was engulfed in war, and it was feared that all the free people of Candor would die under Riht's might." Wael's eyes grew distant, as if he could see a world beyond the burning horizon. "The Five were in full power then, and the Grogans, along with Lotte, Elum, and Preost, were nearly destroyed by their Dominion rule."

Kull rolled all of this in his head, trying to make sense of it. "What did you mean when you said the Five were in power? What are you talking about?"

Wael nodded his head and for a brief second looked very grave, as if he had aged before Kull's very eyes. He answered the question with a question of his own.

"Kull, what do you know of the Dominion War?"

Kull spoke, "I know that it's mostly referred to as the Great War on the datalink files. It was the war that broke the Realms free from Rihtian control."

"That term is not correct, I'm afraid." Wael's voice thudded like a heavy mallet. Kull stayed silent. "There has been a movement within the continent to rewrite Candor's past, to remove facts that some would deem unacceptable to put in the annals of our history. The Five, the Dominion. All of these terms are words forsaken by the history written today, and with them we forsake the truth. Surely, your father told you about them, the Five?"

Kull shrugged. "He barely told me anything about his experience during the Rihtian war, much less the history of the Great War." He smiled as he thought back. "Mom never liked talking about war or anything violent either."

Wael nodded, but Kull read the displeasure that flared on the monk's face. He spoke, his voice echoing through the darkening night, "The Five were the Serub warlords, the Rihtian Kings that created the Dominion, the empire that enslaved our ancestors."

"The Dominion." The word felt heavy as it left Kull's mouth. Kull had heard of the term, but only in whispers in candlelight between his father and his subordinates, loose nuggets that fell from conversations he was not privy to growing up.

Wael continued, "The Dominion annexed the Realms and set their center of their power at Zenith, the capital of Riht. It lies in ruins now. The fact that five rulers could bind the people of Candor under one united regime is amazing. It is truly a feat in itself." Wael's eyes stared intently at Kull. "But now, Kull, it is time for me to hear what you know."

The truck rumbled underneath them, and Kull shuddered at the growing chill in the air. "All I know is what I've read from the datalinks, Wael. The Great War, or as you put it the Dominion War, was a continental revolution that overthrew the Rihtian rule of Candor. It was initiated by the Grogans who came down from their mountain fortresses. They allied with Lotte, and then Elum. The Realm of Preost was then formed to serve as an arbiter to prevent any future conflicts in Candor." Kull's mouth felt dry as he spoke what he had read verbatim.

Wael spoke, "A fair, textbook answer." Wael smiled, but his voice remained serious. "There is much more to tell. The Five Serubs were not just mere Rihts. They were the Exiled."

"Exiled?" Kull had no idea what Wael meant.

Wael continued, "Yes. Exiled. They were the Divines who chose exile from Aether. To take their form, shape, and power in earthly vessels." Wael rubbed his fingers together. "To take human shape and form. They worked wonders in Candor, and it led to our utter ruin. They bewitched our ancestors and brought realities into this world that should have never existed."

Kull shook his head, confused. "Divines? Like Aleph?"

"Yes. For they are Aleph's brothers and sisters who abandoned their stations, longing instead for earthly power and glory. Aleph was abandoned, but through his obedience to his charge, he alone inherited the throne of the Firmament, the Aether. His six siblings forsook their divine duties, and in rebellion made their homes in Candor."

"Six? I thought you said there were five?" Kull's head reeled trying to keep up with it all.

"Yes, Kull." A wide smile grew on the monk's face. "I'm glad to see you are paying attention. There is one who is unaccounted for in the Exile. He regretted his decision and sought the penance of Aleph, seeking to atone for his error, but that is a story for another time. The remaining Five, however, brought ruin on such a scale that it is a marvel Candor and the Realms still exist."

"What did they do, Wael?" He could barely look into Wael's piercing gaze in the low light of the burning fields. "All I ever heard growing up about these stories were that they were mostly mythical. Many say the truth about the war and the Serubs is much less...*cosmic*." His throat went dry as the words left his tongue.

Wael did not respond with anger, but with firmness, "The morels. Let's consider them, Kull. They are a perfect example of a reality that should have never existed on Candor; a reality that the Five brought upon us. So you say that what you've read or heard about the Five is judged as mostly mythical?"

Kull nodded solemnly.

"Well, tell me. What have you been taught about the morels?"

Kull cleared his throat, trying to piece together Wael's logic. "I've been taught that they are the humans who caught the Shambling Plague. Their brains died long ago, and yet their bodies still live. No one can explain why exactly this happens, though it has been thought that there is a virus that controls the plague. The virus controls these dead bodies only to spread the plague further."

"It is a fine explanation from a scientific standpoint." Kull had not expected Wael's response to be affirmative. He listened with piqued interest as the monk continued.

"I doubt you would believe the real truth about them, however. The Exiled in their very natures can render realities that did not and should not exist on Candor. The morels are just one of their works. Tell me, how can the dead live, Kull? It was not always so that the dead could rise, but only after the Five came into power. And let me ask you something. Have you ever seen the dead rise?"

Kull tried his best to control his smirk, but Wael's serious face checked him.

"Well, have you?"

"No." Kull felt his hands twitch with nervous energy. "No, I haven't."

"Precisely. And as Aleph reigns, I pray you will never see it in your lifetime. That is because the Exiles have been bound. They no longer work their nightmares on this plane, though there are still remnants of their work left in Candor. Leftover ranks of the mindless morel armies that they once controlled."

Kull lay back against the back of the truck bed and pushed against the log with his feet to steady himself from the jarring ride. *This is going to be a long ride.* He tried to find the most comfortable position he could as he listened to Wael explain to him the "truth" of the Exiles. After several minutes of being lectured to, Kull's attention drifted towards the eerie dance of firelight on the horizon. He buttoned his jacket as the cool air continued to envelope the convoy. He thought of the events of the past few days.

I can't believe this. I'm sitting in a logging truck with the Mastermonk debating history.

Kull turned back, only to hear Wael *still* talking. Frustrated, he broke in, "It just doesn't make sense to me! You claim that the morels are the remnant of the Exiled army, but I seriously doubt it. Why would anyone want to bury this truth from us? Where is the gain?"

Wael did not answer, but Kull could feel a sudden rift grow between them. The monk simply leveled his gaze out over the open tailgate of the truck and was silent. He lifted his finger and tapped at his ear and then held it to his closed mouth.

Quiet, the motion spoke.

Kull chose to ignore the gesture, "Well? It still makes no sense."

Wael laid back and rested his head on the truck bed and closed his eyes. It was as if a door had been slammed in Kull's face.

Kull's mind danced as he tried to avoid any further thought about the morels and Wael's unwillingness to discuss them further. Every kid grew up with horror stories of the monsters and was warned not to venture out alone, especially at night. No one he knew had ever seen a morel, but then again, he never really asked too much about them back home. They just didn't seem plausible to him. He imagined if someone *did see one* they would probably just keep quiet in hopes they were having a hallucination. It would be preferable to be crazy than to live in a world where the wretched things actually existed.

The truck slowed and turned off the road as it tried to avoid a terribly broken stretch of shattered pavement. Kull reached out to brace himself as the truck's loose suspension did little to dampen the impact, jostling his teeth until he felt they would jump out of his mouth. The driver crudely down-shifted the vehicle, causing it to release a painful grunt within the transmission. The gears reengaged with a loud *clank,* and they were back on the main road, the diesel engine roaring as if it were cursing about the reckless steering. Kull wondered how long it would take until he could finally get out of the old truck. His whole journey had been one long truck ride, and between the choking smog hanging in the air and the eerie burning landscape, Kull decided he had enough truck rides for one lifetime.

At this rate, I could have walked to the Groganlands faster. He looked up from the truck bed, hoping to see some glimpse of stars in the night air, some brief burst of light to help him take his mind off of how terrible he felt. Dense, smoky fog was all that greeted him, hiding the night sky. Frustrated, Kull held his knees to his chest and shivered, praying for an end to this leg of the journey. He thought of his father, and then his mother. His hands reached for the pendant she had given him. He sighed and closed his eyes. Soon he felt his consciousness loosen, and he drifted off to sleep as the desert night overtook them.

The truck jolted and sent Kull face first into the timber across from him. Pain thundered him awake, and he felt sick due to the small amount of deep sleep he earned. He lifted his head and glanced over at Wael to see if he was asleep, but Wael was not sleeping. Wael was not even sitting down. Wael was crouched, looking out the back of the truck, with wild, wide eyes that registered only one thing: fear. Not a sulking, hand-wringing type of fear, but the primal type that rushed from the gut in order to keep you alive. Kull's groggy mind struggled to make sense of the sight of the monk gripping his ironwood staff, accompanied by Rot's vicious barking, the ridge of his back arched up like a banner, his white long fangs tearing into the night.

What...

Kull's head snapped back to the edge of the tailgate. Out in the midnight were the red pinpricks of light, reflecting the truck's red tail-lights. It was what Kull could only have guessed was some pack of wild animals; their eyes glowing like red, dancing flames. The number of dots grew with each passing second. They were being chased. Hunted. Wael banged his staff on the back of the truck and yelled at the driver in a panic.

"MORELS!" Wael ran the length of the truck bed with quick strides and slammed his hand on the back of the truck's rear window. The driver shot a furious glance at Wael in his rearview mirror, but soon realized the desperate situation. He sent a violent jerk through the truck as he hammered down on the gas, forcing Kull to grab Wael by the shoulder. The truck began to shake as it smashed over ditches and shattered pavement. Wael yelled through the chaos, "Whatever happens, stay near me!" His eyes tightened. "Now you can decide whether the morels are real or not." Wael loosed his grip and made a move that Kull did not expect. The monk pulled a knife from his belt and began to cut through the thick ropes holding the massive lumber to the truck bed.

SNAP. One rope dangled in the wind.

Kull held his breath as he forced himself to look back out at the pack of savage creatures chasing them. The creatures were barely humanoid, sunken faces painted in the red of the tail-lights, and even over the din of the engine Kull could hear their labored, jagged gasps for air. Their elongated arms swiped broken, jagged claws through the night air as they tried to grab hold of the truck.

SNAP. The massive rope was now loose and flew off into the darkness. Wael ran to the front of the truck bed and screamed at Kull.

"Kull! Help me!" Without thinking, Kull joined the monk in pushing against the gigantic timbers. "Kull, help me push them out!"

Instinct and a raw surge of adrenaline propelled Kull as he threw his shoulder into the back of the giant log, pushing against the truck cabin with his legs. At first, the mountainous log would not budge, but a quick jolt from a pothole seemed to loosen it. With another heave between them the log slid an inch, then another. Inch by inch they fought to move it, until finally it crashed out into the night, trampling over several of the morels pursuing them at an unbelievable pace.

Kull could hear the cracking sound of the wretched creatures' bones as the log bounced on top of them and rolled off to the side of the road. They writhed in pain, clawing at one another, screaming in agony. Fear filled Kull's heart as he stood dumbfounded at the sight. *They are real. Gods above. They are real.* Wael called out to him.

"KULL! Focus!"

Kull's mind snapped back, and he moved in place behind the second log. A hulking morel lunged for the bed of the truck and Wael's ironwood staff smashed against its jaw in quick succession. The blow sent the creature spinning to the pavement, but as soon as it hit the ground it rebounded, continuing its dogged pursuit. Its jaw was shattered, hanging uselessly from its battered maw, but still it ran after the truck with its blood red eyes glued on the monk.

Wael screamed over the din of Rot's deep barks and the morels' shrieks, "Kull, hurry! We need to push out the second log!"

In a panic, Kull pressed himself against the tree trunk as hard as he could. The second log was larger than the first, and it felt as if it had been bolted down. His legs strained as he drove his weight against the giant timber. The log finally started to give way when the driver slammed on the brakes. The log reversed course, sliding down on top of him. He flung his body to the other side of the truck bed, but not until it came hammering down against his foot.

"AGHHH!" Kull screamed in agony as fire shot up his leg. "WAEL! My leg!"

In an instant Wael was there, pushing the giant log from him, wrenching it away from his pinned ankle. Somehow, the log barreled out into the darkness, trampling into the pack of pursuers, releasing another chorus of ear-splitting shrieks. Kull looked down at his foot in revulsion, pin pricks of light shooting across his eyes. Blood poured out from the shattered place that was once his ankle.

Kull blinked and stared back out into the darkness, rage fueling him. With the truck bed empty, he felt much more exposed than before. Wael sat him down and whispered. "Stay still." He watched as Wael ran back to the edge of the tailgate where Rot was keeping guard for any intruder that dared jump into the truck. *How had he pushed the log out so quickly?* Rot stood now by his master's side with his long fangs bared, both waiting for the night demons to mount another attack.

The morel with the broken jaw somehow avoided the second log and was only a few feet behind the truck. Its eyes never shifted from Wael. Kull's stomach flipped as he saw the creature snap what was left of its jagged teeth together, a twisted ribbon of a shattered smile growing over its fractured face. It made a huge leap into the truck, clawing out for the monk. Wael threw his staff out to the beast, but it countered, landing on the tailgate of the vehicle. The creature slashed his claws across Wael's chest, releasing red blood across his white linen garb. Wael pushed against the beast with his staff as it clawed at him, pale knives slicing for his face. Rot charged, lowering his head like a bull, and sunk his fangs into the ankle of the morel. The beast bellowed in pain, falling to the floor of the bed as Rot pulled the morel off of his master and back deeper into the back of the truck. It clawed for Rot, but Wael hammered his staff deep into the creature's skull with a sickening THUNK. It blinked, twitched, and was gone.

Wael looked at the dog as he gasped for air. "Good boy, Rot," he said.

The truck took another sharp turn and bounced so hard that it threw them all into the air. They landed with a shattering smash, the blow sending a new bolt of lightning up Kull's ankle. Wael and Rot somehow stayed upright through the chaos, remaining balanced precipitously on the edge of the truck bed.

Wael never turned his head to look back at Kull, but instead kept his gaze fixed on the remaining six morels still barreling in on them. The truck seemed to be getting slower and slower until the driver nearly came to a complete stop. Wael did not relent as they came, but swung at the pack as they would lunge at the truck bed snarling, teeth flashing, delirious in their pursuit for flesh. Two morels flanked the truck and jumped into the bed from the side. *He can't see them!* Kull reached out as if he could just tap Wael on his shoulder. Everything happened so fast, Kull could not even scream to warn him. One lunged, but Wael ducked gracefully, sending up his foot in the air, hammering into the creature's nightmare of a face, flipping it back over the truck's tailgate.

The other morel had caught sight of Kull lying in the corner of the truck bed. The fiend bounded after him as swift as lightning, and Kull froze as its dagger-like claws clicked across the metal floor. It bore its fangs and released a deafening scream. Kull swung and smashed his fist into the beast's jaw, but it snapped and bit at him like a rabid badger. Kull let out a primal scream. The beast let out a low, guttural growl, a purr, gloating in its newfound meal. It swiped and grabbed at Kull as he batted away at the claws slicing to grab him. It was as if Kull was punching his fists into a thicket of butcher knives, the sharp claws flying through the air, plunging closer and closer into him.

The pain of his leg was distant now, and Kull felt time slowing. *I'm going to die*. Kull knew it was coming. One quick swipe would relieve him of all of this. It was only a matter of seconds. He looked out desperately for Wael, but he was not there. The morel's teeth clicked, and a long, black snake of a forked tongue flickered out at him.

He must be dead and I will be next. The thought locked in his mind with a dreaded hopelessness. Kull closed his eyes, resolving in his heart that his last sight would not be the monster diving in on him. Behind his eyelids he prepared himself for death, thinking on his mother, his father. Adley.

The sound of bones crunching broke through the darkness behind his closed eyes, but Kull felt no pain. His eyes flew open to see the morel's face, inches away, pull back and flop onto the truck bed like a rag doll. He tried to look around and make sense of what was happening. A blur of black, matted fur stood over the creature, his one good eye blazing with pride.

The morel's horrid body quivered uncontrollably on the ground, and Kull noticed the twisted section where Rot had just severed its spine.

The pit of Kull's stomach churned under the pain of his crushed ankle, but he pulled himself to the back corner of the truck bed, inching himself away from the corpse of the monster that nearly killed him. The crushed leg left him lightheaded and dizzy, the fog of the pain overwhelming. Kull tried to fight out of it, forcing himself to push through the daze, feeling the gears below the old truck churn. *We're moving. We're moving again.* The driver reengaged the transmission and downshifted, punching down on the gas and setting a small bit of distance between the truck and the pack, whose rank and file had only increased. *Aleph above, there are still more of them.* Relief rushed in when he saw Wael still holding his position on the tailgate. *Where had he gone?*

The fight on the back of the truck raged on as another morel managed to jump onto the side of the truck, throwing itself into the bed. It lunged at Wael, but was quickly met by the swift blade of his knife. He impaled the beast and flung it over the opposite side of the truck. Another jumped and clung to the edge the tailgate. Wael gave no ground. Kull counted out in the darkness. *How many are there?!* He could clearly see that there were nearly a dozen of them still left, still hunting them down. Wael was good, but this was a game of numbers, and there was no way they could keep this up.

Kull forced himself to stand, repositioning himself to avoid any pressure on his crushed ankle. Nausea swept over him as the hot iron rods of pain shot up his leg. Any adrenaline he had was fading to a trickle. Wael's staff flew through the night, ricocheting with deafening cracks and concrete thuds against bone, claw, and flesh. The tattered remains of the morel Rot gored still lay in the truck bed in a crumpled heap, a bouquet of decay. The smell, the shrieking din of the beasts howling in the night, combined with Wael's endless fighting made Kull want to give up. *It's hopeless.* Kull could see that Wael was losing energy, gasping for breath with each volley. It would not be long now until they joined the rotting pile of flesh beside him.

Kull saw a sudden movement in the back of the truck bed. He rallied himself. *This is it. Go down fighting!* He turned, expecting his last sight to be the claws of another undead morel, but instead he saw the eyes of his father standing there in the darkness. Kull could feel his chest tighten as his heart thumped with a deafening cadence. *I'm hallucinating. I must be.*

"Kull." It was his father's voice.

Kull stared at the vision and could only whisper. "What?"

His father pointed, and as Kull followed the finger, his eyes landed on the small pack he had lodged in the back corner of the truck bed. *My rifle. How could I forget?* Without looking back at his father, he lunged for the weapon, heaving himself to it. His fingers fumbled in the dark, pulling the rifle up by its stock. His eyes lined down the gun's sights, right onto the head of one of the beasts. A female. She had once been someone's friend or even mother. Kull could see the remnants of the humanity that had long since passed, illuminated from the red glow of the tail-light. She might have even been beautiful once. The monster's loose, pale skin and sagging distant face all reminded him of his mother during one of her deeper sick spells. *I can't do it. That thing is human.* The image tortured Kull as he tried to dismiss the thought that he might be taking down what had once been someone's mother. What if it really was just a sickness, some virus that did this to once normal people? Maybe they could be saved?

Kull's finger eased on the trigger until the beast woman leapt onto the tailgate, bearing her ragged, blood-stained teeth. As much as she made him think of his mother's frail frame, none of that mattered now. She was inches from Wael's back.

He steadied his breath and squeezed the trigger without another thought. *I go down fighting,* he thought to himself. The shot hammered out into the night like thunder, and the bullet met its mark, knocking the female back, her dead body bouncing and rolling on the broken pavement, trampled under her cursed kin. Kull reloaded. He quickly counted nine left. Lifting up his weapon, he aimed again at one of the monsters. This one was an elderly male...or used to be. It ran so fast that it was unnatural. He forced the idea out of his mind and pulled the trigger.

BANG.

Nothing happened. He had missed, and the morel boarded the truck in one swift motion, flailing for Rot. Its claws cut a red path through Rot's fur before pulling back its arm for another blow. The dog yelped, but clamped its powerful jaws on the fiend. Kull heard maddening shrieks as he fumbled for another bullet. Wael was busy grappling with two morels at once. They managed to attack the monk in a wicked display of unison. The older morel was on top of Rot, trying to avoid the dog's powerful fangs, but Rot clamped down on the monster's arm like a vise. The sound of popping bones echoed in the bed as Kull steadied his aim and held his breath for one more shot.

BANG.

The creature did a back flip as the bullet seared through its skull. Kull looked to Wael again as he steadied his stance, blocking the two he fought with his staff, but stabbing them in quick succession with swift swipes from his blade. They went down in an instant. Wael held up his hand and he mouthed over the noise "Hold!"

Wael whistled at Rot, and the two of them leapt off the moving truck and into the darkness. In one bound, Rot cleared the distance between the truck and their remaining pursuers, clamping his massive jowls down on a morel's neck while he was still airborne. The dog greeted his enemies with the happy snap of bone.

Wael landed on his feet and ran straight toward the last four pursuing them. He catapulted his staff from his hand as if it was a spear, and it bolted right through one of the creature's chests. Rot moved on, beheading two more morels in quick succession. Wael grabbed the other end of the staff, unsheathed it from the Shambling's husk, and calmly walked over to the last morel that Rot brought down. Kull could see Wael standing over it writhing from side to side, blindly clawing the air. Kull could not see what happened next as the driver continued to bounce down the road, leaving Wael and Rot wrapped in the midnight beyond the red glow of the vehicle.

Gasping, Kull banged on the outer window of the truck, causing hot pinpricks of light to stream across his vision.

"Cut the engine! I SAID CUT THE ENGINE."

The driver glanced back at Kull. His eyes scanned the truck bed, and he slammed his foot on the brake. He careened the vehicle around and pushed back down the road, shining his headlights on Rot and Wael. The driver brought the truck to a stop, idled for a minute in disbelief only to scramble out of the vehicle in utter amazement.

"Did...did you...jump off the back or fall off? I mean, I saw the way you were chopping those things down. It was, it was, um. I mean. Wow!"

Wael walked up towards the driver and placed his hands on the man's shoulders.

"I'm sorry about your cargo, my friend."

The scruffy driver stared up at Wael and smiled. The smile grew wider and wider until he broke into a string of laughter. Trying desperately to breathe, he looked back up at Wael and croaked, "Cargo. Ha. I'm just glad to be alive! I've driven this road dozens of times and have never seen a swarm like that. Something ain't right. Never in my years have I seen a swarm that big."

Kull was still lying in the back of the truck as he strained to hear the conversation happening between the two men outside. He tried to look from his position, but after losing his rush of adrenaline, the pain in his foot surged

How am I ever going to get to Dad now? The thought sent him careening into a panic. He had seen his dad! He shot up and looked around the truck bed. It made no sense. He had seen him, heard him speak…but yet.

He showed me my rifle. His mind whirled, mixed with both hope and terror when Rot jumped up into the truck bed and began to cover him with slobbery licks and intrusive sniffs, his stump of a tail wagging. The dog's pungent odor hit Kull like a batch of dead fish. Kull gagged and screamed, pushing the dog off of him.

"Get off me, Rot! You smell awful."

The dog panted and bellowed up a howl into the night sky before sitting down on the truck bed. A nasty waterfall of drool puddled onto the truck floor, and the dog happily panted, as if nothing had happened. Kull could not help but laugh at the paradox of the dog's nature. One moment he was dismembering freakish monsters and wagging his mangy tail the next.

"I'm glad at least one monster likes me," Kull said out loud. He could not help but have new respect for the dog that had alone killed five morels in such quick succession. Kull sat up and slowly slid himself to the back of the truck. As he slung his legs over the tailgate, pain rolled up like fireworks and he stopped, lying back down.

"It's broken. Oh, it's broken."

Wael ran up to the truck with the driver and looked at Kull. "There is nothing we can do right now, Kull." He looked at the driver. "Do you have any medicine?"

The driver shrugged. "We don't keep many medical supplies on the convoy. I might have some bandages, though."

"Go get them. Now." Wael pulled a small satchel from his robe. Kull tried to pick up his head to see what he was doing.

"Lie down, Kull."

Kull obeyed, but he watched as Wael pulled out some herbs and leaves. He began to chew it and then he spat the contents out onto Kull's ankle. Relief from the pain flooded over him like a cold wave of water.

Kull wanted to get up and look at his ankle, but Wael held him down on the truck bed.

"You can't move. You need to stay still until we get to a safer place." Wael bound up the ankle with gauze.

"Kull, you did what most young men would not have been able to stomach back there. You have my thanks." The comment was earnest, and Kull could see that Wael was sincere. "How is your leg feeling now?"

"Well, it feels broken, but I've never broken my ankle before, so I can't know for sure. It's busted up pretty good; I mean you saw all that blood."

Kull's mind thought back to Adley. She had been worried that Kull would get himself killed and in less than two days it looked like her worries had almost been confirmed. Kull vowed he would never tell her about this if he ever saw her again.

"We will take a look at it when we get into the Groganlands." Wael spoke to the driver, "We will take a few minutes to rest and collect ourselves, but we will need to start moving soon if we want to avoid being ambushed again."

Anxiety rushed over Kull. He continued to think about the first one he shot down, the female. He never killed anything in his life except for the animals he hunted. The thought that he had just killed what had once been a human overwhelmed him. He coughed violently as his anxiety made way to sickness. An explosion of vomit came from him, slapping out onto the side of the road.

Wael placed his hand on his back and leaned down next to him.

"It is okay, Kull." Wael spoke as if reading his mind. "They are not human. You did what you had to do. If you had not acted we would all most likely be dead right now. We needed your help."

Kull wiped his mouth and looked up at Wael. He spit the remaining filth from his mouth, trying to collect himself.

"They sure look enough like us." He stared at Wael, reading his face. He could tell that he was exhausted and just as undone as everyone else. "I want to get as far from this place as possible. I've had enough."

"Me too, Kull. For this day at least."

Kull let his head fall down on the truck bed where he hoped it would stay for the rest the trip; all the way to Rhuddenhall. His eyelids were heavy, but he feared that if he closed them all he would see were more morels. Sleep won as the truck rambled on through the night, and Kull soon found himself drifting off; dreamless.

He awoke to the first light of dawn. They made it through the nightmare, and Kull could hardly believe his luck. It was a short lived victory as a loud pop and hiss sounded from below the truck, followed by the unmistakable flapping sound of a fresh flat tire.

CHAPTER ELEVEN

Vashti's eyes sparkled with dark anticipation as the key, Seam's most prized possession, tumbled between her fingers. Rubbing the key with her thumb, she leaned in toward him and placed her lips next to his ear.

"We have much to do, my King. Greatness is waiting, and we can finally begin the reclamation process. This key is only the beginning to a new world, *our* new world."

Her words were light, breathy, and soft as satin. She brushed her cheek against Seam's as she continued. The warmth of her skin pushed away the cold night air and left Seam's skin electric and longing.

She stared at him in the dim light. "You have done well, Seam. I always knew you were the one we have been waiting for. We must end the time of binding."

Vashti inched away from Seam, her eyes never leaving his. She took her time to stand, showcasing her warm and inviting figure to the young royal. Her smirk was intoxicating, and Seam would not look away as he spoke.

"What a shame for you to have wasted your beauty with such a dreadful existence up here, Vashti. I certainly would not mind having your *company* at the High Hall."

Vashti's smile broke into a stern grimace, and Seam felt the weight of her answer. "My time has been anything but dreadful, my King. Ever since I was enlightened and left the Alephian order, I made an oath to serve my mistress within the Crossroads until the time of binding ended."

Seam chuckled, his face a mix of shame and embarrassment. "Forgive me. I simply meant that I would have appreciated more of your company. I have always found our visits to be enjoyable in many *different* ways. I am just relieved to know we will be seeing much more of one another now."

Vashti's twisted smile returned as she allowed her robe to slip over her left shoulder. She stood for a moment and bit her lower lip before responding. "I know exactly what you mean. Now, let's not waste our time here. Follow me."

She led Seam down a long, dark hallway behind the temple altar. She grabbed his hand and pulled him into a stairwell leading deeper into the darkness. The old marble stairs were well worn, slick, and beveled after years of use, forcing the young king to watch his footing as he descended.

The two followed the stairs downward, plunging deeper into the shadows. Blackness wrapped tighter and tighter around, their footsteps making hollow echoes in the gloom. Vashti's torch was swallowed in the darkness as Seam's heart raced with each step. Silently they descended further and further into the labyrinth buried beneath the Crossroads. Seam had never been this far under the temple, and yet he felt no fear, no worry. Only anticipation. For years he had dreamt of this moment.

It had not been a mistake that he found the ancient forbidden tomes. It was no coincidence that he met Vashti, who helped him discover the ancient truths hidden deep within the forbidden texts. It had been orchestrated. All of it had been orchestrated by an invisible hand. *Their hands.* Seam knew that he was claiming his place, for he alone was the one the stories foretold. He would lead the revolution that the world had suffered far too long without. He had the key to begin the process of unbinding, and he was holding the hand of the one person who would be able to ensure his success. That was all that mattered.

The stairs poured out into a massive hallway stretching far beyond the reach of the faint torch. Seam felt his breath condense in the cold, subterranean air. Four doors lined the massive stone chamber, bearing deep etchings of ancient runes. The deep carvings coiled in waves, detailed patterns that resembled the rings of a felled tree, concentric circles that grew across the cold stone walls. Vashti tugged at Seam's hand as he marveled at the intricate carvings.

"These are nothing. Follow me. We are almost there."

Seam heard her voice tremble as she pulled him further down the hallway. He marveled at her as they pushed on. Years ago, Hosp arranged Seam and Vashti to meet. Hosp sent her as his ambassador, knowing he could not travel into Lotte without raising suspicion. Ever since that time she lived amidst the ruins of the Crossroads. Yet Seam could tell from Vashti's behavior that this journey was as new to her as it was to him. *Perhaps it is. Perhaps she's never dared to come this far.* The hallway came to an end, cut off by a wall engraved with a massive mural. Vashti stopped and latched her torch on a nearby wall. Her eyes were wide with excitement as she reached out and placed her hands on Seam's chest.

"This is it," she whispered. "*This* is what we have been waiting for." She pulled Seam and pressed her chest firmly against his as she looked up into his eyes and gently kissed him. Her smooth lips glided across his as she continued to pull Seam tighter. "Soon, Seam, and our new world will begin. Are you ready?"

It was impossible for Seam to hide his joy. "I have been ready for far too long."

Vashti spun around and slid her fingers across the stone wall. A pang of disappointment surged through Seam as he reached for Vashti. His eyes lingered on her as she examined the dead-end wall.

Seam finally tore his gaze from Vashti and realized that the wall was not a dead end but another door. Its carvings rippled in the firelight. He examined the etchings, and within the ripple of circles, he noticed that there was an intricate design carved deep within the pattern. Serpents. What had, at first glance, appeared to be nothing more than thin carved lines in the stone, on closer inspection, revealed miniscule artistry. The brood of snakes etched in the wall wrapped around one another in a never-ending knot. Vashti's fingers traveled over the pattern, exploring the wall. Her hand came to rest upon one particular viper whose mouth was open, baring long fangs.

"This is it. Are you ready?"

Seam's hands scrambled for the key, only to realize that Vashti had never given it back to him. A bolt of anger struck him, but he relented. *Not now.*

"I'm ready."

Seam watched as she slid the key between the snake's fangs and slowly turned it. The door let out a noisy crack as it opened. A stale draft of air rushed by them, assaulting them with its odor. The chamber had been shut for a very long time. Vashti handed the key back to Seam and pushed at the wall. The door's weight stood in protest until Seam leaned into it, pushing the massive slab open.

The two stumbled into a dark void and squinted to allow their eyes to adjust to their new surroundings. Light flickered from the hallway behind them, and Seam's heart quickened its pace as he realized exactly where he was. He was standing in the chamber of the Forgotten. No one had been in the room for centuries and now he stood, ready to complete the first task to put him in his rightful place. Seam snatched the burning torch from Vashti and took the first steps deeper into the room.

Seam bounded into the room, leaving Vashti behind. Abandoned sconces with their ancient candlesticks long snuffed out lined the walls. Seam was careful to light them again and turned his eyes towards the room's central podium. The candlelight grew, swelling to reveal a single pane of glass fixed to the floor, in the middle of the sprawling pedestal. A mirror. Aside from it, the room was empty. The mirror reflected the flames of the candles as they danced across its surface. The room stood silent as both Vashti and Seam gazed at the glass.

Seam stared at the mirror. Then he looked back to Vashti who was frozen, her eyes locked on the same fixture. Something was not right, and Vashti was not giving him any clues.

Seam's whisper crept through the room, "Where is she, Vashti?"

But Vashti stood silent. Her lips twitched as she spoke to herself but she would not respond.

Seam's whisper grew, "Where is she?"

Vashti did not turn her gaze. She continued to stare, fixated on the mirror.

Seam threw the torch on the ground, and shook Vashti by her arm. "Where is she?!"

She pointed at the lonely pane of glass that mirrored the candlelight and spoke with a whisper.

"It's empty. Why is it empty? That *is* the portal."

Seam tightened his grip on her arm as he looked back to the glass.

"The prophecy does not lie! It says, 'We wait immortal, locked in glass.' She should be here!"

Disappointment ripped through Seam. The portal was dead, and there was nothing to see. There was *no one* waiting on the other side. The glass mocked him as he continued to recite the prophecies to himself.

There has to be more. I am missing something. The prophecy does not lie.

Seam released Vashti's arm and charged from one step to the next. *I will pull the wretched god from the glass if I must.* Each step brought Seam inches closer to the dead, black glass, and each step brought a new pang of rage. Seam's foot slammed to the platform and as soon as he lifted himself to the apex of the podium he fell backward with a scream and tumbled down the stairs.

"What is it? What's wrong?" Vashti ran for him as he gathered himself. The color washed from Seam's face, and he would not look away.

Seam stared ahead and then back to the empty pane of glass and murmured to himself, "The prophecy is true. *'We wait immortal locked in glass. Descend, rise, and free our hands.'"*

Confusion twisted across Vashti's face as she glanced back at the glass.

Seam whispered, his breath clouding the frigid air, "We are not alone, Vashti. Rise onto the platform and you will see."

Vashti crept one step at a time until she was standing on the platform. She gasped and covered her mouth. Seam stepped back onto the platform behind her to see the image of a shriveled old woman in the reflection of the glass. The same old woman whose image startled him just moments earlier brought a new surge of adrenaline and excitement.

The apparition sat on her knees with her head bent downward. Long gray and brown hair hung loosely, obscuring the prisoner's face. An icy whisper filled the empty air, *"Come closer, my children. My saviors."*

Seam and Vashti stepped closer to the mirror. With each step they took, the woman before them rose her head until she peered out from behind her hair. Her eyes were wild and her mouth hung agape as she stared blankly ahead. The same icy whisper crept throughout the room.

"You are who we have awaited. The Keeper has come, the letting can begin, and the unbinding can commence."

Vashti reached out and took Seam's hand between her fingers. She squeezed his hand and pulled it towards her.

"This is it, Seam. Get the key. She needs the key." Her voice trembled as she tried to whisper. She released his hand and stepped back.

Vashti's mind was a volcano of curses when Seam burst into the dark room. *He is so bold, the fool.* It was a miscalculation. *A foolish mistake.* Seam's unexpected rush into the portico robbed her of her chance, saving him from a dagger in the back.

No matter, she thought, her mind instantly springing for another plan. She feigned ignorance as she descended deep into the chamber with the young king. Vashti could feel him, his desires swelling for her, his mind becoming putty in her hands. She played a convincing role as seductress, and he was buying it.

As Seam stood confused at the empty mirror she too stared into the darkness wearing a convincing mask of confusion and fear, buying more time. She knew Seam would fall for it, happily rushing in to fill the role of protector and champion. He came close to her, and she grabbed his hand.

She baited him with another line. *"She needs the key."* As he plunged his hand beneath his shirt, Vashti gripped the hilt of her dagger. This was it! As she threw the blade at the young king, one thought filled her mind.

Hosp would be pleased.

A hush hung in the air as Seam stood looking at the wretched old woman in the mirror. Her gaze was dead, but he could hear her speaking within him, *"Now, do it now."*

Seam spun on his heels and caught Vashti's wrist as her arm came crashing toward him. Her fingers were locked around a small dagger. She screamed as his grasp clamped around her arm with no mercy. His face twisted into a rage of clenched teeth and demonic eyes. He stared into Vashti's face, forcing her to look away.

He spat the words at her. "*You* are not the first yellow-eyed assassin to make an attempt on my life. Did you think that I am a fool?" Vashti butted her head at him, but Seam, in one fluid motion, pinned her to the ground.

"No, no, no, my dear. We read the very same tomes, and we both know exactly what is *needed* now. I see now that you had no intention to allow me to savor the unbinding. You never intended to continue *together*."

Vashti thrashed as pure panic pulsed within her. She screamed, her shriek only echoing off the carved walls of the dank room. She fought to pull herself away from the king's heavy grip, but Seam was too much for her. She clawed at his face as he threw her against the pane of glass and held her against its cold surface. As Vashti pressed against the glass, the mirror woman stood to her feet. She pressed her hands against the pane of glass, grasping for Vashti like a caged panther. Terror flooded Vashti's eyes as she glanced at the woman pawing at her through the glass and then back again at Seam. His cold stare tore through her. He forced the dagger from her hand and held it in the air as he looked back to her.

"You are beautiful, Vashti, but your beauty is nothing but a cloak to cover your sinister schemes. Don't think I could not see through your intentions. *I am no fool*!" He bellowed at her, "I AM THE KEEPER! Now serve your purpose."

Hot tears stung her eyes as she pleaded for her life. "No! Please! No! I swear I will do anything, my king! Please! NO!"

The whisper that invaded the room roared with rage.

"**NOW! DO IT NOW**."

Seam put his hand across Vashti's mouth to muffle her screams and leaned in next to her ear.

"Your lies won't help you now. Attempting to betray me is the last mistake you will ever make. Now it is time to go to sleep so others can be awakened."

Seam thumped the dagger deep into Vashti's chest without hesitation and fought to hold her still as she whipped from side to side. He muffled the howls of pain that attempted to escape from her lips. He kept his hand clasped around her mouth as her cries morphed into a morbid gurgling. In a few quick moments the struggle was over and Vashti's body slumped over onto Seam. He pushed her to the side and watched as her blood flowed out, sizzling on the platform below him, the aroma of hot iron permeating the cold air, her body's essence smoking in the cold room. The blood smeared on the pane of glass simmered with heat and then evaporated.

The metamorphosis of the trapped visage happened in mere seconds. The old woman in the mirror stood upright before him, invigorated and renewed. Her loose, wrinkled skin tightened in an instant. The haggard façade gave way to a beautiful face of a woman in the vigor of her youth. Her vibrant blue eyes pierced Seam and filled him with an explosion of awe.

She spoke with an authority that caused Seam to shake. "Take me back to Vale, Keeper."

"As you wish, my lady. As you wish."

Bronson's hands shook as he drove in silence back toward Vale. His king was resting in the back of the vehicle, his face hidden in the darkness. Bronson pushed on, reassuring himself every few minutes, but his mind whirled like a hurricane. He could not understand how Seam could be so close to the...*thing* he was transporting back to the capital. How could he even stand to sit so close to it? Whatever transpired between the new High King and the mysterious woman here at the Crossroads was now over, and to Bronson, it really didn't matter compared to the abomination that now shared space with them. *How can I take this to Vale? Aleph above, what should I do?* The entire night had been so unorthodox, first with the woman at the temple, and now *this.* Bronson knew something felt wrong when Seam came out of the temple.

It felt like nothing at the time, just a pinprick of doubt in his mind, like a short blunt splinter that refuses to be wedged out of the finger it's lodged in. It smelled of trouble, and Bronson's intuition blazed with hot caution as Seam emerged from the shadowy ruin. *What had it been that bothered him so much?*

He was smiling. That was it. Seam came out of that dank dungeon with a smile on his face, as if he were in Aleph's gardens. He had been nearly giddy, in fact, laughing like a child who fooled his teacher. He spoke in rapid, short bursts, which were hard for him to follow. Then he heard his king's command.

"There's a mirror I need help fetching, Bronson! Follow me!"

A mirror? From this place? What madness is this? What happened to the woman?

He had been wise enough to hold his tongue as they descended deep into the dark, failing to mention that he sat for nearly three hours while Seam was occupied with the mysterious woman. *Must be a lover,* Bronson guessed. *But where is she now? And now he wants me to fetch him a mirror in a cursed temple dedicated to the Old Ones*. He would sooner fetch all the stars in the sky than to set one foot into that foul place. He shut his eyes in an effort to compose himself and followed his king without a word.

After passing by the altar and main meeting room, Bronson followed Seam to a door obscured by the temple's main platform.

"The catacombs are down here. Watch your footing." Bronson plodded down the slick stairs into the hallway of carved doors. It was nothing Bronson had ever seen before. The etchings forced him to stop dead in his tracks in a potent mixture of awe and dread. Shadows danced in manic forms from the light of Seam's torch. Each carving seemed to vibrate and pulsate with malice and glee, and to Bronson it felt as if the walls were alive, breathing and beating with unnatural life.

This place is cursed. The overpowering stench of mold and rot hung in the place, and the light of Seam's torch was an unwelcome visitor in the dungeon. Bronson's mind whirled around another grave thought. *The girl. Where was the Preost girl?*
All of it made Bronson's head ache with panic. Years of dutiful military service kicked in, forcing him to tamper down his emotions as he followed his king deeper into the darkness.

The vibrating hallway fell into a small portico. A swift sound cracked in the darkness and Bronson saw something move. His hand shot down to his holster for his pistol. He pulled his weapon and threw the sights right on the stranger, only to realize that they too had pulled a gun. Seam unleashed a flurry of curses and screamed at Bronson before he could squeeze the trigger. The deep bellow echoed off the wet stone walls.

"Do NOT break the mirror, Bronson, or it will be your life!"

Bronson lowered the sidearm and stared at himself in the mirror. It was spotless. Among all the dust, mold, and rot the mirror looked as new as any Bronson had seen.

"I'm sorry, sir. It's just that I thought I saw someone."

"I assure you we are quite alone down here." Seam's voice grew calm. "You only saw your reflection...I'm just glad you didn't destroy it." Bronson nodded, but could not shake the feeling off of another presence with them. As if someone else was watching them.

Seam spoke, "We need to transport it back to Vale immediately. Bronson could see that the craftsmanship of the piece was ill suited for the decorum of the High Hall. It was odd, really. To come all this way only to fetch something as plain looking as this mirror.

"Very good, sir."

"We will need to take it up together slowly. It is heavier than it looks."

"Sir, forgive me, but should I call in for some more men? I would hate to have you strain yourself in your recent condition."

"If I wanted a convoy up here, I would have one. Now *help me.*"

With that the two made their way back out of the temple, mirror in tow. As soon as they exited the temple, Bronson thanked Aleph, pausing to breathe in the cool, fresh air. He experienced enough of this night, and he hoped never to have another like it. What if this was going to be a normal occurrence during Seam's reign? These odd, late night excursions.

If the extraction of the mirror was all that transpired that night, Bronson would have laughed the entire experience off. He could have easily chalked it up to the eccentricities of the new king. A man seeking a memento of an encounter with his lover or some other nonsense. These inadequate stories which could have served Bronson well vanished as Seam laid the front end of the mirror down into the truck and let himself in the vehicle.

"Let's get back to Vale."

"Yes, sir." Bronson was pushing the long, thin mirror into the enclosed bed of the convoy and tucking it into safety when he saw her and shock hammered through his entire body.

There before him was the most exquisite woman he had ever seen, staring up at him from within the mirror. Her eyes were a cold blue, and to Bronson they reminded him of an ocean; not soft, but strong. He stared at the woman in the glass, petrified, trying to make sense of the impossibility. She stared back at him and her mouth formed the beginning of a smile. Bronson's anticipation to see such beauty was palpable. Everything in his body wanted to see that smile.

Her lips parted in a slow showcase, not of the pearly neat rows of snow white teeth that Bronson expected, but instead a forest of daggers, serrated and ravenous, the headwaters from which a crimson river of blood freely poured out.

CHAPTER TWELVE

Willyn exposed the dark innards of an abandoned shack as she darted her flashlight through the old cabin's front door. The hovel's floorboards were broken and jutted up like jagged teeth. Willyn and Luken found the building after trailing a fresh set of prints through the thick jungle on the island.

As Willyn eased into the shack she called out to Luken, "I know someone was here recently." Luken pressed through the door as Willyn continued, "Even if it is not Shepherd, you have someone camping out on these islands."

"I'm sure you're quite right," Luken muttered, eying the structure. His gaze lingered on the holes in the floor.

A long gush of wind blew through the trees, and a clap of lightning announced the arrival of a coastal gale. Rain drops galloped across the roof, building into a steady roar.

Luken groaned and looked back out into the jungle before closing the door. "Doesn't sound too good out there. I suggest we stay put. We can keep searching once the storm passes."

Willyn threw up her hands, but said nothing.

"I know what you are thinking, but we already lost his trail. We'll pick up the pieces once this storm blows through. Besides, you wouldn't be able to find your own face out there."

Willyn kicked at a piece of broken floor before picking it up and tossing it to Luken. "Well, if I have to sit here wasting time I might as well be warm. You do have matches, right?"

Booming explosions of thunder rattled the loose timbers of the cabin. Willyn looked out of a small, dirt-streaked window and watched trees bending beneath the powerful winds. Rain threw itself horizontally, and with each rush of wind the ramshackle hut moaned. Several drops of rain fell from the thatched roof only to be swallowed by the white sand that made up the floor of the cabin's back room where the two started a small fire.

"You should get away from the window. Our sea-storms are nothing to tempt."

Willyn lingered and stared out into the night. She closed her eyes and tilted her ear to the glass. Her shoulders relaxed and a faint smile crept over her face.

"It sounds like war."

Luken's face twisted as he answered, "And that is a good thing? You know, it is dark but I can see you smiling."

"Sort of. I am used to it. The thunder, it sounds just like artillery fire. You are pretty safe if you have artillery backing you."

Luken chuckled, "Well leave it to a Grogan to enjoy the sound of explosions. Where I come from, when you hear that sound it means you are dead."

Willyn shook her head and her smile disappeared as she slid onto the floor next to the fire. She wrapped her arms around her legs and squeezed her knees into her chest.

"I just said I am used to the sound. Better to relate to the sound than fear the fact that this horrid little shack will probably fall in on us any minute."

A small smile grew on Luken's face as he looked at her. "So you are scared of the storm?"

Willyn shook her head, "You are impossible. Just let me think in peace."

Luken reclined on the sandy floor and stared into the fire. "As you wish."

The silence did not last long as Willyn stared into the pulsating embers and twisting flames.

"It doesn't add up, Luken," she said as she threw a small timber on top of the fire.

"What doesn't?"

"The tracks. They led to this cabin and nowhere else. They stopped here. Those tracks stopped right here. We searched both rooms but there is no one here." Her eyes locked with his in the firelight. "Why?"

Luken lifted himself from the sandy floor and wiped his pant legs clean. He stood in silence for a few moments continuing to gaze into the small fire. Willyn examined Luken as he stood by, running something through his mind. She could not help but notice how handsome he truly was. Her logic relaxed. *Stop it. You're hungry and tired.* She shook the thought from her mind. After all he put her through there was no reason to find anything about him attractive. *You're exhausted. That's all it is.*

She spoke, hoping her words would bury her thoughts. "What are you thinking?"

He glanced at her, his gray eyes shining in the ember glow. "Actually, Willyn, it does make sense. I should have thought of this earlier."

Luken walked across the room, stamping his heel against the sandy floor. Each kick made a clunk, and a small cloud of dust puffed up into the air.

Willyn smiled at the odd display. "What are you doing? You can tell me so at least I can help."

Luken's eyes sparkled with interest as he looked up at Willyn and grinned. "The floors. He might be under the floor."

Willyn's eyes grew wide with realization.

She began stomping at the floor until she felt something strange. Her foot hit something hard and sturdier than sand, but a hollow thud accompanied the feeling. She squatted down and began to dig away at the white sand.

A wooden trap door.

She laughed at herself and called to Luken, "Hey, come look at this!"

Luken stood over her, and she looked back up at him. He quipped, "You know if he's down there, that means I'm right."

Willyn could not hide her smile. "Well, get me a light and let's find out."Luken handed her a flashlight, and he opened the door with one swift tug.

Willyn lay on the ground and dropped only her head into the hole, her curly red hair hanging all around her face as she shone the light down into the opening. She looked around as the small beam of light illuminated the darkness.

"It's a root cellar, Luken. There are barrels and barrels of stuff down here. You were right about the space under the floor. Maybe bootleggers would hide their goods here until they could sneak it inland."

"Well, hopefully there is more than just bootleg. We are looking for a terrorist after all, not a good time."

"There is only one way to find out!"

"Can you get down there? Is there a ladder?"

Willyn did not bother to respond as she dropped down into the cellar. The small flashlight provided a beam of reference, and as she scanned the cellar floor she saw that the trove of goods was nearly as big as the cabin above her. She opened one of the barrels nearest to her. The sweet smell of dark fermented sugarcane met her, and the glint of dark liquid bounced back her flashlight's glow.

She called up to him, "Well, you were right about one thing!"

"What's that?"

"Guess."

"Bootleg?"

"Yep. Bootleg."

She looked deeper within the dark storeroom, past the lined barrels. Something shifted behind her, a shuffle of quick movement. The hair on the back of her neck stood on end. *Is he really here?* She spun around and examined the corner the noise came from.

Nothing. Just more barrels and plenty of shadows.

She went back past the barrels and deeper into the dark. She could make out boxes stacked in the back corner of the room. Barrels, boxes, and provisions were everywhere, yet there was no sign of Grift.

Another sound of rustling whispered from Willyn's left. She turned off her flashlight and stood absolutely still. The room became a midnight void, and she became stone. The small square of light from the trap door was squeezed out by the shadows. There was nothing left in the room except for Willyn and the sound of whatever was shuffling.

Luken called down to her. "What are you doing down there? Why did you turn out the light?"

Willyn turned to whisper back up the trapdoor but stopped herself as she pushed her back against the nearest wall.

A quick shift of the crates in the far corner caught Willyn's ear again. The sound was too much to be a rodent or a trapped animal. *He's here.* Her right hand dropped to her hip as she reached for her pistol. She slowly unlatched it as she pushed away from the wall and crept toward the sound. New sounds became more pronounced the closer she drew to the boxes. Wheezing. Grunting. Raspy deep breaths slowly lifting and falling. *He's hurt. He lost too much blood. He's probably lying in the corner waiting for me to shoot him.* Then another thought ran through her mind. *It could be a trap. It probably is a trap.*

Her left hand clutched her light as she lifted her pistol and trained its barrel on the sound in front of her. One step after another, Willyn inched closer to the strained breaths, intentionally shuffling her feet. The breathing sounds quickened, and Willyn knew her opportunity was about to present itself. Her nose caught the scent of the battlefield, infection and festering wounds. *At least he isn't dead. I would enjoy cutting off his infected arm myself.* The sounds became soft grunts, almost laughter. The sickening sound of a death rattle threw a knot into Willyn's throat as she readied herself for what was next. The darkness shattered with the sound of a crate smashing to the ground.

Gods! It's not him!

Willyn threw on her light to see someone lunging for her. A quick squeeze of the trigger and the cellar exploded with a burst of light from the muzzle of her gun and the booming echo of the shot bouncing off the walls. Something slashed across her face as the attacker's head snapped back and its body crumpled into a mashed coil of flesh. A warm rush of blood ran down Willyn's cheek, and a familiar stench invaded her nostrils. She knew she had just downed a morel.

Not again! Where are these things coming from?

Luken bellowed below, "What was that?!"

Willyn swung her light to the area the morel had sprung its attack. The boxes scattered on the floor had been hiding the burrow it had come from. There was no visible sign of any additional morels, but as she was shining her light through the tunnel the sound of screams pierced through the depths of the hive.

Willyn looked up to the trap door and her heart sunk as she realized there was no ladder. Another burst of shrieks leapt from the hole. Willyn shoved a barrel beneath the trapdoor and climbed on top.

She only had seconds before she would die. "Morels, Luken! Help me!"

Luken's face appeared a few feet above Willyn, his long, muscular arm reaching down toward her. She leapt and grabbed for his arm but missed, her feet barely managing to land back on the old barrel. She drew in a long breath and focused in on Luken's hand. She had to reach it; there wasn't any other option. She leapt and they connected. His powerful hand locked on her wrist and he pulled her up through the opening.

Willyn slammed the trapdoor and kicked dirt over it as she scrambled for something to block the top of it. Luken joined the scramble, his face grim. The sound of thunder mixed with the torrent of screams below them, creating a chaotic symphony of fear.

Willyn felt her heart slamming against her chest. She panted for air, "I just killed a drone and I heard more behind it. Those things have burrowed into this place. We have to go NOW."

Willyn kept the muzzle of the pistol pointed toward the small wooden door, refusing to turn her back to it. A burst of lightning cracked outside, shooting light through the room as the ocean storm continued its fury.

Luken pointed at the small window pane as nearby branches smacked against the glass.

"Let's go, then." Luken threw open the door just as a loud crack rang out beneath Willyn. The trap door underneath her jolted up with such force that it sent her crashing backwards. A large, scarred morel was clawing at the opening, desperately trying to gain a hold and pull itself into the room. Its red eyes were fixed on Willyn as if it knew she was the one who killed its kin. It flashed its dagger teeth and let out a low call to its hive.

Willyn rolled from her stomach and fired a shot that ripped through the morel's skull and sent it plummeting back down into the shadows of the root cellar. The thud of the beast crashing into the ground below was met with more screeches and groans. A pack was underneath them now, clawing for an entrance. Luken kicked the door shut again and helped Willyn back to her feet. As she regained her footing, Willyn shot off three additional rounds straight down through the brittle wood between them and their attackers.

Luken screamed, "It's no use! Get back to the boat!" Luken pulled Willyn toward the door. "Stay close to me. The last thing you want to do is get lost. You can't shoot your way out of the bogs around here. They will swallow you alive. *Stay close.*"

He opened the door, and the two bounded out into the storm. Willyn stumbled out behind him, struggling to keep a hand on his pack. She refused to lose him, but the stinging rain made it impossible to run without shielding her face. Within seconds, her clothes were completely soaked, and the wind bit at her skin with a terrible chill. The hot and humid jungle transformed in a matter of a few hours to a freezing wetland.

Branches slapped at her as she followed behind Luken, attempting to keep pace with his swift steps. It amazed her that Luken seemed completely unfazed by the weather that was rendering her almost immobile as she stumbled and tripped through the muddy underbrush. The sinking soil and roots twisted and tangled at her feet, and Willyn tripped over every other step. The deep mud sucked at her boots, weighing her steps, but Luken continued to run full speed ahead slapping away branches, only slowing down to call back to her.

The pair ran for a half hour without stopping, splashing through the woods in what seemed no particular direction. Willyn's navigation skills were useless in this weather. The wind and rain mixed with Luken's twisting path had her completely disoriented. Luken turned and shouted back.

"Not much farther now!" He pointed to his right where the trees were thinning out, no more than fifty meters away. The shoreline was barely visible through the deluge, but she could see it. Luken called out to her, "Stay with me!"

As much as she hated the boat that morning, there was nothing she wanted to see more. Willyn set her eyes onto the clearing and ran for her life. A large log lay in front of her path, and in one swift leap, she cleared it. When her feet hit the ground she panicked as the earth gave way beneath her. Her legs fell into a deep viscous pool of earth that swallowed her on impact. She had fallen into a bog. She splashed in desperation as she tried to find some footing, only to sink chest deep into thick, hungry mud. It pressed in on her, constricting her in its secure grip.

Her wet clothes became lead, threatening to pull her under. Her feet were locked in stockades that were sinking with each small movement. She screamed out as Luken's silhouette disappeared from her vision. "LUKEN! Come back! PLEASE." He continued to tear through the woods, unaware. The mud began to creep up around Willyn's neck as she continued to call out for help. "Luken! Please come back!" The sheer weight of the mud made it harder to yell as it pressed against her throat. Everything was becoming difficult; it was harder to think, it was harder to scream, it was harder to breathe. Every shift or attempt she made to push out of the mud only pulled her deeper and tighter within the swamp's grasp.

Mud bubbled up around Willyn's chin and pressed in to swallow her lips. She took in a deep breath and unleashed the loudest scream she could muster, "LUKEN, please!" The slush seeped into her mouth, filling it with the putrid taste of salty mud and rotten leaves. She spat the sludge out and gasped for one last breath. But she lost the last gasp of air as a morel smashed through the foliage in front of her and locked its terrible eyes on her. The constriction of the pit and the terrible sight of another morel gloating over her made it impossible to breathe. Her mind tumbled the possibilities. She quickly decided that she would prefer to suffocate in her liquid coffin than have her last memory be being butchered by a morel.

The large brute pressed forward as it stared at her. It was not a lowly drone, but rather a fighter, rippled with unnatural, pulsating muscles. It was the type that children told ghost stories about, stories that she thought, up until her recent two run-ins, were just stories. The fiend stared at her through the downpour. Flashes of lightning illuminated its sharp, outset teeth as its bloodshot eyes held her in its gaze. It flicked out its long, black tongue and took a resolute step into the mud.

Willyn never feared conflict or even pain, but this was far from anything she had experienced before. She was like a netted animal waiting to be speared by its captor, staring into the eyes of whomever *or whatever* was about to end it all. She clamped her eyes shut, unable to look at the hulking brute that joined her in the hellish pit. She knew it would be over soon. The monster took its time as it carefully sloshed toward her, its long claws grasping out. Her heart quickened with each step it took.

Only one question was asked behind her closed eyes. *Where is Luken? Where is Luken?*

She could not open her eyes. She could feel the beast's breath just inches from her face, sniffing at her, examining its next victim.

A scream shot through the deluge, "NO!"

Willyn's eyes snapped open, only to catch Luken charging out of the woods from the corner of her vision. The morel was face to face with her and turned as Luken pounced on him like a panther, swift and terrible. He grabbed the beast with his bare hands. In one swift motion he locked his arms around the creature's head and dragged it out of the mud pit. The creature wailed in a low, guttural moan as it fought back, trying to pry loose from Luken's barbaric grip. Luken threw his arms around the beast, wrenching down on it without mercy. He broke the brute's neck in half and stared at the creatures that lurked in the bushes beyond the mud pit.

Mud began to push up over Willyn's nose as she tried to breathe in one last small breath. She tilted her head back and closed her eyes again as the mud seeped around her cheeks. Another wave of mud spilled over her lips and Willyn gagged. The bubbling cough made her think of Hagan and his terrible coughing spells.

She had failed. Hagan was alone and dying in a Realm with no one to look over him. Hosp was pushing to eliminate their family's line, and her family's last hope was bound to the woman left to drown in a filthy bog. She failed in her quest to bring back the man with the answers to heal Hagan. She failed her family, her Realm. The pain of defeat collapsed in on her far harder than the bog that covered her, drowning her one cough at a time.

"LEAVE US!" Luken screamed. Willyn could see nothing, and it was difficult to even hear Luken shouting. The screaming stopped and was followed by the sound of footsteps fading into the forest.

What is he doing? Is he running? Is he leaving me? Gods. He's too late…

In a desperate attempt to escape the mud around her, Willyn threw a hand above her head and waved it, hoping to catch Luken's eye. Through the rain she could hear his voice, calm and stern.

"Go limp. Fighting it won't help you. I have you now."

Willyn fought her instinct to try and thrash her way free one last time. She surrendered and relaxed her entire body. Luken grasped her and pulled her out up to her chest. She gasped, desperate for air as she splashed free and spit the horrid sludge from her lips. After a few additional tugs, she was finally free, breathless and sprawled out on the solid floor of the jungle. She clutched Luken's shirt in her hands, refusing to let go, until her nerves settled and she was able to stand. All she wanted was to be close to him, to be safe.

Willyn looked up at him as he sat next to her, panting for breath himself. He did not look the same. Despite the darkness of the jungle wrapping around them, there was enough light to notice that Luken appeared older, aged somehow.

She croaked, her voice searching for strength, "What did you do, Luken? What happened?"

Luken looked away from her eyes and answered. "Nothing. We have to go now. Now stay close! There isn't much more time left." He stood and set back toward the opening in the trees, leading to the beach.

It did not take long for the cold, bitter wind to return Willyn to her senses as she followed behind him. *How could anyone turn away a pack of morels?*

Soon the two were clearing the trees and running across the beach toward Luken's ship. Willyn ignored her earlier fear of water and splashed her way through the shallows back to the safety of the boat. Luken helped her make the swim and got her safely on board. Once on deck he directed her into the cabin to get warm.

"I don't want to be anywhere near the shoreline. If we can make it aboard in our condition, so can they. Lie down and rest. I will find somewhere safe to anchor." The hatch snapped shut, leaving Willyn alone in the dark, cramped quarters of the little boat. As the engines fired to life she slid onto the cabin's solitary cot and closed her eyes.

The small skiff bobbed and swayed as it plunged out into the Endless Ocean. The waves slapped against its hull creating motion that would have normally nauseated her, but the exhaustion hanging over her was too much. It pushed away every sensation other than hunger.

She tore into a box of dried fruit and quickly snapped up several handfuls before lying back down with her back against the hull of the boat. As the skiff started moving through the waves, Willyn surrendered to her exhaustion and crashed into a deep sleep with the rolling thoughts of Luken saving her drifting through her mind.

The sound of a wave crashing jostled Willyn from her sleep. As she shook her head and glanced around the cargo hold, Luken was nowhere to be found. The small hatch to the hold was open as bright sunlight shone into the room.

She crawled out of the hold and back onto the deck where she found Luken steering the boat over the calm, open waters of the ocean. He looked as fresh as when she had first met him.

"Ah, you're awake! How did you sleep? You went through a lot last night."

"Did you ever come down to sleep, or have we been sailing through the night? I never heard you."

Luken could not hide a wry grin as he answered. "Of course I slept. I would have to be a fool to try and steer this sorry ship through an ocean surge all night long."

Willyn stared at Luken, waiting for some further explanation, but he returned to steering the craft in silence. Willyn straightened out her tangled mass of hair and pulled it back into a tight ponytail as she walked to Luken's side and checked the compass at his station.

"East? I thought we still had a few more islands to the west? Plus, we found Grift's tracks back on that island."

"Well, we did. But I don't know that those were actually his tracks. It's possible, but I think it is more likely our little houseguests last night had something to do with those."

"What about his jacket then?"

"I never said he was not on the island, but I have a feeling he moved on. He very well may have stirred up the same morel hive and decided to leave. Can't say I blame him." He flashed a stupid smile. "Plus, we never saw a boat anywhere. No chance he swam to that island, so he must have stolen a boat. If he did, we should have found it somewhere. I circled the island this morning but there was nothing. It's a waste to go back." He paused and then muttered as if to himself. "Plus, we have been called back inland."

"What? Called back? We have three days! Filip gave us three days and we have only been out for two."

Luken's eyes dropped and he cleared his throat. "There seems to be a problem. Normally I only take orders from him, but his son Evan contacted me. He said the agreement was off and we had to head back or they would send gunships after us."

"Gunships?"

"I have no idea why. The only thing that I know is the fact that this boat will not be any use against gunships. Evan left me no choice."

"Since when did Elum threaten a two-man skiff with warships? And how dare he threaten to fire on me?"

Willyn turned and stared off the bow, straining her sight as if expecting to see one of the hulking gunships barreling over the horizon, firing in their direction.

Luken revved the engine and they skipped across the waves. "I agree, something is not right. What is bothering me is my other radio lines are down and I can't reach any of my spotters inland who were looking for Grift."

Spotters? Willyn was intrigued at Luken's unspoken tactics.

The long green coast of Elum peered over the horizon, and the palace grounds rose into view. The morning light set the palace walls aglow and it looked like a swelling fire as they grew closer.

Luken's radio crackled to life.

"Inspector Luken, please bring your ship to a halt. We are sending a guard detail to give you clearance and escort you back to shore."

Luken responded, "Certainly, sir, but what is going on?"

"Our guns are now sighted on your vessel. Avoid testing our patience. Do you copy?"

Luken slammed the receiver into the console in front of him before picking it back up again and forcing a smile as he answered.

"Understood. We copy."

Willyn looked at Luken, but his face revealed nothing. The only thing Willyn could find in Luken's face was agitation. He was not worried or afraid, but it was obvious that he was exasperated by the ordeal.

"What is this about, Luken?"

"If I knew, I would tell you. Trust me."

A long, black dreadnaught rolled through the water toward their skiff, its guns pointed in their direction. A cold, electronic voice bolted out of a P/A system.

"Drop your weapons and put your hands up, Willyn Kara of the Groganlands. You are hereby arrested for the conspiracy and murder of Filip Darian of Elum. Anything you say will be used against you in a fair trial. Come with us peacefully and we will see that no immediate harm is done to you."

Luken glanced at Willyn. "What did you do?"

Willyn stood dumbfounded and mumbled. "I haven't done anything. I have been with you from the moment Filip sent you to me."

Willyn looked out toward the oncoming warship, and her thoughts fell on Hagan. *What am I going to do?*

She stared at Luken, searching for some insight. "*Why would anyone kill Filip*?"

Luken's eyes did not leave the mounted guns of the warship. He held up his hands in surrender. "I was wondering the same thing. So you don't know anything?"

Heat rushed to Willyn's cheeks as she followed suit. "Of course not! I have one man I want to kill, and Filip is of no interest to me."

Luken rolled his eyes. "I wasn't trying to say...I mean. I meant maybe you had some intel of someone who would want to kill Filip."

Willyn's mind whirled, adding up the score. *First...Camden. Then Hagan. Now Filip.*

"Someone is attacking all of our leaders, Luken, and it would not surprise me if it was Grift. But why?"

A shot rang out. A wall of water rushed up only ten yards away from Luken's vessel. Willyn stood as the electronic voice boomed out over the waves again.

"That was a warning shot. We will fire if necessary. Do not move. We are boarding now. You will be taken into custody immediately. Do not resist."

As the security boat pulled up, Luken spoke just loud enough for Willyn to hear.

"Red Deaths." He stared at her looking for recognition, but she looked at him blankly.

"What?" Willyn had no idea what he was talking about.

"Listen to me, Willyn. You must trust me now."

"Luken!" The soldiers were beginning to board.

He whispered, barely audible. "Be patient. I have friends who can help. Just do as they say."

Five Elumite soldiers held their guns on the duo. One of them flashed metallic handcuffs around Willyn's arms and led her off the ship. She glanced at Luken who stared back.

A thought burned in her mind, a thought that sounded like Luken's voice.

Don't make this situation any worse. Trust me. I'll be there soon.

CHAPTER THIRTEEN

Every step was a new pang of torture. Kull's ankle ignited with each movement he made as the party continued their monotonous march across the arid desert. His legs felt petrified as he willed them to keep up with Wael, Rot, and their driver, Arik, who were all walking steadily ahead of him.

Wael called back, "We need to keep moving, Kull. We can't stop."

All Kull wanted to do was stop. It took all of his willpower not to scream as the pain continued to ratchet up his leg. Nothing could sway Wael's firm resolve to keep moving through the shimmering heat of the Wasteland. He said nothing because in truth, he realized he had no choice. Stopping meant the possibility of another morel swarm. That would be the death of them without the truck for protection, like falling into a barrel of spinning razor blades. The thought of *them* made him quicken his pace as much as he could. They had made steady progress during the morning hours, but with the heat of the afternoon Kull wondered how much he could keep going. The abandoned vehicle was miles behind them, and as the hours passed by, Kull could not shake the daydreams of riding in that dented, unloved rust bucket.

The march was painful but uneventful. The landscape shifted in terrain as the day grew late. The desert dunes morphed into rolling rocky crags that pushed into a full valley of blistering red rock. Jagged walls of crimson rose around the road and shut out the wind and sun that had been beating down on them. Arik craned his neck up to gaze to the top of the canyon walls. His messy tangle of brown hair kept falling in his eyes as he spoke.

"Always felt small in my truck. Now I feel like an ant. Welcome to King's Canyon, kid. Almost there."

Kull forced a smile as he leaned in on his makeshift crutch. The ironwood staff he borrowed from Wael was an intricate totem of engraved symbols and runes etched deep into the dark grain of the wood. There was some sort of pattern to the pictures, but Kull could not begin to decipher their meaning. It was a wonder the old staff held up even after beating back the hoards of morels that attacked them the previous night. Kull's eyes darted across its carvings as he hobbled along. It was unbelievable to think any piece of wood could come out of the last night's chaos without a scratch.

"Hey Wael, how much farther?" Kull's eyes mirrored Arik's trailing up the high ridges of the canyon. "Not too crazy about being closed in. You know, just in case."

He took one last look over his shoulder worrying that the thought might bring *them* closer. He kept pressing forward, waiting on an answer.

Rot bounded next to his master and looked back at Kull, but Wael did not answer. The party soon made their way through a winding valley, and Arik spoke to fill the void.

"Don't worry, kid. I promise we are almost there. I have driven this road a hundred times. We aren't far." Arik pointed at a distant ridge ahead. "Just look up there; it's the Hangman's Pass. We will be there soon."

Kull looked up at the cropping of rock that spread from one side of the canyon's ridge to the other. Dozens of chains draped over the ridge, clinking in the breeze.

"Hangman's Pass?"

"Yep. That's the spot where the ol' Grogans used to hang the prisoners of war they were finished with. Figured if someone wanted to invade they might think again after seeing their buddies hanging there. Pretty brutal, huh?"

Kull's eyes shot back to the rocks, his mind fearing what he would find there. Visions of his father flew in his mind, his body hanging there off the overpass, dead eyes staring blankly at Kull. A nightmarish scene shouting of his failure, his cowardice. His father's mangled body, swinging in the wind, and his mother's cries of agony. He shook his head, trying to throw the thoughts out of his mind, but he could not help but to gaze up into the waterfall of nooses overhead, sighing to see that each of them was gratefully empty.

I will not fail, he promised himself. *They won't take you, Dad; I'll hang from that rock before you do. I won't stop until I find you.* His hand reached for his mother's pendant, and he said a silent prayer for her. *I hope Eva is taking good care of her.* His mind flickered between his mother, Ewing, and Adley, but he ran from the homesickness that trailed him in the horizon of his mind.

They kept walking, and after another hour Kull was glad to put the grim ridge behind them. Wael stopped without warning and turned to Kull, his face calculating. Even after fighting off a horde of morels and leading them through the desert the man still seemed fresh and full of energy. Kull read Wael's face. Something was wrong.

"What is it, Wael?"

The monk spoke. "We have a problem, Kull. There's something we must do to continue safely." Rot, in a show of strange understanding, let out a high-pitched whine.

"Problem? What kind of problem?" Kull asked.

Wael's response was quick and calm, "You, Kull."

"Me?" Kull was shocked. "What do you mean?" His thoughts swirled to his defense. "If I am such a problem, why did you even bother to bring me in the first place?!"

Wael placed a hand on Kull's shoulder.

"Calm down. You are a Lottian. Your appearance is that of a Lottian. Hangman's Pass marks the border of the Groganlands. You have no reason to be here in a time of war. Arik is a licensed transporter and my source of transportation. He is known, but you, Kull...for you I had no answer for your presence. Until now."

Wael unsheathed his knife and unrolled his white, pristine outer robe. He cut at the robe's seams.

"What are you doing?" Kull asked as he tried to examine Wael's handiwork.

Wael finished cutting and handed the long stretch of cloth to him. "Put this on," he said.

Without notice, Wael ran his hand through Kull's thick brown hair. "Next we need to cut your hair. The Alephian order commands one must keep their head shaved."

In that moment Kull resigned himself to what was happening. If he was going to go any farther this would be the cost. Better to be bald than on display, strung up on Hangman's Pass.

He nodded. "Do it. Whatever it takes, let's just hurry up and get there. I don't want them dragging Dad to that ledge."

"As you wish." Wael held out his blade and raked it over Kull's head with skillful precision.

Kull could not feel any more out of place standing beneath the shadows of Rhuddenhall's massive gates. He was bald, his head shining like a beacon in the desert sun, with ash smeared across his face, wrapped in the strange white garb of a monk. They slowly approached the massive city built with rock, cement, and steel. *Gods above, what an ugly place.* The Red City baked like a scab in the desert sun, keeping its watch over the once contested border of the Groganlands and Riht. Beyond the Red City, filling the horizon with gray giant peaks of treacherous mountain ranges, laid the Groganlands. This country was nothing like his own; all of it looked dead, dry, inhospitable, and barren. His only comfort was the weight of his rifle strapped against his back.

The canyon gate was empty. There were no guards posted and no border patrols to contend with. In fact, it appeared that the gate was abandoned, its doors standing wide open. This was not what Kull expected. Fifty foot gates weren't made to stand open unguarded.

The three stood stunned as they examined the gate, confused by the lack of military presence until Wael spoke up. "Stop here. Wait on my command."

They stopped meters away from the gate. No one spoke. No one moved. Kull's eyes darted across the canyon walls, searching for a sign of a hidden sentry, but he saw nothing. Something wasn't right.

The snap of gunfire broke the silence. One round gave way to another as a fresh burst of violence filled the air. Screams followed the gunfire and an explosion echoed off the canyon wall, adding to the chaos. Kull and Arik scrambled for cover, but there was none to be found. They were trapped, and there was nowhere to go. Kull lay prone on the red dirt and fumbled for his rifle, only to see Wael still standing, a tall pillar of resolute peace.

"Get up." Wael lowered his arm down to Kull and pulled him up to his feet. "Those shots were not meant for us."

"What?"

Kull tried to make sense of the sounds as another shot popped off. Wael spoke again. "The violence is coming from *within* Rhuddenhall." The monk's face was grave. "We must hurry."

Wael waved for them to press through the gates. Kull gingerly sprinted behind Wael, Rot, and Arik as they dove through the open mouth into the Groganlands' capital. He was ready for whatever was waiting for him; anger and adrenaline fueled his resolve.

You came to my home and burned it to the ground. You murdered my people. You stole my father from me and wrecked my life. I am here to return the favor.

Wael whispered to Kull as they made their way down the main cobblestone street, "Stay close to me! I have no idea what we are running into." Rot's hackles rose as he kept up with his master.

Arik spoke in disbelief as they made their way through the ruined and littered streets, his voice filled with fear. "What happened here?"

The sound of gunfire and explosions bellowed again as the three pressed down the long street lined with single story cement structures. Pillbox buildings dotted the streets and led to a massive courtyard that was glowing red with fire. The heart of the city was in flames.

Rot's back arched fully and a rumble of growls escaped from behind his fangs. Wael pointed to a side street, directing them to follow him as they darted for cover. Arik and Kull followed close behind Wael and Rot as they traveled deeper into the city. The street offered a narrow alley between the cement boxes that ran parallel with the main street. A small channel of dark, oily water ran down the center of the alley through a shallow trough dug between the buildings. The narrow channel was littered with debris and trash; boxes, garbage, and scrap bits of broken machinery. At the end of the alley Kull could catch a glimpse of the churning chaos taking place in an adjacent courtyard.

Civilian men and women were firing onto armored guards who stood above them guarding a massive complex overlooking the square. The rioters created a barricade of burning vehicles, a wall of fire that covered the square with a blanket of smoke. The smoke made it difficult to lock onto any one figure as they darted across it, slipping in and out of view like gray phantoms. Each of the men and women wore strips of tattered red cloth across their face or arms.

Some of the Red Cloths fired on the army that was gathered at the far end of the square while others lay dead in pools of their own blood. The attackers were not any part of the Lottian forces. They were not from Elum, or even Riht. They were some new entity, but from the look of their features they appeared to be Grogan. The reality left Kull speechless. The Grogans were killing one another.

Kull pushed next to Wael and spoke just loud enough to be heard, "What is happening? We were only out in the desert a few days. *This is insane!*"

Wael's wide eyes were full of dread. "I don't know. This is not what I expected." Kull's fears escalated into panic. *What were they going to do? If they were killing one another, what chance did his dad have?*

Wael glanced back down the alley and then to Arik.

"Arik, did you hear anything on the radio about this on our way in?"

"The radio?" Arik tried to smile, "That ol' truck hasn't had a working radio for years."

Kull slipped back to the edge of the alley to glance back out over the square, hoping to uncover a clue as to what started the infighting. Kull spoke over the chaos, his mind full of disbelief. "They wage war on all of Candor, and it's still not enough for them. So now, they kill each other."

A strange voice answered, "You're right. We don't mind killing anyone. Not even a child, such as yourself."

Kull spun around to be greeted by the barrels of five pistols trained on him. A man with a red bandana wrapped around his face grunted and lifted his gun toward Kull's face. His bright green eyes bore into him. Kull glanced quickly back. The Red Bandanas surrounded them all in a flash.

Their leader spoke, still holding his gun at Kull's head. "How about you explain to me what a Preost monk, his runt, and some Lottian slug are doing in Rhuddenhall before I put a bullet in your brain?"

Wael answered, "We are here for peace. We seek to speak with…"

"Shut it, monk," the man interrupted, "I want to hear it from your punk kid and his smart mouth."

Kull's mouth went dry with fear. The bandanna man laughed. "Oh…now I see your lips are not as loose. The cat must have gotten your tongue."

The man's eyes were filled with hateful fire and pride. Kull knew that this man would probably enjoy killing them and then go about his day killing his neighbors without a second thought. Kull stepped forward and locked eyes with the masked man, looking past the gun's barrel aimed at his forehead.

Wael tried to step forward and put himself between Kull and the interrogator.

"I will speak for the boy. I am his elder. He does not understand."

One of the larger grunts beside the leader swung the butt of his rifle into the side of Wael's head and sent him sprawling to the ground. Rot lunged for the soldier, pinning him to the ground and flashing his fangs. Low rumbling growls paraded out of the dog as the man below him screamed in a panic.

"Call your dog off, monk!" the green-eyed leader commanded.

Wael calmly called for Rot, and the beast left the man lying on the ground and returned to his master. Wael stood, holding his head with pain.

The leader spoke. "If that dog lunges again, all of you are dead. Do you understand?"

Wael said nothing, but nodded, still holding his head. To Kull's surprise, the leader grabbed Wael's attacker and stood him up, only to throw a hard fist in his face. He fell to the ground as his leader sent a barrage of blows over him, cursing him. The man was lying on the ground in a heap until his leader gave one final swift kick to his ribs that let out a deafening crack of bone.

The leader turned back to the party and spoke, "I apologize for my colleague's rudeness to you, monk, but I told you *I want the boy to speak*. Now this is your last chance before you all die."

Wael conceded and nodded at Kull. Kull stepped forward with the weight of their lives on his shoulders. His answer would either bring them closer to his father or kill them.

Suddenly the words flowed out of his mouth like a cool stream. Kull heard his voice, but his mind felt as if it had taken a backseat to whatever was happening. "We are here for peace. We have come to seek counsel with Hagan, leader of the mighty Grogans."

The alley fell silent. The sound of explosions and gunfire was absorbed by the vacuum caused by Kull's strange words. Kull looked around into all the attackers' faces and saw something he had not expected: shame.

The leader of the pack blinked and lowered his pistol. "Hagan is dead, boy. The Grogan Council has placed surrogates over our Realm and they have exiled General Willyn Kara."

That name. Where had Kull heard that name? As Kull tried to register what he had been told, Wael spoke again, ignoring the small river of blood flowing down his forehead. "And who do you represent? Whose cause have you taken?"

The masked man let out a low chuckle. "Isn't it obvious? We support the rightful rule of Willyn. We would have killed you had the boy not mentioned the name of Hagan. The Grogan Council has crossed the line. We believe they killed Hagan and now are trying to dispose themselves of Willyn. We, the Grogan people, will not stand for such treachery."

The men around them nodded their heads and shouted, some firing their guns into the air. Their anger, solidarity, and frustration reemerged again in full force, and Kull glanced at Arik. He could see the fear growing on his face.

What is Wael doing?

Wael ignored the displays of aggression and continued, "Have you had any talks with the Council? Have any terms been set?"

The Red leader strutted up to Wael and pulled down his bandana, revealing a long trenched scar crossing his face. He spat, his whole body vibrating with rebellion.

"What does it look like to you, monk? No, there have been no talks with those traitors. They motioned to surrogate and all of Rhuddenhall erupted into chaos. Even now we have armies marching down from Candor's Spine to retake the city and put Willyn Kara on the Sar's throne. There will be no talks until all of the Council hang from the Pass. We'll let Aleph sort them out."

Laughter and snickers filled the alley, but Wael still showed no signs of anxiety. Kull wondered what could make this man so brave in the face of this bloodthirsty mob.

"You speak of Aleph. I am Wael, and I serve as the Mastermonk of Preost. Aleph is my master." The air's electricity was grounded. "As my protégé said, we come to bring peace to this land, and bring it in the name of Aleph. Name your terms, and I will meet with your Council. I come on Lotte's behalf, but I will represent your party as well, if you will have me."

Silence flushed the alley. The Reds stood, glancing at one another as the volleys of bullets and explosions continued to erupt in the background. All of the Reds looked to their leader, watching him as he stared at Wael, considering his response.

The Red leader spoke, "What then, Mastermonk, do you suggest?"

"I would suggest that you and your men cease fire immediately and allow me and my party to convene with the Grogan Council members. Name your terms to me and I will represent you. You must give peace a chance."

No one spoke as the leader stared into the dirt in front of Wael's feet. He raised his head with a furrowed brow and spat on the ground. "There will be no peace. My men will ensure your safe passage on our territory, Mastermonk, as a matter of our respect for you, but we do not seek your representation. Go and represent Lotte, but you will not represent us." The leader then stuck his finger in Arik's direction, "And what of this one? He doesn't look like any monk to me."

Arik raised his hands in the air and motioned to his pocket, "I am a registered transporter, got my papers right here. I don't care one bit about your Council and I prefer not to be tied up in any wars. I won't be any problem so long as you can get me home. I was just the monk's ride here until my truck got busted up."

The man tightened the bandana back around his face as he called for one of his followers, "Take him to the trains and let him ride back with the baggers." The Leader's eyes smiled menacingly. "They shouldn't mind his company."

Arik sighed and dropped his head, "This trip just keeps getting better and better. Morels, desert hikes, a civil war, and now a bunch of stinking baggers." He looked back at Wael and Kull. "Good luck, you two."

Wael nodded. Kull spoke, "Take care, Arik."

Arik let out a chuckle. "I'll have to. My foreman probably won't believe the yarn I have to tell. He don't take too kindly to canceled shipment, morels or not." A smile flashed on his face. "Mind that beast. He's liable to get you into trouble."

Rot shook the nub that served as his tail as Wael rubbed the scruff of hair on his head. The monk whispered to Rot, and the beast began to follow Arik and his escort.

"Actually, Arik, from here I need you to watch Rot. Deliver him to Arthur Ewing. He should be in Vale, and he won't mind Rot's company," said Wael.

Arik's face twisted in confusion as he spoke, "I don't know that you want to trust that dog to me. He's liable to run off."

"He will stay right by your side," said Wael, "He is safe with you, and he will keep you safe on your journey back to Lotte."

Arik looked at the dog, his eyes full of questions. Finally he nodded. "I'll give him to Ewing." Without another word Arik left with Rot trailing behind. Wael raised his hand, giving a silent blessing to both Arik and his trusted friend, Rot.

"Touching." The Red leader looked back to Wael.

Wael spoke, his eyes resting on the determined Red leader, "For seeing our transport back to safety, you have my thanks. You are generous, and I will be generous in turn. My offer still stands. For Aleph's sake, may I represent you before the Council or not?"

The leader's voice huffed from under the bandana, "My answer remains firm. Thank you for the offer, but we don't need your services, Mastermonk. We will handle this problem on our own. The peace of Grogans is purchased in blood, and we seek it to be paid in full." All the men screamed in unison, and Kull felt a cloak of darkness fall over the alleyway.

Wael spoke, his voice rumbling over the cheers of the Reds' cries, shaking his head with contempt. He pointed his finger in the leader's face and whispered with electric intensity.

"That is your decision. Know that I have come to offer you Aleph's blessing and you have rejected it. Twice. It will not be offered a third time. May Aleph have mercy on you all."

The Reds exchanged glances but remained silent.

Wael then looked to the Red leader and spoke without a trace of judgment or anger in his voice, "You are a man of your word. I can see that. I will take you by your word. Show us the way to your Council."

He nodded and led them out into the Red City as it shook and smoked with the chaos of war.

Kull blinked under the dim lights of the underground bunker. A Red soldier led them deep into a labyrinth of underground tunnels that snaked beneath the city. Despite being underground, the space was permeated with the electric smell of gunpowder, blood, and ash, a combination that made Kull feel dizzy with the memories of Cotswold burning. He leaned heavily on Wael's staff, but the pain was long past unbearable. He did his best to keep up with Wael as they followed the soldier through the blind depths. A long sigh of relief fell from Kull's lips when the party finally stopped at a bunker located off one of the tunnels.

"This is the rendezvous point. I've been ordered to leave you here. The Council dogs will meet here shortly, once I get back to HQ. Our couriers will send word to them."

Wael nodded. "We will gladly wait for them. Thank you for leading us safely through the depths, soldier."

An earth-splitting eruption shook the bunker, and Kull could feel the ground above him quake. *It's going to cave in. We are going to die down here.* Kull's stomach flipped and he fell to the ground, hot tears pouring from his eyes, not from fear but from his crushed ankle.

"The Council is shelling above. I know it might not seem like it, but rest assured you will be safe here. I have to leave."

Wael nodded, and the Red soldier left them in the dim light of the bunker chamber. Kull decided it best to stay on the ground. He stretched himself out on the cold metal floor and let out a low moan, the hot, dull pain of his ankle finally catching up with him.

Other than the buzz of the subterranean lighting, the bunker was quiet. Kull thought about how far he had come over the last few days and all he encountered. *I've come so far, but I'm still no closer to Dad.*

Wael's voice interrupted Kull's thoughts. "Kull, we have finally made it to Rhuddenhall. We should have several hours before the Council members meet with us, and I need to lay out a few ground rules about any interaction we have with them."

Kull opened his eyes. "Okay...I'm listening."

"We must be on the same page when it comes to talking to the Grogan Council members. It is extremely important that we correspond with them according to protocol, but before I go into that, let me see your ankle." Wael leaned down next to Kull's throbbing bandaged ankle. Kull gingerly rolled back the impromptu wrapping that Arik devised from the few supplies left in the transport.

It was bad, and Wael's face confirmed it.

"It's badly sprained, but not broken." Wael slowly reapplied the bandages across the injury, causing Kull to wince.

"Well, what are we going to do?"

Wael looked at Kull and reached for a small satchel hanging below his right arm, "I will take care of the swelling and pain. You should be just fine."

The satchel was holding an assortment of small glass vials and tan parchments which Wael carefully inventoried before setting aside three of the containers. He handed a small black vial to Kull.

"Drink this."

"Why didn't you give this to me before?" Kull's nostrils flared as a wind of vindictive rage blew threw him. "My foot's been killing me this whole time, and now you think this is the time to give me some painkillers?!" He eyed the vial as he held it up to the dim lighting above.

"You will understand once you take it." Wael held out the small glass vial and smiled.

Kull popped off the vial's top and peered at its contents. Inside, he spied a viscous, vile-looking substance as dark as midnight. Kull gagged as the putrid aroma of rotten flesh filled the room.

"Ugh, how do you expect me to down that?"

Wael answered, "Do you trust me, Kull?"

"Of course I trust you, Wael." His anger diminished and he spoke, forcing himself to become calm. "Yes...I trust you. But are you sure this isn't rotten? It smells awful."

Wael laughed. "That's because it's Death's Balm. The sap harvested from the ironwood trees in Preost. Here. This will make things a bit more bearable." Wael mixed the Death's Balm with two other vials he pulled from his satchel.

The monk continued. "It is rotten, in fact, but that is the point. From death, comes life. Now, hurry up and drink this quick!"

Kull obeyed and slogged down the potion, which swirled with long ringlets of black. As soon as he swallowed the foul concoction he realized why Wael spared him the aid. The elixir went down fast, and Kull could feel the room start to spin beneath him. A cold sweat broke on his forehead. He looked over at Wael as his heart began to thump at double speed, his eyes desperate. "What is this?"

"Lie down, Kull. The sensations will pass in a moment's time."

Laying down only made things worse. The floor became fluid and sloshed him from side to side.

He blinked and realized that he could hear his heart beating inside him. *How can I hear my heart beat?* Panic and fear bolted through him when he realized that the drumbeat within him was beginning to slow down, the beats in his chest lengthening.

He stared up at Wael with desperation, the world before him spinning around like a carnival ride.

"Don't be afraid, Kull. I will see you on the other side."

Kull's eyelids felt weighted like anchors. The rhythm of his heart dragged to a near halt and pulled him into the deepest sleep he ever knew.

Kull gasped.

He shot up and looked around him. The metal, riveted walls that surrounded him reminded him of where he was. *I'm in the bunker. The bunker under Rhuddenhall. I'm not dead.*

"You're awake!"

Kull spun around, fearful of who was there, only to see the kind face of Wael.

"What happened to me?"

"You were out for several hours. How do you feel?"

"I feel fine, but what happened?!" For some unknown reason, Kull felt a rush of panic and paranoia in his mind. It was as if all his fears exploded in his mind in one fell swoop.

Wael came over to him and laid his heavy hands on Kull's shoulders. He stared deeply into his eyes. "Your leg. Tell me how your leg feels."

Kull had forgotten all about his leg. He looked down at his ankle. What had been a putrid playground of mottled blue and black was now a clear field of healed, white snow. Kull stared at what had once given him so much pain and then back up at Wael's ashen face.

"What did you do?" The awe and wonder could not be contained from Kull's voice. "That is amazing."

Wael let a long smile escape from his lips, "I simply helped your body heal and accelerated its normal abilities. Now, don't sit there staring at me with your mouth hanging open. I am no magician. Had it been broken there would have been little I could have done. Now stand up and test it out."

Kull popped up and walked around the room. At first he was afraid to step too hard on the ankle, but when he finally faced the fear he put his full weight on it. It was tight. Stiff in its motion, but not painful. Soon Kull paced from one side of the bunker to the other, enjoying his newfound freedom and relief. He laughed with delight but was stopped in his tracks by the sound of the loud, metallic click and grind from the bunker door. The Surrogate parties were coming.

"Kull," Wael shot a whisper as the door began to pry open. "All I need is for you to remain silent. You *must* remain silent. One misstep can end it all."

Kull blinked and nodded. "Okay. Easy enough."

"Good."

The dim light did little to reveal the strangers as they approached them. Four large shadows surrounded a shorter, thinner frame. As they came closer it was apparent the four larger men were soldiers, their lights glowing from their rifles as they swept them from one corner of the room to the next.

The apparent dignitary in the middle bowed his head and spoke. A thin whisper pierced through the room, making Kull's skin crawl with disgust. "Welcome, Mastermonk, to Rhuddenhall. I am Hosp, the newly elected Surrogate to the crown of the Groganlands. My apologies I cannot welcome you with the appropriate formalities. I presume you have been informed of our country's recent loss." The man's smoky eyes held no grief as the last words slipped from his pale lips.

Wael bowed his head and stepped forward with his hands spread open. "I come to you with empty hands. They carry no weapons, and I invite you to empty your hands as well. In the name of Aleph, I ask for you to extend peace to your brothers in Lotte."

"I am afraid Lotte has already decided that war is what it wants. When our beloved Hagan was poisoned and killed, they left us with no other option. We will not rest until their new king crawls to us and kisses our feet, begging for a truce. They struck us first, and we will not back down."

A thunderclap of mortar explosion shook the ceiling, and Wael pointed upward.

"Is this what you want? A war with Lotte and with your own brothers and sisters? Your own people? This violence *must stop*. You have already killed countless men and women in Lotte. Innocents have been murdered and you have even taken hostages. This must be undone. All prisoners must be freed. Aleph takes no pleasure in such destruction."

Hosp's eyes narrowed as he stepped within inches of Wael's face.

"I will have you know that one of those hostages, Grift Shepherd, helped Willyn orchestrate this entire fiasco! Now both have fled these lands into Elum!" The man's words rang out against Wael, "No, Mastermonk, the only way I would release him to you is if I held his severed head in one hand and his limp body in the other."

Wael was unflinching as he stared down at the whisper of a man. Kull's hands shook, but he kept his eyes lowered, stomaching the desire to slam his fists into the foul man's face.

Hosp continued, "Willyn wanted this war. It was her opportunity to showcase her potential, but she was greedy. Greedy and foolish. She would not stop her apparent conquest and is now rotting in Elum for the murder of Filip. Soon the Elumites will find her cursed Lottian accomplice."

Wael's eyes flared, but he did not break his gaze from Hosp.

Hosp continued, "Grift and Willyn are allies, you see? Together they wish to annex the Groganlands and Elum into Lotte's territory! She is in league with that new Panderean king who sits up in Vale, and their schemes have sparked this horrible civil war! My people are killing one another, twisted by that red-headed witch's lies!"

Kull's heart exploded in his chest. *Grift has escaped. Willyn. The girl who captured him is with him.* All of it began racing in his mind like an uncontrollable pack of wild horses. *Is he is safe? Is he hurt?* Before he could contain his speech, Kull stepped forward and locked eyes with Hosp.

"How can we help you catch this man? We are trusted and we seek peace. It is obvious that his capture is what is needed to ensure peace resumes in Candor."

Wael let out a small sigh, throwing a sharp glare at Kull.

Hosp snapped his head to the side and shot a glance back to Wael as he placed a cold palm on Kull's cheek, making his skin crawl.

"I like this boy, Mastermonk. *He seems to be particularly wise on foreign affairs.*"

Wael placed a hand on Kull's chest and ushered him back behind him. Kull rubbed his cheek, trying to wipe away the feel of the man's touch. His eyes looked back at the dirty hand that just touched him. There, on Hosp's finger, was a prominent gold ring. Even from this distance, the pattern was undeniable. It was a snake eating its own tail. Something about it made Kull's stomach reel.

"He has spoken without permission, Surrogate. Please forgive his interruption. We *will not* seek further violence even if you offer peace in return."

A smile slithered back across Hosp's face as he stepped back and started to turn for the door.

"But didn't I just overhear you telling the boy that from death comes life? Eh?"

Kull's heart sank. *They had been listening. Monitoring them.*

Hosp began to slide toward the exit and barely looked over his shoulder to address Wael one last time.

"Don't be too stubborn, Mastermonk. If you have half a mind like this boy here you might actually be of some use. I will let you think things over. Call for me if you change your mind. Otherwise, I believe we are done here."

The men disappeared back through the doorway, and Kull and Wael stood in silence.

As soon as the doors closed behind the men Wael grabbed Kull's arm and whispered into his ear.

"This is much bigger than the wars we can see, Kull. There are powers at work that I did not foresee."

"What do you mean?" Kull mind buzzed with questions.

"Not now. We must leave Rhuddenhall as soon as we can."

"But Wael, where are we going to go?"

"To Elum. We need to get to your father." Wael turned and sprinted out of the bunker, following the winding pathway back up towards the surface.

"Follow me!"

CHAPTER FOURTEEN

Seam paced the floor, his heels threatening to dig a trench down the middle of the room. His eyes were fixated on the tall, plain mirror hanging on his chamber wall.

"Appear to me, goddess in the glass." He stood proud, studying his own reflection. His eyes unfocused, scanning past his own reflection, drilling deep into the mirror. He stood waiting for her to appear. His mind refused to rest during his long journey home from the Crossroads. Instead it swelled like a flooding river with visions of glory, chronicling his rise to power. Soon his many questions would have answers.

The Serubs will secure my place as the ruler of all Candor, he thought to himself. *They will be my rod and my scepter, and soon all will look on me with fear and wonder, as all the prophecies come to fruition. Seam of Lotte. The Keeper of the Keys.* The inner monologue continued to swell like a rising tide. The world would once again come under order.

His order.

Seam stood at the glass's edge, lost in his thoughts. Time gave way, and Seam became conscious of his idleness. Five minutes passed. Then ten. Thirty minutes passed and still she did not appear to him. A firestorm of anger ignited within him as he stood staring at himself in the mirror, unable to understand why she did not show herself when *he* beckoned. His fists balled in over themselves, and he shouted as an avalanche of rage exploded inside of him.

"APPEAR TO ME, GODDESS IN THE GLASS!" He stood shaking as newfound mania washed over him. Had he somehow broken the mirror as he transported it back to Vale? *No.* His mind whirled back, replaying the events that transpired at the Crossroads. Back to Bronson. To the catacombs. To Vashti.

Vashti. He slid his hand from its black leather glove and held out his bare palm to the mirror. He drew out his knife and cut the tip of his finger. He winced at the bite of the blade where the small bead of blood grew.

He flicked it onto the mirror, and the small, crimson drip sizzled as it hit the glass face.

She appeared in an instant, causing a pang of fear to hammer in Seam's heart. Her long, regal face stared down upon him, her eyes shifting colors until setting on the orange-red of twilight. These twilight eyes set deep onto Seam like daggers, causing fear to overtake him.

"Know this, King Seam of Vale. I and my kin are subject to no one, not even you. If you want to commune with *us,* there will be a *cost."*

His response came faster and more assured than he expected. "So I take it that I am to barter with you in drops of blood?"

The woman's face fell into a scowl. "You are a fool if that is what you think, for surely you have no understanding of what you speak. I will drink rivers of blood, for *no one in Candor can satisfy my thirst*. No sacrifice can meet the obligation owed to me and my kin." She placed her long hand up to the mirror's edge and glared at him. "This mirror is the only thing that protects you from me. *You would be wise to know to whom you speak."*

Seam slipped his glove back over his bleeding hand and pressed his palm back to the mirror. He stared coldly into the dagger eyes that attempted to pierce him.

"Abtren, I understand the prophecy's truth and I know very well the appetite and obligations that must be fulfilled."

"So you do know my name," she glared at him through the glass, her yellow-red eyes glowing like stoked furnaces. "You think yourself very wise don't you, *High King*? Do not fool yourself into thinking that I am utterly powerless in this prison." Her face grew in the glass, filling the whole mirror. "You do not know power. You do not know strength. You do not know fear. You are but a *boy."*

Seam searched in vain for a response, when suddenly he found himself enveloped by mirrors on all sides. Abtren's voice echoed in a panoramic swell. The sunlight within Seam's quarters evaporated, and the chamber fell under a tide of darkness. His skin turned cool as he stood surrounded by the circle of mirrors that appeared around him; a hall of glass. Within the mirrors stood men and women whose faces bore the likeness of animals, each of them a beast. They opened up their horrible maws, roaring with desperate hunger. Seam stood motionless amidst the faces of a lion, snake, boar, and hawk. Abtren stood in her mirror directly in front of Seam at the head of the others, like some twisted queen ruling over this nightmare menagerie.

"You see, High King. I have many powers, even behind this glass." Her face transformed before Seam's eyes into the horrific face of a wolf. She bore a fanged mouth frothing with malice. The beast before Seam spoke in a voice that sounded like a thousand screams harmonizing into words, "**I am sure that *we* could find a good use for you and *our* purposes on Candor.**"

Seam straightened his back and took time to examine each of the creatures before setting his eyes back on the wolf-beast. He continued to stare into the glass and spoke quietly.

"I am unconcerned with your purposes, Abtren." He reached deep within his shirt and pulled out his father's key. He held it out before him like a weapon. The beast let out a low rumbling growl and winced, only to let out an ear-splitting howl. The vision mirrors shattered all around him, sending out an explosion of crystal fragments through the room, disappearing into the night air like a memory. As soon as they appeared, the other nightmares vanished, leaving Seam once again in front of the mirror. Abtren was there, and her eyes burned with rage.

Seam held up the small gold key and smiled. "You *are bound*, Abtren of the Serubs. Bound to *me* and *my* purposes. Bound to my destiny. You know history as well as I do, and your fairytale creatures are not to be feared. One must fear the Keeper. Because I will wield absolute power in my hand." Seam looked down at the key in his palm. "I will rule with the hand of *Aleph*."

Abtren screamed, her shrieks making Seam's head rattle in pain.

"Do not speak that name to me. Do not speak the name of that false god."

Seam spat at her in full rage, "If you try to defy me again or try to manipulate me, Serub, I will repeat *that name over and over until you submit to my will.* Candor has been waiting on direction and unity, and I will finally bring it to this broken planet. I will bring it even if I have to *enslave* you and your brethren to do it."

The wraith in the mirror stood in silence, staring at the key dangling from Seam's hand.

She sighed, not daring to look him in the eye.

"You have...*my support*. You have indeed studied the prophecies well and understand the power you hold in your hand." A spark lit in her eyes again as her eyebrows twisted, "Just remember one thing, King Seam. *You need us*."

Seam stepped away from the mirror, folded his arm behind himself, and tipped his head. He left his head bowed as he spoke.

"I understand your power, Abtren, as well as that of your kin." He looked up, facing her again, and whispered toward her with absolute authority. "But *I am not subject to you*. I understand my place and you *will* understand it as well. The people of this world are mindless and can accomplish nothing more than to stoke the fires of chaos when left to their own free will. The prophecies call for a new rule, a new order, and I will be the one to finally bring that balance back to this forsaken planet. But I cannot do it alone." He raised his eyes, his face a painting of some sick cheerfulness, and smiled, "We will make a wonderful partnership. Candor will soon fall under a perfect order."

Abtren began to shrink back into the shadows of the glass but never let her fiery eyes fall from Seam. "As you see fit, *High King*." The last of her to disappear was her knowing, yellow-red eyes. Seam stood staring at the mirror, turning the small key in his hand until a knock at his door interrupted the silence.

A familiar voice beckoned, softening the tension that coiled within the room.

"Seam, dear, do you have a moment? I need to talk."

Seam cracked the door. His mother's frail frame was slumped

in the dim light of the hall behind her. She was still draped in one of Camden's robes, its fabric swallowing her shoulders. This was one of the few times that he could remember that she actually ventured out from her room. Seam smiled as he opened the door wider.

"I see you have been able to escape your prison, Mother." He hugged her. "You have me worried."

Aleigha afforded Seam a small grin, and her eyes showed a glimpse of their old life. She placed a warm palm on Seam's cheek before taking his hand.

"Seam. I know you have, but I need you to know that grief is not what shackled me for so long. Your father and I loved each other very much. He would not want me to suffer over him."

Each word brought an ounce of Aleigha's former self back from the shadows. She squeezed Seam's hand and looked at him with a stare that demanded his full attention. She wanted to say something to him, but Seam could not guess what.

"What is it?"

Aleigha sighed, and took in a shallow breath. "I've been meaning to talk to you for many days now, Seam." She hesitated, but consented. "There is a fear that has been building within the darkness of my mind. I have tried to understand its source, but I have failed. My dreams are dark, and I cannot focus enough to pinpoint it, but I cannot shake the feeling that something evil is lurking."

Seam placed his hand on his mother's shoulder and sighed as he straightened himself before her. He ran a thumb along his father's cloak and said, "Mother, of course evil is lurking. We are in a time of war and Father was murdered. This world is full of evil. But believe me, I will do whatever I can to change that, and I will keep you safe."

"My fears do not involve this world, Seam."

Seam glanced at his mother with earnest concern. "What do you mean?"

"I haven't slept well in days, Seam. I keep having the most horrible dream. It comes every night, and every night I wake fearing for your life. I need to talk to you about it."

Seam chuckled, his face igniting into a smirk. "Am I a soothsayer as well as the High King?" Aleigha's face stayed firm, refusing to acknowledge her son's rebuttal.

"This dream concerns you, son. That is why I am here. Every night I see you staring into a mirror, a mirror which opens up like a doorway, and every night you walk through that doorway."

Seam's mouth went dry.

She continued, "Through the door you encounter a stone staircase. Yet each stone is made up of hundreds and thousands of mangled bodies." Fear welled in her eyes. "Horrible, murdered innocents."

Seam swallowed as a shiver went down his spine. "Mother. This is insane. What you are saying…"

"Let me finish." Seam's mouth snapped shut. Aleigha's eyes wandered as she continued to recall the dream. "This staircase is both alive and dead, and each stone screams out to you, blaming you for its fate. Blaming you for this abomination, the staircase descends deep down into the darkness. The staircase, somehow, though I don't understand it, never leads up…" she looked up at him, a mixture of fear and pity in her eyes. "Yet you have no problem walking on these living stones. In fact, you don't even notice them, Seam." Her eyes began to fill with desperation. "You just keep descending...and where the staircase ends…" Hot tears welled up in her eyes now, and she let out a deep, mournful sob.

"What, Mother? What is at the end of the staircase?"

Aleigha stared deep into Seam's brown eyes. "Your father. Camden is at the end of the staircase. He stands to block your path; he says he has something to tell you, but you...you…" She could not bring herself to the words.

"What do I do?"

Aleigha stood, her face cold and rigid. Finally she answered her son, "You slit his throat…and his blood pours out on the ground."

"What did he want to say to me?"

"He wanted to tell you to stop. He wanted to tell you that he loves you. He wanted to tell you that you can still find peace."

Seam took a step away from her, closing his eyes. He could feel his hands shaking, and the room began to spin. A sense of timelessness and youth filled his mind, and for a brief moment he felt as if he were just a child, not a king or a prince, but just a boy. A whole world of possibility lay before him, and there was nothing that seemed pressing or too serious. There was not the burden of war. No plots, no politics. No mirrors, no murder. Only peace. The feeling wafted over him in an instant, wanting to linger. One word was spoken in his mind at that moment, from the depths of Seam's very soul.

No.

He opened his eyes and met his mother's deep gaze. Seam smiled at her, brushing the tears that welled in his own eyes. He pointed over his mother's shoulder to the empty hallway that led to the throne room behind her.

With a cracked voice he spoke to her calmly. "It was just a dream...a horrible one at that. Many kings and rulers before me have tried to manufacture peace, Mother, including father. No doubt his ghost wants exactly what I want, but I will finally end the chaos that has been ruling Candor once and for all. I have always known I would do something great, and I believe that I am not far from obtaining what many have thought to be impossible. Peace will come again to Candor, Mother. Peace of my making."

Aleigha's eyes left Seam's face and her smile withered, only to be enveloped by a look of terror. Aleigha pushed past Seam, barreling into the small room. She stared into the tall mirror standing against the wall. She stood without a sound before reaching for the pane. Seam ripped her arm back and placed himself between his mother and the mirror.

"NO! Don't touch it!"

Seam forced himself to look past the knowing, penetrating gaze of his mother. "Why can't I touch this mirror, Seam?" The simple question made him want to ring her neck.

He stammered out a hollow answer. "It's just that it is quite the antique and I don't wish it to be disturbed." A warm smile grew on his face, but his eyes were locked in a cold, threatening stare.

Aleigha's face fell. "Tell me, Seam. How does one *disturb* a mirror?"

Seam said nothing.

"How long has *it* been here? This is the same mirror I saw in my dreams...the one that swallowed you whole and took you down into that hellish place. "

He screamed at her, "You need to leave...now!"

Seam tried to corral her back out the doorway, but she refused to be moved and pushed his hands away from her as she continued, "I want you to TELL me how long that has been here! It does not belong in this palace!"

Seam laughed at her, but his eyes burned like hot coals as his hand clamped down on her. In one swift motion he forced her out of the room. "Come, Mother. You mustn't be upset." She stiffened in protest at his touch, but he was finally able to get her out into the hallway as she continued to struggle in his grip, looking back over his shoulder, back into the room.

"Seam Panderean." Her voice was high and pleading. "You MUST destroy it. For Aleph's sake, you must break it into a thousand pieces!"

Seam's voice took on a patronizing, sorrowful tone. "Mother, you are clearly *stressed*. Are a few bad dreams all it takes to make one act like a madwoman? Will you have me chop up the throne for firewood next? I don't understand why you would be so concerned about an antique mirror that was given to me as a gift. You must have seen it in passing and placed it into your terrible dreams."

"A gift? *Who gave that to you*?"

Seam smiled and placed his hands back on his mother's shoulders as he tried to get her moved further into the hallway, "A very powerful ally, Mother." His face softened as the protective rage he felt began to fade. "You have nothing to worry about. As a matter a fact, I don't intend to keep the mirror here. If you don't care for its appearance, I will have it moved very soon."

Aleigha fought to catch another glimpse of the mirror as Seam continued to usher her down the hallway. She spat her rebukes at him. "I don't care what the thing looks like. You think I'm a fool, don't you?" She stared at him, trying desperately to read him. "What are you hiding from me? You don't understand what was given to you. That mirror is the source of my fears. It is evil! I don't want it moved. I want it destroyed!"

Seam held her with one arm and pointed back to the open door of his chamber. "Mother, I understand very well what was given to me. It is a priceless gift and one I am grateful for. No mad dream is going to change that. Now, *you need to rest.* I don't like seeing you like this."

He paused, trying to control himself and assure her.

"We are okay and you are okay. I will keep you safe, that I promise. I know I could not keep Father from dying, and your cursed dreams continue to remind me of that failure, but you are safe now, and you will stay *safe*. Now, let me have Bronson help you to your quarters and I will have the staff bring you something to eat. You need to rest."

Seam tapped at the datalink on his wrist and called for Bronson as he continued to walk with his mother toward her room and away from his chamber. Bronson appeared around the corner and rushed to Aleigha's side.

"Please allow me to assist, Your Highness. It would be my honor to escort you back to your quarters."

Aleigha took Bronson's arm but looked back at Seam and said, "Destroyed. *I want that mirror destroyed.* I don't care who gave it to you or what value you might think it has. I am no fool, son, and my dreams are not madness. I need you to listen to me."

At the mention of the mirror Bronson's face went white as a sheet. He gathered himself quickly and without a word reached for Aleigha's arm. "Let's give the king his peace."

Seam turned without addressing his mother again and made his way back into his chamber. As he stepped back into his reclusive lair he forced his mind to let go of his mother's dreams, the vision of warning from his late father. *That man was a fool anyway. A foolish king too concerned with the traditions and the old ways, never seeking to seize the opportunities that lay before him to actually make a difference. Camden was a coward. A coward with no vision.* He found himself again staring into the mirror, his eyes enamored at seeing himself.

"But I," he whispered quietly to himself, "have more vision than can be contained." He pulled off his black leather glove and without hesitation sliced open his palm with his dagger. He slammed it on the glass, ignoring the pain shooting up his arm, and let the hot, wet blood pour out over the mirror's face. It sizzled and smoked relentlessly, as if it was being funneled into a fire.

"Your dreams have no merit here, Mother. Mine, I'm afraid, are the only ones that matter."

CHAPTER FIFTEEN

Willyn's prison cell was a far cry from the lush vineyard estates and mansions she had seen during her journey into Elum. The floor of her cramped cell was cold and damp, leaving her little choice but to stand. She whittled away the hours examining the fine lacework of green moss that wove on her dirty cinderblock walls. Cracks crossed through them like spider webs, and drops of salty brine bled out from the gaps, slowly running toward the middle of the floor where it pooled. The overwhelming stench of mildew was enough to make her want to scream.

The steel iron cuffs around her ankles clanked an audible reminder that she was caged. She rubbed her eyes. She had studied the moss-covered walls long enough. It was time to examine the door again. Three days had passed since she was arrested from Luken's ship. *Or was it four?* It didn't matter. It might as well have been an eternity. She stared at the door, a sigh escaping through her lips. She ran her fingers up the rough, rusted features of the iron door, taking time to explore the hinges for any signs of weakness.

The small window near the top of the cell's door was a dim beacon for the room, offering only a withering portion of light for Willyn to ration out during her days. This slim arrow of daylight was precious to her. It was the only thing she had that could cut into the stale, murky fog that hung within her cell. She tried in vain to stand on her toes, doing her best to peer outside, but it was no use. The window stood too tall and offered no clues of her whereabouts. All she could make out was a long, narrow hallway outside the cell, constructed of the same cinderblocks that surrounded her. As she tumbled thoughts of escape through her mind she thought back to Luken. His face seemed to push out the monotonous grind. She remembered his promise to her. He promised he would come back for her. That promise and her rationed daylight were the only comforts she had.

Willyn sat back against the far wall of her cell and stared at the iron door separating her from freedom, from Luken, from seeing Hagan again, and from her hunt for Grift.

Grift. She nearly forgot him in the midst of her imprisonment. *I've got to get out of here,* she thought to herself. She blinked, forcing herself to focus. An idea leapt up from the darkness of her mind.

If he could escape, so can I. The thought rolled in her head like a stone, but she dared to think it again.

Yes. If Grift could escape my prison…surely I can escape this one. But how?

She closed her eyes, searching for an answer. She willed herself to relax, to allow her subconscious to engage the problem. Her mind whirled and clicked for days, but there were no immediate solutions. There had to be something else. She held her breath, losing herself in the sound of that dank place. The slow drip of brine was the first thing she could hear. She pushed herself further down the hall, allowing her ears to see all that she couldn't.

Yes. The distant sound of the guards shuffling their feet could be heard echoing down the far hallways. Then she heard something she wasn't expecting. The sound was faint but distinct. The slow lumbering rhythm of waves. Willyn could hear them whisper, crashing against the rocky shoreline. It was a sound she heard before. The answer fell into her mind.

Filip's palace. She was under Filip's palace. Even though the guards blindfolded her upon her arrest and then taken their sweet time delivering her to her current location, she knew she was right. She could feel it in her bones. She knew that they had come right back to where she started.

So what do you do with that? The question was like a splinter throbbing in her mind. She determined where she was, but how could that knowledge benefit her?

She pondered this idea silently, but no more sounds and no more ideas visited Willyn in her cell for hours. She sat in complete silence, not wanting to even hear her own voice. The fatigue of the days prior settled into her shoulders like a lead weight. She was exhausted, having only escaped the morel pack within an inch of her life. *Thank you, Luken,* she thought, brushing away the thoughts of the brute that had come after her in the bog. The waves beating in the distance began to lull her to sleep. Yet sleep brought no comfort to her.

She dreamed, and in her dreams she took on the form of a young girl. Hagan was there, but his form was not right. Her older brother was haggard and dying, coughing up putrid green bile and wasting away with each painful heave of his brittle chest. He looked to her child form and wiped his mouth. His voice croaked out, its hollow sound causing her to scream, *"This is your fault. You left me to die!"*

One nightmare led to another. Another dream came, and Hagan was no longer lying on his deathbed but was shackled and chained. Hosp was dragging him across the ground and turning to beat him and curse at him with each faltering step. Willyn attempted to run to save her brother, only to realize that again she was bound within the body of a small child. She charged after her enemy, doing all she could to save her brother, but with each advance she was countered by a swift kick or punch from Hosp who cackled at her futile attempts. His eyes were glazed over with hatred, and they burned brightly, like crimson yellow orbs of fire.

"Your family is cursed, Willyn Kara," he yelled. *"Cursed! You are powerless and unfit to lead. There is nothing you can do!"*

To her surprise Grift Shepherd appeared out of thin air. He attacked and overtook the screaming phantom. But her joy fell to despair when she saw Shepherd slowly and willfully stand over Hagan, pulling his pistol out of his holster. Willyn screamed but no voice could be heard as Grift leveled the revolver and pointed it straight at her brother's face. She forced herself to look away, startled awake by the crack of the pistol firing.

Willyn's eyes shot open with the bang of her brother's execution still ringing in her ears. She clawed her way to her feet, covered in a cold sweat. She fought to catch her breath as she tried to chase away the nightmares. As she gathered herself, a small plate rattled beneath the door.

Food. They had brought her food. That had been the sound. The vision of her brother being murdered along with the terrible smell of the room robbed her of her appetite. Despite this, she forced herself to retrieve the hard crusts of bread.

Her voice croaked, echoing off the damp walls, "You could have done better than *this*. I am the general of Groganlands! I swear all of Elum will regret this day!" Laughs and jeers boomed back at her from behind the thick iron door. Rage filled her mind and she fired back at them, "Why don't you come back so I can smash this plate through your skull?!"

Stop. Stop giving them what they want. She quieted herself, her teeth working on the thick rind of the dry bread. *There is nothing you can do here.*

The guards left, and the hallway was once again quiet. The silence was maddening. Pacing was the only thing that seemed to help. Willyn worked her way around the room, following her small orbit of exploring the room, each rotation a new attempt to reveal some small flaw; something to leverage.

Willyn.

The sound of her name stopped her dead in her tracks. Her footsteps could not drown out the fact that someone had called for her. She stood silent, but there was no sign of anyone nearby until the voice came again.

Willyn.

It was surreal. She could have sworn she was hearing her name, but it felt like it was only a part of her earlier dream creeping back into her mind. But the voice. She heard it before.

I am here. Sit quietly and I will join you soon.

"Who is here?" Willyn said. Her eyes shot around the room. "Hello? Hello?"

Willyn continued turning in a slow circle, waiting for movement, ready to attack any sign of intrusion in her cell. A chill ran down her neck as she slowly circled, waiting for the fight that was sure to come, but nothing came. There was nothing but silence. More silence.

"Hello?" she called out one last time. *You are going mad, Willyn,* she thought to herself. *It's only been a few days and you are already losing it. Get it together.*

Willyn sat back down in the corner of the room and tried to focus on the sound of the waves again, hoping that the meditation would help calm her nerves. As she closed her eyes and took in a deep breath, the sound of her cell's lock snapping open rocketed her to her feet. She braced herself for a fight, but her mouth fell open when she saw who it was.

"Luken? How did you..."

He interrupted. "Never mind that. I have to be quick. What have they told you, Willyn?"

Willyn did not understand.

"No one has said anything since they charged me on your ship. How can they think that I killed Filip, Luken? It's impossible. I'd been with you the whole time."

Luken blinked and then stared at her. He let out a low sigh.

"Willyn...I..."

"What is it?" There was something in his eyes. *Gods above.* Something was wrong.

"I didn't want to be the one to tell you."

"To tell me what?" Fear fell over her like a waterfall.

"Your brother..."

Willyn screamed, full of shock and panic. "What about Hagan?!"

Luken's eyes dropped. "He's dead, Willyn. Hagan is dead," he whispered.

A cold void filled Willyn's collapsing lungs, and the room began to spin. She saw little white pinpricks of light, white fireworks streaking across her vision, and everything, all the colors, sounds, smells, all at once seemed to blend and bleed together. She picked up the words that were just spoken. She struggled to make sense of them. "He's dead, Willyn. Hagan is dead."

There was no way to process the news that she lost her only ally, her only friend. The weight of her world collapsed in on her like an avalanche, choking her of breath. Her hands went numb as she stared down to the floor of her cell, trying to somehow forget Luken's words. Hoping that all of it was a bad dream and that somehow she did not really lose the only person who mattered to her.

"Willyn, did you hear me?" Luken grasped one of her cold hands. She was silent but her eyes were screaming out. It was as if she left her body, as if the words had been too turbulent that they *pushed her out*, leaving only a hollow shell.

Luken closed his eyes and inhaled. He called out to her, his voice again penetrating her mind.

Willyn, come back. Come back.

In a flash Willyn threw herself at him screaming, clawing at him like a panther.

"HOW DARE YOU!? How could you let him die? He was all I had!" Luken grabbed her wrists, but she quickly pinned him down on the damp, dirty floor. He screamed at her. "Willyn! Calm down!"

She laid into him, "How dare you come in here and tell me that! Is this not enough? Are these chains not enough? You had to tell me that Hagan is dead? Why?!" She stood up and backed away from him. "And then on top of that you pull some witchcraft on me, talking inside my head?" She leapt off of him, recoiling at his touch. "Leave! Leave now! Just let me die here in peace!"

Luken blinked at the word. *Witchcraft.*

Hot tears streamed down her face. She heaved for air, the panic of it all finally receding. In between deep, haggard breaths, she spoke. "I was a fool to have trusted you. You ran me around searching for the man who poisoned my brother, knowing that time was all that was needed to kill him. *You* stole that time from me. You and your witchcraft can burn in the hell you came from."

Luken gritted his teeth. Anger flared on his face, and he stiffened his back. A moment passed and it dissolved, but Willyn had seen it. He spared her from something, but she did not know what. He whispered to her, reaching out his hand.

"Willyn, please."

She slapped his touch away. "What is your problem? *What makes you think you can do this?"*

Luken winced and shook his hand. "Willyn, I'm here to help you. You have to calm down and listen."

"NO. You will get no listening from me. You dragged me across creation after a ghost, and now..." The weight of the situation completely eclipsed her. Stammering, she choked out what she knew was true..."my brother *is dead."*

Her tears shook her to the core, leaving her gasping for breath, only to quake again in her heart. Her chest ached, and she felt as if it were splitting open with each heave for breath. Her soul ached for Hagan, for his advice, his friendship, his leadership, his love. In losing Hagan she lost everything. Everything except for her duty to lead the Groganlands. All she wanted was one last word, one last exchange with her brother, but she knew no words would ever come.

Hagan was gone. She wailed until there was nothing left in her, until she had nothing left to give. Luken sat silently beside her in the dark.

When the sobs ceased, Willyn held her hand over her eyes and banged her head against the cell wall. She let out a moan and looked at Luken through red, tired eyes.

Luken laid a soft hand on her shoulder and pulled back her tangled mess of hair. "I am sorry, Willyn. I am truly sorry." His words brought little comfort, but his soft touch spoke louder than he ever could. Despite her rage, she knew he was sincere. Despite everything, he was the only person she could trust now.

His gray eyes met her. "It's time. We've got to get you out of this cell and find who is really responsible for this. These people are set to see you hang on the gallows tomorrow. I can't let that happen to you."

Willyn's voice cracked out a small whisper. "What difference does it make? Hagan is dead; his murderer is miles from here.

And I am being framed for regicide." Her voice was cold; all of her hot, unruly emotions were left on the wet floor. "Dying could be better. I'd be free from my shame. I'd be free from failing Hagan."

Luken grabbed her shackled ankles and inserted a small, thin wire into the lock. "That's enough of that talk, sacker of cities." He made a few swift strokes with the device. His grasp on her leg was firm but comforting. The same electricity she felt on the ship seemed to transfer from him again as he held her. She was mesmerized by him.

Why is he helping me escape? He has nothing to gain.

Her mind drifted as Luken continued to fight the locks. She thought back to Hagan and remembered his crippled body lying in his bed, withering away. But the image faded and a new one took its place. She could see Hagan in her mind's eye rise from the bed. He was well once more and full of his former strength. He was as relentless as the waves crashing against the shores of Elum.

He is at peace. Where this realization came from, Willyn did not know. The thought was a small one, but it calmed her heartache like a soothing balm.

He would not give up had I been the one who died. He would have his revenge before the end. The thought was true and gave her comfort.

A resounding clang sprang from Willyn's locks as Luken laughed.

"Got it! Come on, let's get out of here!" Willyn's mind snapped back into the present as she rubbed her swollen legs. Silently, she promised to herself that she would avenge her brother, no matter the cost.

Luken took her by the hand and led her out of the cell and into the narrow chamber. Five Elumite guards were splayed out on the floor like rag dolls.

"You made quick work of them. I didn't even hear them struggle when they fought you."

Luken smiled. "They were knocked out before they knew I was there. But don't let them fool you; we are not out of the woods yet."

The chamber led to a staircase that circled up into what Willyn assumed would be the main palace courtyard above her, the same courtyard where she had first been greeted by Filip. As she rose up the stairs, thoughts began to flow into her mind.

Three leaders of the Realms were now dead. Murdered. Camden, Hagan, and now Filip. This cannot be a coincidence.

This new reality crashed over her. All of this was more than another territorial conflict between Lotte and the Groganlands. It was bigger than Grift Shepherd. He had to be someone's pawn...

Someone or something is killing the leaders of the Realms. But who is leading it and why? How can Hagan's death and Filip's be related?

The thoughts receded as Luken led Willyn to the top of the staircase. The courtyard that opened up in front of her was breathtaking. The immaculate white stucco shone bright in the midday sun, and the heavenly smell of fresh orange blossoms wafted from the trees lacing the lush gardens. Gulls and seabirds cried, calling in chorus with the thundering waves. Luken released her hand and stared into her eyes. "You must listen to me and do exactly as I say. We only have one chance," he whispered.

She nodded as she allowed her eyes to scan the terrace that lined both sides of the courtyard.

"My boat is at the dock, right outside that entryway." He pointed to the wide arch that opened up toward the sea. "When you run out of there you will see that there are seven flights of stairs that run down the cliff face toward the docks.

"I remember, Luken," she snapped at him.

"Willyn, there are snipers lined on top of the roof now. If you run, you'll be shot down."Willyn cursed under her breath and squinted at the rooftops, trying to glimpse the possible nesting spots the snipers would have chosen. She was able to pick out at least five optimal spots and figured each one would have at least one rifle with a bullet waiting for her.

"Is there no other way around? A hallway or something less open?"

Luken shook his head and gestured toward the courtyard. "Unfortunately, this is the only path. Believe me, I have been planning this little rescue from the day they plucked you off my ship, and this is the best way out."

She actually allowed a chuckle to escape. "Thanks. That makes me feel much better." She forced a grin and went back to examining the roof line.

"Luckily, I've got the perfect distraction. When you *hear* my distraction, run. Run like you've never run in your life. When you get to my ship get in the cabin below and lock yourself in. I'll unlock it when we are at sea."

"So that's the whole plan? Just to run and hope for the best?"

Luken smirked, "Do you have any better ideas at this point?"

"Not at the moment, but it seems a bit farfetched to think I can outrun at least five snipers."

Luken laid his hand on Willyn's shoulder and leveled his eyes with hers. "Willyn, I need you to trust me."

"What choice do I have? No one else is trying to save me." She smiled.

Luken's face was grim, his normally playful expression solemn.

"Trust me when I leave now. Trust me when you get on my boat. Trust me when you get into my cabin."

"What?"

"There is no time to explain. Get ready. You will know when to run. Just wait for it. Trust me!"

Luken ran, ascending the staircase up on the second floor above her. She swallowed her fear and waited. A minute went by, then two. Willyn sensed a change. Whatever Luken was going to do, he had done it. She felt a calm silence penetrate the courtyard and knew it was time. Everything within her told her to run, but she stayed pinned within the small doorway, staring out over the courtyard. She felt naked and vulnerable with no weapon, no rook, and no defenses. Just instructions from a stranger to run across a courtyard lined with snipers. She stayed hidden inside the doorway until she heard Luken's voice ring through her mind again.

Now. Run now!

Willyn bolted from the door and sprinted for the line of trees running parallel to the compound's terraces. They would at least provide some cover. After about forty yards, a deafening explosion roared behind her. She glanced back mid-sprint to see the second floor of the palace engulfed in flames. *Keep running.* Willyn cleared the cover of the courtyard and sprinted out the open archway. The sheer drop of the cliff face took her off guard. She had not remembered it being this steep when she first got on Luken's boat several days ago.

There, carved in the red rock were the seven flights of slippery steps descending down the red stone ridge. She saw the waves far below her and fought to catch her footing on the slick stones. Fiery debris rained down around her from the smoldering palace, the deafening memory of the blast still ringing in her ears. Her fear of the slope and its uninviting descent collapsed once she noticed a red dot skip across her chest. She saw it for only a split second, but it was enough. A red laser sight was always followed by a bullet. She threw herself down the stairs as the cannoning thunderclaps of gunshots rained down on her.

One flight.

BOOM.

Three flights.

BOOM. BOOM.

Willyn took a chance and jumped off the side of one flight, sliding down the rock face to a small landing several flights below. The move saved her time and put her out of the line of fire for a brief moment, but she had to fight to keep from losing all her footing and tumbling off the landing out onto the jagged rocks.

Three bullets careened off the nearby rocks and whistled by her head.

She could feel the snipers' eyes focus on her as she ran with all her might. She was on the main platform and could see Luken's boat.

BOOM.

An explosion of red blood came from Willyn's left hand as she screamed. She knew there would be nothing left. The bullet hit her hand like a sledgehammer, and she would not dare to look down.

She did not pause, but ran, as more bullets licked at her heels. With each step she felt her heart heave with force as blood plunged out of her mangled hand. She gripped it down with her other arm, stomaching the throbbing pain.

You're...almost...there!

She barreled over the edge of the ship and expected the pain of another shot to wring through her, spilling her life out into the ocean floor below.

But it did not come. Shaking, she slid open the cabin door and threw herself in. The sound of bullets thumped against the tiny ship's hull but none broke through. She gasped for breath and braced herself, forcing herself to look at her hand and assess the damage.

Blood poured out of her with each heartbeat. She still had a hand, but she needed to stop the bleeding and get help. She clamped her hand in her other armpit, cringing with pain, and scurried around the dark cabin searching for binding. Her vision was becoming narrower, and she struggled to find anything to stop the bleeding—a blanket, rag, or towel. She struggled to even hold herself upright. She reached out to open up a trunk when someone grabbed her wounded hand. Pain shot up Willyn's arm as tears streamed down her eyes.

"Hold still. I've got you. We've got to get this dressed."

Her eyes trailed up the rough hands pressing down on her wound and up to the face they belonged to. She fought to focus her vision, but it was soon apparent who it was.

Grift.

It was Grift Shepherd.

CHAPTER SIXTEEN

Kull had never seen such a hulking, menacing machine. Its black paint shimmered bright in the hot, dry sun, but this was not the feature that captivated Kull the most. It was the armor. Thin, nearly translucent, sharp quills covered every square inch of it. Kull took a daring step closer toward one of the small, hair-thick pins.

"*Don't* touch it, Kull," said Wael. "Those quills would likely kill you."

"What is it?" Kull asked, disturbed by the tenor in Wael's voice.

Wael answered, "It's a custom railcar, made by the Grogans. It's designed specifically for protection against morels. The baggers enjoy some comforts in Candor, after all. The rise in attacks the last few years must have finally motivated the Grogans to protect them."

"The railcars have been attacked?" Wael nodded without a word. "Well, hopefully it will keep us safe and get us out of here."

The two were terribly out of place mixed with the crowd of baggers. Wael towered over the mass of people pooling in through the main toll gate, and his wardrobe did nothing to help him blend in with his new neighbors. The quickest way out of the Groganlands was sitting in front of Kull and he could not help but feel his heart beating faster and faster as he and Wael waited to stow away on the train. It was obvious that they stood out, but the guards patrolling the platform did not seem to pay them any mind, at least for now.

"Hey Wael, are you sure this is the right line?" Kull peered up and down the platform trying to read the different signs pointing to each track.

Wael nodded, "This is the one. If Grift is in Elum, then there is only one person your father would run to for help. This train will deliver us to him."

An old man shuffled past Kull and bumped into Wael who chuckled and gently ushered the elder past him. The man whistled and laughed and pushed closer to the car.

Baggers were a rare sight in Lotte, and most people did well to avoid them. Most were a landless people, descendants of the Rihtians who had been defeated by the Grogans in the Great War, though their number swelled following the more recent Rihtian War. For generations they spent their entire existence riding the rails of Candor searching for their next job and meal, continuing a never-ending cycle of summer mining in the depths of Legion's Teeth for the ore and iron the Grogans required, harvesting crops in Elum in the fall, building construction projects in Lotte in the winter, and spending the spring planting again in Elum. The three Realms shared the baggers, even through times of war. It was the one thing in Candor that was agreed upon; the Baggers were to be free and unrestricted. They came and went, and their coming to the Realms was like the coming of the tides; consistent and necessary.

To Kull, the sea of day laborers, craftsmen, and vagrants flooding the platform reminded him of a memory from his childhood. It was the time he first saw cattle-beasts, herded into Cotswold from Elum for trade in Vale. Baggers brought the gentle giants, coming in a caravan of ramshackle vehicles of suspect construction, driving the cattle across the countryside toward the capital. Kull was with his father at the main market square when the herdsmen skillfully appeared over the horizon. The beasts sounded like thunder on the cobbled streets, their lows and bellows ringing in his ears. Grift pointed out the skillful bagger ranchers who directed the herd into the round pen just outside the market square. They made it look so easy.

Grift let Kull inch closer to the pen so he could experience the cattle beasts' size firsthand.

Kull could still hear his father speaking to him:

"These creatures could easily stampede. They could break down this crude fence and break rank from their drivers. They are so strong that they could easily kill their captors."

Kull had stared at the herd for a long time. "So, why don't they just run away? They're huge!" Kull would never forget his father's response.

"Fear."

The memory forced Kull to examine the faces of the drifters passing by him as he waited to load into the rail car. Many of their faces carried the same heavy burden as those beasts. They were driven by a silent master, one of their own making.

A bagger woman in line ahead of them turned around and pointed to the rail car. A string of bouncing language that Kull could not understand tumbled from her lips. She wore an intricate pink headdress and her entire face was veiled by long strands of ancient silver coins that rattled around. Behind them, Kull saw beautiful yellow eyes staring at him, and his heart jumped in his chest.

"She says that it is rightfully called a *hedgehog*." Wael smiled as he translated.

"A hedgehog? What's a hedgehog?"

"It's a species of animal that long went extinct, but the baggers...they remember them. They used to be a type of pet."

The doors of the "hedgehog" opened, and soon the crowd of baggers filed in, choosing their seats, laughing and singing in their melodic language. Kull and Wael entered their car and sat in one of the long rows of seats. They were cramped, the seats quickly filling with baggers who rattled and laughed, danced and spat, and blatantly stared at both Kull and Wael, pointing and gesturing toward them without shame. A wall of gagging smell soon surrounded Kull. Bathing, it seemed, was a luxury that these people could not often afford.

Kull sat silently next to Wael, doing his best not to offend or be offended. He breathed slowly, allowing himself time to readjust to the strangers. Soon, the hedgehog rocketed from the station toward Elum. It was there they would find his father, or at least that is what Wael said after their meeting with the Grogan leader ended short. Kull tried to remember the man's name, tumbling names through his thoughts before he stumbled over the right one.

Hosp. Something about that snake of a man caused the hair on Kull's neck to stand up and his stomach to pool with dread.

Since the train left Rhuddenhall, Wael had been mostly silent, keeping his eyes trained out on the empty hills rolling by their view from the window. After the meeting with Hosp he had become even more stoic and introverted than usual, so much that it was painfully obvious to Kull that something was wrong. Wael seemed to be piecing together something as his eyes peered out into the wastelands, but everything happened too fast for Kull to have any idea what it was.

A bagger leaned over and flashed a smile of rotten teeth.

Surprisingly, he spoke in the common tongue. "Want a bite to eat?" he said as he held out a peach to Kull. "It will do you good, boy. Tis' a long ride."

"No thank you, but you are kind to offer. I don't want to go taking your food." Kull smiled as he held up his hand politely to gesture the gift away.

"You sure?" the old man whistled. "These good. Hate you miss out. Straight out of Elum's orchards. Rare beauty."

Frustration grew in Kull's mind as he refused again, more firmly. "No thanks, really. I am fine."

"Take the gift."

Kull's head spun around to Wael. "It would be rude to refuse his gift," Wael said.

Kull grimaced and whispered, "Well, I mean, he is a bagger. I feel bad taking..."

The bagger interrupted, "Ah, phff, boy you not taking a thing. Lot to learn, lot to learn." The old man laughed and rolled the peach to his feet. "Now eat."

Wael let out a low chuckle as Kull picked up the fruit. Wael's eyes soon went back out into the desert and he fell silent again.

What is wrong with him? What is he not telling me? The questions gnawed at Kull.

He tried to break the silence with small talk. "Hey Wael, looks like we are in Riht. I don't think I've ever seen so much...nothing."

Wael gave a small nod, but remained silent. His eyes never left the horizon.

The bagger sat down and wiggled about as he enjoyed his small triumph of getting Kull to accept his precious gift. A smile twisted across his lips as he settled back into his normal spot. Kull held the fruit for a moment, inspecting it on each side. He plunged into it and tasted its sweet flesh. Juice rolled down his cheek and an intense, sweet flavor exploded in his mouth. After the ride in the back of the truck and eating nothing but jerky and crackers for the past few days, it was extremely refreshing.

"Thank you." Kull managed to mumble through a mouth full. "It *is* very good."

The old man nodded, smiling widely, and then entertained himself by whittling a small block of wood. Kull turned to face Wael and made another attempt to break the silence.

"Wael?" Wael did look at him, but his eyes were still occupied with some unspoken thought. "What is it? You said back in Rhuddenhall that this was much bigger than you could imagine. What were you talking about?"

Kull took another bite of the peach, waiting for an answer, but none came. Frustrated, he swallowed and whispered.

"I have been dragged around for over a week now, Wael. My hair is chopped off, and I'm stuck on a train with a bunch of baggers. My dad is lost out there somewhere, my mom is sicker than ever, and I can't get any answers out of you. *Now* we are heading to Elum. I've never seen this much of Candor in my life, but the fact is that you've told me nothing of what's going on. How does my dad fit into all of this? I know there's something you're not telling me."

Wael closed his eyes and gently nodded. He let out a small sigh as he turned from the window and walked toward the opening of the car. He pushed by the wall of baggers and motioned for Kull to follow. The two slid out of the railcar into the opening between it and the adjacent unit. The small platform was barely large enough for both of them, but Kull followed Wael out onto the ledge. He would go anywhere to finally get answers. Wael closed the door behind them. The desert heat was suffocating, and the din of the railcar's speed made it hard to hear anything. The desert flew by them like a passing thought, and Kull marveled at how fast they were going.

Wael stared at Kull as the train wheels scratched and squealed along the tracks. His continued silence and awkward gaze seemed to drown out everything else until he finally spoke.

"Kull. What do you know of the Legacy?"

Kull leaned in, bending his ear toward the monk over the noise.

"The what?"

"Did your father ever mention other Keepers?"

Kull let out a groan and threw up his hands.

"Wael, I don't know what you're talking about! My dad never said anything about a legacy or keepers or anything like that! What does any of that have to do with him?"

Wael's face was blank as he weighed his response. "I wish he had, Kull."

Wael dropped his head as the roaring railcar filled the silence between them.

Then he spoke, "The Keepers have everything to do with your father. He is a Keeper. So am I. Let me be frank with you, Kull. Your father and I have known one another for many years now. The Keepers are a secret brotherhood that spreads across all the Realms of Candor. In fact, the Realms were originally founded and are maintained to keep the keys safe, but that bit of history has been lost amidst all of the petty skirmishes and wars we've had. Despite them, nothing has ever broken the brotherhood of Keepers. No war, no conflict. Nothing."

Kull's mind buzzed. *Keys? What keys?*

Wael continued, "The true reason for these things has faded out of memory, I fear. Now the Keepers are at a precipice of near destruction, and no one in the Realms has the knowledge to know what is actually happening." Wael stared at him. "Your father, Kull, kept one of the two keys that stayed in Lotte. I fear he was arrested for far more than suspicions of murder."

Kull stepped back against the train and shook his head as he tried to piece together everything Wael was saying. A brotherhood, keys, a legacy? Nothing seemed to have anything to do with the war with the Groganlands or Grift's kidnapping.

Kull stammered, trying to keep up. "Wael...what keys are you talking about?" Why had his dad never told him any of this? Did his mom know? Why was he left in the dark all these years? Why did he know absolutely nothing about this if it was all as important as Wael was implying?

Kull strained to speak over the roar of the tracks. "The only thing I can tell you is that Dad was never the sort of man to instigate a fight. He always taught me that it was important to learn to fight only to defend yourself. He wouldn't lead an assault on another Realm and kill their leader. No matter how terrible the enemy was. What Hosp claimed does not match his character. I also know that King Camden was not the sort of man to condone this kind of violence. I don't know what Dad was doing when he left me in Cotswold other than he was on patrol, but I never suspected him of conspiracy or murder."

How long had it been since his dad went on patrol? How long had it been since Cotswold exploded with the sound of missiles and fire? Two...no...three weeks ago?

Kull closed his eyes and sighed. He had been on the road for such a long time, and it seemed that his journey was only beginning. His father had left him only one thing; aching questions.

"Please...Wael. *Just tell me what I need to know.* I am tired of these guessing games. What are these keys? How is my dad involved?"

Wael's concern shifted to one of resolve as he stared back at Kull. His eyes looked like they carried a titanic burden, a burden of knowledge that could crush his soul.

"This is all the work of The Old Ones, Kull. The Serubs, the Legion. The Five. The Five Terrible Kings are mounting a return to Candor. For generations my order, *your father's order,* was established to prevent them from escaping their prisons, but someone is changing things. It is apparent now that this war is not a war between Lotte and the Groganlands. It is a war on the

Keepers." Wael stared into Kull's face. "Your father and Camden were its first casualties."

Kull could not hide the grimace of surprise, embarrassment, and revulsion he felt.

"Serubs? You mean to tell me that the Five are behind all of this? This war, my dad being captured, is all because of some old legend in your religion?" Anger swept over him. "That's crazy. If this stuff was so important, Dad would have told me about it."

Wael's gaze did not waver as he responded.

"You said the same thing about the morels, Kull." Kull's eyes fell, and Wael continued, nearly shouting over the clacking rails beneath them. "This is no fairy tale. *This is history*. History that mankind has long worked hard to forget. The Serubs are *real*, Kull, and they have powerful followers, followers who have been waiting, conspiring for a time to reveal themselves. Your father, like me, was set apart as a Keeper to prevent the Keys of Candor from falling into their hands."

Wael's words made Kull's brain rattle. *Serubs, the Keys of Candor, Keepers.* Kull shouted over the loud rattle of the hedgehog's wheels below them.

"I have one question, Wael."

"What is it, Kull?"

Kull looked out at the landscape speeding before him, his mind lost in thought. "If your order was such a secret, how did anyone know who the Keepers were? I mean, my own father told me nothing of this, but *someone must have.* Otherwise, how could they mark and kill the Keepers like they have?"

Wael's face fell and his eyes lost focus as he began to retreat back into his thoughts. He shook himself free to answer Kull.

"That, Kull, is what has haunted me this entire ride. I am afraid I know exactly who the source of information was."

Kull straightened his back and set his gaze on Wael, "Who is it then?"

Wael shook his head and dropped his gaze, "I am not willing to accuse anyone at this point. I need closure, though, and must speak with someone once we enter Elum. But I will admit my suspicions are terrifying me."

"You can tell me, Wael. Come on!"

Wael stiffened and took a deep breath before answering, "No, Kull. I am afraid I cannot. Not now."

Frustration with the whole situation boiled to the surface of Kull's skin as he groaned at Wael's secrecy. *All these secrets. Here I am stuck in the middle of this mess, and no one is willing to talk.*

Kull huffed at the monk, "Can't we just go back inside? This noise is driving me crazy and I can barely hear you."

Kull reached for the handle to re-enter the train car, but Wael whisked it away.

"We will not speak a word of this around our Rihtian brothers inside. They, of all people, remember the truth behind the Serubs and would riot if the word left your lips. I am not going to cause a panic in there. We still have time, but we need to make haste once we arrive in Elum. I think I know where your father may have fled."

"How much longer until we get there?"

Wael looked up at the desert sun, his mind calculating, "At this pace we have another day's ride before we arrive."

"What makes you so certain about the whole Serub thing? Was it something that Hosp guy said?"

"No, Kull. It was nothing he said. It is what he was wearing. His ring. It bore the serpent's signet on it. No one wears the sign of the Serubs unknowingly. That ring was enough to cause me significant worry, but it was what the Reds revealed that worried me most. The Sar, Hagan, is dead. A Keeper. Willyn Kara has been convicted of killing the Elum dictator, Filip Darian; another Keeper. Camden, the High King of Lotte, is also dead."

"But wouldn't Camden's son take on the mantle of Keeper?" Kull asked the question to help calm Wael's concern.

Wael shook his head. "That does not give me comfort, Kull…I have often felt concerns with Seam's fealty to Aleph and to the Order. He has a restless spirit, full of ambition and pain, and his father never settled on a new keeper to follow him. Even he did not trust his own son."

Kull swallowed. "That leaves only you...and Dad."

Wael nodded, "Precisely. We are in more danger than I thought, and we are running out of time." Wael looked deep into Kull's eyes, his face grim.

Kull tried to brush Wael's warning away. "Danger? Wael, if it weren't for you I would have been dead back on that truck when the morels attacked. I'd rather be with you and take my chances. How can you say that?"

Wael placed his hand on Kull's shoulder and measured his response.

"That man, Hosp, is behind these attacks. I sense he murdered Hagan and was behind the death of Camden and your father's kidnapping. Don't you see, Kull? *They are rounding us up to take the things we bear in secret*. This war is the cover they need to distract Candor from their true agenda." Wael lowered his eyes, his face set like a grim stone. "These are *Red Deaths,* Kull. To murder a Keeper is a heinous crime; a Red Death is something that Aleph himself will not forgive. It is a precursor to dark days. Terrible things are coming; the Five are amassing their strength." Wael shook his head and pinned his eyes on him. "Do not think that you are safe with me. I bear the most important piece of the Keys of Candor. I will be hunted down, and now Hosp knows where we are going."

Wael slid back the right sleeve of his tunic, revealing an ancient steel arm brace that was intricately crafted with the weaving of iron ivy vines, serpents, and sunrays. The elaborate design of metal danced in the desert sunlight, the patterns moving and shimmering across the brace, as if it were alive. Nestled inside the living weave Kull could see a small key. Next to it were open slits just large enough to fit four additional keys. Kull's heart beat fast, his breathing slowed, and his eyes filled with wonder.

'This is the last Key of Candor, Kull. This is the only key that keeps the Serubs locked in their prisons, sealing away our world's doom. If it falls into Hosp's hands we will never again see joy in our lifetime, for the world as we know it will burn with the Serubs' hate and malice for all mortal life..."

Kull's mouth dried with fear. Seeing one of the keys filled his mind with a surge of panic he was not expecting. "I don't understand. I mean, why can't we just bury this key or just melt them down?"

"I wish it was that easy, Kull, but we have all been sworn to protect the keys with our lives, and they cannot be destroyed with any technology we have today. *They were made by the Serubs,* forged in another age, and the technology that could destroy such things has been lost to us."

"Why would the Serubs even make the keys? I mean, they keep them imprisoned, don't they?"

"It was the Serubs' folly that they made these keys, for it was Aleph himself who imprisoned them using their own creations. When the Five rebelled, they quickly conquered all of Candor, but their lust was not satiated. They wanted to reclaim the thrones that they left and destroy their brother who refused to fall with them. So they made portals to the Other Side. These keys were crafted in this world to serve as a bridge into the next. Remember when I said that the Serubs ushered in realities that should have never existed in Candor?"

Kull nodded.

"These keys are a prime example of that. They form a bridge to *the other side*. The Serubs' ambition and desire was to destroy Aleph and reclaim the thrones that hold this very universe together. Their lust for power and worship was not quenched when they trampled our planet. But we must not lose hope." Wael stared into Kull's eyes and continued. "*There is a prophecy*. It has been prophesied that the Serubs would one day return so they could finally be destroyed, though I never thought it would be in my lifetime." Wael held out his wrist for Kull to inspect.

"This key, Kull, I have kept bound to me since it was last handed down by the Order to me. This, I fear, is all they need now. We need to try and find your father as soon as we arrive in Elum and ensure that he is not only safe but that he also still holds his key."

Kull's mind throbbed as he tried to piece everything together.

"Why didn't Hosp just attack us then? I mean, if that is what he was after he could have just had us arrested right then and there."

Wael reached for the door handle to re-enter the train car.

"He might yet, Kull. The machinations that move that mind are greater than our own, I fear. Mark my words, he has something planned. I can only assume that *he wants* us to go to Elum. So when we arrive we must be cautious, but we need to regroup with your father and come up with a plan. We must move quickly."

He held his hand on the door and looked back at Kull.

"Let's get back into the car. We cannot discuss this further, but we must make every effort to rest. What lies ahead of us, I cannot see, but I know that we will both need to save our strength. So rest and wait. We will discuss this further when we arrive in Elum."

Kull nodded and entered the train. He sat back down in the seat that the two had occupied and let out a long sigh. As the hours rolled by he saw the sun run its circuit in the sky and disappear beyond the horizon. The stars blinked into existence across the dark blanket of the night sky. It was clear, and it was beautiful, but to Kull, all of this seemed as distant as his mother and father. Wael was asleep and had been for hours, but Kull would not rest. Rest was impossible after learning the truth. The truth about his father. The truth about Wael. The truth about the Serubs. He kept feeling if he could take one deep breath the anxiety would subside, but nothing brought relief.

Are they really real?

The question burned in Kull's mind as he weighed out the possibility of what Wael had told him. If it was real, then the entire cosmos was in flux and he was in the middle of a war that was about to be waged. In the same hand he weighed out whether Wael was insane. Those two choices seemed to be the only rational options.

Wael is not insane. Kull knew Wael was coherent and honest. *That only means that the Serubs are...*

"Real." He whispered to himself, staring out into the deep desert darkness that covered the world outside the hedgehog's window. *How did I ever find myself here?* Kull thought to himself as he tried to close his eyes.

The desert night swept by them, and the blanket of stars continued its rotation, unaware that their existence and the powers that kept them spinning were in danger.

CHAPTER SEVENTEEN

Seam's gaze locked onto the acute gray eyes of the man approaching him. For many months they carefully calculated their moves, surgically plotting within the Realms they both influenced. Their plans had worked, each move confirmed by destiny.

It is meant to be, Seam thought to himself. *My path is clear.*

"I hope your journey was pleasant, Surrogator." This first meeting felt disjointed, awkward. It was the first time Seam met with Hosp face to face. The Surrogator of the Groganlands had an unassuming if not diminutive look to him, a slight build, and wore a simple black robe that shimmered in the hot desert wind. His robe flapped in unison with the thin waterfall of hair that clung to his forehead. He was enveloped by a legion of Grogan bodyguards, whose eyes swept over the horizon.

Hosp bowed his head, showing the respect due to a High King. "My journey was long, High King, but I came as soon as you summoned. I am glad to see our two Realms can begin the peace talks. It is long overdue." Seam's skin bristled knowing that their charade would soon bear marvelous fruit. Seam walked in tandem with the Grogans toward a tent that had been pitched on the outside of the ruined city of Zenith, the long abandoned capital of Riht. The sight of the desert metropolis was breathtaking. Even the bones of the abandoned city skyline caused the men to stand in awe. The city's broken buildings towered higher than anything ever constructed in the other Realms. They stood proud, still penetrating the heavens with boldness, refusing to be swallowed by the desert, refusing to let time forget the glory and the power of what was once the Rihtian empire.

The two autocrats stared out over the empty city sprawl in silence, the desert wind whipping around them like a hot, dry river. Bronson exited the tent and saluted the two leaders, "Welcome to Zenith, Master Hosp. King Seam, the tent is clear to enter." Hosp spoke as he waved off his bodyguards, "At ease, men. I must talk to the High King privately. You are dismissed until further notice."

The two plunged into the tent, leaving the guards to deal with the rushing desert heat. In a checked whisper Hosp spoke, "*You've brought her, yes*?" Seam's skin crawled at the sound of Hosp's voice as he mentioned the Serub. *Such unquestioning adoration.*

"I would very much like to see *her.*" An unashamed, hungry statement.

This sudden shift in Hosp's conversation grated Seam. Here was the new sovereign of the Groganlands asking to see the goddess in the glass as if she were a treat to be doled out to a child. *Fool. You have no idea what you are dealing with.* Seam pointed to the dark inner chamber of the tent.

"Of course I brought the portal. The first of the five. I would have been unwise to leave it behind. There are already others hoping for its destruction."

Hosp's eyes grew wide as he pressed past Seam toward the inner chamber. Seam reached out an arm to block Hosp's path and stepped in front of him.

"You will meet her in due time, my friend. But first, we must discuss how we will obtain the final keys. Our business is not yet complete."

Hosp pushed past Seam's blockade. "Our business *can wait,* High King. For hundreds of years my people have been *denied* our sacred practices." He stared at Seam and sneered, "Have I not done enough for you?" Shameful venom began to drip freely from Hosp's lips. "After all, didn't I set the chain of events into motion that put you in your current station as High King?"

Seam threw out a small tense smile. "I am very grateful to you, Hosp, but what we must continue to focus on…"

"NO. No." Hosp pointed a thin, crooked finger in his face. "Seam Panderean, you owe me this after all I've done for you. You at least owe me *this* opportunity."

Seam shifted and looked away from the eyes boring into him, swallowing the fire roaring in his chest. "Fine. You have done much, Hosp, to help me, but the mirror is mine. I will allow you to enter…" Hosp smiled like a starving dog. "…if you give me what I most desire."

"Only name your price, High King."

Seam's mind whirled, and he forced himself to remain calm and cordial, burying his excitement. "Your keys." Seam knew that Hosp held not only the Key of the Grogans, but also the Key of Elum. Filip Darian hadn't bothered to instruct his son of the Order's importance. It was a duty that could wait until tomorrow, washed away with the never-ending bottles of liquor that Filip loved. That tomorrow never came for Filip, and Seam had it on good authority that Elum's priceless heirloom had been given over to Hosp without a second thought from Evan upon his father's death.

Hosp scowled, his eyes drawn into daggers. "So, this is how it is then?" Seam did not break his stare, but only held out his hand.

"Fine. If this is your cost, I gladly pay it." Hosp handed over two small keys, one as red as Rhuddenhall, the other shimmering with a translucent blue-green of the ocean waves. Seam could not believe it. Hosp handed over the two keys as if they were nothing. He looked down at the objects, his heart stoked with joy.

He turned to Hosp and asked, "I take it that you know how to summon her, then?"

Hosp let out a low chuckle. "Of course. I come prepared to make an offering on behalf of my people." His hand fell down to a dagger housed on his belt.

Seam nodded, but his eyes locked on the dagger's hilt. It was the same in appearance as that of his attempted assassin. "Well, then I will leave you with her. I will wait outside the tent, but we must soon discuss the details of the remaining keys. We are running out of time."

"I understand. Thank you, High King. You are most *generous."* Hosp's voice trailed off as he let himself into the back chamber of the tent, leaving Seam alone with his thoughts.

Seam stood outside the entryway and weighed his options. *I do not trust him.* His grip tightened on the two new keys. A kinder voice came into his mind. *Let him look in the mirror. What can he do?*

Yet, he still was not convinced. *No.* Hosp could not be trusted. Even though he handed over the keys without hesitation, Seam long understood that to deal with Hosp was like taming a cobra. A skillful dance of checks and balances that, in the end, might lead to death. *Not my death.* With that one thought, Seam slipped between the layers of the inner tent and positioned himself in a dark, far corner of the inner room where he could observe Hosp's true intentions. Hidden in the darkness, he observed his cunning ally.

Despite the heat of the desert invading the outer chambers of the tent, the inner chamber was unnaturally cold. The portal sat at the back wall of the room, inviting Hosp to penetrate deeper into the shadows. Hosp took his time approaching the mirror pane, sliding his dagger from its sheath. His breathing deepened with each step. His eyes were locked on the mirror. It was the only thing separating him from his god.

He reached the portal and ran his hand down the glass, looking into the clear reflection. Even in the darkness Seam could not help but notice the grin that crept across his countenance. Hosp reached for his heart and could feel it pounding as he leaned in and placed his cheek against the shimmering pane.

"I have come, my Queen. I am here," he said. His whispered tone was so quiet he could barely hear himself, "I knew you had to be the first. I have dreamt of this day. You have my full loyalty and service. I give myself to you and your cause."

Hosp grasped the blade of his dagger in his hand and sliced his palm. Blood flowed from his open hand and dripped to the desert earth. He pressed the wound to the mirror. The mirror clouded and sizzled with violent energy. The mist of the mirror gathered into a shroud that encased the form of Abtren, hiding her pure countenance from his vision. Her form stood stoically as Hosp bowed his head, keeping his palm pressed to the glass in silence.

Her words cut through the darkness. "I know who you are, Hosp of Intryll. I know your journey. I now know your pain. Why have you awakened me?"

Hosp lifted his head and stared at the vaporous form on the

other side of the portal. He strained to see past the mirage for a glimpse of Abtren herself.

"Abtren, my Queen. I come as your humble servant. A servant of the coming Dominion. Your Dominion. I have come to free you."

The aberration slammed its fist against the glass, causing Hosp to flinch, and Abtren's voice grew stronger than a thunderstorm.

"*WORDS*. How can I trust that you are able to serve me? Your promises mean *nothing* to me."

Hosp's countenance firmed as he gazed deeper into the portal. He lifted his bleeding hand from the glass and firmed his grip on the dagger.

"I came fully expecting to prove my allegiance and my strength, my Queen. I merely wanted to ensure the portal was legitimate and that Seam was truthful in his claims. I will pour myself out to you, to the point of death, and I only ask for one thing in return. *I beg to see your face*."

His request was met with cold silence as the form stood motionless behind the vaporous cloud that shrouded her. Hosp grasped the knife and recklessly plunged it into his stomach. The dagger's bite drove deep. He drew it out, wet with blood, only to let it drink again, slicing open his arm. A waterfall of crimson poured on the ground beneath him, rushing toward the foot of the mirror where it seeped into the glass with an acidic sizzle.

Excruciating minutes passed as Hosp panted and bled in silence. Each heartbeat brought on a new surge of sacrifice, and he fought to maintain his footing. He supported himself against the mirror. The cold air of the room was replaced with a ferocious heat that radiated from the glass, causing sweat to drip from his brow as he waited, staring with a fading hope for a sign from the figure behind the fog, for something. *Anything*. The gloom of death wrapped around him, and his vision choked in the darkness. His heart continued its fatal duty, pushing out his life with each rhythmic beat. He realized that it would be over soon. He would either fade away, merging with the darkness that circled him, or his eyes would see the glory that his ancestors once knew. He grasped the mirror's edges with all his strength and braced himself for what would come next. A single pinprick of white light broke through the hazy fog that swirled in the mirror. It grew exponentially, filling the darkened tent with hot, radiant light.

The coming burst of light forced Seam to retreat from his hiding place for fear of being discovered. The thought of Hosp being alone with the mirror turned Seam's stomach, but he knew he had no choice.

Abtren's emergence was captivating, and Hosp wheezed with anticipation as she appeared through the dissipating fog. Her beauty was indescribable, and her naked, full form was exposed to Hosp as he fell in fear and devotion to his knees. Her skin glowed like lightning and her eyes looked like the deep furnaces of the sun.

Her voice thundered in Hosp's ears, yet they were filled with an unspeakable tenderness, "You have done well, Hosp. If you are strong enough to survive your sacrifice then I may yet have a use for you."

She ran her hand down the glass and pointed behind Hosp.

"Know this. You are my protector now. *No one* must come between us. Especially not the High King of Lotte." Her voice turned grim, "He is not one of *us.* Conspire and plan what you must, but you must *eliminate* him. He holds the key that binds me to this cursed prison."

Hosp crumpled to his knees as he grasped at the mirror. Hot tears mingled with his own blood.

"Of course, my Queen. He is seeking out the other keys. He believes that he is the Keeper and has dreams of restoring order back to Candor."

"And you must help him. Help him find the other Keys of Candor, for only when he holds all of them can we be released. Yes, you must help the young fool find all of the keys and release my kin. *And then you must strike him down.* My brothers and sisters have been calling out to me, for they have sensed my awakening. They are...*hungry* for justice. *For revenge.*"

Hosp whispered, his mind exploding with awe and desire.

"Direct me where I am to begin, my Queen, and it will be so!"

Abtren smiled and spoke softly. "I know where only one of my brothers is bound, faithful Hosp. Arakiel's portal is buried deep within the bone field of Zenith. He is so very close to us; I can feel him calling out to me. He alone knows where the others may lay."

"I will find where he has been kept, my Queen."

"Hosp of Intryll, you are the man of destiny. Take your rightful place and you will know more of me and the Dominion that is to come."

"You have my word. You have my life. I am yours, my Queen."

A smile slid across Abtren's face as the vapors of the mirror began to swallow her. She left with one last word.

"Very good. Your sacrifice is noted, and it has given me much strength. I will require no more blood from you this day, faithful servant. I look forward to our meeting outside this cursed portal. *Serve me well.*"

The mirror went dark and Hosp collapsed to the floor, swallowed by a pool of his own blood and sweat. He climbed to his knees and crawled for the door where he finally called out for Seam.

Seam burst through the curtain to the sight of Hosp lying prostrate on the floor with a trail of blood leading to the mirror. The air in the room had grown frigid, and Hosp's pale skin had become sickly white. This was worse than he expected.

Seam recoiled at Hosp's mangled body. "You fool! I thought you said you knew how to summon her. What were you thinking?"

Hosp grinned as he looked up at Seam and said, *"I know exactly what I am doing."*

Seam lifted the Surrogator from the ground and ran him back to the outer room of the tent. He set Hosp down in a small chair. In the light of the room, Seam could not believe the damage that Hosp rendered upon himself. It both disgusted and terrified him. He screamed out for help, his eyes unable to turn away from the deluge of crimson pouring out from his ally's body.

Bronson broke through the door and stopped in shock at the

sight of Hosp's bloodied body and the trail of blood leading to the inner chamber. He did his best to shake the realization that Hosp had nearly been killed in the mirror room. The horrific image of Abtren's face that night at the Crossroads hammered in his memories. He stammered as he fought to hold onto his sanity.

"What are you waiting on, you fool? Get help!" shouted Seam.

Bronson broke himself free of his nightmares and shouted for help.

"MEDIC!"

A medic rushed in and went to work without a word, spraying a disinfectant and wrapping thick layers of gauze tightly around the open wounds on both Hosp's palm and wrist. Blood still poured out of him, and Seam grimaced as Hosp smiled like a wild man, wild-eyed and oblivious at his own condition. Bronson slipped from the tent, knowing he had to find an escape from these dark matters. His exit was unnoticed as everyone poured over Hosp.

"Will he live?" Seam asked, full of doubt.

The medic flipped down his eyenocular visor and took a quick scan of Hosp's body. "The knife nearly got his stomach, but it looks like he's safe. It's just a puncture wound, a bad one, but it only cut through flesh."

"Good," the word came out quick, but rang hollow to Seam's ear.

The medic pulled out a vial and loaded his syringe-gun. He shouted to Hosp who writhed on the floor in a show of disturbing ecstasy. "This will be painful, Surrogator, more painful than the wound itself. Brace yourself." Hosp nodded and the medic thrust the metallic gun down into the gaping hole in Hosp's stomach. With a loud bang, he emptied its contents. Immediately Hosp's flesh began to grow over itself, and he howled out in pain. In a few minutes, a hot-white scar bubbled up over the wound, singeing his skin with new growth.

"That is only a patch, Surrogator. The skin will be soft, weak, and thin. Please take precautions not to overexert yourself, or I guarantee you it will open again." Hosp kept his eyes shut but nodded. "As another precaution, I'm calling in a transfusion for you; your scan indicated that your blood count is severely low."

"Thank you, medic," Seam whispered, wiping the sweat off his brow and glancing around the room. He leaned in close and whispered to the doctor. "It is *vital* that you keep this...this little incident off the record. The Surrogator's well-being will not be compromised to the Grogan forces here, is that understood? Please ask Bronson to report back to me as well."

The medic nodded and stammered out an affirmative response before leaving the tent. As soon as the two were alone again, Seam yanked Hosp to his feet.

"What are you trying to do?" Seam looked over his shoulder to the tent doors. "We are trying to begin the process of ending this charade, not send it into oblivion! How am I to explain a dead Surrogator of the Grogan people in the midst of peace-talks?"

Hosp chuckled and made an attempt to brush Seam away as he stumbled into a nearby chair. He looked back to the opening that led to the mirror as he lowered himself into the seat.

"Seam. I am no fool. I have dreamt of that moment since I was a boy. I knew full well what I was risking, and I know the risk you and I will both have to make to continue our plans. These are risks worth taking, and there will be *many more* in order to fulfill our destinies."

Seam paced the floor, looking back to the door, waiting on the reappearance of the medic with the transfusion needed for Hosp. He lowered his voice as he spoke.

"You know what we need. The two remaining keys. Once we have them secured we will be able to secure the remaining portals and re-establish the Dominion. We have both studied the black book. It is not a question of if, but when we gather the keys."

A smile snaked across Hosp's face as he nodded in agreement. The sound of approaching footsteps led him to lean in close to Seam's ear and whisper, "I know where to find Arakiel. She told me."

Seam's eyes grew wide in awe as Hosp sat back in the chair with a victorious smile. The medic burst into the room with two blood bags in each hand. As he set up the transfusion equipment, Seam's gaze never left Hosp's face. His smile was not that of a liar. *He's telling the truth. He knows where to find the next Serub, but there is something else. Something he's not telling me.* Despite hearing part of Hosp's secret conversation, he knew Hosp was hiding something from him. Seam fought the urge to throw the medic from the tent and strangle the secret from Hosp, but he knew that he couldn't. He needed Hosp to finalize this war.

Seam put his arm on the medic toiling over Hosp.

"Please do whatever you can to ensure his comfort. We have a very important announcement to release to the entire continent of Candor within two hours. Will he be stable enough by then?"

The medic nodded, "Not to worry, my king. I can use some stabilizers and adrenaline to make sure he is ready." He reached for a syringe and several capsules. He loaded the syringe and plunged it into Hosp's leg. Hosp winced, but his eyes were still filled with uncanny ecstasy. The medic emptied and reloaded the syringe, "Surrogator, you will feel terrible tomorrow, but as for two hours from now, you will be as good as new."

Hosp offered a congenial smile and nodded, "Thank you."

Seam excused himself from the tent and stepped out into the desert sun to think over what he just witnessed. Hosp knew something. That much was clear, but Seam had also learned a new secret. Hosp was no Grogan; he was from Intryll. The snake he long tried to tame was an imposter from Riht.

Bronson approached Seam and bowed his head. "The medic sent your summons. How can I be of assistance, High King?"

Seam smiled and motioned his head toward the tent, "Keep an eye on that one, Bronson. Be covert, but watch him. I don't trust the man."

Bronson's heart sank to the depths of his stomach as he tried to imagine some way to escape from his duty, to leave Seam behind, but he was trapped. His destiny had been tied to a mad man. He let out a sigh as he answered.

"Yes sir. As you command."

Every datalink and service screen throughout Candor flashed to life as a force feed was pushed out over all the network servers. The screen was focused on Seam and Hosp standing with Evan, Filip's son and the new leader of Elum. In addition there were several Alephian monks and Rihtians standing amongst them. Behind all of them a new flag flew in the desert air, flashing red and blue, the colors of Lotte and the Groganlands intertwined. A shield made of flames burned squarely in the center of the new banner.

Seam stepped forward and addressed the cameras, "To the citizens of Candor and all the people in all of the Realms. Today is truly a momentous day, and it is with great pleasure that I address you all here in what was once Zenith. Today is a new day for our world, for this pronouncement is not just for the denizens of the Groganlands and Lotte, but for all people who are on the continent. Too long have our nations been at war. Too long have our people, all of our people, been subject to bloodshed. We have marched for generations to the steady, never-ending drumbeat of war. This ends today, my friends, my countrymen. The most recent conflict between the Groganlands and Lotte, I am happy to announce, is now over."

Silence filled the pregnant pause between Seam's statements all over Candor. The masses braced themselves for what would come next.

"The Kingdom of Lotte and the mighty people of the Groganlands have agreed upon not just a ceasefire but also an Alliance, and this Alliance is supported and held up by our brothers in the nation of Elum, the Order of Aleph presiding in Preost, and the remnants of the once proud nation of Riht where we now stand. Our world has been groaning in pain for peace for hundreds of years. Wars, disease, and disasters have threatened to wipe us all from this planet. We have survived, but as the human race we have struggled far too long. We must stop our selfish self-destruction. This day we make a new vow. A vow that we shall not threaten our species' existence anymore. Finally, we shall stand united!"

The soldiers in Zenith burst into a roar of applause. Cameras buzzed overhead, capturing the euphoria unfolding as both Grogan and Lottian soldiers laid down their weapons and began to shake hands and embrace one another.

The broadcast feed focused back onto Hosp as he approached the wide podium set before the two men. He lifted his hands as he spoke, "To all of my fellow citizens of Candor, welcome to a new world! A world that is built upon diplomacy and honesty and a willingness to share our burdens and joys with one another! We have identified and punished those responsible for our most recent conflict. However, we ask for your help and support as there are a few conspirators still on the loose. The armies of Lotte and the Groganlands are performing an exhaustive pursuit for a trio of co-conspirators that sought to create confusion and incite aggression amidst our people." Hosp paused, as if weighing his words carefully. "Once their plot was uncovered Seam and I knew that our fighting must cease and that peace must prevail. We cannot allow terror to bind us any longer. We must be set free from our bondage of fear; our bondage of hatred and bigotry toward one another. We must band together to stop these radicals among us, these traitors that kindle the flame of hatred and distrust between our mighty nations, reigniting the fuse of war. They may have lit the fuse, but, my friends," Hosp smiled broadly, "we have snuffed out their fire before it destroyed our world."

The roar of the crowd died down. Seam stepped to the podium again and pointed to the screens flanking the stage.

"I want all eyes in Candor to look at the faces set before you. These three individuals have led an assassin's guild aimed at the destruction of peace. They sought further power and control through the weapon of fear. We have lost too much to their bloody hands. Hagan, the mighty leader of the Groganlands, was poisoned and killed by their conspiracy. Filip, the rightful ruler of Elum who has long championed for peace and diplomacy, was struck down. And I..." Seam paused as his voice cracked with emotion. "I lost my very father to their murderous hands. I want everyone to see the faces of these killers and bring them immediately to me."

The data feed changed over first to an image of Willyn as a mechanical female voice announced her name and nation of origin. "WILLYN KARA OF THE GROGANLANDS." Willyn was followed by an image of Grift Shepherd. "GRIFT SHEPHERD OF LOTTE." Finally, the screen froze on the image of Wael. "MASTERMONK WAEL OF PREOST." The image of Wael brought an audible gasp of discontent from the crowd of soldiers at Zenith, and a buzz grew before Seam readdressed the broadcast.

"I know. It is terribly unsettling to have learned that our own Mastermonk of the Alephian Order was involved in such a terrible plot. However, sources from both Lotte and the Groganlands' intelligence have linked Wael of Preost to the other two individuals shown. He cannot be trusted and is extremely dangerous. If you see him, notify enforcement officers immediately. Do not attempt to apprehend any of these individuals on your own! Notify your local authorities! Though their actions have leveled untold amounts of pain and loss on our nations, we must apprehend and investigate in a civil manner. You, dear people of Candor, are better than them, and we ask that you not resort to their level of violence."

The murmur of the crowd continued until Hosp spoke again, taking the microphone. "This news is troubling indeed, but we must not focus on the negativity of these terrorists. Their goal has been to undermine our sense of security and ensure that the old ways and the old seats of power were preserved. It has worked until this day. We must now rejoice and celebrate our new peace. Those responsible have now been marked and will soon be brought to justice, but today, my brothers, my friends, rejoice in your new freedom and peace. We have entered into a new age!"

Seam pointed to the flag that was tossing behind the stage and concluded the broadcast with his final announcement, "Before you now is Candor's new banner. The flag is a symbol of our new peace and of our new continental unity!"

The crowds roared back to life. Across all the Realms seas of people began to celebrate. Peace had finally come. Safety had finally come. Revelry had not been seen in Candor like this in hundreds of years, and fireworks soon lit up the night skies. Each magnificent explosion of sound and light spun the people up into a frenzy of freedom. For one night, they would forget their troubles because soon all would be made well. The constant projection of Grift Shepherd, Willyn Kara, and Wael would be ignored for only one night.

CHAPTER EIGHTEEN

"You."

The bullet that seared through Willyn's hand felt like a distant memory, and the bullets thumping against the boat's hull meant nothing to her. All that mattered now was that Grift Shepherd stood next to her. The man responsible for Hagan's death was within her grasp again.

She slammed a kick across his face, causing him to fall in a crumpled heap. She threw herself on top of him with her eyes glazed over in white fury. Her hands clawed over him, hunting for his throat. She gripped onto his windpipe like a vise, ignoring the searing pain that blazed from her mangled hand. Grift grunted and stared at her.

Fear. Good. Let him be afraid here at the end. She did not care about the cost. If the cost was her own life, so be it. It was more than enough to know that her brother's assassin would be crushed beneath her own hands.

Grift's face turned a hot red before it descended into purple, and his body shook underneath her, flailing on the cabin floor like a fish out of water. Despite his strength, Willyn continued to pin him down. Nothing would cause her to release him. A long, crooked smile grew on her face as she saw him diminish before her eyes. *Only a few more seconds.*

A fist fell on the back of her neck, and a jolt of pain shot up from the base of her skull. Grift kicked himself free and crawled away, heaving for breath. She saw stars and turned around to see Luken standing over them.

"We don't have time for this!" he screamed at her.

As she turned back, Grift pounced on her. She screamed as loud as she could, but soon she was locked in Grift's arms. He held her, locking her into a choke hold. She flung her head back with a snap, hammering it against Grift's face, releasing a trickle of blood from his lip.

The hit failed to loosen Grift's grip. *"Willyn. You need to calm down."* Grift's voice was ragged. He held her down and repeated himself. He would only stop to spit another mouthful of blood to the side. He was not angry. He behaved more like a parent trying to calm their child as he fought Willyn's attempts to break free.

She spat and cursed at him like a frenzied animal in a cage.

"You are losing too much blood." Grift's white eyes flashed up at Luken. "Do something. *She's losing too much blood!"*

Luken ran out of the cabin and back to the deck of the ship without comment as bullet spray continued to pummel the hull of the small boat.

Willyn looked down at her hand as stars began to cloud her vision. Her hand was a shattered mess, and blood was beginning to pool, sloshing beneath her on the cabin floor. It was much worse than she thought. She whispered at her captor as she felt the ship's engine ignite and roar with life.

"You'll pay for what you've done to me." Overcome with emotion, her voice cracked. *"To my family."*

Grift's grip held her firm, but his voice became soft with pity. It made her skin crawl. "My dear girl, I had nothing to do with Hagan's death. Hagan was my ally. Just calm down and listen to me."

The engine roared, and Willyn felt the boat rocket away from the dock. Luken could barely be heard from above deck.

"GRIFT! I need you out here! Now!"

Grift let out a sigh and spoke quickly, "Willyn, I'm going to release you, but if you come at me again, I will knock you unconscious for your own sake."

She wanted nothing more than to try and attack again but she could feel her body trembling as chills ran over her skin. She knew she lost a large amount of blood, and her attack on Grift had not helped. Her head began to feel squeezed and pressured with pain as she explored the cabin for a space to sit.

"Lie down," Grift said, "I have to get on deck, but let me help you first."

Willyn snatched her hand away from Grift as he reached for the wound.

"Don't dare touch me," Willyn said, "I will take care of myself."

Grift shook his head and pinned Willyn's arm before pointing back to her hand. "I am afraid you will need some help getting that shrapnel out. No way you can pull that out on your own."

Shrapnel? Willyn took time to inspect her shattered hand and saw the pieces of metal embedded deep within her flesh. She looked up to Grift who started gathering medical supplies from different cabinets and drawers.

"I thought I was shot," said Willyn in disbelief.

A small smile crept across Grift's face as he poured a solution over Willyn's hand. It felt as if her hand was plunged in a hornet's nest. Her jaw clenched as Grift spoke.

"It looks to me like they got just close enough with a mortar. You're lucky it was just your hand and not your head. Now lay down. This is going to hurt."

Willyn retreated from Grift, her face flickering with rage.

"I said I will take care of this myself! Leave those supplies and get up there with Luken. You won't touch me again."

Grift shook his head and dropped the scalpel. He sighed as he shouldered his rifle. Willyn braced herself in the small seat with a scalpel and a bucket of water, preparing to dig the shrapnel out.

"Have it your way, but mark my words, it would be easier if you accepted my help."

"*I don't want your help.* I don't want to have anything to do with you."

"Trust me, I wish that were true, but fate, it seems, has other plans for us. I know you don't trust me, but there is a lot that you don't know." Another volley of bullets rattled across the port side of the vessel. "If we survive this, we will have a lot to talk about."

Grift bolted up the stairs and slammed the small cabin door shut before she could respond. The sound of his rifle joined the chorus of the ship's engine as they tried to escape whatever was pursuing their vessel.

Willyn groaned as she looked down at her mangled hand again.

Maybe a little help would not have been a bad idea.

For several minutes she paused until she finally took a deep breath and began to cut away at the shrapnel. Each incision sent a blinding swell of pain up her forearm, causing her to yelp. Even though she was only cutting at her hand, her shoulders and neck ached in unison, a sickening accord of shocks that swelled with each shard of metal she managed to dig out of herself. The rocking motion of the boat compounded her unsteadiness, and she fought the urge to vomit with each new slice.

As far as she could tell, her hand had five separate pieces of metal lodged inside, but after the fourth piece was removed, her arms shook in a riot of defiance. Her hands and feet were soaked in blood in a scene that fit well with the worst of nightmares. She toiled over the wound and the final piece of alien metal, but she was losing the fight. She grasped at the scalpel to make one last pass but her vision blurred together. She knew that there was no chance of successfully proceeding. Her strength was exhausted. Her body revolted at the thought of her continuing to torture herself.

She dropped the scalpel and gave in to the rushing darkness that embraced her.

When Willyn woke, she was still in the dimly lit cabin of the boat. Consciousness came slowly, but when she finally came around, she saw her hand mended with a bulk of gauze and bandages.

"You're lucky you passed out. It made my work much easier." Grift smiled as he spoke and sipped at a cup of coffee. Both he and Luken stood over her, their faces tired, but relieved.

She started to sit up but Luken put his arm out. "Lay down, Willyn. We're safe, but you need to rest."

"Where are we? Did we get away?"

"Yes, we got away, barely, but we are safe enough now," Luken said as he flashed a quick smile. "If not for Grift's help we wouldn't have made it."

Willyn slowly sat up and fought to steady the room as it spun around her. She looked again at her bandaged hand and then again to Grift and Luken. She pointed at Luken and wished her index finger was the loaded barrel of a gun.

"You *lied* to me!" She tried to sit up but her body refused to cooperate. All that transpired had spent her energy. "You knew Grift all along and played me for a fool running me from one island to another while Hagan died."

Luken's smile faded as he stood and placed himself between Willyn and Grift.

"I never lied to you. In fact, I was hoping to find Grift as badly as you were. My intentions were different from yours, but I *never lied*."

Willyn had none of it. "What's the matter, Luken? Does it bother you that I called you out on this charade? It's very easy to play games, isn't it, when you can somehow barge into people's minds! Who exactly are you both working for anyway? Were you paid to kill him off, or do you have plans for me as well?"

Luken sat back down and shook his head as he passed a glance to Grift. "You have no idea what is going on, Willyn. You're lucky to even be alive. *This is much bigger than you think.* Why do you think we even bothered to save you?"

Grift cleared his throat and stood up between them.

"It's time that we finally cleared the air with you about your brother's involvement with our group. You are correct to suspect us as culprits in your brother's murder, based on the evidence you've seen. But now it's time to tell you the facts." Grift paused, waiting for some response to shoot out of her mouth like cannon fire. When none came, he continued, "Hagan was a Keeper. A Keeper of one of the five Keys of Candor." Again he paused, but Willyn stared at him with no response.

"Do you know anything about the keys? Have you heard of the Five Kings?"

Willyn rolled her eyes and croaked, "Of course I know about the Kings. The Great War, all of it. These are the legends of my people." Her mind began to boil over. "But I have no idea what you're talking about when it comes to five keys. Hagan never had any keys. What are you talking about?"

Grift sighed, "It's a long story, but to answer your question, the keys were created by the Serubs for one purpose. They were not content with their rule on Candor, and they set their eyes elsewhere."

Willyn did not understand. "Elsewhere?"

Luken interrupted. "Home. They wanted to go back to Aether and overthrow the only Celestial left there. Aleph."

"Aleph?" Willyn did not hide her skepticism. "So, you're saying that Hagan, along with you and some others, was tasked to keep these keys made by the gods?"

Grift nodded without a word. Willyn stared at the two men in the small boat's cabin as it bobbed in the Endless Ocean. No one moved. They simply absorbed the silence.

Willyn spoke, "So, you two actually believe these myths of the Five Kings? That the Five were *actually* Celestials before coming to Candor?"

Luken nodded his head. "Yes. The keys serve as the gateways into Aether, into Aleph's Realm. Once the portals were constructed, the Serubs entered them, only to be bound there on the outside. The Keeper of the Keys locked them in their portals."

Willyn nodded her head, but a wide smile was planted in defiance on her face. "Yes, I do know the old myths, but this bit about the keys is news to me. It's amazing that I've never heard this, after all my years of instruction in the Alephian religion." Her voice descended into a low growl, "What is more amazing, however, is that I am with two grown men who believe these stories as literal facts."

Grift ignored her and continued to forge ahead. "The fact is, Willyn, that your brother himself believed these same things, as well as his father before him, because it is your family that has served as the Keeper of the Grogan Key...until now." He reached underneath his shirt and pulled on a necklace. There, threaded on a worn leather string, was a small, onyx key, shaped like a dagger.

Willyn looked at it, suspicion flowering on her face. "This is one of the keys that our Order has sworn to protect. That your brother also swore to protect."

Luken spoke, "Yes, Hagan was a Keeper. So were High King Camden and Filip Darian. They were all Keepers, and now they are all dead. Three Red Deaths."

"Red Deaths?"

"To murder a Keeper is to commit a Red Death and a sign that the Serubs are regaining their strength. Already three keys are outside the Order's protection. Once all five are in one's possession, nothing can stop them from unlocking the Fallen. The one who holds all five becomes the Keeper of the Keys and wields power that is truly unimaginable. "

Willyn's mind felt like a barrel in a rushing river, tumbling over the knowledge drowning her. If Grift had not been her brother's murderer, then who was? Her mind arrived at the answer in a second and filled her with rage.

"*Hosp*. Aleph above, it was Hosp this whole time, wasn't it?"

Grift nodded and spoke. "It was not just Hosp, but it was also Seam Panderean, whose alliance, I must admit, eluded us all for far too long. They set the board game, engaged in a false war in order to hide their crimes, and now are planning for something much more sinister. The two must have been orchestrating these attacks for years. We are just now seeing the first fruits of their labor. It did not all come together for me until their recent datalink feed."

"What are you talking about?"

Grift played the datalink transmission that was sent throughout the entire continent. Willyn slammed her good fist into the wall and turned her back to Grift and Luken. She felt like a fool. Her face became flush as she fought back hot tears. *I failed you, Hagan. I was blind. Played like a pawn. How did I miss it?* Her hands trembled and she fought to maintain her composure, but it felt impossible to look back to the man she chased for so long. The man that Hosp convinced her was the one who poisoned her brother.

Grift's voice was soft, "Willyn. There is nothing we can do to bring Hagan back, but he fought hard to survive. We did everything we could to remedy his condition, but even medicines from Preost could not stop the poisons from spreading."

Willyn laughed as she thought back to the surveillance video she used to incriminate Grift. She wiped a tear from her cheek.

"So, you mean to tell me that your trespass onto Groganlands soil was to deliver medicine to Hagan?" The irony fell on her like an avalanche. She kept her back to Grift and waited to hear the words that would tell her what a fool she had been.

"Yes. I trespassed in hope of helping to save Hagan. He contacted me and I sought what help I could offer. Unfortunately, it was not enough. I still ask myself if I could not have possibly done more."

Willyn cleared her throat and rubbed the tears that refused to be denied. She turned back to the men. "That makes two of us, Grift. At least we have that in common."

She could not remain in the room anymore. She forced herself up from her cot and reached for the door. She took her time climbing the short staircase onto the ship's deck, leaving the two men behind. She looked out over the waves that tossed the small boat from side to side. There was no land in sight as they bobbed up and down. The vast, empty ocean only compounded her overwhelming sense of isolation.

I have no one. I have nothing. I have lost. I failed Hagan and I failed my country. Willyn leaned over the railing of the boat, imagining what it would be like to sink to the bottomless void below when a hand grasped her shoulder.

Grift pulled her back, "You are not alone, Willyn. You still have your country. Many men and women are still fighting for you and for Hagan. We have to hide for now, but we will do whatever we have to do to get you back to your people. *They need you.*"

Willyn spun on her heels and searched Grift's eyes. The man was earnest and determined. She felt like such a fool. Her face was flushed as she swept her eyes from his gaze.

Her face clouded over with sorrow when she thought about her homeland and her people. "What are you talking about? My country is following that mad man now."

Grift shook his head and pulled his datalink from his pocket.

"Not all of your country. A lot has changed since you left. When you began your search for me in Elum, Hagan succumbed to the poison. Hosp wasted no time in naming himself Surrogator. It was not long after that unrest broke out amidst many of your people calling for you to take the lead. Hosp did his best to suppress the opposition, but once you were announced as a traitor and conspirator, all hell broke loose."

Grift flashed videos of mobs firing pistols and throwing firebombs at Grogan military within the walls of Rhuddenhall. Willyn watched as men, women, and children were tazed, beaten, and dragged into the city square for execution following their attacks.

"There is a remnant of Grogans who are calling themselves the Reds who continue to press against Hosp's regime. They would have you as their leader."

A firestorm of anger and pride began to swell within her. All Willyn wanted to do was find Hosp and choke the life from him. Not only had he killed Hagan, but now he was ripping her Realm apart.

She shook her head, "I was a fool. I played right into his trap and left my brother. I left my people, and now Hosp used that opportunity to poison Hagan and the entire Groganlands with him." Her eyes fell on the distant, blue horizon. "I have to kill him."

Luken spoke up, "In time. But first we have to get to the port of Falal. I am afraid if we don't get there we will not stand much of a chance to do anything."

Willyn swung her head toward Luken. "Falal? Why are we headed to Preost?"

"Because that is the only Realm that has not bought into Seam and Hosp's charade. We need their protection, and if we are fortunate the final Keeper will also be there."

Willyn looked to Grift, searching for an answer.

"Who is the final Keeper?"

Grift spoke, "Wael. The Mastermonk. He is the longest standing Keeper, and leader of our Order. If we can make it to him safely then we can at least safeguard the two final keys. From there we can work to re-unite you with the Red resistance in the Groganlands. It is our last opportunity to stop Seam and Hosp before they gain any more power."

Luken stepped to the boat's railing and stared out over the eastern horizon. He ran to the boat's controls and punched the throttle. The boat pushed forward, offering the last reserve of energy it had. Luken picked up an assault rifle and adjusted its scope before using it to spy back over the water.

"Grift. I hate to be the bearer of bad news, but it seems our plan might have just become a little more difficult. We have several drones on the horizon."

"Aleph, help us," Grift whispered.

CHAPTER NINETEEN

The sound of screeching brakes jolted Kull from his sleep. He sat up and looked out the open door of the rail car. The outline of large buildings flashed by in the night. It was difficult to make out much detail, but the moonlight lent a faint light that revealed the massive nature of the passing structures. Wael was standing in the doorway, craning his neck to see further out into the darkness.

"I thought you said we had more time until we reached Elum," Kull said.

"This is not Elum. I know exactly where we are, and we are in danger," Wael answered. "Now, take off that robe and ask a bagger for a change of clothes. We don't have much time."

Kull's mind filled with questions, but he knew it would be no use to ask them. He tried to press for the door to see the city, but Wael placed a large hand on his chest.

"Kull, we don't have time. Listen to me and change your clothes *now.* Your life and any chance you have of finding your father depends on it."

The rail car was quickly losing momentum and the whine of the brakes stirred most of the baggers from their sleep. Men and women sat up and chattered, trying to learn why they were making an unexpected stop. A thought fell in Kull's mind. *They have found us. They are stopping the car to arrest us. To take Wael's Key!* The Preost garb would not do them any favors.

He tapped a young bagger on the shoulder who looked to be close to Kull's age, about fifteen or sixteen. The boy was big for his age, bigger than Kull, but Kull figured if anyone in the car would have clothes he could borrow that this was his best chance. The boy turned, flashing a grin full of rotten teeth.

"Can I help ya?"

Kull swallowed any sense of awkwardness as he spoke, "I need a pair of clothes. Do you have something I could wear?"

The young man's grin grew even larger and he chuckled as he looked over Kull.

"Gonna cost!" he said, "How many credits 'em got?"

Kull shook his head, "None. I have no money, but you can have my tunic. You could sell it."

He held up the long robe that flowed from Kull's body, rubbing his finger over it. Kull could see the numbers whirling in the boy's mind. "No, no. Not good 'nuff. Need credits," the boy whistled through his rotten smile.

Wael stepped behind Kull and lifted a small satchel to his ear. He shook it and looked back to the boy.

"Fifty credits enough?" Wael asked. "It is all we have."

The bagger's eyes flashed open and he laughed out loud as he turned and dug through his satchel. He pulled out a worn pair of field pants and a bright new linen shirt. He tossed them to Kull and reached for the bag of credits. Wael handed the purse to the boy and leaned in close to the young man.

Kull could hear him whisper in the bagger's language. The boy's eyes grew even wider and he flashed a knowing grin to Wael. Wael placed his hand on Kull's shoulder and looked back out the door to the buildings that were barely creeping past them now as the train continued to slow.

"What did you tell him?"

"I simply told him that you are his brother if anyone asks, and for our secret he now has one hundred credits instead of fifty."

Kull chuckled as he began changing clothes. "I never thought I would see the day that a Preost monk would bribe someone to lie. What is this world coming to?"

Wael's normally stoic expression melted into a smile for a moment and he laughed.

"Ah, Kull, I did not pay him to lie. We are all brothers, whether we realize it or not. I asked for no lies. Now hurry. *Change*. We don't have much time."

Kull switched into the bagger's clothes and again tried to peer out of the hedgehog door. He was able to make out the outline of black figures forming a perimeter around the rail car. Grogan infantry were waiting for the line of rail cars.

Speakers outside blasted a message into the car, "All passengers, prepare for boarding and inspection. Interference will not be tolerated. By order of the Groganlands' Council and the High King of Lotte, this train has been commandeered for inspection."

He looked at Wael with eyes full of confusion. *The High King and the Grogan Council? What was going on?* The car erupted with confused expressions and questions as all the baggers looked outside to find the source of the announcement.

Wael looked back to Kull and grasped his hand. Kull could feel something cold pressed into his palm.

The Key. He looked up into Wael's hollow eyes. He wore the look of a man walking toward his execution, given one brief moment to speak.

"Kull, they are coming for me and no one else. They seek the Key. It is yours now; protect it with your life. Do not let them unlock the Kings."

The next few moments blurred together in a swarm of chaos. Eight faceless soldiers wearing black riot gear galloped into the car. Wael stood up amidst the baggers, as if to greet guests to a hosted dinner party.

"Aleph's blessing on you. I know you are here for me, so here I am. Take me if you must."

The guard at the point of the pack answered Wael with a crushing blow across his face. Wael stooped, his face willfully receiving the blow. Despite the attack he arched his back straight and recovered, his head held high. His eyes lowered on the man and in an instant, Wael seemed like a titan in the presence of his enemies. He spoke loud enough for all to hear.

"I will not risk you hurting these people. Do what you must, but do not hurt the others."

The soldiers began to pummel Wael with their clubs, sending him to his knees. A waterfall of violence fell over the monk, and he lay on the railcar floor in a broken crumble as the eight soldiers tore through him. Kull's throat twisted in a knot as he held his scream. The horror of seeing Wael fall and submit to such treatment overwhelmed him, freezing him in a horrific trance. Finally the soldiers ended their thrashing and tazed him. The smell of burnt flesh filled the car, and baggers tried to flee. Wael screamed as they sent lightning through his body, but he offered no resistance to their attacks. The boy who sold Kull clothes pulled him back into the crowd as the soldiers continued to swarm over Wael. Kull and all the others were ushered out of the car, but the sight of Wael's crushed face would not leave Kull's mind.

Following the capture, everyone on the hedgehog was detained for several days. The soldiers said they had to do a full examination of the railcars' contents. Two days went by full of anxious waiting as the coalition of Grogan and Lottian forces ripped the hedgehog apart. Soon, the baggers were loaded back on the railcar and carried to a desolate patch of desert dirt. Without explanation they were all put on work detail in the desert. The soldiers claimed the work was being commissioned by the Groganlands Council and that all who assisted would be rewarded, but as baggers started to collapse and die in the desert heat, Kull soon knew that this was a lie.

The heat of the desert swallowed the mass of baggers as they dug through the dry, brittle skin of the earth. It gave way without hesitation to the hollow scrapes of shovels and picks. Dust and sand filled the air, covering the workers from the harsh rays of a cruel sun overhead. After hours of digging, they had formed a massive crater. As they dug deeper, the dark brown sand of the desert gave way to a bright, chalky, white powder.

Kull stooped down as sweat poured off his brow. Perspiration soaked through what had once been his new linen shirt. He stooped down to examine the change in earth, allowing his fingers to rub the new white substance. It was not sand, but it seemed familiar. He could not place it. He leaned on his pick and glanced around the labor camp. There were hundreds of them, all of them digging in this one spot. Grogan soldiers stood surrounding them, their pistols and rifles ready in hand for *redirection.*

"A cla on morte de vellu! A cla a morte de vellu!" One bagger called out to the other workers. The guards swarmed over to him. A single gunshot rang out and a command blasted over the loudspeakers:

"You will not stop digging under any circumstances. Loiterers will be redirected."

The baggers' chatter was cut, and Kull threw his head down, dipping his pick back into the strange white soil. His shoulders, his arms, and his back felt like hot iron. He had been in the camp for several days, and all they had done was dig at gunpoint with scarce food and little water to keep up their strength. He placed his hand on his chest. Behind the sweat-filled linen shirt hung a small key, looped on the same chain as his mother's emblem.

It is still there. You haven't lost it. Touching the secret held around his neck sent a wave of grief over him, over what happened to Wael and the uncertainty surrounding both of his parents. None of them had given up, and neither could he. He buried the grief within his mind and made himself take another swing into the earth. He focused on his pick's landing with each swing, allowing his mind to rest as his body toiled. The white chalk continued to fall away, but instead of powder, it broke off into more uniform chunks. Kull studied the clumps of white soil. The white powder was not rock, soil or sand. His eyes darted over the white ground. *What is it?*

His pick landed, and the earth gave way. Over and over again until there, in the ground, the hollow visage of a skull stared back at him, smiling gleefully at the sunshine filling its dark, hollow sockets. Kull dropped his pick and fell to his knees. He looked back at the chunks of earth, a silent scream boiling in his mind. *Bones. A mass grave. Aleph above, why are they making us do this?*

All around him, the baggers' silence erupted into screams of protest. They, too, were uncovering the awful truth. The sound of bullets rang out along with the robotic voice droning over the intercom.

"You will not stop digging under any circumstances. Loiterers will be redirected."

A Lottian guard was making a line for Kull, his hand wrapped around his pistol, ready to use it. Kull stood to his feet and began swiping at the ground again, trying to look away. The guard continued to press forward until another bagger started screaming at the site of an uncovered set of bones. The guard smacked his gun down over the bagger and then opened fire.

Kull cringed and slid deeper into the crowd, beyond the eyes of the guard that he knew had a bullet saved for him. He dug at the ground and took quick glances to try to gather any clues from the pit. Nothing stood out. There was only pain, exhaustion, and bones. The digging endured for several more hours until the loudspeaker cranked back to life.

"Shift change. Mandatory rest. All loiterers will be redirected."

The guards corralled the mass of baggers in the pit back to the rail cars. The hedgehogs had been pulled to inactive rail lines and parked with their doors wide open. Kull followed orders as he climbed into the vehicle and sat down. People collapsed all around him, panting and trying to cool themselves. The guards prowled outside of the cars like panthers.

Kull whispered to the man next to him, "Any idea what we are digging for?"

The man shook his head and refused to make eye contact with Kull. Kull turned to another bagger and asked the same question.

"No talking. Want to live," was the bagger's only response. Kull slumped against the wall and took in a deep breath. He closed his eyes and thought back to the moments before this new, confusing nightmare began. *What would Wael have him do now?*

The digging continued for another excruciating day. Ten hours of work were followed by two hours of rest. The regimen was hellish. It was as if they were digging bones out of a furnace. As soon as the sun set, the baggers began to get restless, throwing down their tools and looking mad-eyed at their captors. Surely, they thought, they would be able to sleep through the night. The hopes were in vain, as the rumble of generators echoed through the frigid night air, causing artificial light to pour in from overhead. The work would continue regardless of the conditions.

Never in Kull's life had he fought so hard to keep his wits about him. The toil of just this one day was enough to make him forget his mother and father. Enough to forget Wael. Enough to forget the Key resting under his thin, sweat-soaked shirt. This was labor meant to rob one of all hope and make them wish for death. He did not know how much more of it he could take because he knew that as soon as he would sit and rest, the vicious cycle would begin again. By the end of the first day and night Kull witnessed at least twelve shootings and twice as many people falling victim to the heat or to the cold. The guards who surrounded the pit stacked the victims' bodies into orderly piles. Kull found the sight horrifying, but after another seven hours of work, he could feel his mind unhinging. Accepting the bodies, accepting the murder, accepting his fate. To dig until he died.

Focus, he thought to himself. *You have to focus.* As his shovel ate at the bone meal soil, his mind flickered up a picture of his dad. *Dad would know what to do.* What Kull would give just to have his father by his side. He could hear his voice during their extensive trainings, "Keep *pressing on. There is always an opening, always a weakness. Use it for your advantage."*

Kull began to steal glances as the desert night gave way to the dawn. The sun crept over the horizon and drowned out the lamps that buzzed with artificial light through the night. He knew that another rotation was going to happen with daybreak, and he observed the guard shift restlessly at their post, ready to make the change. The shift change came, and Kull was pulled from the night detail to the railcar for his regimented two-hour rest. All around him the baggers fell to the ground, some passing out from exhaustion. Kull leaned his back to the metal car, balancing into a squat. He could feel his eyelids swaying with weight, but he forced himself to notice the changes taking place in the dig workflow. He started to see the different shift of baggers moving throughout the dig site.

There has got to be something I'm not seeing. There has got to be an opening. He stared out, looking for an answer. An hour passed, and Kull remained, determined not to let sleep take him under. He looked around at his fellow laborers and the guards' blatant weakness became apparent. The soldiers were well-armed, but they were outnumbered. In fact, there were hundreds of baggers to the twenty soldiers that stood guard over the work camp. Hundreds of baggers armed with shovels and picks. The thought fell over Kull, and he pondered his next move. *I have no choice,* he thought. *They will bury us here.*

Glancing through the railcar he looked to see if anyone was awake. Kull knew that there was no way he could do this on his own. He had to make allies and quick. There, in the same car, was the boy who sold him clothes. He was awake and their eyes met with sudden purpose. The bagger motioned for Kull to come near, and Kull slinked back further into the car.

"You're awake too, eh?" Kull nodded but said nothing. He had to play this very carefully.

He considered his words and spoke, "What do you think they are making us do?"

"What, besides unearthing a bone yard? I know not, man. I know not."

"There has to be some purpose to it, don't you think?" Kull's mind began to spin at the sheer insanity of it all.

"There is a purpose, ya. Must be, but I don't know." He shook his head with exhaustion. He looked at Kull and whispered, "What's your name, 'brother?' We got to get through this; I should know your name."

"I'm Kull. You?"

"Duncan. Nice to meet ya, Kull. Sorry 'bout your friend."

Kull shifted in his seat and hung his head. "Me too. Thanks for your help when it happened." Duncan's help seemed so far off, as if years transpired in the days out in the bone pit.

Duncan laughed and smiled a big toothy grin, "A lot a good a hundred credits is going to do me out here!"

An old crone shuffled from behind them and whispered, "I tell you what they are a'doing, boys."

Duncan looked behind him, and Kull shifted in his seat. "Well, what is it, gran-ma?" said Duncan, raising an eyebrow.

The old woman cackled like a dying dog and smiled wide, a hollow cave of gums. Kull could scarcely believe that this woman had survived the past few days. She cleared her throat and whispered, "Not so fast young-un. What's me hear you say someting about one hundred credits?"

"Oh, put a sock it in, gran-ma, I ain't buying no stories off ya this day." Duncan turned away, rolling his eyes. Kull blinked his eyes as questions rose in his mind but said nothing.

"Suit ya self, but you'll never know why the last thing you'll do is dig up dese here bones. If this be our last days, I just thought you'd want an answer. I'll tell you the answer fer only fifty, a real bargain since I know how much you got." Her eyes squinted in a smile, but they were sharp like daggers. Kull could not help but smile at the crone's bargaining, even now.

Duncan huffed. "I'll give you fifteen for your story, but that be it."

"Twenty and I'll tell you everything I know."

Duncan looked at Kull, who shrugged.

"Fine." Duncan fetched the money and put it into her claw of a hand.

"Such a good boy, such a wise boy," she cooed as the money changed hands. "Thank ye. Thank ye."

Duncan huffed, "Well, go on, spill it. I want to know how foolish I am."

Kull forced down another laugh and looked carefully back outside at the workers. The past few minutes made him forget where he was, in a place where it seemed wrong to laugh at all. He stared at the crone, waiting for her answer.

"Mark my words, boys; we are digging up a blood hex." Kull looked at Duncan to try to catch the reference. Thankfully, Duncan was just as confused as he was.

"What in Candor are you talking about, gran-ma?"

"Boy, twearnt you ever told about de desert witches? They work blood hexes all up and down the Rihtian desert, making themselves powerful magic from the bones of their enemies. Mark me words, dis here be a blood hex. Made to ward others off, to keep people out, especially other witches. There's something here that dese soldiers need, but they making us dig for it."

Kull spoke, "But what would a desert witch be hiding?"

The crone laughed and shook her head. "I don't know, boy, *but it is something bad*. The tales say the desert witches will hide powerful totems with a blood hex. Sometimes treasure too. But I ain't ever heard or seen of one this big. I never seen the like of so many bones. Trust me, 'dis is ill tidings. Ill tidings."

Kull whispered another question. "What will a blood hex do?"

The crone whispered in the dark. "Terrible things for those who fall upon a blood hex. Some say the fools that step into one will go blind. Others say they will die right on the spot. Still others say that the hex only works on the true enemy of the witch, so it won't hurt the innocent. Who knows what type a magic we are dealing with."

Kull looked at Duncan, who remained unimpressed. "Gran-ma, you are crazy. We are in the desert digging up bones when we should be in Elum picking peaches." He looked out at the soldiers and shook his head. "These boys aim to work us to death or kill us first, whichever is easiest. It's the baggers' lot to suffer, and this new friendship between the Grogans and Lotte, well, it don't think much of us. *It don't think much of us at all.* Must be better for them to round us up and make us die." A cloud fell over his face, vanishing when he turned back to the old woman. "The sun's rattled what's left of your brain, but you do tell a good story. I just wish it hadn't taken me so many credits to hear it."

Kull winced at Duncan's words as they stung at his heart and filled him with grief. As a boy he had not thought or cared much for the baggers. The past two days changed that, and it filled him with regret.

The hag nodded and smiled, ignoring Duncan's insult and

slipped back into her seat. "Blessings upon ye both," she whispered. "When we hit the marked bones, ye both will see the truth in my words."

A whistle blew out from the pit. The work shift would change again. Kull stood up with the other remnant of ragged diggers and cursed under his breath. He wasted whatever opportunity he had to conspire with Duncan. The crone's distracting story made him lose his focus.

Focus. You have to focus.

Soon they were all corralled together, digging, scraping, and pulling the remains of bodies that had long been entombed below. The previous shift plunged the work another ten feet or so further into the earth, and still there was nothing but ragged, dry bones. Kull's mind dissipated in the oncoming desert heat, and he realized that his dream of revolt was completely foolish. Another day of this and they would all be dead. Many could barely pick up their picks to swing, and those who couldn't or refused received a bullet in their temple. *There is no way to do this. There is no way out of this.* He glanced around at the hundreds swarming in the pit, moving the layers and layers of the dead out from the earth.

He looked and saw Duncan a few rows down from him, continuing to swing and break through the earth. Beside him was none other than 'gran-ma.' Her energy was fading fast. The shovel she held wavered in her weak arms, and she slowly pushed it into the chalky, white earth. Duncan whispered to her, and even though Kull could not tell what he was saying, he could see that he was trying to encourage her. It was painful to watch as Duncan kept trying to keep her going. Kull's heart sank into his stomach as a soldier began to flow up through the rows of laborers, like a shark approaching his prey. Kull slid through the crowd toward Duncan and the old woman. Whatever was coming, he would be there to defend these two. He forced his exhausted body each step of the way through the mob.

Don't let him get there first. She can't die. Not now. Move faster!

Kull fell in line just a few feet from Gran-ma and Duncan as the guard made his approach. The man raised his face shield and barked orders at the old woman. Duncan continued to work but kept peering from the side of his eyes. After a failed swing of her shovel, Gran-ma dropped her shovel and fell to her knees.

The soldier un-holstered his pistol. It was as if time slowed to a standstill. Kull had no time to think about what was coming next.

First he looked at the guard, whose mouth, face, and eyes twisted up in a savage collage of power and hatred. The soldier reveled in holding his pistol to the head of this poor, weak woman.

Kull's mind went through the possibilities. A flickering thought flew within him. *Let her die and live!* He could not stomach it. He knew what he would have to do. *Aleph, forgive me.* It was his last thought before he made his choice.

Kull pulled back his pick axe to take a swing at the ground, but at the last moment spun around, and his eyes met with Duncan's for a brief moment that seemed like an eternity. He powered through his swing and rocketed the pick through the soldier. Kull's mind flashed back to his father. *A time will come when you have to use whatever weapon you have.* The pick was bulky and awkward, but deadly efficient. As the pick nailed his enemy to the ground, the soldier held up his pistol and fired a single shot up into the air.

In that instant the world within the pit erupted. The baggers who saw Kull's brave act turned and poured out of their prison, pulling, clawing, and scraping their way up toward their captors, fighting for their freedom. The soldiers, slow to respond to the mad rush, began to rain a lethal spray of bullets down on the pit. Kull fell to the ground and covered his head. The soldier he struck lay beside him breathing weak, hollow breaths on the bed of bones beneath him. He stared at Kull as the light left his eyes. The soldier was Lottian, and Kull was filled with remorse as he saw the life leave him. Instincts took over and Kull swept up both the rifle and pistol of his fallen enemy and took aim at the pit's ridge. His finger flickered over the rifle's trigger five times and he watched as three more guards fell to the ground. The soldiers posted to the train abandoned their positions and flooded toward the pit.

Several baggers managed to get hold of the sentries' rifles and began trading fire with the remaining guards. The men trying to wield the guns were sporadic and firing in no particular direction, but it drew the attention of the majority of the soldiers lining the dig site.

Kull scrambled to find Duncan. He was huddled over Gran-ma, who was trembling and heaving for breath. He covered her, shielding her with his broad shoulders.

"Duncan! Is she shot?"

"No, but she needs help. She's having a panic attack, a bad one."

Kull flashed a glance back to the perimeter of the pit where the baggers were clearing out and fighting the remaining guards. There was a wide opening on the near side of the crater where he sniped the guards. As far as he could tell there was a clear line to the looming skyscrapers not far beyond the pit.

"Duncan. Have you ever fired a gun?"

Duncan screamed over the chaos, "No, man! Never!"

"Well, you will today. You keep her safe. I will see you again."

Kull handed the rifle to Duncan, who took it and tried to hide the terror in his eyes.

Kull scrambled for the ridge when he heard Duncan calling back for him. He turned back and saw him standing, shouldering the rifle.

"Why did you do this? No one fights for baggers!"

Kull's mouth opened and words flew out faster than he could comprehend. "That changes today. Aleph fights for you, and I with Him."

Kull offered a nod before running as fast as possible to the lip of the crater. As he crested the ridge he was greeted by the boot of a Grogan guard. The kick sent him rolling back down the side of the rocky bone pit. He caught himself and sprung to his feet.

The guard was bleeding from his shoulder. Kull's earlier shot had not finished him off. The soldier had a club in hand and lunged for him. Kull ducked and kicked his feet out from under him. The man thumped to the ground and lay in the mix of bones and blood. As he tried to gather his feet, Kull shoved him to the ground and tried to grab the club. As he reached for the weapon, the soldier slammed the club against Kull's face, and he fell to the earth like a load of bricks. He forced his eyes open as the soldier pulled him up by the shirt and landed a heavy punch in Kull's stomach. Kull lurched, heaving for air. The soldier then hammered Kull's head back up against the earthen wall and pulled out a long combat knife. He held it to Kull's throat.

"You think you can start a riot and live, boy? Huh? Not so big now, are you? Now I am going to gut you...slowly."

Kull threw his head into the soldier's face. The crack of Kull's head butt sent the soldier sprawling. The trooper reached out and grabbed for Kull, but only grasped the chain around his neck as he fell. The chain snapped, and the key tumbled to the ground and fell into the pit. Kull's stomach dropped, and his hand reached for the broken chain. Kull breathed a slight sigh of relief when he realized he still had his mother's pendant. The relief evaporated as his eyes swung back to the key. He had to get it back. He could not lose it.

Get the key. Get the key.

As soon as the key hit the bones, the pit quaked, and all the bones began to rattle with some unseen energy, releasing the sound of a thousand hollow drums clanking together in eerie unison. Kull shook his head, trying to fight the new vision as he questioned his sanity. The fighting ceased and the conflict stood still. Everywhere, each and every single bone joined in the chorus of percussion until it became deafening. A skull emerged from the pit, hovering off the ground right above where the key was laying. The skull floated as more bones began to join it, forming a mosaic of white death. Kull fell to his knees and tried to close his eyes to fight the onset of madness. He was certain that the heat and exhaustion had finally broken his mind's last stronghold, but even as he fought to focus, the chorus of bones continued.

The skeletal pillar stood ten feet high, and the original skull was swallowed within a flood of white faces that vibrated and undulated in unison as a hollow-socketed terror. Beneath the skulls came femurs, ribs, and vertebrae that connected and fused into one nightmarish body. As it moved it took the shape, form, and movement of a serpent. The beast roared with unnatural life, its many jaws moved in unison, speaking with a thousand voices.

"THE KEY. RELEASE ME. COME, KEEPER, AND UNLOCK MY PRISON."

Kull snatched the key from the ground and held it up to the face of the bone serpent. He could feel himself being lifted by an unexplainable energy. He took a step toward the behemoth and shouted, "I will die before I release this key. You will not be awakened as long as I live!"

The hundreds of jaws opened and closed as the serpent circled Kull, a chorus of clicking and popping bone. The thousand voices began crying out to one another, screaming with rage. Kull tightened his grasp on the key as the white-boned beast constricted in around him.

"THEN DIE AND JOIN THIS PIT OF BONES. JOIN THE ONES I HAVE SLAIN."

The beast began to spin around him, sending waves of death over him, trapping him beneath its coils. *It's going to bury me!* Kull pressed against the walls of bones, forcing himself through the sea of death. A strange instinct took over, and Kull held up both the Key and the emblem of Aleph. He screamed.

"Release me! By Aleph's name, release me!" Kull heard the words leave his mouth, but it was as if someone else was speaking through him. The bone beast let out a horrific scream and began to lose its form. Its once unified body began to disintegrate, and Kull held onto both the key and emblem with everything he had. The living nightmare rattled and collapsed to the ground with one last deafening scream, sending up a huge cloud of white dust within the pit.

Kull stood, shaking all over, as the dust cleared. The sound of the dead was replaced by the chaos and violence of the living still fighting for their lives. Kull was motionless, his mind still trying to process what he witnessed there at the bottom of the crater. He could not move. All he could do was clutch the key and emblem to his chest. In an instant a battalion of reinforcements crested the ridge, the barrels of their rifles lowered directly at him.

They called out, "You there! Lay down your arms! You are charged with inciting rebellion! Do not resist!" Surrender was the only option. Kull lifted his hands up, still holding his precious items as the soldiers swarmed over him.

CHAPTER TWENTY

The lights lining a lonely hallway flickered to life as Seam and two of his guards approached a solid iron door at the corridor's end. One of the guards popped a key into the door's lock and clicked the bolt open, squealing its rust-caked hinges. Kull was chained in the corner of the room. The thin stream of light from the open door was enough to illuminate the anger on his face. His cheek bore a deep gash and his left eye was welted in a sickening hue of purple and black. As Seam paced into the room Kull's one good eye bore into him with the look of a beaten dog ready to retaliate. The two guards squeezed into the quarters and placed themselves between them as they continued to stare holes through one another.

Kull fidgeted with the bindings around his wrists and grunted as he tugged at the wall. Seam smiled and chuckled.

"Well, now I meet Kull, the son of Grift Shepherd. You have your father's features, that's for sure. No doubt you would love to kill me, just like he would." Seam's lips uncurled in a mocking smile. "That is what you would like to do, isn't it? You Shepherds seem to revel in murder. The families of the guards you killed in the work camp will be happy to know that you will pay for your crimes. Justice will be rendered very soon."

Kull could not contain his anger. "Justice? *You come to me to talk about justice*? Where is the justice of putting women and children in work camps under gunpoint? Where is the justice for the baggers who lost their lives in the desert? You and your soldiers are monsters!"

Seam stiffened, "Monsters, now? Bold words for a murderer. The men and women watching guard over that work detail knew it was filled with dangerous criminals such as yourself and that monk. The work provided was to be paid, but proper precautions had to be taken. Our guard detail proved to be most prudent seeing that you attempted to start a mindless rebellion with those baggers. If there are truly monsters in this world it is none other than people like you and your father."

"Don't speak of my father!" Kull lunged at the king, but the bindings snapped him back to the wall. "You call me a *murderer?* After all you have done and conspire to do?"

Seam blinked. *What does this whelp know?*

Kull smiled madly, allowing the truth finally to reveal itself. "I know what you want, Seam. I know your secrets. I know what you did to your father, and I know what you seek to do." Kull looked at the guards standing next to the High King. "He wants to free the ancient Serubs for his own power. These wars, these deaths across the Realms; everything we have experienced is *his* doing." The guards shot uneasy glances at one another, but remained mute. Kull continued, "I know you conspired with..."

Seam's fist smashed against Kull's cheek and reopened the gash under his eye. Kull's head bobbed back and he opened his mouth to speak again before Seam landed another blow across his face. Kull slumped over as Seam reached and grabbed his face. The High King's eyes simmered with hatred.

"Don't you dare accuse me of warmongering! You are a fool and have no idea what you speak of. If you ever speak to me that way again, I will personally end your life."

Seam tossed Kull's head back as his eyes began to flicker back with consciousness.

Seam spoke, brushing himself off, "That monk seems to have been quite effective in brainwashing you with his religious nonsense." He drew in a deep breath and motioned for the guards. "No matter. You and your lot are precisely those who would want to keep us straddled in this dark age, where division takes root. Your petty religion shuts out our only hope for true salvation; *ourselves.* Your kind would keep us in a world of war. But your time left on Candor is short." He barked his commands to the guards, "Take him to the Spire's pinnacle. I want to make sure he witnesses Candor's bright new future before he dies for his crimes."

The guards stooped down and unlocked Kull's bindings from the wall. Each of the hulking soldiers locked a binding to their belt before standing him to his feet. Kull fought to lift his aching head and spat at Seam's feet.

"Wael was right about you."

Seam lunged and grasped Kull's neck. Slowly, he began to squeeze. As Kull coughed and sputtered Seam leaned in next to his ear and whispered.

"The Mastermonk is a fool, and his little charade with you has failed. I think you will enjoy getting to see him again. Please, when you do, be sure to tell him how you could not keep his little secret safe."

Seam released his grasp and drew out the thin chain hanging from Kull's neck. He grasped the key and held it in front of Kull's face. The corners of his mouth curled up in a sneer as his eyes slid from the key back to Kull.

"You failed, Shepherd. Just like your father. You failed."

With one quick swing he snapped the key from the chain and tucked it away in his pocket. His mother's emblem and the broken chain fell to the floor, but all Kull could do was stare at the key with agonizing rage. He jumped for it but was thrown back to the cold floor by the soldiers chained to him.

"NO! Give that back!"

A heavy hand slammed down on the back of Kull's neck, sending him face first into the cement floor. Through the fog of his swollen eye and aching head, Kull glimpsed his mother's emblem. At least he could hold onto the memory of her, even if he was destined to die at the hands of Seam. He slid his hands to steady himself and clasped the necklace before making one more lunge for Seam. The guards hurled him back to the ground and laughed at his desperate attempts.

"Take him upstairs, men. I will return shortly."

Kull was pulled back and dragged down the hallway. Seam looked back over his shoulder as Kull was taken away. All Grift Shepherd's son could do was scream for his release.

Kull's rage felt incredibly distant to the High King, whose

hands shook as he held another Key of Candor. He tried to calm himself from falling into a panic of sheer joy.

Breathe, Seam. Breathe. It is almost time. Mankind has been waiting for this moment. The hour is near. Human weakness will be broken and order and perfection will soon be within reach. Breathe. Just breathe. This is your moment.

There was only one key left. The one that eluded him the longest. The one he thought would have been the easiest to possess, even easier than the key he received from his father's unfortunate end. The one held by Grift Shepherd.

He pressed his datalink and it came to life with a crackle.

"Yes, sir?"

"Bronson, I want a report on Grift Shepherd's whereabouts immediately. Have you found any trace of him in Elum?"

"Sir, I just received word that Shepherd has...well...it appears he has freed Willyn Kara from Filip's palace. They have escaped by sea. I've called in a small fleet of cruisers for pursuit."

"Excellent, Bronson. Route them and hold them in position. I want you to send an extra detail of soldiers to reinforce the Elumite navy. I want to capture them *alive.*"

"Understood, sir."

"I also want to ensure that you take a recording team. I want all of Candor to witness this final capture. Lotte will watch me bring this traitor in myself."

There was a long pause on the other end of the datalink. "Come again, sir?"

"You heard me, Bronson. I'm going to Elum. Make sure an airlift is ready for me within the hour. I plan to land on the lead cruiser. I will deal with Grift myself."

Grift peered over the broadside of Luken's ship, squinting against the glare of the sun bouncing off the waves. He sighed and hung his head.

"The horizon is clear, Luken. No sign."

Luken shook his head. "They are coming, Grift."

Grift threw his hands down on the handrails of the vessel, squeezed them, and walked away.

Luken spoke, his voice void of emotion. "We have to make a decision. We don't have the firepower to stop an entire fleet. We don't have the speed to evade them either." He glanced down to the cabin beneath them. "Willyn is too weak to be any aid to us. What were you expecting us to do? I tried to tell you we needed to stay close to the coast."

Grift ran his hand through his shaggy, graying hair and breathed in the salty air.

"We have to outrun them, Luken. We have to try to make it to Preost. It's our only hope."

The Endless Ocean stretched out below Seam's transport, and he could make out the shape of Luken's skiff on the horizon. It was being followed by over twenty-five mammoth warships. As the plane made its descent to the lead vessel's deck, Seam reactivated his datalink and dialed in a new contact. Hosp's pale face filled the screen. His recovery was ongoing but slow, and his glossed over eyes gave evidence to his pitiful state.

"I have them, Hosp. They should be in my hands upon the hour's end."

"See that you bring them in alive, Seam." Hosp's head bobbed as he struggled to keep his head lifted.

"Of course." The sight of Hosp's pathetic physique provided Seam with a burgeoning sense of power. He labored to produce a façade of concern, "Hosp, your condition looks poor. Are you sure you are well?"

"I am fine. Contact me as soon as you have the terrorists in your hands." Hosp coughed.

"Understood. How is the conflict with the Red resistance?"

"Tumultuous, to say the least, but that thorn will soon be plucked from our side, given enough time. My forces still hold

Rhuddenhall and are pressing into the Reds' territory."

"Keep it quiet. The last thing needed is word to spread of a civil war during this time of peace."

"It is handled, Seam," spat Hosp as he broke into a fit of coughing.

"See that it is." Seam shut the datalink screen as the plane landed on the carrier's runway.

A torrent of Elum navy officers spilled out onto the deck of the warship to greet Seam. As his plane landed, Seam saw the crew line the landing zone and salute. As soon as the plane stopped Seam slid back the plane door and stepped onto the deck. An Elumite admiral bobbled over to him. He was a slim, sickly looking man with a weasel face. Seam read him in an instant. *Subservient. Manipulative.* His small, squeaky voice only sealed Seam's opinion of him.

"King Seam, we have the terrorist vessel in our sights. If it would please His Royal Highness, we can commence to firing on them immediately."

Seam snapped his head back and laughed.

"Absolutely not, Admiral. These are not mere terrorists who deserve death. They are terrorists who must be tried in the court of law. After all, how can we legitimize our continent's new peace if we do not honor even our enemies? Prepare your men to board their vessel. I want them all taken alive."

The admiral saluted the king with an awestruck stupor. "Very good, your highness."

Seam could feel the warship's rotors engage as it jettisoned toward his prize. He smiled and sealed his thoughts with a nearly silent whisper.

"I have you now, Grift."

Grift peered through a pair of binoculars to scan the ocean's choppy horizon. Grift cursed at the site of the ships growing on the horizon and called out to Luken, "How many rounds do we have?"

Luken was fumbling beneath him in the cabin of the ship, causing a racket underneath. He called back sarcastically. "Do you really want to know, Grift?"

Willyn stood by Grift's side, her arm bound in a sling. She stared at him, the man she chased all over Candor. He evaded her against impossible odds. She allowed herself to look out into the sea. The armada presented itself over the horizon and the distance between the vessels was shrinking by the minute. In front of them were the taunting tides of the Endless Ocean. The question that burned in her heart could not be silenced anymore.

She spoke, "Grift, how long will you let this go on?"

She was met only with a hot glare and cold silence. She stared at him and shook her head.

"Grift, you know we can't win this. We will be surrounded!"

His eyes burned as he stood up straight and pointed to the ships coming from the horizon. "They are planning to make a spectacle of us, Willyn."

Willyn threw her hands in the air. "So what are we supposed to do?"

"I don't know!" He stood looking over the water at the oncoming ships, his mind piecing together a plan. "Well, if it's a show that they want, let's give them a show." Grift called below deck. "Luken!"

A muffled reply from below reverberated beneath them.

"LUKEN!"

"What!?"

"Get back up to the helm. Bring the ship about. Let's force their hand. Let's see how peaceful their alliance really is. Let's have all of Candor witness this *new peace* that Seam and Hosp offer our people."

Luken climbed back up to the deck and shook his head as he chuckled.

"I did always like your style, Grift." Luken looked at Grift and Willyn. His hands flew over the ship's controls, setting the course. In one swift movement, the ship changed directions, turning to face the oncoming fleet of the Elum navy. "Our course is set. We will make our last stand below deck! Let them come down to meet us!"

The three made their way below deck and braced themselves for what was to come.

Seam stood at the bow of the lead battle cruiser and from a distance he could begin to make out the shape of Luken, Grift, and Willyn moving from the cabin to the deck and back again on their small craft. Adrenaline charged through his body, surging down his arms as he gripped the bow. The small yacht only sat out about half a league in front of them, and they were pushing forward.

Soon all the Keys of Candor would be his. He would be the Keeper of the Keys. He would command the power of the Serubs and control his destiny. He would control the world's destiny.

In a flash, Seam saw Luken's small ship's boom fly across the deck as its sails quickly emptied out of the wind and then refilled, rocketing the small vessel as it turned around. The ship's stern leaned precariously as it swung into its bold maneuver.

What are they doing? The bold decision to charge caught Seam off guard. After all, there were over twenty-five vessels in their fleet. What could possibly compel them to make such a foolish move?

"Sir." The squeaky mouse admiral appeared, awaiting instruction. "The targets are heading straight to us. I await your orders."

Seam's composure remained stone cold. "Very good, Admiral. Command your men to batter into their vessel. You and your troops will come aboard and disarm them. My detail will then personally escort me onto their ship, and I will apprehend these terrorists myself."

A flash of shock flew over his face, "But sir, are you sure..."

Seam cut him off. "You have your orders, Admiral."

The admiral's mouth hung open until delivering an affirmative,

"Yes, sir."

The yacht bounced across the water and quickly approached the cruiser.

"Now, Admiral, measure your approach accordingly. Grift is known to be quite crafty. Disable their engines and do what you can to put holes in their sail. I don't want to smash through their vessel. I do not want them dead. The people of Candor need to see the bloodied faces of those who started this whole conflict, but I don't want it to be messy, understood? Now, cut their engines."

"Yes, sir."

The admiral scurried away from Seam and began chirping commands to the gunners overhead. The metal artillery chutes groaned to life as they positioned to fire on the renegade boat challenging the king's fleet. Seam looked up to see the barrels of the large guns swing into position. The ship's deck began to vibrate softly underfoot. A high-pitched ringing sound rolled out of the cannons that began to charge, their barrels glowing a dark blue.

Gunners on large machine guns unleashed a torrent of gunfire that ripped through the small vessel's sails, tearing it into a shredded collection of rags.

A low thump blasted Seam's eardrums as six cannons fired simultaneously, sending their payloads over the waters. Four of the six EMP charges hit the waters around the yacht, sending bolts of energy flying across the water, skipping over the waves like a glowing blue sea serpent. Two of the shots registered, slamming into the boat, cascading blue arching energy from bow to stern. The yacht showed no sign of structural damage, but the rounds met their mark. The ship's pace abruptly slowed, leaving the vessel helplessly bobbing in the waters, waiting to be overtaken.

There was no movement on the deck, and the small boat sat splashing and rocking in the water like a child's toy. Twelve armed guards assembled behind Seam awaiting orders to board.

The fleet surrounded the yacht with their cannons trained on it, ready to annihilate anything or anyone that dared challenge the oncoming capture. Four small vessels carrying a dozen soldiers dropped in off the side of the lead battleship. Soldiers clad in black swarmed over the side of Luken's boat and onto its deck. They slid effortlessly across the vessel and positioned themselves around the cabin door.

"Hold. Hold." Seam cried out. "I need to board. I want to ensure they are taken alive."

The soldiers shuffled around the door as they waited for the next set of orders. One of the men in the unit broke off formation and took a vessel back to Seam's ship to allow him to board. As he climbed down into the black raft, the soldier dipped his head and addressed his leader.

"My apologies, sir, but we were under the understanding that we were to clear the boat, apprehend the suspects, and then allow your entry. We don't desire any injury to the king."

Seam rebutted, "I understand, Lieutenant, but I believe that now more than ever the people of Candor need to see their leaders are not afraid of punishing those who wish to harm them. I will allow your men to go ahead of me, but I need to be on that boat as we make the capture."

The soldier saluted and answered, "Yes, sir. We will breach, enter, and call once all clear."

Seam nodded, "Very good."

The skiff bounced against the side of Luken's yacht and Seam pulled himself aboard. The media drones hovered overhead as Seam climbed on deck, the terrorists still alive and armed on the boat with him. Seam's heart raced knowing the entire continent was about to see his bravery. After the capture of Grift and Willyn, no one would be able to question his authority. This one act would cement his standing as the true head of the new alliance.

Grift and Luken locked eyes as the sound of feet thundered above them. Grift took point with his pistol trained on the cabin door while Luken stood close behind. Willyn was lying behind her overturned cot with her rifle's sights pointed and waiting.

Grift flashed a smile in Willyn's direction, "You have a gun, but it doesn't give you license to shoot me in the back. *I'm watching you.*"

Willyn rolled her eyes and spoke, "If I wanted you dead I would have shot you by now."

Grift chuckled as he brought his eyes back to the door, "Well, it's settled then. I guess we are friends."

The three waited in silence, measuring the distance of their attackers as their footsteps surrendered their proximity to the hatch.

The cabin became a vacuum as they waited until the hush was shattered by the cabin door exploding open. The wooden hatch hurdled through the room and smashed into the cot shielding Willyn. Soldiers poured into the room with their rifles raised.

Grift wasted no time and shifted to the side ripping off a series of shots that leveled the first two intruders. The third man collapsed under a bullet from Willyn's rifle.

A grenade bounced into the room and exploded with blinding light. The flash bang forced Grift to fall back deeper within the small cabin. Luken pressed closer to the door, waiting.

"I can't see anything!" screamed Willyn.

Grift pulled beside her as he wiped at his eyes. "Don't move your rifle. Just shoot!"

Willyn's trigger finger fell and sent the rifle into a red hot fury as it spat bullets through the open hatch. Four lifeless bodies tumbled through the door, but two men managed to push in and charge for them. Luken, hiding by the portal, smashed a club against one soldier's face while catching the other's oncoming fist. He grappled with the second man while a third pushed in behind him with his rifle aimed at Luken's spine. Luken spun in an instant and threw the soldier into the opening fire of this third attacker. With his other hand, Luken hammered the club into the man's helmet, buckling him to his knees. The first soldier he had downed got back up and lunged for Luken, tackling him to the ground.

The datalink on Seam's wrist flickered to life as he stood upon Luken's vessel, waiting for the chaos below deck to cease. An electronic intercom screeched in.

"King Seam?" It was the sniveling admiral again.

"Yes, Admiral?"

"It appears that the onboarding crew is taking heavy losses. Should I intervene?"

Seam smiled coolly and responded. "Not yet, Admiral. We still have other options."

As Grift's eyes began to regain focus he ran and slammed his boot into the ribs of the soldier who had jumped on top of Luken. The man groaned and began to scream out, but Grift did not afford him the chance to finish his plea for help. One quick shot finished the man.

Just then a small metal cylinder hit the floor.

Grift's eyes flared open. "Oh no."

The canister whirled like a dervish as white hot smoke billowed into the cabin. Attackers continued to pour into the room despite Willyn's covering shots at the door. More smoking canisters were thrown in, followed by another round of flash grenades. Within seconds the cabin exploded into chaos.

The dense fog of smoke and thunderous explosions made it impossible to see anything, but Willyn caught site of two grenades rolling next to Luken. She tried to call out, but was too slow. The first grenade ripped a hole in the side of the boat while the second explosion hurdled Luken's charred body out to sea in a fiery blast. The salty ocean rushed into the vessel and mixed with the cloud of bullets, screams, fists, and blood.

Willyn kept her hand on the trigger despite it all, but the sight of Luken being ripped from them destroyed her will and strength. Just like Hagan, Luken was gone. A chill ran through her bones as she cursed the fact that everyone she ever opened up to had been snatched away from her. She cursed madly, pushing away her despair. She would not stop fighting. She would die fighting.

In Vale there was a tumultuous din of whooping and cheering as crowds ran to the nearest broadcast screen. Word had spread that the last of the traitors was about to be rounded up by none other than King Seam himself. The screens displayed an overhead view of the yacht while side bar screens showed a schematic of the ship as the commentators speculated which cabin the terrorists might try to hide in. The screen flashed between the overhead view and a view from a camera mounted on Seam's shoulder.

Ewing stepped into a cafe that had a small, public datalink flickering with the broadcast. His newfound companion, Rot, followed on his heels and lay at his feet. Nearly a dozen people clustered around the screen, clamoring for news about the capture. Ewing settled into a corner booth to observe the excitement from a distance. The banter filling the room orbited around one person, Grift Shepherd. It went back and forth as most attendants argued on how Grift was a murderer, a traitor, or whether he was innocent.

Ewing's heart dropped as he looked up at the screen and saw Grift's face enlarged on the screen alongside all the charges brought against him. The list was almost too much to bear; treason, murder in the first degree, inciting rebellion, resisting arrest, trespassing, everything down to petty theft. Ewing fidgeted with a piece of peacetime propaganda that had been left on his cafe table. His eyes scanned the smiling faces of the men and women in uniform and the bold red letters reading, "For Unity." As he turned the leaflet in his hands he muttered under his breath.

"Oh Adley, girl, I don't know why you ever signed up with these people. This is a mess and a rotten lot." He glanced down at Rot and tousled the hair on his head, "In fact, Rot, this peacetime talk smells worse than you." Rot whimpered and laid down underneath the table.

Ewing fired another glance at the screen before lighting up his pipe. He grunted, exhaled, and shifted in his seat. He flipped open his datalink and skimmed through several pages but nothing matched what he was looking for. There was not a single feed related to Kull or Wael. Despite Seam calling for Wael's capture, there was nothing showing up about him. It was as if they vanished. All he knew was Arik arrived a few days earlier with Rot and told him that the two were to meet with the Groganlands Council.

A loud explosion ripped Ewing's attention away from his search. The attack party breached the doors and thrown in flash bangs and what appeared to be some type of gas grenades. Even Seam's shoulder-mounted camera was of no use as the haze of gas obscured the view, but the sound of gunfire, screaming, and pounding feet rang out from the loudspeakers. The sound of the conflict sent the hair on the back of Rot's neck on end, and he let out a low, rumbling growl.

Soon the sight Ewing feared was before him. Grift's bloodied face was on the screen as Seam was holding him by the shoulders, yelling at him that he was being arrested for the murder of his father. The announcement brought a roar from the people on the square watching as they screamed in approval. Seam then turned to Willyn and announced that she too was to be tried for assisting in the murder of her own brother and for conspiring with Grift.

The cameras then pulled away to show the raiding party abandoning the sinking ship, dragging out Willyn and Grift, and then throwing fire bombs deep into the ship's belly, sending a gush of flames pouring out of the door. Seam appeared back in front of the cameras, his face full of gleeful pride, addressing all who gathered to watch.

"To my brothers in Lotte, Groganlands, Riht, and Elum and the covenant group of Preost. We have seized and captured the traitors. Willyn Kara of the Groganlands and Grift Shepherd of Lotte are now in our custody. They will be held captive and tried for their crimes. Just as Lotte and the Groganlands have partnered to end our war, we will partner in bringing these criminals to justice." Ewing shook his head as Seam exclaimed his pronouncements to the world. "We stand together as we fight against terrorist tyranny. We will have justice for those who attempt to bring about war through division. My friends, this is a time for unity and we will make an example of those determined to destroy our continent. I will work with the leaders of each Realm to ensure that the proper judgment is rendered to these who have sought to destroy us. This is a new day for all of Candor, and I am honored to be your king."

Seam then held up his hand and saluted the camera before signing off the broadcast, "For Unity."

CHAPTER TWENTY-ONE

"You must unlock Arakiel first, High King." A kaleidoscope of deep golds, greens, purples, and oranges danced within Abtren's eyes as she stared out from her glass prison.

"Why?" Seam could feel himself being *pulled,* drawn into the hypnotic fire that channeled out of Abtren's presence. He willed himself to force his eyes away from her so he could gather his wits and channel his own mind into order.

"It is the way it must be. Arakiel is the first, I am second. We are essential in unlocking the others. You must have faith in us." She blinked and laid her hand on the back panel of the mirror, the form of her body pressed as close to the glass as possible. All the beauty of the world seemed to pour out of her. *"You must have faith in me."*

Waves of energy swept through Seam. A furnace of heat and desire washed over him. It took everything in him to squelch it, to bury it, and destroy it.

"The only faith I have, Abtren, is in myself and the destiny I have been called to fulfill." Seam let out a low sigh, briefly allowing his eyes to fall on her again. "But I will do as you say." He pulled up his sleeve to reveal an intricately sculpted iron bracer. Snakes and ivy were threaded over it, only broken by sunbeams. "I am the Keeper of the Keys now, Abtren. I am your rightful Lord and Master, and I will lead your kin. Your allegiance is to me and me alone."

Abtren bowed her head, but said nothing.

Seam ushered an order through his datalink.

"Bring me Arakiel's mirror."

Soldiers wheeled in the pane of glass, recently unearthed from the dry desert outside Zenith. Seam looked at it, his reflection off the glass still dirty with fresh earth, his mind filling with a fever of maddening thoughts.

"Bring in the sacrifices." He looked at Abtren and smiled. "It will soon be time to feed Arakiel."

The ancient streets of Zenith had been revived. The corpse of the former city had found new life as trainloads of soldiers, citizens, and servants arrived day by day. Kull's earlier revolt in the King's Pit had been quieted and forgotten. The riot was squelched, and those who opposed the work detail were quickly addressed and buried in a mass grave. A quiet and hushed determination pushed back into the city. Free men and women from all of Candor flowed into Zenith, happily toiling for its reclamation. The Groganlands and Lottian alliance's new nexus would be here, and after hundreds of years of abandonment, life once again filled the alleyways, courtyards, and plazas of the once-forgotten metropolis. Abandoned wells were reclaimed, and water flowed through the city's aqueducts. Black and gold decor adorned the signs and screens erected throughout the city directing new settlers and laborers throughout. There was little silence. Excitement filled the desert with hope for a new peace, a peace that called for all the citizens of Candor to take up the honor of rebuilding the city. Only the most skilled laborers and soldiers had been hired through a massive public selection process, broadcasted via datalink, while baggers were piped in by rail line to fill in the roles less desirable.

With each passing day, Zenith was being resurrected for all to see. The former bones of skyscrapers began to shine once again in the desert sun, pillars that served as symbols of the continent's growing power and privilege. The city's central building, known as the Spire, was the High King's primary focus. The king had begun work before the announcement of peace, making way to a new order and coalition between the Realms, as it would serve as the perfect backdrop for his announcement. In that time, work crews managed to restore the majority of the tower's outer windows and support beams. Soon, the monolith of glass and mirror twisted into the desert sun and gleamed with a brilliance that was matched only by the excitement of the people working tirelessly below.

Kull's eyes flickered open. His head pounded with a thumping wave of pain that swelled from ear to ear. He tried to lift his head to take in his surroundings. As his blurred vision came together he felt his hands locked in place. He was shackled in the center of a large round room. Troughs ran from where he was chained to five different platforms; two of which held long, tall mirrors.

Kull was bound too tightly to move his head, and his swollen eye cut his peripheral vision, but he could feel that he was not alone. Someone else was bound in this place with him. He could not see them, but he could feel their presence and hear them breathing, heaving, fighting for air. Kull's heart quickened its pace as he whispered.

"Wael?"

There was no response, only heavy breathing and a stirring of the chains.

"Wael, is that you?"

Kull's second question was followed by more groans and a stirring, but no coherent answer. A loud voice shot out from the back of the room.

"Shut up, worm! If you so as much say one more word, I will personally wipe you off this floor."

The sound of heavy boots fell against the metal floor and a burly guard came into Kull's line of sight. He unsheathed a baton, lifting it toward Kull's chin.

"Your face could bloody up this here club very nicely. Now shut your mouth or I will shut it for you. I had fun convincing your friend here to keep his mouth shut." He glared down at him; his face was a foul mixture of pride and sick pleasure.

Kull dipped his head, "Yes, sir."

The guard spun around with a wide smirk inching across his plump face, "That's what I thought."

Kull's whole body ached from the labor and from the beatings he endured over the past few days. He forced himself to stand, the bindings around his arm and neck tightening with his movements. He passed the time watching the shadows shift on the floor as the sun paced across the sky. The view from the panoramic window was breathtaking. Whatever building he was in, it was surely the tallest on the continent. It was as if all of Candor gathered under this one spot to be evaluated and observed, bowing before the tower. To the north he could barely see the Asban Mountain with its clear blue river flowing out from Lotte. He knew Vale was there, and below that, Cotswold. Kull took in a deep breath as he thought of his mother and the fact that he failed to bring his father back to her. Now he would most likely die, leaving his mother sick and alone and his father still missing. It felt like a lifetime passed since he had been captured by the Grogans. The pain of it all fell on him like lead weight, and Kull pushed his eyes away from the distant horizon that he knew held Cotswold. To the west he could see the desert borderlands of Riht and the Dagger Mountains of the Groganlands. Rhuddenhall, despite its vastness, seemed like a miniscule dot from this vantage point, a blot of blood on a dry brown canvas.

Where in the world am I?

He thought over what he and Wael discussed during their time on the hedgehog. He had only heard a few stories about the Serubs, the Kings, all of which he dismissed, if not mocked, growing up in Cotswold. But there was a tale that Ewing told that he could never, ever forget. A tale that now revealed a horrible truth.

He could still hear Ewing's low, droning voice by the fireplace in his old shop.

"You've heard tales of the Five, haven't you lad?"

"Oh come on, Ewing. Not another Serub tale."

The fire crackled and popped, the sparks filling Ewing's dark, old eyes with amber. "So you don't believe in the Serubs, do ye? That's what many people used to think, until they died by the Serubs' hands."

Kull had rolled his eyes and clicked his tongue.

"Do you know how the Serubs stayed alive, Kull?"

"What do you mean?"

"So you've never considered how the Serubs remained on Candor? What sustained them on our plane of existence?"

"Can't say that I have...but I'll bite. How?" Kull flashed a smile to prove to Ewing his bravery.

"Human blood." Ewing stared deep into Kull's eyes. There was no smile on his face, and his stare was so intense that it made Kull's gaze retreat into the fire.

"You see, Kull, the Serubs cannot stay in their physical form on Candor. They weren't made for this world. So when they left the Aether and made their dominion here they had to find a way to sustain them. The only way to stay in their physical form was through sacrifice."

"Sacrifice?"

"Aye. Sacrifice."

"What do you mean?"

"I mean precisely what you think I mean. Legions of folks, Grogan, Lottian, Rihtian, and Elumite were slaughtered to keep the Five Kings alive. To keep them on this plane of reality."

Kull had sat in silence. He went to bed that night deciding it didn't make sense to believe in such nonsense. He sighed as he realized that Ewing was trying to prepare him all along. For the key he would one day inherit. Despite the fact that his father never mentioned the keys to him, Ewing was trying to drop breadcrumbs to bring Kull to the truth. Those were the early warning signs, the ones he failed to give much attention. The platforms, the troughs. Kull could add it all up. *Sacrifice.*

"I did not come this far to die," he whispered to himself. Briefly, hope flared up within him like a single match light. It burned brightly for a time, but as the sun set in the horizon, it was swallowed in a sea of darkness. Kull hung his head, allowing it to go limp against the chains that held him in place.

Death, it seemed, would be his only escape.

Seam sat in silence in the helicopter that was taking him and his final trophy back to Zenith. He twisted the final Key of Candor between his fingers. After months of frustration, the dagger-key of Riht was finally his. Grift Shepherd had done an admirable job of keeping it from him. Seam chuckled when he thought of a punishment worthy of his adversary. His eyes flitted across his prize. The Key's edges were razor-sharp, crafted from shiny black obsidian. Out of all of the keys, this was his favorite.

He unbuckled his restraints and slipped to the pilot's chamber.

"Captain. How much longer?"

"We will be hitting the tarmac in less than half an hour. From there we have set up a faster air transport to Zenith. You should touch down on target no later than midday."

"Very good. Make sure that there are no delays in transfer. Ah, and captain, any word on the captives' transport?"

"Yes, sir. They were loaded only a half hour behind our departure. They should be landing an hour or less after we do."

Seam smiled and patted the pilot on the shoulder. "Thank you, captain. Please make sure that they use the utmost caution. We are transporting some very dangerous individuals."

"Yes, sir. I will link with them now to check."

Seam slinked back into his seat and slid back his sleeve to examine his bracer. His fingers trembled with anticipation as he slid the dagger Key into the final, empty slot. The key dutifully clicked into place, just like its brethren, and completed the collection that had been separated for so very long.

Unsure if it was only adrenaline or something supernatural, Seam could feel a raw energy coursing through him. His muscles tightened and his body tensed. He felt powerful. Imagination or not, Seam knew exactly the power he had unlocked, his pulse quickened with the thoughts of a destiny that were now his.

The thumping sound of the helicopter's motor was comforting. It had a similar rumble to that of a rook, and it made Willyn feel at home. Despite her shattered hand and shackled arms, she allowed herself to disappear within the droning hum of machinery. Either she was in shock or her body was simply exhausted of sending tendrils of pain to her brain, but Willyn's hand had long stopped hurting, and she was able to plan her next moves. The important thing was she could think.

The cabin she was in was dark, but she could make out the slouched figure in front of her. Grift. The attacking party had been so much harder on him. Maybe they felt bad attacking her because she was female. *Fools,* she thought. Grift hadn't moved since they pulled the two out from Luken's boat, and this fact alone was worrying her.

As her eyes examined the broken figure of Grift, her thoughts trailed back to Luken. A choking pain swept over her at the thought of the grenade exploding and ripping through him. *He is dead, Gods above.* The thought of Luken burned alive and sinking into the Endless Ocean flashed in her mind, and she fought back the emotions that came over her in the dark. He had been a most unexpected ally. *He could have been something more.* It felt wrong to think it, but it was true. And now he was gone. *Dead.* Willyn saw what happened. As much as she wanted to hold onto some foolish shred of hope, no one could have survived that.

Rest now, dear friend.

She pushed away the excruciating image of Luken's lifeless body drifting in the ocean waves and forced her mind back into the present. Her only restraint was a basic hand lock that was tethered to the helicopter's floor. She let out a small laugh and glanced around the dark cabin. It was empty other than Grift, which suited her perfectly. It was another foolish mistake by her captors.

She dislocated her thumb and slid her good hand out from one of the shackles. She was free, as easily as she had been trained in the Grogan military school. She was never more grateful to have had someone break both of her thumbs as a young girl than she was in that moment. She slid her hand back into the hand lock, content that at least one thing was working in her favor. No need to waste that advantage now. When the time was right she could free herself again within seconds.

She slid her foot out and kicked Grift. He lay motionless on the floor in a heap. As she kicked him, he raised a single eye to her, and with a low, defeated voice grumbled.

"What?"

"I can get out of these bindings. We have to escape." It was not a suggestion.

Grift let out a series of horrible coughs. He spat blood on the floor. His voice could just be heard over the engines of the helicopter.

"There is no escaping now, Willyn. Seam holds all the Keys of Candor." Grift closed his eyes, revealing their black and bruised landscape. "Our only hope is to remain with this party, wherever they are going, and wait for one last attack. Save our strength."

"How can you be sure we will be in the High King's detail?" Willyn asked with an earnest voice.

"Trust me, if we are the prisoners of Seam Pandarean, we will have to be publically humiliated, judged, and executed in his presence. His ego will stand for nothing less. His pride will not allow another option." A dark determination fell on Grift's face. "I know my enemy, and I know him well. It will be our last stand." His eyes locked with Willyn's, his voice filling with regret. "I wish we had not been enemies for so long, but I'm glad Aleph saw to it to reveal the truth to both of us."

Willyn's mind conjured up the journey she had faced. The death she caused and the death she had seen. Again, Luken's body floated in the Endless Ocean of her mind. "Why do you bring religion into this, Grift? If there ever was a god who worked wonders on Candor, he has lost interest in us long ago. Try telling Luken that Aleph is watching over us."

Grift nodded, but weighed his words. "I agree. It certainly feels like that is true." He let out another string of violent hacks and wheezes. "But right now, Aleph is my only hope against such darkness. The evil coming is not like that of war, famine, or corruption. It is something different entirely. The Serubs will butcher our world like a calf set for slaughter, and all its inhabitants with it." His bloodshot eyes pierced through the darkness, locking on hers. "That is, unless Aleph intervenes."

Willyn said nothing, her lips remained pursed. She was no theologian, nor was she a devout believer in anything religious.

"Well then, if what you say is true, then I guess we have no choice but to wait."

Grift nodded. "Wait and hope. We must make our stand. You will know when it is time."

Willyn nodded.

The rest of the journey was spent in silence.

Kull watched as shadows slid across the floor. They grew longer with each passing hour and extended like long, black fingers from the two mirrors that stood across the metal floor. *A sacrifice.* The realization still made his throat dry and his mind cloud with fear.

The room's silence was finally disturbed by the sound of the door sliding open. The guards shuffled, and Kull could overhear them questioning the new entrant.

"State name, assignment, and clearance level."

The short, bold answer stabbed a saber of shock through Kull.

"Adley Raynor of Lotte. Royal medic. Level silver seven."

Aleph above. Adley? Here?! Kull's fears of the Serubs and of Seam vanished like fog in dawn's light. He nearly screamed with relief to hear Adley's voice and had to will himself not to call out to her.

"Afraid this area is restricted. Come back when you have the right credentials," the guard snapped. This lot was smug, enjoying all the authority bestowed on them in protecting the King's precious Spire.

A moment of silence passed before a new voice cut in, "You will allow her to advance, and you will stand down. That is an order. She is here on command of the High King."

The guard stammered, "Commander Donahue. My apologies. But no one said anything about her coming."

Adley fired back, "Your business, I would assume, is to guard, not to know everyone's itinerary. Now, I have a cart of meds for these prisoners. I was instructed to ensure their vitals held until the King returned. You can scan if you want, but don't touch anything. I have direct orders. Thank you, Bronson, for making sure I was cleared. I will hurry."

The man's voice was short, "Be quick. The King wants no time wasted. Report back to me when you are finished so I can report. I will be tending to the convoys."

Kull could hear shuffling feet and a few grumbles as the guards examined the contents of Adley's cart. Her footsteps clicked against the cold metal floor. The steps stopped, and Kull strained his neck to try and catch a glimpse. *She's checking on Wael.*

"Gods! How long has this man been like this?" Her voice was laced with horror.

The guard shrugged his shoulders. "Dunno. Since we brought him in."

Kull heard Adley's voice raise with panic. "That does not answer my question! I asked how long?"

Kull's heart sunk to his stomach. *What did they do to Wael?*

"Pipe down," grunted the brute. "Eh, it's been about five hours." The guard's voice fell into an awkward excuse

"Shouldn't matter. He is still alive and where the King wants him."

Adley stamped over near the guards. Kull could see her in his mind's eye, her eyes blazing with contempt. "Of course it matters! These men are to *be alive* when the High King arrives. This one is on the edge of death. *They are no good dead!"*

Kull tried to process what he just heard. This was a major disconnect from what he expected. *What did she say? Is she somehow a part of this? How could she speak about us like this?*

Kull could hear Adley pulling supplies from the cart. She addressed the guards again and the anger had not receded from her voice, "I will be giving them a few shots to ensure their vitals stabilize. I hope for your sakes that it is enough to keep them alive until it is time for them to die."

"Do what you have to, medic. We're not worried." The other

guard chuckled in agreement.

Kull could hear Adley whisper, "*You should be.*"

Adley labored over Wael for several minutes and afterwards Kull's heart jumped at the weak voice that simply told her, "Thank you." The voice was thin and strained, but the voice was undeniably Wael's. Just knowing he was still alive caused a glimmer of hope to pulse through Kull's veins, but the hope was tempered by the thought of his old friend supporting Seam's insanity.

A thousand thoughts ricocheted in Kull's mind. How could Adley, of all people, follow and join Seam's order? What had happened to her?

After several minutes she was standing over him. Kull dared to look up at her face. Her long brown hair was pulled back, and she wore a black and gold uniform. Kull flashed a broken smile, but Adley showed no signs of recognition. No signs of friendship. It made Kull sick to his stomach, and he wanted to look away from her, his heart filled with shame. Shame for himself and for her. Something shifted between them, and he wondered if it could ever be repaired. Kull felt guilt as he wondered if he and Ewing's lies had partially driven her to follow Seam's leadership. Her face was still vacant as she filled a large syringe and held it in her hand.

She stepped close to him and looked him over from head to toe. Kull winced as she touched him, taking his pulse at his neck. *Say something,* he thought to himself. *You must say something.* Tears welled in his eyes as she reached down and drove the shot into his neck. He yelped as she pushed the plunger down, the burning liquid rushing under his skin. His neck locked up, and it felt as if his entire body would go into convulsions. He could feel the injection explode down his neck and fall deep into his shoulders.

"*Argh*. What are you doing?"

Kull shuddered under the pain. With his one good eye, he looked at her. Adley slapped him across the face and injected another shot into his shoulder.

"Shut your mouth. I don't answer to you," she said.

The guards chuckled and talked beneath their breath to one

another as she reached for his arm to check his pulse. As her hand fell on his wrist he felt her slip something into his palm. She then turned back to the cart and picked up an ophthalmoscope. She peeled open Kull's swollen eye and peered in. As he growled in pain she whispered to him.

"Get out. Back of the Spire. A transport is waiting." Kull looked into her eyes, which softened with concern.

Kull smiled and whispered back, "Told you I wouldn't get myself killed."

"Fine job you're doing of that."

She stepped away from Kull to address the guards, "Well, this is all I can do for these two. I hope for your sakes that the King is not upset with their pitiful state when he is ready for them."

As quickly as she entered, Adley exited the room and left Kull behind. The pain searing down his neck quickly faded and gave way to comfort and a renewed strength. He could feel his body being rejuvenated by whatever torturous concoction Adley injected into him. His fingers fumbled around the object she gave him. *A lock pick.* The serum continued to work within him, and he felt his hands steady to the point that he was able to begin working at the bindings.

A silent prayer bloomed in Kull's mind as his hands struggled with the lock. He had never unlocked anything without a key in his life, and here he was in a place where everything depended on the next few moments.

Aleph above. Please, help me.

Kull threaded the pick into the open lock. *I haven't asked you for much, but I need you now. I've needed you this whole time.*

He held the pick with his thumbs, and bit on the small metal wire, plunging it deeper into the lock. He could feel it pressing against the springing pins. Fear began to set in. *Even if I get my bindings unlocked, what will I do? What can I do?*

He closed his eyes and forced himself to breath. *All of this is just so hopeless. I...I don't know what to do.*

Suddenly the door opened behind him. He let out one last sigh and pressed in on the pick as one last prayer left his lips.

Click.

The bindings around his wrists popped free. A patrol of many footsteps approached outside the room, and Kull felt like his heart might beat a hole in his chest. There was hope. He was nearly free. His mind filled with thoughts of what to do next, knowing his hands were unbound. He could feel the guards shuffling in the room, and could feel their tension and silence. *The King is coming.* Kull knew that whatever fate awaited him it came alongside Seam Pandarean. His chest tightened as he fought to keep his composure, until he thought back to one of his many sparring lessons with his father.

"Don't always take the first shot. Wait for the right opening. A hasty choice may very well be your last."

Wait for the right opening. Patience was his answer. Kull knew that his only opportunity was to wait for the right opening to present itself.

"Long live the King!" The guards chanted.

Seam's voice rolled out like a victorious banner, "At ease, men. How are the prisoners faring?"

"Still alive. We await your orders, sir."

Kull took a deep breath, his hands trembling. He waited and listened, trying to get a sense of who entered into the room, how many he would have to deal with. Kull had been thankful to have his back to the room as he picked the lock, but now everything was a guessing game as he tried to determine how many guards he might have to face.

Seam spoke with an elated voice, "I have brought the remaining fugitives with me. They will stand on trial for the crimes they have committed in Candor. Bind them to their places. Now!"

Kull heard the shuffling of chains being moved. To his right, he caught a glimpse of the girl who attacked Cotswold, the red-haired warrior who captured his father. The guards forced her to her knees and locked her hands to the floor. She looked over at him, but showed no sign of acknowledgement. She seemed almost amused, and it was clear her mind was occupied.

Then Kull looked to his left as another prisoner was locked to the floor. His mind froze when he registered the face. It was his father. In an instant, Kull's whole body was shaking with a storm of emotions. Tears stung his eyes as he saw him, broken and bound.

"Dad." Kull could not contain himself anymore.

Grift looked up. Shock and fear ignited over his face, as he stammered. "Kull...I…I, I didn't know...I."

Kull tried to reassure himself and provide some sliver of hope, regardless of how hopeless it really was. "I'm here to get you home. Mom is waiting for us."

"SILENCE!" The guard sent a steel-toed boot into Grift's gut. Grift's eyes never left his son's.

Kull whispered over to him "It's okay, Dad. It's okay." A smile flashed on Kull's face, despite it all. Grift smiled too, remaining silent. They were finally together. That fact alone made things better, no matter what was waiting them.

Silence passed for a moment as Kull heard slow footsteps approach him.

"Touching, really, to see this reunion." Kull looked up and was face to face with the High King of Lotte once again. Seam Panderean looked down at him as one might look at a worm or a dead animal. He reached down and patted Kull's cheek before letting out a sigh and turning to the mirror facing them.

"Ah." He looked over at Grift. "So nice to have both father *and* son."

Grift's eyes filled with fire, but he remained silent as Seam turned back to Kull.

"Your family has been quite a thorn in my side. Destiny, however, cannot be stalled." He paced toward one of the tall mirrors that stood near them. He ran his hand down the glass, his deep brown eyes turning back, surveying all of his captured prisoners. He screamed at them, "I plan to make you ***all*** into an example of those who choose to voice their ***opposition***! Candor and its newfound unity will not tolerate sedition!" He looked at Kull and then to Grift. "Grift, I am going to enjoy seeing your son gutted."

Grift raised his face toward the King, his yell echoing through the chamber, "LONG LIVE KING CAMDEN!"

The entire room went completely silent.

Grift stared at the young royal, "My son is more of a man than you have ever been, you worm." Kull stared at his father, his heart overflowing with awe, fear, and pride. "He is a warrior and a man of great valiance. He has, to the end, remained loyal to his King and to his family. *I am so very proud of him.*" Grift's battered face looked on Kull for a moment, his eyes filling with tears. He shot back at Seam, his voice filling with deep disdain. "I wonder, *High King,* what Camden would say about you?"

Seam's face went pale.

Grift did not relent, "Better yet, Seam, what would dear Aleigha think if she knew that it was *you* who murdered her husband? *All because of your lust for his throne.*"

Seam flushed with rage. "SILENCE!" Seam turned to the guards behind Kull. "Put the Surrogator on the screen. These trials will commence *now.* As for the rest of the security detail, stand down. I will call for you once you are needed." Seam stared over at Grift, daggers shooting from his eyes.

A long, panoramic window filled with the large, pale face of the rat-like man that Kull met with in the Groganlands. The red-haired girl threw herself against the weight of her chains and screamed like a wild animal.

"HOSP!"

A broken, digitized voice filled the room. "Ah, High King Seam, it looks as if you have secured everyone that we need."

Seam spoke, "It is time to conduct the trials, Surrogator. Where should we begin?"

Kull kept his mouth shut but allowed a torrent of curses to flow through his mind against his enemies. *Wait for the right opening.* Seam turned and faced Kull and then looked at Grift. Everything on his face made his intentions clear.

"My dear, Hosp, let's start with the boy. Grift Shepherd's son."

Kull's stare softened as he looked over at his father. Terror flooded Grift's face.

Kull did the only thing he could think of doing. "Dad," he whispered, "it's okay, Dad."

"It is time to pronounce our judgment over you, Kull Shepherd of Lotte." Seam tapped into the datalink on his wrist and read off the list of charges for Kull.

"Kull Shepherd, you are hereby found guilty for inciting sedition, revolt, and terrorism. Your actions and conspiracy led to a massacre in a bagger work camp, costing many civilian police their lives, not to mention that of the baggers who were employed there."

Willyn could not stand it anymore. She fired out, "This isn't a trial! Where is his chance for a defense?!"

Seam turned to Willyn. "Silence! Your crimes will be read for you in time, Willyn Kara."

Rage overflowed from her mouth, *"Oh, please, don't hesitate.* Tell me these crimes I have committed against Candor and this new peaceful unity. I want to hear them come from your divine mouth, *most glorious High King."*

"Fine," Seam turned to face Willyn. "It will be as you wish."

Tapping his datalink, Seam glanced up at the large projection of Hosp. "For the murder of Sar Hagan and for the insurrection of the Red militia, this court finds you, Willyn Kara, guilty of high treason."

Willyn threw herself against her bindings. "I did not KILL my brother!"

"For these crimes, Willyn Kara, and for so many innocents whose blood is on your hands, you are hereby sentenced to death. I believe the Surrogator supports this sentencing?"

Hosp's eyes grew wide as he sneered into the datalink screen, "I could not agree more, King Seam. Her crimes have ravaged our once proud Realm, and her betrayal of her own brother is unimaginable and unforgivable."

The two guards flanked Willyn. Seam pulled a long, black sword from beneath his robes. Kull knew that it was time. *This was it. This was his moment.* Was it adrenaline, or maybe Adley's drugs? It didn't matter as his mind locked into a new state of clarity. *This is my chance. I have to move now.*

Kull threw his arm bindings down and snapped the pick into the lock around his neck. The second lock was much easier to navigate than the first. He offered up one last prayer as he felt the springs dance beneath the pick, and the bindings sprung free from his throat. *Thank you, Aleph.*

He scanned the room. First he spun around, and his fears were confirmed. Wael managed to lift himself to his knees but was still trembling and weak. Kull knew he did not have time to free him, and even if he did, Wael would not be able to fight.

This is it. Kull stood, ready to attack Seam from behind. The soldiers who saw him first pointed and yelled. Seam began to turn around, when suddenly the world began to slow. In Kull's mind it was as if the entire world was stopping to a standstill, locking in stasis. Kull looked at Seam, the guards, Willyn, his father, and Wael. They were all frozen. Kull carefully stepped around the room. *How is this happening?* He stared at each face in the room. They all stood as still as statues.

"What are you doing, child?"

The mirror. Kull's mind exploded with the reality. *They are kept in the mirrors.* He turned to face the pane of glass that carried the voice. It shimmered like the surface of water, and a face appeared, a radiant face that was intoxicatingly beautiful. The woman's eyes glowed with the colors of swirling starlight, as cold as comets.

Kull's mind felt like a rope had noosed around his sanity, and it was being stretched to its limits as the woman spoke to him.

Kull slammed his eyelids shut and took a deep breath. With his eyes still closed, he called out to her.

"I know what you are, and I will not allow him to free you."

"You are sadly mistaken, for we are destined to be free. The keys have all been collected. This is the time for our unbinding." Kull opened his eyes as the woman's face crept into a sinister smile, "And I must say, thank you for delivering the Key of Preost to us. Now, return to your place at the altar."

From the corner of the room, behind the second mirror Kull could sense movement. Amid everything else frozen in place, something moved *outside* the mirror, a shadowy figure shifting against the wall. In a flash he ran toward it, but nothing was there. When he turned back he saw the mirror filled with the woman's face. She smiled and opened her mouth. From it, hundreds of snakes began pouring out, crawling toward him and filling the room. It was as if the whole floor had become alive with nightmares. As his mind strove in vain to make sense of this, he saw that within this living sea were not just snakes, but worms, maggots, flies, and centipedes. A full menagerie of darkness and death was sweeping over the room, racing toward him. It became impossible to move as Kull stood petrified by fear. The hoard got closer until it overtook him, wrapping him within a biting, stinging blanket of a thousand teeth.

This can't be real, this can't be real. He slammed his fist against the mirror.

"Get out of my head! GET OUT OF MY HEAD!"

The woman in the glass laughed maniacally, and Kull pushed himself away from it. He stared down at his body. The carpet of creatures that covered him completely disappeared, even though he could still feel the pain of a thousand mouths gnawing on him. Absolute madness was on the brink of overtaking him. *Wael was right. Wael was right about these things. How could I have been so stupid?*

Kull blinked and found himself on his knees again, back on the altar. His arms were unbound, and the collar around his neck was still locked. It was as if he never stood up. He looked over and listened as he freed the lock from his neck.

"For these crimes, Willyn Kara, and for so many innocents whose blood is on your hands, you are hereby sentenced to death."

It was uncanny, the feeling like he had seen the future or traveled back to the past. Was it a dream? Kull glanced up at the mirror where she had been. Ice cold fear hit him in an instant. There she was, standing over him, but instead of starlight within her eyes, black blood poured out of her eyes, and her mouth opened wide to reveal a cavern of daggers.

Kull held his face like flint against the horror before him. The Serub was trying to get him to stop, but it was too late. Kull knew this was the opening he had been waiting for. He stood, unlocked his binding, and turned to Seam.

"STOP!" he screamed.

Seam turned around from Willyn and saw Kull unbound. "Guards, seal the door!"

The datalink connection crackled in with static. The face that filled the screen was clearly flustered with worry, "Seam, what is going on?!"

The two guards drew their pistols and aimed them directly at Kull's skull as he dove behind the nearest mirror. Adrenaline hammered through his heart as Seam screamed out to his men. "DO NOT FIRE YOUR WEAPONS! THE MIRRORS MUST NOT BE HARMED."

Seam ran to the platform with his sword in hand. "Kull Shepherd, I'd advise that you come out. You are outmanned and outgunned. Don't play games with me."

Kull crouched behind one of the mirrors and waited. Seam paused, the two only separated by the single pane of glass.

Seam had barely glanced around the portal's edge when Kull slammed his fist underneath the King's chin. Kull followed with another shot to his eye before tackling Seam to the ground. In the fray Seam's grip loosed from his weapon. Rage, adrenaline, and purpose flooded into Kull as he struck Seam again, smashing his fist against the King's mouth. The blow split Seam's lip and a trail of blood pushed its way down his face. He landed an elbow to Seam's cheek before hammering his fists down on his face again. Kull pushed every ounce of rage that was pent up in his chest out through his fists as he continued to land blow after blow on the King's face.

The guards did not risk firing, but ran at him armed with clubs. Willyn, pressing her advantage with the distraction, slipped her hands free and kicked the legs out from under the guard closest to her. As his momentum carried him down, she hammered her knee into his face. There was no hesitation as she snapped up his pistol and fired three rounds into the other guard. He was dead before he had time to realize she was free.

Seam managed to gain an advantage by pinning Kull to the ground, but the shots broke his concentration enough for Kull to push free and land a kick to his head. Kull had no idea whose side the redhead was really on, but he took his chances. He threw the lock pick in her direction.

He nodded toward his father and Wael. "Free them both. There is a transport waiting at the Spire's base. Get them out of here!"

Willyn scrambled for the pick and moved to Grift. "I am not leaving until I kill Seam myself. My brother's blood is on his hands. You can take them, and I will finish this."

Seam regained his footing and flicked at the datalink on his wrist. The room immediately went black. Sirens cranked open with a deafening howl. Kull squeezed his eyes together to try and focus in the dark. The only light was the dull glow offered by the rolling static screen that was once the datalink projection, but it was a terrible help.

A small red blip of light flickered to Kull's right. *Seam's datalink.* Kull ran full speed and collided with him, tumbling through the shadows. The two fell to the floor again and Kull swung wildly. His fists struck flesh and the metal floor. He could feel his knuckles swelling and splitting under the force of his blows, but he did not relent. The King swung an arm around and grasped Kull's neck. Despite Kull's assault, Seam's powerful grip pressed down on the air in his throat like a vise. As his breathing became more and more labored, each punch was losing power. Seam began to laugh.

Another light flickered on, and Kull could see Willyn fighting to finish with Wael's locks. Grift was standing next to her helping lift Wael from the floor. She noticed Kull and screamed to him.

"Keep fighting him. I almost have them out!"

Seam's grip continued to tighten on Kull's throat in the darkness. His eyes were filled with anticipation and hatred as he waited to watch Kull's life slip away beneath his grasp. Kull sent his fist into Seam's datalink, and suddenly the room was engulfed in hot white light. He threw a jab into Seam's face once, then twice, and then a third time. He focused every ounce of energy he had left on trying to connect every heavy throw. By the fourth jab, Seam's grasp broke free and Kull pushed himself away, gasping for air.

How is he still fighting? No one can take this kind of beating.

Kull's adrenaline was wearing thin, but the sound of the last of Wael's bindings popping free offered him hope. Seam slowly stood to his feet and pulled a dagger from his belt. He wiped at the river of blood flowing from his nose and lip.

"I have had enough of you, boy. This ends now."

Seam lunged for Kull and grabbed his arm. He used his momentum to throw Kull into the empty pane of glass. As he thudded against the portal, he could feel the low chanting of a voice from behind the mirror's edge. *There was another one in that glass, too.* Kull's mind filled with horror when he recognized the voice. It was the one from the King's Pit. Kull tried to push away from the mirror but Seam had already leapt on top of him like a panther, doing his best to thrust the knife into Kull's gut. Kull held it at bay with what little strength he had left.

Seam's voice changed into a sadistic growl as he pressed down on the knife, "It's time to wake the King. Arakiel is thirsty."

Kull's arm screamed with protest as he held back the dagger, preventing it from falling in on him. Seam leaned down, putting his whole weight behind the blade when a deafening thunderclap rang out. Seam snapped back and crumpled to the ground, grasping at his chest. Blood splattered against Kull and the mirror. An intense heat grew out from the glass as the beads of red liquid sizzled into its surface. Grift stood a few feet away, smoke still swirling from the barrel of the gun in his hand.

Kull glanced into the mirror and saw a new face begin to appear, morphing from the sagging, drawn face of an elderly man to the strong chiseled face of a warrior. He scrambled for the knife that Seam dropped and yelled out to Willyn and his father.

"You have to get out. NOW!"

"Not without you!" Grift screamed.

As Grift called out, the door split open and a wave of guards flooded into the chamber. Their rifles were drawn and leveled down on each one of them.

Kull heard Seam stir and he looked down. The King was starting to stand and *he was laughing*.

This is impossible, thought Kull. *How is he not dead?*

Kull surveyed the room, quickly counting twelve new soldiers. His mind whirled with possibilities, but he chose the only one that would work. In a flash, Kull sprung behind Seam and pressed the knife's blade against his throat. All the guns in the room were focused on him.

Kull screamed out, "This ends now! I will kill your King unless you let these prisoners walk!"

The guards stood, their long, black riot masks concealing their thoughts. They shuffled, but did not lower their weapons.

Kull screamed out again, positioning himself behind Seam. "I said they go free!"

He cut into Seam, freeing a flow of blood from his neck. Seam shouted out in pain, and the guards pushed in closer. A soft voice full of fear escaped from Seam, "You heard him. Let them free."

Without hesitation, Kull dipped the blade back into Seam who howled.

"Say it louder so they can hear you!" Kull bellowed, his mind alive with rage.

"Let them go free, NOW!" screamed Seam who shook under Kull's grasp.

The guards slid to the side, allowing Willyn, Grift, and Wael to pass, but Grift pushed past them all and ran for his son. Before he could reach them one of the guards smashed the butt of his rifle into Grift's head, causing him to collapse on the floor.

In a panic Kull yelled, his eyes wild, "I SAID THEY GO FREE! Did you not hear me? Or do you think I'm joking?" He slammed the dagger down deep into Seam's shoulder. Seam buckled under the blow, howling. "They all leave safely or the King dies!"

The guards retreated a few feet and opened a path to the door, but the opening provided no guarantee that they wouldn't all be shot upon exiting. Kull examined the scene as his father lay motionless on the floor. Willyn's eyes kept darting back and forth from one guard to another as she assisted Wael. His face was bruised and swollen. The three were surrounded by an army of guards, hungry for the command to open fire.

Kull stammered, "I want to see them go free or he dies. Bring up their feed on the datalink screen. I will watch them leave freely or this blade cuts your King's throat the rest of the way."

He pressed in further with the knife, bringing a desperate cry from Seam who flailed his arms in agony, trying to swat away at the knife.

"Do as he says! Now!"

The guards spread as Willyn pulled Wael through the door. One of the soldiers lifted Grift's limp body and dragged it close behind. The datalink screen ignited, showing a black and white feed of Willyn, Grift, and Wael making their way down and out the Spire. Guards stood by, their weapons lowered. Soon they were outside, and Kull could see them far below from his vantage point on the Spire. A transport rolled up, and Kull could see the outline of a figure running out to assist them. *Adley.* Adley was helping them up into the transport. Soon the vehicle sped out into the desert without anyone trailing them.

Grift rubbed at his head as he regained consciousness. He blinked the shadows from his eyes and searched the truck bed for Kull.

"Where is he? WHERE IS KULL?"

Adley laid a hand on his shoulder and tried to pull him back into his seat. She said nothing, but her face was painted in grief.

Willyn broke the silence, "We had to leave him. There was no other way."

Grift eye's flared open. "You left him!? How could you leave him?" He cried out before stumbling back, fighting for balance until Wael reached out with a heavy hand and grasped his wrist.

Wael's voice cut through the dark desert night. "Grift. *Kull saved us all.* He made his choice. It was his choice to make. Not yours." His face was stern as he continued, "Kull gave us a gift. A chance to fight back. It is now up to us to decide what to do with this gift."

A thunderstorm of grief erupted over Grift's face. Wael's strong hand stayed on his arm as painful sobs ripped through his body. "But he is just a kid. He doesn't understand…"

Wael lifted himself to level his tattered face with Grift's, "He is no child. Only a man would have done what he did. He made a promise with Rose that he would guarantee your return. He made his choice."

Grift fell back into his seat and wiped the tears from his eyes. "He's all we have, Wael. He's ALL WE HAVE. I am supposed to protect him and I failed. I failed to protect the key! I have failed!" He screamed, allowing all of his pain to roar through him. "I've FAILED!"

Wael turned to face the back of the truck, toward the Spire shrinking in the distance. "We have all failed, Grift. I am afraid that I have failed us most of all."

Grift shook his head as he answered, "What are you talking about, Wael? How can you say that?"

Wael's face dropped and his gaze drifted back to the horizon as he spoke. "I am afraid I provided information about our Order to Seam's informant. My own flesh and blood has betrayed us into Seam's hands, and now the Keepers are no more. Vashti has betrayed me." Hot tears began to roll out of the stoic monk's face as deep, untold pain quaked over him. Grift held his friend as the dark desert rolled by. The rest remained silent. Wael wiped his face and locked eyes with Grift and spoke.

"But your son has succeeded in freeing the few people that know what has to be done to fight this evil. Kull is in Aleph's hands now. *Strong and mighty is his grip.*"

Grift grasped Wael's wrist. "Then it's time we fight."

Willyn sat up and glanced between the members of the company, "Sorry to interrupt, but how do we fight them? Look at us!”

Grift’s face turned to stone. Whatever terrible grief that had overtaken him looked as if it had been thrown into the bottom of the sea. He took a deep breath and paused before turning to her, “We find and destroy the rest of the mirrors before Seam gets to them. Then we make him pay for what he has done to us.”

Kull lifted his eyes to the dozens of guns trained on him. He lifted the knife from Seam’s throat and dropped it to the ground. He had done all he could. He trusted that his father would fight to finish what he started. Even though they lost their keys, at least he and Wael were alive. That was enough for him. They were more equipped to continue the fight than he could ever hope to be, and he knew Grift could protect his mother better than anyone else.

The guards pressed in around Kull and soon he felt the razor sharp pains of electricity traveling up and down his spine and a barrage of clubs beating down on him. He collapsed to the ground and looked out one last time over the horizon. The last sight he had before everything went dark was that of the transport's dust trail cresting the horizon, leaving him behind to die in their place. It was the only way.

As an avalanche of pain fell over him, his hand reached up and held his mother’s pendant, still hanging on his neck. Somehow he had not lost it. He rubbed his finger on the small etching of Aleph’s rune.

There was no regret.

He took his only opening.

Thank You For Reading!

We hope you enjoyed Keys of Candor: The Red Deaths and we look forward to connecting with you. We love hearing from our readers and taking in your thoughts and feedback. We invite you to write a review at www.Amazon.com to let us know what you liked.

Also, please feel free to connect with us at the resources below, we love interacting with our readers:

Online: www.keysofcandor.com

Facebook: www.facebook.com/keysofcandor

Email: eanesandervin@gmail.com

Twitter: @keysofcandor

Be sure to subscribe to our monthly newsletter at www.keysofcandor.com to get exclusive content, news about our upcoming books and chances to win an advance copy of Sea of Souls!

COMING SOON

KEYS OF CANDOR: SEA OF SOULS

The Serubs have been unleashed and Seam's power grows as Willyn, Grift, and Wael try to stir the remnant surviving Seam's oppression in hope of mounting a resistance and bringing peace back to Candor.

Be sure to subscribe to our monthly newsletter to get exclusive news on the next installment in the Keys of Candor series.

ACKNOWLEDGEMENTS

This has been a labor of love for us over the last few years. A lot has changed during our journey writing together. New jobs have been secured, children have been born, and life keeps on going. If it weren't for the belief and faith of our family and our friends, I'm afraid Candor would have never seen the light of day. This book is a testament to the love and support that they have offered to us every step along the way, and we want to acknowledge that.

We both especially want to acknowledge our beautiful wives who allowed us to journey with Kull, Willyn, and Seam for so long. Devin and Janet, there would be none of this without you both. Thank you for believing in us.

We also want to thank our beloved beta-readers who contributed so much to this project. We appreciate each of you and value your friendship and contributions so very much. This story is immensely improved because of your input.

There is more to tell in the world of Candor. We hope you'll stick around to see what's next.

Until then,

-Seth and Casey

ABOUT THE AUTHORS

Seth and Casey grew up together in North Carolina, and are lifelong friends. In "real life" they hold their posts as a librarian and a banker respectfully enough, but have always had deep interests in creating art, music, and now stories.

Keys of Candor: The Red Deaths is their first collaboration.
It won't be their last.

52802445R00192

Made in the USA
Charleston, SC
27 February 2016